By TJ KLUNE

NOVELS
Bear, Otter, and the Kid
Who We Are

Tell Me It's Real

ELEMENTALLY EVOLVED
Burn

Published by DREAMSPINNER PRESS
http://www.dreamspinnerpress.com

D1258312

Tell Me It's Real

TJ KLUNE

Dreamspinner Press

Published by
Dreamspinner Press
5032 Capital Circle SW
Ste 2, PMB# 279
Tallahassee, FL 32305-7886
USA
http://www.dreamspinnerpress.com/

Tell Me It's Real
Copyright © 2013 by TJ Klune

Cover Art by Reese Dante
http://www.reesedante.com

ISBN: 978-1-62380-353-7
Digital ISBN: 978-1-62380-354-4

Printed in the United States of America
First Edition
February 2013

If you have ever been told that you're not skinny enough, smart enough, straight enough, beautiful enough, strong enough, masculine enough, or any other "enough" that made you feel less than you actually are, then, man, do I have something to tell you: this one is for you because you are perfect just the way you are.

CHAPTER 1
Way Too Much Information About My Anatomy

JUST so you know, I don't have a gargantuan penis.

Shocking, I know, right? Most of the time when you hear stories like the one you're about to, the narrator is this perfect specimen of man, whether he knows it or not. If he doesn't know it, it's because he's most likely damaged and needs some hot piece of ass to bring him out of his shell and to help him realize his outer beauty dwarfs his inner beauty. Or he *knows* he's attractive and uses it as a weapon until the object of his lust-fueled heart breaks down that narcissistic wall with spooge and flowery words. Then they frolic off into the sunset and go live in Everything's Perfect Land where everyone has a ten-inch cock and big balls that can create semen by the bucketful every hour, on the hour.

But if we're going to be honest, I'm not small either. I was fourteen when I first noticed other boys in the locker rooms at school (and when I say "first noticed," I actually mean when I first allowed myself to look to see if they would give me a stiffie—which they did), and I realized penises were like snowflakes—no two were exactly the same. Some were big, some were small. Some had hair around them and others were smooth. Jacob Sides had one that curved wickedly to the left, and every time I saw him in the hall, I couldn't help but think, *There goes Captain Hook*, and would blush furiously, sure he would know that I was thinking about his frank and beans.

So the point is, I don't have a Coke can for a dong, but I don't have a Mike and Ike either. I'm somewhere in the middle. Average, if you will. Regular. Normal. Ordinary.

But then that describes the rest of me too.

I guess you should know what you're getting into before we go any further. If you leave before the story is finished, I wouldn't blame you. Too much. Okay, okay, I'll probably call you a bitch behind your back.

But hey, it's *behind your back*, so you won't even know about it. So feel free to walk away. Bitch.

Anyway, here's the rest of me. Sorry for the info dump I'm about to take all over you.

I don't have huge pecs, nor do I have stone-hard abs that you could attempt to grate cheese on. Those two things are so stereotypical amongst gay men that it's almost offensive. I watched a porno once where this little twinkie dude went to some haunted house in the middle of nowhere (which really looked like a set from an all-white elementary school production of *The Wiz*—if you get the reference, you'll know it's not racist). The little twinkie had little pecs and abs and a huge penis that could have posed as a third arm if he tried hard enough. Anyway, the little twinkie dude then got gang-banged by fourteen ghosts (guys that started out wearing sheets with holes cut out for eyes and ended up wearing nothing but spunk), and I swear to God, every single one of them had pecs and abs that went on and on. For *days*. So after I finished watching said porno (which, by the way, wasn't scary at all, especially since it was supposed to be about ghosts. Where was the *story*?), I decided that I could easily get pecs and abs, so I went to a gym not far from my house, intending to sign up with a personal trainer who would let my outer beauty shine through.

On the way there, I got distracted by the fact that a Dunkin' Donuts had opened up right down the road from my house and they were giving away *free donuts*. It was as if God himself saw that my intention was to make my outer self match my inner fabulosity and didn't think the world could handle such an explosion of amazingness. So instead of letting me get to the gym where I would have transformed myself into a walking sex god, he created a Dunkin' Donuts out of nothing and then *gave them away for free*. I didn't make it to the gym. I had a bear claw instead. And a maple bar. And some donut holes. And then some more donut holes.

So, I don't have pecs or abs. Not even close. As a matter of fact, I probably have a bit more around the middle than I should. I'm not *fat* or anything. I'm more… husky. My doctor told me I could stand to lose ten pounds (okay, okay, he said fifteen) and that it would make me a healthier person. I thought he was a cute older thing, maybe forty, forty-five, and I flirted with him until I realized he was calling me morbidly obese.

"That's not what I said," Dr. Suddenly Getting Less Attractive said with a knowing smirk. "I said you could lose fifteen pounds and then you'd break all the boys' hearts."

I glared at him. "How do you know I don't break their hearts now?" *Kind of like how I want to break your stupid face.*

"Do you?" he asked.

"All the time," I lied. "I'm really a way hot bear. Bears need to have a little extra junk in the trunk and a bump in the front in order to maintain the bear lifestyle."

Dr. I Don't Know When To Shut My Mouth almost rolled his eyes. "You? A *bear*? You have, like, three chest hairs," he said, reaching out to pull on one. It came off my bare chest almost immediately. "And this one's a cat hair!" Which was weird because I don't have a cat.

"It's a new thing," I said, insulted. "No-hair bears. We have monthly meetings and talk about how smooth our skin is and how our leathers start to chafe because of it. We're thinking about switching to denim chaps and vests. Sort of an old-school look. I suggested we also get denim gloves, but it was agreed upon that was too much denim."

"Paul." Dr. Not As Gullible As He Looks rolled his eyes and said, "My partner is very active in the bear community. There's no such thing as no-hair bears. Trust me. I would know."

"You're a homosexual?" I screeched at him, trying to put my shirt back on as quickly as I could. "I demand a straight doctor so he won't judge me!"

"Can you even grow a beard?" he asked me, obviously judging me.

"It takes a few weeks," I admitted. "I thought puberty would be the end of all my miseries, but it just gave me zits on my butt."

He looked like he could have done without that information.

Story of my life. I tend to say things without thinking them through. It is my gift. It is my curse.

"Not anymore," I told him hastily. "I'm almost thirty. I don't get butt zits anymore. Or zits anywhere else." That was a lie. I'd gotten a zit the other day in the middle of my forehead that I glared at in the mirror until it went away. You don't need Proactiv when you have the sheer force of will. Justin Bieber is a liar and a fat mouth.

"Uh-huh. Paul, I just want you to be healthy. It won't hurt you to get some exercise."

"Well, it *would* hurt *you* if I punched your face off," I grumbled.

He stared at me. "What?"

"What?" I asked innocently, batting my eyelashes at him.

So, seriously. I'm not fat. I could stand to lose a few pounds. There's just a bit more of me to love.

Wow. That sounds way lame.

All right. So you know I have an average penis and I'm not a ripped Adonis, nor am I hairy bear man. That's a good start, I think. What else is there?

Well, I have black hair that I keep short because it starts to curl when it gets longer and looks like a homeless poodle died on my head. Sometimes, when I'm feeling really adventurous, I spike it up with gel, but usually, I don't do a whole lot with it. I don't have dandruff, which is good. And my hairline is not receding (yet), which is even better.

I have blue eyes and I could tell you that they're the color of ice that covers a frozen lake in the Himalayas, but that wouldn't be exactly true. I bought contacts to give myself ice-blue eyes one time, but they made it look like I had big cataracts in my eyes, so I took them out. Nothing says "Hey, would you sleep with me?" like milky cataracts. But mine are just a plain old blue, like most everyone else in the world.

Um, what else. Oh, I'm five foot ten, though I like to tell people I'm actually six feet tall because it sounds so much bigger. I don't wear my glasses like I'm supposed to because I think they make my face look too wide, so I tend to squint a lot. I can be shy around people I don't know, unless I'm drunk and then I can't seem to shut up at all. I like video games and loud action movies that pretend to have plots but really are about blowing shit up (oh, and just between us, I've probably seen every romantic comedy ever made—hello, I'm gay. It's a requirement that we pretend to like Jennifer Lopez when she's playing a maid in New York who still happens to look like Jennifer Lopez. J-Lo, no one believes you when you try to play working class, so knock it off). I tend to have a bit of a swish when I walk, and sometimes I wave my hands too much when I talk. I'm a homo, but sometimes I can be a *big* homo. I'm not effeminate. I'm just… animated. But I can be totally butch if I wanted to. Like, way butch. Like "going outside and taking off my shirt to chop some firewood for winter" butch.

As you heard earlier, my name is Paul and I'm almost thirty years old. My last name is Auster. Family legend says that our last name was Austerlitz, but it was changed after World War II because my dad's parents didn't want anyone to think they were Nazis when they fled Hamburg to come to America. I suppose I should thank them for that. I don't need people asking me if I'm related to Hitler.

That would not be a good start to a friendship.

But my grandparents are dead and I never met them, so I can't thank them unless I was into psychics and mediums. I'm not. Well, not anymore. Not since I dated a guy who told me my house was haunted with the spirit of a woman who had her period over and over again and moaned continuously about menstrual cramps while she wandered between my bedroom and the bathroom.

George lasted six dates before I couldn't take it anymore ("There's just so much *blood*!" he'd moaned to me, huddled in the corner of my couch). I kicked him to the curb and went on the Internet to find out how to get rid of menstruating ghosts. Funny, no one could really tell me. So I just bought a box of heavy flow tampons and made a big deal about putting them under the bathroom sink, telling my ghost Flow that she could use them whenever she wanted. Needless to say, two weeks later all tampons were still accounted for and I was slightly disappointed that I didn't really have a ghost haunting me, even if she was on the rag all the time.

Am I worried about turning thirty? Nah. Maybe. Sort of. Okay, I'm freaking out. Because when I was sixteen, I'd sit in front of the mirror and sing "Some Day My Prince Will Come" while brushing my poodle curls, sure there was a big strong man out there for me, just waiting to whisk me away to his castle on a beach in Cabo San Lucas. One who would pick me up with his massive arms and cradle me against his chest and tell me, in varying accents (sometimes he was Cuban and other times Chinese—I didn't use the Chinese one too often because I couldn't stop giggling at the Chinese voice I'd hear in my head. Don't ask me to do it. It's way wrong.) all the things he just couldn't wait to do to me once we got to my Dream Castle. We'd live there happily ever after and he would love me for the rest of my days while feeding me grapes and tickling my nipples.

Oh, by the way, I have very sensitive nipples.

I certainly did not expect to be almost thirty and working a dead-end job as a claims adjuster for an insurance company. I'm not going to tell you which one; suffice it to say you've probably seen our commercials on TV and chuckled once or twice until they played over and over and over again and you wanted to dropkick the stupid little animal spokesperson. You think the commercials are bad? Try working here. Sometimes, they have some idiot dress up in the animal mascot costume for human resource events. The person in the costume is always chipper and waving hysterically as if they're under the impression that if they stop, their hands will be chopped off. I hate that damn costume. And, I'll admit, it scares me a bit. I was the kid who never wanted to have birthday parties at Chuck E. Cheese because I was sure the animatronic monsters that were Chuck and his friends were actually real and when my parents weren't looking, they'd jump down off the stage and snatch me, taking me back to their dungeon where they would eat me slowly. I was the life of every party, let me tell you.

Sorry. I got distracted again.

Where were we? Oh, yeah. My job.

My soul is slowly being sucked dry in a cubicle that is smaller than a prison cell. Trust me, I measured it. But of course, management was not impressed when I brought this up. They tend not to like it when I speak at staff meetings. I understand why, though; what starts as a simple observation usually leads to another of one my "tirades." Their word, not mine. I can't help it. I get loud about things that matter to me ("We're donating to the Salvation Army *again* for Christmas? They *hate* gay people! Those bell ringers are nothing but homophobic ex-junkie fascists in disguise! Why are we even donating to a religious organization at Christmas! *Jesus was born in April!*"). So yeah, they prefer if I don't speak in staff meetings.

I never expected to still be living in Tucson, Arizona, land of the Border Patrol (aka the Fascist Regime), home of 115 degree temperatures (*but at least it's a dry heat,* we always say). I'm too pale to live in the desert. I don't tan. Instead, I get pink, so much so that I look like one of those oddly disturbing hairless cats that nobody wants to own. I went to a spray-tan salon once, but the woman at the front desk was orange and I was convinced that I would get melanoma just by breathing the same air as her, so I left immediately, after accidentally telling her she looked like a perky blonde carrot. She didn't think that was very funny. Either that or she normally looks like she's perpetually pissed off.

When I was younger, I thought I was going to get a ten-picture deal from Paramount, where I'd be paired with all the handsomest leading men in Hollywood and travel all over the world in my yacht. After a hard day of filming a gay action adventure along the lines of *Romancing the Stone* (called *Fluffing My Jewels*) we'd all retire to my yacht and have an orgy filled with riotous passion.

Instead, I live in a small adobe house right smack-dab in the center of a middle-class neighborhood. The neighbors to my left are a husband and wife, and they're seventy-year-old nudist racists who like to have swinger parties in the hot tub of their backyard. They've invited me over for a couple of the parties, but I've seen the type of people that show up. When that much of your body has fallen because of gravity and you're still wearing clothes, I can only imagine what your balls will look like hanging down by your ankles. I politely decline each invitation. Each time there is a party, though, I sit at my front door with a spray bottle filled with water, ready to spritz any randy old people who want to have a bone sesh in my driveway. So far it hasn't happened, but I did wake up one morning, went outside to get the mail, and found an empty travel-size lube packet near my mailbox. I went back inside, got gloves and bleach, and scrubbed down the mailbox, trying hard not to gag at the images in my head of two old people wearing chaps boning against it.

After that guy told me I had a ghost who perioded (that's a word I just made up; doesn't it sound gross?) all over my house, I thought it best that I get a pet to protect me and keep me company since I decided to swear off men for at least seventeen years. I briefly considered getting a cat, but then decided against it because I didn't want to be one of *those* people. You know what I mean. My grandmother, Gigi (Mom's mom), was one of them. She'd make tuna fish and then sit in her old chair, which smelled like Bengay and broken dreams, and chew it, then open her mouth and let her cat eat it right then and there. She said it was because Mrs. Tingles was too old to chew her own food and she wanted to give her a treat. I told her I was the only person in the world who had a grandmother who made out with her cat and smelled like fish while doing so. My grandmother wondered aloud if that made her a lesbian.

When she died, I was kind of sad. The cat, not my grandmother. Gigi is still alive. She has a homophobic parrot now. His name is Johnny Depp.

When I went over to her house to meet him for the first time, the first thing Johnny Depp did was squawk at me, "Pray the gay away!" while my grandma giggled from behind his cage. Gigi swears up and down he was like that when she got him, and I almost believe her, because she doesn't have a hateful bone in her body. She likes everyone, for the most part. But it's kind of hard to go to see her now, since Johnny Depp screams, "Here comes the rump ranger!" every time I walk into her house.

So instead of getting a cat to make out with or a parrot that is one step away from committing hate crimes, I went to get a dog. I told myself when I went to the shelter that I was going to get a big dog because big dogs make you manlier. No teacup Chihuahuas for *this* homo, no, sir! I stomped into the ASPCA and told them in my deepest voice that I was there to adopt a German shepherd! No, a Rottweiler! No, a *pit bull*! I told the lady I would take the manliest pit bull they had and that I would name him Snarl or Stab or Meat Eater and I'd get him a collar with spikes on it.

The lady at the front desk asked me calmly if I was part of a dog-fighting ring. I felt properly rebuked and apologized, telling her no, I just needed a dog to live with me and my menstrual ghost. She must have thought the phrase *menstrual ghost* was somehow referring to me because she asked if I was pre-op or post-op transgender. I almost reached over and plucked the two gross black hairs growing out of her chin. But she looked so pleased with herself that she was showing the world how open-minded she was that I couldn't bear to rip out those gnarly hairs *or* break her heart, so I told her I was post-op and that my name used to be Chaz Bono and that I missed my menstrual cycle more than I thought I would. She reached over and rubbed my arm soothingly and told me she'd help me find an "animal companion" to help me forget all about the vaginal bleeding. "After all," she said, laughing, "we women have to stick together, even if one of us has an artificially constructed penis now. Girl power!"

A golden retriever named Duke caught my eye almost right away. His coat was so bright and pretty under the lights, and he sat there and preened when I smiled. He chuffed a bit, obviously playing up his part. He knew he looked good and he knew I knew it. I almost said he was the one, but then I heard a squeaking noise coming from the next cage. Duke turned his head to the right and growled and then looked back at me with soulful eyes. The squeak came again and Duke all but snarled.

I was curious so looked into the next cage. Inside was a mutt of some kind, pretty small and scrawny-looking. He was almost all black except for random white spots of hair on his back and face. His front right leg was white, like he was wearing only one sock. But then I saw he didn't have back legs and that the squeaking sound I'd heard were the wheels of a little contraption that hooked to the back of his body and allowed him to move. When he saw me looking in at him, he started wiggling his butt back and forth, causing the wheels to tilt every which way and clack on the cement floor. It was only then I saw he didn't have a tail, either.

"What happened to him?" I asked the woman.

She smiled fondly down at Wheels (I'd already named him in my head—highly, *highly* original, I know) and told me he'd been hit by a car months before and had to have his legs and tail amputated. No one had claimed him and the shelter couldn't find anyone to take him. Since he'd been a survivor, they called him Lucky, which I thought was the stupidest name ever.

Duke, the golden boy in the next cage, was pissed he wasn't getting more attention from me and growled at Wheels. It was then I understood that Duke was nothing but a big golden bully and Wheels was the little guy that no one wanted. I was just enough of a sentimentalist that I could relate, so of course I adopted him. And named him Wheels. No child of *mine* would be named Lucky! We would make our *own* luck!

I was feeling pretty good about myself when I brought Wheels home. I turned my back for a minute, listening to his wheels squeak throughout the house as he explored while I set up his food bowl and water jug thing that the cute stock boy at Petco said I just *had* to have. I went looking for the new addition only to discover he'd pooped in the middle of the living room and then tracked it through the rest of the house after rolling through it with his wheels. I threw up in my mouth a little when I had to clean it up, but I figured it was still better than a homophobic Johnny Depp calling me a fudge packer.

So, yep. This is my life. Sorry about the info dump I just took on your chest. If you don't want to keep going, I'll totally understand, though that still gives me the right to call you a bitch behind your back.

And, of course, you'll miss the rest of the story and won't get to hear about Helena Handbasket, drag queen extraordinaire. You'll miss out on meeting my parents (though, that might not be the best way to entice you—they are so damn weird). And you'll totally miss out on the way I thought I'd gotten Freddie Prinze Juniored, only to discover that a sexy man named Vince was the best thing that ever happened to me and that maybe, just *maybe*, I'd get my happily ending after all.

But of course, a bunch of crap will happen before then. I can't help it if I am a walking drama magnet. It just happens that way. So, one last chance for you to get the fuck out.

You still there? Cool. Wasn't that person that left already such a *bitch*? Seriously. You could totally tell by the way they walked that they had a stick up their ass.

All Right. You ready? Sweet.

Let's rock and roll.

CHAPTER 2

The Evils Of Whiskey And Twinks

"WOULD you hand me that tape there so I can tuck my penis and testicles back to give the illusion that I'm a woman?" my best friend Sandy asked, just to fuck with me. He was already in full makeup, the fierce red eye shadow and blush spreading around his eyes, like a wild mask, that he always wore when he was doing his Lady Gaga numbers.

"I still don't get how you can push all your junk back like that," I said with a shudder, handing him the double-sided tape. "Balls weren't meant to get squished like that."

"They're squishy by nature," he pointed out, pulling off a piece of the tape and shoving his hands down his loose boxers. A grimace came over his face as he twisted his hands, and I had to look away before I felt sympathy pains.

We were sitting in the upstairs dressing room of Jack It, one of the few gay bars we have in Tucson. And out of the three or four bars we *do* have, Jack It is the only one with a dance floor, though I don't really dance. There's a major difference between dancing at home in your underwear, and then dancing at a gay bar with all the go-go boys in *their* underwear. It's enough to make a man feel self-conscious. Trust me.

Sanford Stewart, the man doing evil things to his boy parts, is pretty much the best friend I have in the entire world. He's a skinny thing, but tall, over six feet. One might look at him as a man and not see anything remarkable. His blonde hair is just yellow enough to be flat-looking. His brown eyes are chocolate left out in the sun. He's cute, but in that almost immediately forgettable kind of way. He could stand to gain at least twenty pounds. I tell him all the time he needs to eat more and he says he will if I will. He thinks I look good just the way I am, even though my ego won't let me believe it.

I think he's beautiful no matter what he looks like, but most don't, for whatever reason. As a man, he's perfect in my eyes.

But when he's in full-on drag as Helena Handbasket? Holy fireworks, Batman.

There's no one in this entire fucking town that can hold a candle to her when she's performing (notice the pronoun switch: when he's Sandy, he's a "he"; when she's in full drag, she's a "she." Queens can get vicious if you don't respect the pronouns). Helena Handbasket is an absolute legend in Arizona, with a reputation starting to grow around the country as well. She's been asked to perform at a few pride events outside the state, and next year, she's considering competing in Miss Gay USA.

What's funny about Sandy is that when he *is* Sandy, he's quiet and unassuming. He sometimes stutters over his words and he can be shy, almost as much as I am. He tends to watch people rather than contributing to conversation. Some might think him cold, but he's really just listening. When he does speak, his words are carefully chosen. We grew up together, and when we got old enough, he dragged me into the gay bar scene, even though I would have rather had bamboo shunts shoved under my fingernails than be in a large group of people. He said it would be good for the both of us, though there were plenty of times we ended up as wallflowers—standing and not speaking much while sucking down vodka cranberries.

But when she's Helena Handbasket? Holy. Shit. When she's in full-on drag, you would swear to God she is the biggest fucking diva in the history of the world. Her costumes are completely outrageous, and a testament to the amount of time we spent pawing through thrift stores and the fact that he's a wiz with a sewing machine.

She moves with the fluid grace of a trained dancer and can lip-synch with the best of them, but it's her trademarked snarl, as she tears through her routines, that sets her apart. Sandy Stewart might be a quiet twenty-nine-year-old man, but Helena is a hard-core bitch who doesn't take shit from anyone. It took me a bit to get used to the whole split-personality thing that most drag queens seem to have, but once I did I never looked back.

You're probably wondering if Sandy and I were ever anything more than best friends. Eh. For maybe, like, two seconds. We got drunk one night at his old apartment and started making out, which somehow led to all of our clothes on the floor. When we realized that we were both bottoms, and didn't feel like bumping assholes, we decided we were better best friends than boyfriends. Sandy's brutally protective of me. Everyone knows not to mess with Helena's "bitch boy," as he calls me affectionately. Bastard. He's all class, that one.

Even when he's reaching to tape his balls to his taint.

"I don't know why I watch every time you do that," I said to him. "You look like you're trying to fist yourself and it's not going too well."

He gave a little huff. "It's the most unladylike thing about becoming a lady," he said, giving his wrist a little twist.

"It rubs the lotion on its skin or else it gets the hose again," I intoned.

"That stopped being funny the first thousand times you said it," he grumbled at me. "Keep saying it and I *will* put you in a hole in my basement."

"You don't have a basement," I said, trying to smooth out the feathers on the boa he wore during his opening number.

"I'll dig one," he promised. "Lace me, please."

He turned, the white skin of his slender back facing me. I slid my fingers through the ties of the corset, pulling them tight, cinching each one up tight like I knew he liked. It helped create the illusion of cleavage so he wouldn't have to wear falsies in this outfit. Once he added a little blush to his chest for shadowing effect, it'd look like he was rocking some knockers.

"You going to come down and watch?" he murmured, then looked in the mirror to fix the makeup around his eyes.

I sighed. "Not tonight," I said quietly. "I'll just stay up here and watch your show, okay?" I didn't want to go down and mingle with all the hot boys and men who wouldn't even look at me twice. If you ever want to find out if you're attractive or not, go to a gay bar. Within the first five minutes of walking in on a busy night, trust me, you'll know whether you're hot. I was one of those that could slip through the crowd without anyone trying to stop me by grabbing my ass, or smiling wickedly and asking if they could buy me a drink. The only reason anyone ever looked at me is because of Helena.

Oh, man. I sound way bitter. I'm not, I promise. It's just how things are. I don't question them anymore. I just don't like being reminded of it constantly. The only reason I went to Jack It as much as I did was because Helena performed on Wednesdays and Saturdays.

He sighed too, but it sounded sharp with exasperation, and I knew "he" was slipping into "she." Sandy took my shit for the most part. Helena thought I was an idiot. "You know," she said (yes, definitely *she* by the tone of her voice), "the more you hide out up here, the less you'll be seen."

"That's kind of the point," I reminded her, finishing with the corset.

Helena glared at me in the reflection of the mirror as she handed me a makeup brush to put a bit of glitter on her shoulders. "That's *not* the point," she growled at me, her voice going low and throaty. Yep. Helena was here. "How many times do I have to tell you that you are perfect just the way you are?"

I fought against the need to roll my eyes. "You're a bit biased," I reminded her, making sure her shoulders sparkled beautifully. She'd look like a disco ball with fabulous legs by the time I was finished. "You going to open with 'Poker Face'?"

She wasn't fooled by my feeble attempt to distract her. "Two songs," she said. "Come down for two songs. Stand amongst the other boys and girls and let yourself feel like you're a part of something instead of staying up here in your tower."

"Rapunzel, Rapunzel, let down your hair."

"Be serious for one damn minute," she snapped at me, eyes blazing. She was pissed at my evasiveness yet again.

"What do you want me to say?" I asked, trying not to sound hurt.

"Other shoulder, please," she said. I move to her other side. "I want you to say that you'll try. I want you to say that you'll do something different. I want you to say that you'll allow yourself to take a chance." She leaned forward to wipe away a smudge of mascara clumped in the corner of her eye. "You're not getting any younger, Paul. As a matter of fact, on *today* of all days, I would think you'd want to turn over a new leaf."

I scowled at her, not bothering to reply. I don't even want to think about today, but once Helena Handbasket got going, it was best to keep your mouth shut or she'd trample all over you. I learned that the hard way. Repeatedly.

Her eyes soften in the mirror. "Honey, I just want you to be happy."

"I *am* happy," I say, trying to sound convincing. "I have you and Wheels. My parents are still alive. My grandmother made a deal with the devil, so *she's* still alive. I have a job and my own house. My car is paid off. What more could a guy ask for?"

"Hope," Helena Handbasket said. "You could ask for some hope."

Ew. Gross.

I rolled my eyes. "You just after-school-specialed all over my face."

"Someone has to," she retorted. "Nothing else is going all over your face."

"You don't think that's hot, do you?" I asked, stepping back, making sure her shoulders shone evenly.

"What? Spunk on your face?"

"Yeah. I know it's supposed to be pornographically hot, but isn't there just something kind of gross about getting frosted like that?"

Helena leaned forward to fix her false eyelashes in the mirror. "Ruins my makeup," she muttered. "Those queen chasers think its *sooo* hot to see my makeup run when they nut on me. It gets them off even more, for some reason. I can't stand it."

"But you do it?"

She shrugged tightly. "Might as well. Helena likes herself some cock."

And that right there was another difference between my best friend and his alter ego. Sandy wasn't the type to let a guy nut on his face (sorry for the overuse of the word "nut"; "ejaculation" makes it sound so clinical). As a matter of fact, I don't think Sandy has ever had a guy do that to him while he's Sandy. Sandy's more like me than Helena is, although since Helena would do things that Sandy wouldn't even consider, I don't think that can be considered hypocritical. You can't call a drag queen hypocritical because they have two different personalities. It's like Clark Kent becoming Superman. Except a whole lot gayer. Okay, actually, now that I think about it, it's probably like Clark Kent becoming Superman and then going into the phone booth and stepping out as Wonder Woman. *That's* pretty damn gay.

Oh, by the way, I might also be a comic book nerd, for those of you keeping score of just how cool I am.

Anyway, Sandy wouldn't ever do that, but Helena? I can say with no reservations that Helena is a *whore*. For some reason, whenever Dr. Jekyll turns into Mrs. Hyde, the gloves come off (and then, if we're speaking honestly, the rubber gloves get pulled on; apparently Helena is very kinky that way). There are some guys, the queen chasers, that while still gay/bi/whatever, love to see lipstick marks around their dicks. And who else can provide such a service but a drag queen who has lipstick colors named things like "Dick Lip Red" and "Prussian Blue Balls"?

The queen chasers understand that queens like Helena aren't *exactly* women, but for some reason their kink is to *see* her as one. Apparently there are quite a few married men out there who want to get their rocks off with an illusion. To each their own, I guess. Helena doesn't talk about it a whole lot, and I try not to ask.

"Yeah, well, you can have some cock for the both of us," I told her. "I'm fine just the way things are."

"I know you are," she snapped. "And that's the problem. You've become complacent. Stuck in your routine."

"This whole tough-love thing is kind of hard to take seriously when you just taped your balls back in front of me," I said.

Helena stood up and gave herself one last look over. "Go ahead, Paul. Make jokes. Brush it off like you always do. But deep down, you know I'm right. I harp on you because I love you and I worry. I don't want to see you alone and full of regret after having wasted your life by shying away from the chances you could have taken."

"How could I possibly be alone?" I asked her quietly as I tried to look away. "I've got you."

She looked at me in the mirror for a moment before turning her sad, expertly sparkled eyes to me. She stayed rooted where she was, but leaned forward and kissed me gently on the cheek. I knew she'd left the perfect imprint of lips there, like she was Marilyn Monroe and the most perfect specimen of womanhood ever. "And you will always have me," she whispered in a throaty voice. "I love you, baby doll."

I grinned at her. "I love you too." And I did. I do.

"How does Momma look?" She stood up straight and preened and posed in front of me.

"Like the hottest, most fiercest thing to ever walk the face of the earth," I told her in all seriousness. "There was never one more beautiful than you."

"You're too good to me," she breathed dramatically. "What would I ever do without you?"

"Find another homo to stroke your ego?"

"No one strokes me like you do," she purred. "You sure I can't convince you to come down?"

I shook my head. "I'll just stay up here with Charlie." Charlie heard his name mentioned and grunted at us. He's the old guy who handles the spotlight and video camera for the drag performances. "You'll be my boyfriend for tonight, won't you, Daddy?" I called over to him.

"Whatever you say, boy," he rumbled at me without even looking. We all think he used to be some big Tom of Finland leather queen back in the day, though no one knows for sure. He's got to be in his seventies or eighties now, but you can still see the striking big man buried under all that saggy skin. I'm one of the few people who can get away with calling him Daddy. There's nothing sexual about it; I just think it makes him feel better. I do what I can for the elderly.

"Did you hear that?" I whispered to Helena. "He called me 'boy' again. Maybe this will be the start to our beautiful D/s relationship and I'll call him Master or Sir and we'll live out the rest of our sadomasochistic days together in perfect fisting harmony. My asshole is all aquiver just thinking about it."

Helena gave a very unladylike snort. "Yeah, I remember when you thought the Dom/sub route was going to be your next big thing. That leather daddy bent you over his knee to give you your first spanking, and you tried to lecture him with statistics on domestic abuse in Arizona."

I scowled. "It's not *my* fault he misinterpreted my intentions. *I* just wanted to get tied up for a bit. How was I to know he was going to go all hard core the first time around?"

"Oh, darling," she sighed. "If spanking is hard core to you, then it's probably a good idea he didn't introduce you to a cock cage to start out with."

"I don't even want to know what that is," I assured her, even though I kind of did. A cage? For your *cock*? Like it was some sort of chicken?

"Helena, you're up in two," Charlie called over his shoulder.

"Showtime," she said as she took a deep breath.

"Break a falsie."

She flashed me a wicked grin before she headed down the stairs.

I listened to make sure there was no *thump thump thump*, the telltale sign of a drag queen in high heels falling down the stairs. There wasn't, so I moved to the balcony that overlooked the dance floor and stage and sat down next to Charlie.

"You going to need that spanking, boy?" he asked me with a twitch to his lips.

"Oh, Daddy," I said as I blushed.

Moments later, she took the stage and the show was on. I'm sure you're thinking that if you've seen even one drag queen perform Lady Gaga before, then you know what to expect. But it's not even close. There's just something about Helena that forces you to watch her work the stage and the runway, stealing kisses in exchange for dollar bills. Drag is not an easy thing to do, especially if you're an athletic performer like Helena. It's more than just strutting about and lip-syncing. It's *art*. It's *performance*. And, in the case of my best friend, it's also *gymnastics*, and I winced slightly as she did a cartwheel and then fell into a full-on split during the middle of "Poker Face." Of course, the crowd went wild, and I was probably the only one worried about her balls. But, as the best friend, if I didn't worry about them, then who would?

Even though I'd seen her perform this same routine countless times, it never got old, and I watched with rapt attention, anticipating the next steps in my head. *Okay, front kick. Land. Twirl. Give some sass. Give some sass. Give some sass. Walk away, walk away, and sexy pose! Two. Three. Four.* And, as always, she executed it flawlessly.

But then, the funniest little thing happened.

"Poker Face" segued into another diva with the words, "It's Britney, bitch," and the crowd screamed its usual roar of approval. I clapped quietly, not wanting to interfere with the sound on the video camera, knowing that Sandy would watch the recording with a hawk's eye, wanting to point out all the little mistakes he felt Helena had made (and he would, too; no one was harder on Helena than Sandy). I sat back and got ready for her Britney routine (sans all the head-shaving crazy. Dear Britney: thank you for taking your super fun-time medicine now. Love, the gay community) when I felt a curious thing.

You know that prickly feeling you get when you just *know* someone is watching you? I've often wondered *how* we can know this. Is it like some sixth sense kind of thing? Or are our bodies so in tune with each other's that we can pick up on actual heat in a gaze? I don't know. I can't explain it. I may never know.

What I *can* say is that I got that prickling sensation—that slightly odd feeling of being watched. I pushed it away, knowing it was probably just people down below glancing up at Charlie and me, wondering who the VIPs were and why we got to sit where we did. I focused back on Helena.

But it wouldn't... go... the fuck... *away*. I was starting to get slightly annoyed and maybe even a little uncomfortable. *It's probably nothing*, I told myself. *Probably nothing at all*. But I couldn't get that feeling to leave, so finally, inevitably, I looked down to the crowd and saw him.

Oh sweat balls, I thought.

Standing near the wall, surrounded by what looked like a group of total fratty jockish dudes, was a man. A very *fine* man. He looked a few years younger than me, with brown hair that fell all over his head in an artfully messy way that looked like he might have just rolled out of bed, but you *knew* was done on purpose. He had thick, pretty lips that were made for sin, stretching into a delicious smile that showed even teeth. Dimples. *Fuck me up, we have dimples!* Deep, deep dimples that I wanted to put my tongue into. I blushed a fire red, but I didn't stop my depraved up and down assessment.

Tight white T-shirt pulled against a strong chest, the sleeves of which strained against his meaty biceps. Since he was standing against the wall, I couldn't see his ass, and I was slightly disappointed, as I am an ass man through and through. But I could see his front, and I have no shame in admitting that I checked out his package, what little I could see given the fact that strobe lights were going off and there was a moderately large lesbian with a mustache blocking part of my view. *Move your labianical ass!* I wanted to scream at her, but somehow I was able to fight the words back. After all, one does not scream at lesbians in Doc Martens unless one wants to receive a penis kicking.

And so I let my gaze rise back up until I locked eyes with the man I'd already dubbed Mr. Yes Please. I couldn't tell what color his eyes were, but I pretended they would be green, the sharpest of all emerald greens. I couldn't remember ever thinking that noses could be hot. But he had a hot nose. Made for... well, whatever sex things noses are made for.

His grin widened.

Dimplepalooza. Dimplefest. Dimplenator 3000.

He winked.

And then I realized that I was blatantly eye-fucking what had to be the hottest man of all time, to ever exist, anywhere, ever, and that I was still *me*. I was Paul Auster, slightly effeminate, slightly husky, very ordinary and boring and any other adjective I've already thrown at you. I was *nothing,* and it was like my Pavlovian conditioning had kicked in and he was my bell. One of his frat-jock buds said something to him and he looked away for just a split second, but it was enough to break whatever spell he'd tried to cast over me like a level-thirty warlock hell-bent on getting my Crystal of Zyanthia. But then the fact that I'd just compared him to a *level-thirty warlock hell-bent on getting my Crystal of Zyanthia* caused me to hyperventilate a bit further, knowing that he was so far out of my league that it wasn't even funny. I didn't date guys who had *veins* bulging out of their arm muscles. I didn't date guys who had *muscles*. I didn't *date!*

Then I recognized this for what it was, that I'd totally misconstrued the whole look. It was just one of those things where we'd looked at each other at the same time and he was being polite while I drooled all over him from afar. *He probably gets people falling over him all the time,* I thought. *He's probably used to humanity begging to suck on his dimples, so he was just letting me enjoy the moment of being able to bask in the awesomeness that is him.*

Or maybe he wasn't even looking at me. Maybe he was grinning and winking at Charlie. Or the ceiling. Or maybe he wasn't grinning and winking at all, and it was just a facial tic brought on by having a slightly chubby man practically ovulating right in front of him. *Take my fictitious eggs!* I wanted to bellow at him. *I will carry* all *your babies to full term!*

He wasn't looking at you, I told myself. And even if he was, it meant nothing.

But then that heated sensation into the side of my head was back.

I refused to look.

For three seconds. Then in a performance that would have made Daniel Day-Lewis proud, I stretched, popping my back, yawning and all the while squinting my eyes partially shut. Once I was in mid-stretch/pop/yawn/squint, I looked down briefly and saw that Mr. Yes Please was watching me yet again. *He's probably just wondering how big my nipples are*, I thought as I continued what undoubtedly had to be the longest stretch/pop/yawn/squint ever. *He probably thinks that I'm quarantined up here because I've got the biggest nipples in the world. If he even can spell quarantined. He might be hot, but he's probably dumber than a box of rocks covered in cocaine. Ha, ha! Crack rocks. I'm funny as shit. Why am I still stretching?*

So I stopped stretching, but Charlie must have seen what was going on because he started making a weird chuffing/grumbling noise he made when he thought something was *really* funny. I glared at him. "Real smooth, boy," he said as he chuffed/grumbled, somehow able to move the spotlight perfectly over Helena as she prowled the floor even though he was watching me. "Don't let anyone tell you that you don't have game."

"Shut up, Daddy," I groused.

I looked down again, and Mr. Yes Please was laughing silently up at me, but for some reason, I got the feeling he wasn't laughing at me as much as he was laughing at my blatant disregard for subtlety. I blushed again and looked away, determined to watch Helena perform and not watch the hotness watching *me* for some damn reason.

It almost worked.

Of *course* I gave him a quick glance every now and then. Okay, it was more like every few seconds. With how much my head was going back and forth between him and Helena, you would have thought that I was trying to dance really awfully along with the music. Sometimes he was looking at me, other times he was laughing with his perfectly perfect friends. Once or twice, our gazes locked and clashed and my breath caught in my throat and I had to tear my gaze away before I jumped on him from the second floor and demanded that he take me right there.

Halfway through Helena's set, one of the shirtless twinkie barbacks walked by him carrying a tray. Mr. Yes Please stopped him and spoke with him. The twinkie (Eric was his name, stupid perfect little twinkie Eric) started to put a little sex in his pose. His jeans hung low on his hips, so low that it was obvious he was circumcised. His tanned skin glittered wondrously in the strobe lights. Mr. Yes Please laughed at something Eric said, and Eric reached out and playfully gripped Mr. Yes Please's large bicep.

It was about that time that I pulled out my phone and googled how much time you got in prison for premeditated murder in the state of Arizona, all the while watching Eric out of the corner of my eye getting so close that I'm sure his normal-sized nipples were rubbing up against Mr. Yes Please. Google told me it was twenty-five years to life, and I weighed my options. I knew if I ended up in prison I'd just need to find the biggest, baddest guy in there and immediately become his bitch so that I wouldn't get shanked or shivved by some guy named Boisterous Frankie. But at least the twink would have felt my wrath.

On the other hand, I could avoid prison altogether instead of getting oddly jealous over Eric touching a guy who I hadn't even known existed less than ten minutes ago.

I was still debating this when someone said, "Paul," right next to my ear.

I jumped. I turned and saw Eric standing right next to me. "You bitch," I hissed at him, unable to stop myself. I glanced down at the floor and saw Mr. Yes Please watching us. *Did he send Eric up here to tell me to stop staring at him like a crazy person? Well, then, I will send Eric down with a message back saying that the only reason I was staring at him was because I was wondering where one bought steroids because muscles that big are gross. Sort of.*

Eric didn't seem to hear me slander him, or maybe he was just used to it and tuned it out. "Compliments of the guy downstairs," he said, handing me a shot of something from his tray. "Who the hell is he?" You could tell what he *really* wanted to say was *how the hell did you pull* this *off?*

I stared at the shot glass, confused.

"You gonna take this, Paul?" Eric asked. "Seems like a waste, given how hot the guy is. If you don't want it, I'll take it." He smiled an evil smile. "And then I'll go back down and thank him properly, if you know what I mean."

"He would, too," Charlie huffed. "Eric's ass is so loose it sounds like wind blowing over a cave entrance when he walks."

"Oh, Daddy," I said, laughing.

Eric didn't think it was funny. In the slightest. He sort of huffed and thrust the drink in my hand, spilling a bit of it before turning and stomping back down the stairs. "He's a bit bitchy today," Charlie observed in that dry way he has.

"Maybe he found out he has crabs," I said.

"That was last month," Charlie said. "He needs to be a bit more careful, otherwise he's going to wind up in a world of hurt." There was affection in his voice, however. Charlie's a big old softie, and I'm sure Eric looking the way he does helps that just a bit. Charlie's not a creepy lecherous old man, but he does have eyes. "You going to drink that?" he asked, arching an eyebrow. "Seems someone fancies you."

"This has to be a joke," I grumbled. I look down to the floor below and saw Eric reach Mr. Yes Please. Eric made sure I was watching with a little glance over his shoulder and then leaned in far too close to Mr. Yes Please, giving him a bit of the old bump 'n grind, whispering something in his ear but nuzzling a bit too. I wanted to stand up and tell everyone that Eric apparently had crabs last month, but even I'm not that mean. Out loud, anyway. In my head, I'm the meanest bitch who ever walked the face of the earth.

What bugged me a little bit (even though it had no damn reason to) was that Mr. Yes Please didn't exactly seem to be pulling away from Eric. He even seemed to be smiling a bit to himself as Eric fucked the air around him with his mouth, the dimples flashing in the strobe light. His friends over his shoulder were grinning at the two of them and whispering to each other, obviously sure that Eric was going to get down on his knees and blow Mr. Yes Please right there.

"He's a big fat slut," Charlie told me, obviously not missing a thing. He reached over and patted me on the shoulder as Helena stood in one place and did this pretty little twirl.

"Shouldn't your eyesight be failing by now?" I asked him, watching as Eric did a little twirl of his own, pressing his ass up against Mr. Yes Please's crotch, bending over and then grinding against him as he held the tray perfectly level. Mr. Yes Please stared down at him, not touching him, but not junk-punching him either. People began to give them room, backing out of the way as Eric worked his whore magic. Mr. Yes Please glanced up at me, an undecipherable look on his face.

"Cheers, Daddy," I said to Charlie, raising the glass to Mr. Yes Please and knocking back the shot before I even tasted what it is.

And as it hit my tongue, I realized it was whiskey.

I can't *stand* whiskey. Makes me sick. Makes me feel gross. Can't stomach it.

Which is why my throat closed up.

Which is why I spit it out of my mouth, forgetting I was on the balcony.

Which is how it sprayed off the balcony.

Which is why it landed right on Eric's head, splashing a bit onto Mr. Yes Please.

Even though it was an accident, I couldn't have planned that better had I done it on purpose.

Most people didn't even notice, their attention still on Helena Handbasket, who was doing this awesome backflip thing, pressing her feet up against the wall. But Eric sure as fuck noticed, snapping back up and glaring at me. Mr. Yes Please had the weirdest look on his face as he watched me, as if he couldn't decide if I was awesome or the grossest thing he'd ever seen. Charlie was busting up laughing, obviously not caring if it messed up the sound on the tape still recording.

And what about me, you ask?

I was fucking mortified.

I tried to sink down into my seat, my face going as red as it'd ever been. I really wanted to run down the stairs and get the hell out of here, but the stairs curved around and the door to the dance floor was right near where Mr. Yes Please and Eric stood. I decided in that moment that I was never going to leave the balcony ever again and that I would live up here for the rest of my days. People would come from everywhere to see the Gay Who Wouldn't Leave Because He Couldn't Handle His Alcohol And Spit It Onto A Stupid Slutty Twink. There would be lines to take my picture as I roamed the balcony, bemoaning my apparent lack of any kind of social skills.

But then the crowd roared as Helena Handbasket did her big finish (the one where she did this creepy/sexy upside-down crab-walk thing down the middle of the runway, all the while thrusting her taped junk toward the ceiling in writhing time with the music). I turned my attention back to my best friend and clapped meekly, praying that she would feel like staying up here for a bit before we went back downstairs.

But then I saw her glance up at me with a determined look on her face and I knew I was fucked.

"She wouldn't dare," I said to no one in particular.

"Wouldn't dare what?" Charlie said innocently.

"Daddy, what did she do?" I snapped at him.

He shrugged annoyingly. I looked ahead, horrified at what was about to happen. My secret shame. She wouldn't fucking *dare*.

Someone handed her a microphone. "How you bitches doing tonight?" she shouted, panting slightly from all the exertion.

The crowd roared back.

She smiled beautifully. "Oh, my lovelies. You are all so wonderful." Her face dropped into a sneer as she looked at a guy up front. "Except for you, honey," she said with faux disdain. "You were just sad and pathetic and just sat there. Kind of like you did last night too."

The crowd laughed. The guy she was picking on blushed and shook his head ruefully, in on the joke.

There was still time. I could still run. I just needed to—

"Oh no, you don't," Charlie said as he grabbed my arm and pulled me back into the seat. "You keep your ass right where it is until you are told otherwise."

"But, *Daddy*," I said, my whine coming from a panicky place. It did not sound cute at all.

"But, pretty boys and voluptuous girls," Helena said, "there is *one* thing left before we clear to dance our asses off for the rest of the night. Isn't that right, Charlie?"

"That's right, Helena," he said, pulling the microphone out of thin air, still holding me back. Every single goddamn person in the room turned to look up at us. Including Mr. Yes Please. I tried not to look at him. "One thing left, though you might want to hurry because he's starting to get a bit… fidgety."

"Oooooh," Helena moaned into the mike, playing it up. "Just the way I like him." She licked the microphone and the crowd hooted at her. "Boys and girls," she said, "today is a very, very special day. Do you see that *delicious* hunk of man sitting next to Charlie up there? That is my very best friend in *all* the world. And do you know what today is?" She grinned up at me, all teeth.

"Oh, you *skank*," I mumbled. Mr. Yes Please was staring at me again, a serious look in his eyes, Eric seemingly forgotten. I blushed even further as another spotlight turned on me. It was bright. I was sweating and turning red. *So* not attractive.

"It's his *thirtieth* birthday!" Helena shouted. "Paul, get your hot ass down here!"

The crowd started cheering, really only because Helena told them to. Or maybe they were just that damn excited about my life being totally and completely over, given that I was now the oldest thing in the world. I thought again about making a run for it—screw Mr. Yes Please; he wouldn't want a geriatric specimen such as me, anyway—but even before I could get to my feet and hightail it the fuck out, Charlie grabbed my arm. "Oh no, you don't," he growled at me in the deep, manly man voice of his. "Helena went to a lot of work to keep this secret, and I'm not going to let that go to waste. I'm getting pretty tired of seeing you standing in the shadows, boy. You deserve to be up in front of everyone so they can all see the real you."

"Now *you're* after-school-specialing all over my face," I said weakly, still hearing the cheers from below.

He chuckled. "Once upon a time that may have been so, but I'm just an old fart now." But then his gaze grew steely and I shivered a bit. "However," he said grimly, "I'm not too old to put you over my lap to give you the spanking you deserve if you don't get your butt down there now." And as if on cue, two shirtless barbacks appeared (thankfully, neither were Eric; I'm pretty sure he wanted to scratch my eyes out). They grinned down at me with grins that almost made me think I was about to get a hand job, but instead they grabbed me by the arms. I gave a very unmanly squawk as I was pulled down the stairs, Charlie calling after me that I'd better be a good boy or I'd answer to him later.

Before I knew it, I was down the stairs and out into the crowd, which parted in front of me as if commanded. Everyone was still clapping and hollering at me, and I couldn't help but think I was about to be sacrificed so all the gays could keep their ethereal beauty. I realized I'd probably seen *Indiana Jones and the Temple of Doom* one too many times when I saw Helena standing on the stage, and I expected her to reach for my heart and start chanting, "Kali-maaaaa! Kali-*maaaaaa*!"

But that was all completely forgotten for one brief, shining moment when I saw *him*.

As I was being dragged down the middle of the gay bar by two shirtless hunks (*Oh, the things that happen to me,* I thought to myself), I scanned the crowd frantically, trying to find a sympathetic face who'd help me escape my capture and flee with me. All I saw, for the most part, were drunken grins staring back at me, happy and wide. No one looked like they had my weapons of choice on them (ninja stars and/or nunchucks—don't ask), so I figured my escape could only be accomplished by sheer force of will and hand-to-hand combat. Since the last time I'd punched anything was a wall at work, after I accidentally tripped over my own feet and slammed into it with my fists, I figured fighting was out. I was about to offer each of the barbacks the seven dollars I had in my wallet (and, for some reason, an expired coupon for a loaf of bread; why I thought I needed the carbs at the time, I'll never know. I felt like an old Jewish lady for having it there), but that all went far, far away when Mr. Yes Please became Mr. Right Fucking Now Please.

Our gazes locked again like it was meant to be. He was only about five feet away now, and even in the dark, I could see his eyes were a chocolate brown, just like his hair. He grinned at me, a smile I thought was for me and only me, even as stupid twinkie barback Eric tried to get his attention with his whiskey-wet hair. The dimples came out to play as everything disappeared around me, the noise of the crowd fading to nothing until it was just me and Mr. Right Fucking Now Please staring at each other like we were the only people in the world. I could hear my own breath in my ears and I saw his lips move slowly, forming a single word: "Paul."

And, of course, I looked away. I had to. No one had ever looked at me like that before. It wasn't real. I knew it wasn't a real thing. It couldn't be, at least not for me.

So I just pushed it away.

I was forced onto the stage, and while the cheers started to die down, Helena reached out and grabbed my hand and squeezed. Without moving her lips from that big, showgirl of a smile, she muttered, "On a scale of one to ten, how pissed are you?"

"Seventy-two," I murmured back, trying to smile, but most likely looking like I was sneering. I have a weird smile. Oh, and I'm also not the most photogenic person in the world, so I'm sure all the photos that were being taken with phones and cameras would later need to be destroyed given how I probably looked like I was gassy and holding it in.

"Thank God it's that low," she said, her smile going wider. She raised the microphone again as one of the barbacks appeared with two more shots. They looked red, which meant they were probably fruity and I wouldn't have to spit it out on Eric, though he deserved it for trying to crawl inside Dimples. The lights were in my eyes. "Okay, boys and girls," Helena shouted into the mic as she handed me one of the shots. "You all know what to do! Ready? Haaaaaaaappy birthday to youuuuuuuuu...."

Is there anything more embarrassing or awkward than having "Happy Birthday" sung to you? Think about it. You're the center of attention for fifteen to twenty seconds while people sing horribly off-key at your face (with some wit most likely adding in his or her own words to make the song even longer: "Happy birthday to you, cha, cha, cha"). What are you supposed to do during that time? Do you sit there with an idiotic grin on your face while people sing about the day you came out of your mother's vagina? Do you look down at your hands? Do you sing along *with* them, only to realize it's sort of dumb to sing "Happy birthday to me"? And don't even get me started about the way people clap when it's over and smile at each other, like they're thinking what wonderful people they are for singing to you like that, like those fifteen to twenty seconds absolved them of all their sins.

So the entire bar sang to me and I stood up on the stage, looking like I had to fart. When it was finished, I was bright red and sweating like a roasted pig. My only consolation was the fact that I was able to take the entire shot down by the end. Helena thanked people for coming out to the show and the crowd began to disperse, giving way for the barbacks to clear the stage so it could be converted back to the dance floor.

"We love you!" a group of Muscle Maries told Helena.

"Thank you, baby dolls," was her reply with a lascivious smirk.

"You bitch," I told her once her adoring fans had gone out to the patio.

She snorted. "It wasn't *that* bad, was it?" She grabbed my hand and started pulling me across the floor. I looked for the hot guy, but he was nowhere to be found. I knew I was sort of okay with that. He was probably out back with the rest of the crowd or at the bar. Hell, maybe he'd even left already with all his hot friends and they were going back to their frat to bang some hoes and brag about how they worked up the courage to go inside a gay bar. Whatever was going on with him couldn't have been what I thought it was. I was just being stupid. Things didn't work out like that for me.

"It was like you flung battery acid at my face," I snarled at her as I followed her back up the stairs.

"You are such a drama queen," she huffed. "It's about fucking time something happened, and since you weren't going to do it yourself, you left me no choice."

"Meddlesome homo," I muttered.

"Paul!" she snapped. She was a little pissed off, I could tell. Nobody can rage like a drag queen. "You need to come out of your shell or step into the light or whatever other clichéd metaphor you would like to use. It's high time people got to see the real Paul Auster and love him for who he is."

I knew I was being a bit of a whiny ass, and I knew, of course, that Helena only wanted good things for me, but I couldn't help but feel attacked, pushed outside of my comfort zone without my consent. It rubbed me the wrong way. "I don't want to," I sulked. "I don't care about stuff like that. Why can't you accept that? I like the way things are. Besides, I'm pretty sure you are overestimating what would happen if I did what you asked. It'd probably be like expecting a beautiful butterfly to emerge from a cocoon, only to have it actually become a mentally disabled giraffe with eczema."

Helena twitched her lips and I knew I almost had her. She'd break and laugh and hug me and tell me she loved me and then we'd go back to the way things were until the next time she got a bug up her ass. "Giraffe, hmmm?" she murmured.

"Mentally disabled," I agreed. I leaned over and rubbed my nose against her cheek and hummed. She chuckled.

"What about that guy?" Charlie asked.

Helena reared back. "What guy?" she asked, looking suspiciously excited.

I whirled around and glared at Charlie. "I will put you in a retirement home and no one will visit you!" I hissed at him.

"What guy?" Helena barked.

"Some guy bought Paul here a shot and had Eric bring it up," Charlie said casually, as if my threat meant nothing. Which it didn't. "A very... *fit*-looking fellow."

"Ouch," I said, my feelings slightly hurt.

Charlie rolled his eyes. "That wasn't a dig against you, boy. You need to stop thinking that everything is about you."

"Ouch," I said again, my feelings more hurt.

"Where is he?" Helena asked, looking down to the lower floor, where people were starting to trickle back in. "Seen him before?"

Charlie shook his head. "Fresh meat, I think. Was hanging out with Darren and his group."

Helena looked at me, astonished. "You have a hunky *jock* wanting to jump your ball sac and you *stayed up here?*"

"He spit his shot down onto him," Charlie said helpfully.

Helena was horrified. "You did *what?*" she shrieked at me, going all Xena: Warrior Lesbian on me.

"It was *whiskey,*" I said in my defense. "And it didn't get on him. Mostly. It was all on Eric!"

"I think that boy gave me crabs," Helena muttered, scratching herself obscenely.

"*That's* who you were doing last month?" I said with a grimace. "Ew. Show some respect for yourself. It's fun to have *standards.*"

"When was the last time *you* got laid?" she retorted. "Let's go find this guy. I want to know who he is."

I took a step back. "Uh." I looked down at my hands and blushed, my shyness returning in full force. "No, thank you," I mumbled.

"Paul," she said, taking a menacing step forward in her red vinyl platform boots.

"Just drop it," I said, not looking at her. "It wasn't like that."

"And how do you know that?"

I was getting mad again. Meaning I was getting whiny again. "Because guys like that don't go for guys like me. It was a fluke. A joke. And even if it wasn't, the lights probably played tricks on him, making him see something I'm not."

"Paul...."

"No, Sandy," I snapped at him, breaking one of the cardinal rules of drag: in costume, she is Helena and she is a lady. But I was too pissed to care. I could see through the makeup to the guy who'd been my best friend for as long as I could remember, and it was *him* I was pissed at. "I'm sick and tired of you trying to change me. Why can't you just let me be? I *like* the way I am." Okay, that last might have been a bit of a lie. "I'm sorry if you don't, but that's not my problem."

His eyes flashed angrily at me, but then he seemed to deflate. "Oh, baby doll," he said. "I think you are perfect just the way you are. I just want others to be able to see how perfect you are too."

I refused to look at him.

"Go down with me?" he—*she*—asked quietly. "I'll buy you a frou-frou drink that comes with an umbrella in it."

"I think I'm going to stay up here for a bit," I said. "Keep Charlie company."

She sighed and stood up straight, becoming full-on queen and angry again. "Fine. You stay up here, locked in your fucking ivory princess tower. I'm done trying to help you."

"I never *asked* for your help," I reminded her. "You tried to do it anyway. If I'm so good the way I am, then why are you trying to help me do *anything*?"

She didn't say another word and pushed past me, stomping down the stairs as loudly as she could. Even above the dance music that had started to play, I could hear the door slam.

"Boy...," Charlie said, shaking his head.

"Not in the mood, Daddy," I grumbled at him. I pulled my chair off to side and in the shadows so I could still see down onto the floor but no one could see me. Eventually, the floor filled again and people started dancing. Mr. Nice Thought While It Lasted came in with his friends. I couldn't help but notice how he seemed to be looking for someone and would glance up at the balcony every now and then. I started to get this weird warm feeling in my stomach again, but it was gone the moment some big, muscley bear-looking dude came up and started rubbing up on him. He had a spark in his eye as Bear Dude leaned over and whispered something in his ear. He tipped his head back and laughed, and they started dancing all sexy-like, Bear Dude getting a nice handful of his ass as they moved. I looked away.

Charlie sighed but didn't say a word.

Happy thirtieth birthday to me.

CHAPTER 3
Dear God: Fuck You

THE next day, Sunday, I awoke in my own bed. Alone, of course.

Well, not *completely* alone. When I first got Wheels, I'd built this ramp thing that led up to the bed from the floor so Wheels could get up whenever he wanted to. It took him a while to get used to it, and his wheels squeaked when he was climbing up the ramp, but it was better than waking up in the middle of the night because he was trying to jump on his wheels to get onto the bed.

So I opened my eyes, not even remotely hungover, remembering I was now thirty, in a fight with my best friend, and had probably missed meeting the man who would undoubtedly be the love my life but was now probably waking up in Bear Dude's bed, all because I was a gigantic vagina. Not that he'd actually been looking at me seriously.

Blargh.

"You still love me?" I asked Wheels, reaching up to scratch behind his ears, his tongue lolling out in that way he does when he knows he's going to get his scratch on.

In books and movies, when asked a question by his lonely owner, a dog would most likely reach up and lick his master's face in a way that let the master know that the world might be scary sometimes, but it would all be okay eventually. But my life is not a book or a movie and instead of licking my face, Wheels farted and then barfed up the section of carpet he'd been gnawing on when I'd gotten home last night.

"Augh!" I cried, trying to roll away. Of course, Wheels thought we were playing a game and tried to crawl after me, running his cart through his own vomit, spreading it over my sheets as he rolled. "No, you gross two-legged monster!" I shouted at him, but he was already distracted by his own vomit and started to eat it and I gave serious thought to urking up a bit myself, but then I realized I would just be feeding him even more, and I had to turn away. As soon as I got myself under control, I heard my phone ring.

"Hello," I said, running to the bathroom to get a towel.

"Hi, baby!" my mom said.

"Hi, Mom," I sighed. "Listen, now's not the best—"

"Your father is on the line as well," she said, interrupting me.

"Dad."

"Hello, son," Dad said.

Ah, Matilda (Matty) and Lawrence (Larry) Auster. My parents. You can't say I haven't warned you.

"How did last night go?" Mom asked. "Did you get any play?"

"It is way too fucking early for this," I muttered, grabbing my bath towel and warming it under the water.

"Language," my father warned.

"Sorry."

"Well?" my mother demanded.

"Sandy called you, didn't he?"

"Oh yes," she gushed. "He asked me how much I thought you would try to murder him if he pulled you down on stage with him."

"And what did you tell him?"

"That you'd probably crap yourself on stage," she said.

"Language," my father snapped.

"It was fine," I said through gritted teeth, walking back to the bedroom. Wheels had the decency to look at least a bit contrite as I walked over to him. He hung his head a little bit, and I started to feel bad for the way I had glared at him, but then he farted again and I didn't feel so bad anymore.

"It was fine," I said. "Not that big of a deal."

"You did it?" my mother squealed. "I am so proud of you!" And she was, in her weird, weird way. Both of them were. I hear horror stories all the time of people coming out only to be rejected by their families and kicked out onto the streets and told never to return. I was scared, yes, when I was seventeen and trying to work up the courage to out myself to my family. Sandy had already come out to *his* family and received indifference, so we figured we could expect the same from mine. Boy, were *we* wrong. Being their only child, of *course* they were upset. For, like, two seconds. Once my mom got over her tears and my father stopped frowning, they went online to look up two things: where the closest chapter of PFLAG was, and the proper way to use a dental dam. "For all we know," my mother had said, "you may be into rimming now. We just want to make sure you are safe."

I love them completely, don't get me wrong. But they like to meddle just as much as Sandy does. They keep asking when I'm going to give them grandbabies. "We're not getting any younger," my father once growled at me.

"Well, I'm not quite fertile enough yet," I had growled right back.

I don't have the heart to tell them that I don't have ovaries like they seem to think I do.

"You got up on the stage?" Dad said now, sounding surprised. "Did you take off your shirt?"

"It's not *that* kind of a club," my mother scolded him. "He wasn't being auctioned off like some piece of meat. This isn't Phoenix."

Apparently I went to the wrong kind of clubs. When you're auctioned off, does that still make you a prostitute? Money is still exchanging hands, so it sounded kind of whorish to me. I decided right then and there that I would not want to be a prostitute. Besides, I still had all my teeth and I didn't look good in fishnets.

"Phoenix," my father grumbled. "Such a blight on the world."

"Did you shake your groove thing?" Mom asked me.

"No," I said, picking up Wheels and wiping off his paws. He just grinned up at me adoringly, shaking his butt where his tail used to be. "You're gross," I told him.

"I don't think shaking your groove thing is gross," my mother said, sounding baffled.

"Maybe that means something different than it did years ago," Dad said. "Like maybe now it has to do with unseemly things, like fisting or nipple clamps. Which," he said, directing his stern words at me, "you better not have been doing in public. You could get arrested for that kind of thing, even if it was in a sex club."

"It wasn't a sex club," I said, trying to scoop up leftover doggie discharge. "You've been there before, remember? For pride? You thought that leather bear had a neat vest and you asked him where you could buy one and he told you that he'd take you for a ride on his motorcycle?"

"Oh yeah," Dad said thoughtfully. "The floor was sticky there."

"From drinks," Mom said. "Not semen."

"Well, that *you* know of," Dad replied.

"How does it feel to be thirty?" Mom asked me as I scooped up the sheets from my bed and headed to the washroom. "Hungover from any... *whiskey*?"

"I didn't drink that much last night," I grumbled and then I froze.

"Did you meet anyone last night?" Dad asked casually. *Too* casually.

"What?" I asked, trying to buy time. "No." Then it hit me. "You already spoke to Sandy, didn't you," I accused them both.

"Matty," Dad sighed, "I think we need to work on our subtlety."

"Of course not, dear," she sniffed. "We're as subtle as the day is long."

"Yeah, if the day is in Antarctica during the winter," I muttered.

"What?" Mom asked.

"What?" Dad asked.

"She said you guys were subtle as the day is long. And I said only if the day was in Antarctica in winter."

"We heard that, sweetheart," Mom said. "We're not deaf."

"Days are really short in Antarctica during the winter," I ground out, shoving the sheets into the washing machine.

"That's nice, dear. Did you want to go there or something? That seems really far away. Consider going somewhere closer first, like Iowa. I hear the people there are very... Iowan."

"Maybe it's on his bucket list," Dad said. "You know, now that he's thirty, he's trying to figure out all the things he wants to do before he dies."

"Like have grandbabies?" my mom asked hopefully.

"That's why I got a dog," I said, hearing Wheels rolling his way to his dish in the kitchen.

"Granddogs?" my mother said, perplexed. "Not quite the same. Now, who was he?"

"Who?"

"Don't do that, Paul. It's annoying."

"Yes, Paul. Don't annoy your mother because then she annoys *me*."

"Really, Lawrence, try to be a bit more sensitive."

"I'm the most sensitive man you know."

"No, Paul is. He always has been, ever since he was a little boy. I don't know why we were so surprised when he came out. We should have seen it coming."

"Like the time he wanted to be Cinderella for Halloween when he was ten?"

My mother sighed. "Though, now that I think about it, he should have been the fairy godmother."

"Mom!" I choked out, as my dad started to crack up. "That's not funny!"

"Oh course it is, sweetheart. I'm the funniest person in the world."

"That makes me so sad," I told her.

"What was his name?" she demanded.

"If you talked to Sandy then you know I don't know," I said. "I don't want to talk about it."

"Why not?" Dad asked. "I don't understand why you're so quiet. Or so shy, for that matter. You're just as good as any of the other homosexuals in there. Better, even."

"The best," my mom said fondly.

I tried not to let them know how their words affected me, only because I realized that this is why they had called to begin with. We didn't speak on the phone that often, and if we did, the conversations were short and sweet. But Sandy must have told them I was upset and this was them trying to make me feel better, and I'll admit, my eyes were burning a bit. All my anger fled at that moment, and what I really wanted was my mom and dad.

"I don't know," I said, my voice a bit rough. "You guys are just biased."

"Well, even if we weren't, we'd still love you to pieces," Mom said. "We know you're shy, Paul, and maybe you'll always be like that. But one day, someone is going to come along and sweep you off your feet and it will be like magic. You'll open up like a blushing, virgin flower filled with rainbows and sprinkles"

"Rainbows and sprinkles," my father agreed. "The most sprinkliest virgin flower ever."

"I love you guys," I told them honestly, even if they were batshit insane.

"We know, sweetheart," Mom said. "Feel better?"

"Yeah. A bit." And I did. Dog-vomit eating and all.

"Good, because Sandy is sitting in your driveway, waiting for us to make you not mad at him anymore."

I groaned. "You set me up!"

"And it was surprisingly easy." Dad laughed. "Geez. I don't know how you weren't kidnapped as a child by a stranger who offered you candy. You're so gullible."

"Lawrence," my mother admonished. "What terrible thing to say. Accurate, but terrible. Now, Paul, are you done being mad at Sandy?"

"I guess," I allowed.

"Why don't you ask *him* out?" my dad asked. "He's already like one of the family. It'd just be so perfect! And then you two would be married and your mother could borrow that one outfit he wears that has the tail...."

"Larry!" my mother shouted, but even I could hear the smile in her voice.

I tried to scrub that image from my head, but it worked its way in. It's a weird kinky pony-play outfit he found at some sex shop that he wears when he does Marilyn Manson at the club. It's scary, but a little hot. "We're not like that," I told them. "Sandy and I are best friends. Like brothers. We tried it once, but it was just too weird. Not our thing. I love him, but not that way."

"It'd be easy, though, right?" Dad asked.

"Oh, Larry," my mother sighed. "Love is never easy."

Oh gross. Not this kind of conversation again. You'd swear there were three people on the phone with a uterus instead of one. "And on that note, I gotta go. Sandy, and all."

"Okay," Mom said. "Don't forget next weekend going to Nana's for your birthday."

"Wonderful," I said. "There's nothing greater for my self-esteem than to hear Johnny Depp call me a fanny-bandit."

"That bird," Mom said. I could hear the frown in her voice. "It needs therapy."

"Is there bird therapy?" Dad asked, and I hung up gently, knowing *that* conversation would go on forever.

I thought I'd let Sandy suffer for a bit longer, but it was May, and it gets very hot very quickly in the desert. Part of me was vindictively gleeful at the thought of him sweating horribly, but then I realized he had air-conditioning in his car and he hates to sweat. "Guess who's here," I said to Wheels in a happy voice, getting him all riled up. "Guess who's here! Is it your Uncle Sandy? Is it?" Wheels about shat himself when he heard the name Sandy. They'd bonded over a Milk-Bone and been soul mates ever since. The mutt pretty much hates everyone else. He's very… *picky* about who he loves. Which, to be honest, was just a nice way of saying my dog is a jerk.

I opened the door, a little startled to see Sandy standing in the entryway. He eyed me warily. "You still mad?" he asked. "Because if you are, I brought you a breakfast burrito from Los Betos, which is your most favorite thing in the world."

It was, but I wasn't going to let him off that easy. I stared at him.

He sighed and went a bit further. "And I also brought *Transformers* on Blu-ray, because you don't seem to own it for some reason." He dangled it in front of me.

The man knew his way to forgiveness, especially through Michael Bay and burritos. I stood aside and let him through the door. He looked instantly relieved, and only then did I notice the bags under his eyes, like he hadn't slept well. I wondered if it had to do with our fight, and I immediately felt like an ass. I placed a swift kiss on his cheek as he passed me by. I caught his small smile as I closed the door behind him.

"DO YOU even want to know his name?" he asked me an hour later, tucked into my arms on the couch, lying with his head on my chest.

"Who?" I asked, watching as Optimus Prime kicked some major digital ass.

"The guy from last night."

I took a deep breath and let it out, trying to remain calm. I paused the movie and the house got eerily quiet. "You talked to him?"

He shook his head, a little tense against me. "I asked around. Tried to get some info."

"Why?"

"Because I love you, you big idiot," he said softly. "More than anything in the world."

Asshole. Going straight for the heart is so unfair. I just grunted at him, unable to use my words.

He took this as a go-ahead. "Apparently he's from here. Went to the U of A before moving to Phoenix. Then he moved back here a couple of weeks ago."

I shuddered. "Thank God he moved back. Do you think he still has his soul or did Phoenix steal it away?" There's a strange rivalry between Tucson and Phoenix, one that probably goes back to the dawn of time when people from Phoenix crawled up out of the pits of hell and tried to destroy the paradise that was Tucson. It's not something you're supposed to question. If you live in one place, you automatically despise the other city. It's a desert thing.

Sandy laughed quietly to himself. "He's twenty-eight. Apparently not the sharpest tool in the shed, but he's supposed to be sweet as all get-out, not to mention he looks as he does. Single, doesn't appear to be too much of a slut. Couldn't quite nail down his type, but I don't think you'll need to worry about twinks like Eric. Besides, even if you did, did you see his arms? I'd kick anyone's ass for that. I think he could probably bench press a moose if asked."

I snorted. "We'll be sure to test that theory out," I said before I could stop myself.

Sandy sat up, eyes wide, that familiar smirk forming. "Does that mean…?"

I blushed as I shook my head. "Doesn't mean anything. I'll probably never see him again." I tried to ignore how my heart thumped a dance beat in my chest. And I didn't want to know his name. Not at all. To hear it would make him real, and to make him real would make it hurt all the more because nothing would happen. I didn't stand a chance in hell, especially with what all his friends looked like. I'm pretty sure you have to be a shallow jerk to look like they do. It's part of the "I'm So Pretty" contract God makes all the beautiful people sign. I groaned as I realized I was going to ask anyway.

"What's his name?" I asked, avoiding eye contact.

Sandy grinned and I saw a bit of Helena spark behind his eyes. And then, in a low and throaty purr, he spoke the name that would change everything. "Vincent Taylor," he (or was it she?) said. "Goes by Vince."

Vince Taylor. "God," I groaned, unable to stop myself. "That's so fucking *hot*. It's so not fair. The least he could do by looking the way he does is be named something horrible like Leslie Poofington or George Bush. God *hates* me."

"It does sound very sexy," Sandy agreed, laying his head back down on me, snuggling closer.

We stayed like that for a time, in the quiet, me rubbing his shoulders slowly, him humming softly to himself in that way he does when he's content. Then something bugged me (as usual) and I had to ask. "Sandy?"

"Yes, baby doll?"

"How come you didn't go talk to him?"

He turned his head, his chin on my chest, staring up at me with his pretty blue eyes. "Should I have?"

I thought for a moment and then shrugged.

He nodded. "I didn't, because I knew that'd piss you off. And I don't like it when you're mad at me. Makes me feel all funny inside, and not in a good way. Ever since my parents... you know...." He sighed and looked away, biting his bottom lip.

I did know. His parents were killed in a car wreck when we were sixteen. I'll never forget the look on his face when I was called into the principal's office, the way he shook, his hand squeezing mine so hard that I had bruises for a week afterward. The look he'd given me was one of heartbreak, yes, but it was also of a boy who was completely lost. I promised myself right then and there (as I had over and over again for years) that I would always take care of him, for the rest of our days. And I liked to think I'd kept my promise, at least as best as I could.

"I know," I said softly, rubbing his shoulder.

"There's not so very many people I trust, and even fewer that I say I can trust completely," he said. "But you're number one, you always have been. And I push because I want everyone to see you as I do, this bright and shining star that would take their breath away. But I get scared one day I'm going to push too hard and you'll leave me too. I don't know where the line is and I don't think I ever want to find out."

"Hey," I said, grabbing his chin, bringing his bright eyes to mine.

It'd be easy though, right? my dad had said.

Maybe. Maybe not.

I leaned forward and he sighed, and his lips brushed mine and…

… we both burst out laughing.

Definitely not.

"No spark," he said as he giggled.

"None whatsoever." I laughed. "It's like incest."

"If only, right?"

I nodded, brushing his hair out of his face. "No one's gonna love me as much as you do."

He stopped laughing then, suddenly serious. "You just wait," he said quietly. "I promise. You'll see." He kissed the tip of my nose and sank back down onto my chest. "Besides, we're both bottoms. What would we have done? Bumped boy pussies?"

I groaned and rolled my eyes. "Shut up and watch the movie."

And he did exactly that, right where he belonged.

Vince Taylor.

I sighed like a forlorn school girl waiting on her sparkling vampire boyfriend.

Oh sweat balls.

MONDAYS suck.

"Mrs. Jackson," I tried for the sixth time. "Mrs. *Jackson*." I lowered the volume on my headset, waiting for Mrs. Jackson to finish.

"Do you know who I am?" she screamed into the phone. "Do you know who the fuck I am? You better do what I say!"

I bit back every single sarcastic remark I could have possibly said and took a deep breath. "Mrs. Jackson, this is the *tenth* time we've had this conversation. There is no coverage for your accident because you let your insurance policy lapse. When you don't pay your insurance bill, you don't have insurance."

"Are you being condescending?" she shouted. "I know my *rights*. I am an American *citizen*."

"I'm sure you are," I said. "But I don't know what that has to do with this conversation. You could be from Botswana and we'd still be having this conversation."

"You better hope I never see you on the streets," she growled. "Because if I did, I would *cut* you."

Gee, another threat. "Mrs. Jackson," I said, trying to keep the boredom out of my voice, "it seems I have to remind you *again* that these phone calls are monitored and we take threats very seriously." Well, we didn't, actually. I don't think I know of anyone that has been murdered doing my job. Plus, she lived like three states away, so she would have had to take a bit of a road trip if she was going to really cut me.

"You gonna fix my car?" she snapped at me, ignoring me completely.

"No, ma'am. We can't give you something you haven't paid for."

"You mother is a *whore!*" she screamed at me before she hung up.

"Yeesh," I muttered, hanging up the phone and taking off my headset.

"What'd she threaten you with this time?" Sandy asked, looking over at me from his jail cell… er, cubicle, across the way.

"She's going to cut me," I sighed.

He grinned. "How wonderfully ghetto. You're the only person I know of who works here that gets people to threaten you with physical violence."

I rolled my eyes. "What can I say? The melodious sound of my voice obviously brings out the best in people. When are we going to quit and open up our surf shop?"

Sandy laughed. "Well, first we have to move to a place that has water. Then we have to learn how to surf. Then we need to learn how to operate a small business. Then we need to find the capital to open such a business. And *then* we can open our surf shop."

"So… tomorrow?"

"Tomorrow," he agreed. "But, on the bright side, it's now 8:32 in the morning, and we only have eight hours until we get to leave."

"So much time," I moaned, banging my head on my desk. "This place is sucking out my soul. I should have been a romance novelist by now. Or, at the very least, had my own reality TV show where cameras follow me around as I get into all kinds of shenanigans."

"What would your reality show be called?" Sandy asked.

"Paul's Hour of Power."

He grimaced. "That sounds like you'd spend your whole time getting fisted."

I threw a paper clip at his head. It didn't even make it halfway across the aisle. It was a good thing I never wanted to play baseball, because I threw like a girl. Who didn't have arms.

"What time's the new guy getting here?" Sandy asked, not even bothering to make fun of me for the paper clip.

"Nine. I don't know why I have to be the one to show him how to do crap. He's coming from the Phoenix office. It's not like they do things differently up there in Hell."

"Maybe he'll be way hot," Sandy said, waggling his eyebrows.

"Have you seen where we work? Knowing my luck, he'll be straight, won't have any teeth, and will spend the entire day telling me how pretty and perky he thinks his stepdaughter is."

"Oh, Paul," Sandy said sympathetically. "You are brain-damaged."

"I love you too."

I didn't even notice the next twenty minutes going by. Time supposedly flies when you are having fun, but time also jumps around weirdly when you're trapped in the limbo that is an office job. Some days, I'd look at the clock and be surprised about how quickly the time had passed. Other days, time slowed down so much that it moved backward and I could feel myself breaking piece by piece until I was nothing but a pile of corporate American sadness.

Paul's Hour of Power: speaking the truth, doing it fabulously.

So I wasn't really paying attention when I heard my boss call my name. I said, "Yeah," but I didn't look up from my computer while I tried to pretend the new system that they'd made us start using weeks before made sense and wasn't a train wreck like the rest of us knew it was ("This will make your jobs so much easier" turned out to be code for "We may not have known exactly what we were doing, but we put too much money into it, so you'll kind of have to suck it up and work with it, even though it's so broken that it makes your jobs ten times harder." I thought about writing to the ACLU to complain and have them intervene, but then Sandy reminded me that it wasn't civil rights related. We tried to think of a way to spin it that the new computer program was homophobic, but then we got distracted by the UPS guy, who happened to have a different kind of package we wanted to sign for, and the ACLU was forgotten. Cock tends to make things bearable).

So I was distracted. I kept getting a stupid error message on my screen, and I was about to chuck the keyboard across the room when I heard Sandy begin to choke. I looked over at him, ignoring the two people standing in front of me. Sandy's eyes were bulging from his head as he stared up at our boss and the other dude. I frowned at him. "Are you okay?" I asked.

He nodded as he started coughing, his face turning read. I didn't know what the hell his problem was, but he didn't seem to be dying, so I figured he was okay. I swiveled in my chair to face my boss and my nine o'clock distraction.

My boss, Chris, smiled at me. "All right. This is—"

"You've got to be fucking kidding me," I almost shouted.

Chris took a step back. "Pardon me?"

But I wasn't even listening to him. He ceased to exist. All I was aware of was the sharp buzzing in my ears, how my palms became instantly sweaty. I knew I was turning red and I was fighting a losing battle to curl up in on myself. I knew when (*if*) I spoke next, my voice would be soft, so much so that my words would be unintelligible. My shyness and awkwardness were trying very, *very* hard to take over, and I was fighting against them in a losing battle.

Because, oh *because,* standing in front of me, dressed in expensive-looking slacks, a crisp white shirt adorned with a silk tie and suspenders (really? *Really? Suspenders?*), looking like he just walked out of a photo shoot for a magazine called *I Look Better Than Anyone Ever,* stood the man I'd spent the last two nights fantasizing about. Mr. Yes Please. Dimples, of course, on full display.

"Paul," Vince Taylor said, his voice deep and looking inordinately pleased about *something*. "How nice to see you again." He grinned at me like we shared a great big secret.

My boss looked confused.

Sandy continued to sound like he was dying.

"Fuck," I whispered.

CHAPTER 4

I Am Going To Freddie Prinze Junior You So Hard

"GOD hates me," I groaned to Sandy at lunch later that day. We sat at some restaurant that was supposed to be a hip and trendy vegetarian place. So, of course, all I could think about was how hilarious it would be if I went next door to Burger King and got the biggest bacon cheeseburger they had and ate it in the vegetarian restaurant in front of all the hip and trendy vegetarians. I suck like that sometimes. "It's like he got bored and thought, 'Hmmmm. I don't want to mess with Africa today, and I don't want to send Hurricane Ebonica to wipe out Florida, so I'll just fuck with Paul.'"

"Hurricane Ebonica?" Sandy asked, his lips twitching.

"I thought the hurricane could use a bit more ethnicity," I muttered. "They always sound so white. It's not fair to other races. You always hear about hurricanes called Carl or Diane, but you never hear of Hurricane Rodrigo Sanchez or Ji-Ting Kao."

"Only you would fight for the civil rights of hurricanes," Sandy said, smiling sweetly at me.

"Someone has to," I insisted, wondering just how we'd gotten to this point in the conversation, but realizing it was probably my fault.

"Let's focus on Hurricane Paul for a second," he said.

I looked at him, horrified. "Are you saying I should suck *and* blow him?"

Sandy looked startled for a moment. "Paul Auster," he said, chuckling. "Just when I think I know you completely, you can still say shit that surprises me."

This pleased me for some reason, but I ignored it. Instead, I frowned.

He reached over to pat my hand before diving back into his salad. I looked down at my own. I guarantee you there has never been a single person in the world who ate a salad and said, "Gee, I am so full now.

Thank God I just had *that*." It's just not possible. My body needed bacon to live.

"Next time we come here, I'm bringing my own Bacon Bits," I threatened Sandy. "You may have your girlish figure to maintain, but I'm a man. I need steak."

He snorted into his radicchio, which I admired because it was a pretty purple. The radicchio was purple, not his snort. Just in case you got confused there. I don't think it's possible for people to snort colors. We're not unicorns, after all. "You're all man," he agreed. "So, I had to go to a meeting. What happened with your boyfriend?"

I blushed and mumbled threats at his person.

"What was that?" he asked. "Couldn't quite hear you."

"I said I'm going to cut you."

"Ah. That's what I thought you said. So what happened?"

"God hates me," I said again. And he did. I don't know what I ever did to God (maybe the Christian Reich was correct and God *did* hate homosexuals; that could be the only possible explanation as to why he was torturing me so).

I couldn't tell Sandy what had happened when Vince arrived because I didn't *know*. Everything from the moment I saw him until the moment Sandy snapped his fingers in front of my face, asking me to go to lunch, was a haze. A deep, murky haze, punctuated with little flashes of light, like the moment Vince sat down next to me and extended his hand to shake mine, his grip calloused and warm. This was followed by words he said to me with a grin: "Quite a small world." Then, everything went dark for a bit until there was another flash of light when he leaned forward and said in a low voice, "Not a whiskey drinker, eh?" The haze descended again until my phone rang and I picked it up, hyperaware of just *how close* he was sitting next to me, his knee *accidentally* brushing against mine. I don't remember the phone call in the slightest, and I don't know if I told the person on the other end that I'd give them a million dollars to go fuck themselves or not. I heard Vince chuckling next to me, and I didn't know what was so damn funny, but it didn't *matter*, because his laugh was a low, throaty thing that sort of rumbled out of him as if it'd crawled from the depths of his stomach.

After that, it was white, white bliss until Sandy started trying to get my attention. I didn't even remember Vince leaving or where he went.

"Oh, Lord," Sandy said when I admitted this all to him. "You've got it *bad*."

"I do not," I said defensively. "Got what?"

"You're crushing on him."

"*What*? I am not!"

"You so are."

"You shut your mouth, you bitter queen."

"You *loooooove* him."

I scowled at Sandy. "What are we, twelve? You act like I want to get his picture and put it on my Trapper Keeper."

Sandy squealed. "And then you could write all over it with things like Mrs. Paul Taylor over and over again like you did with Zack Morris from *Saved By The Bell* when we were in the sixth grade."

"Oh, Zack," I sighed. "You were too good for Kelly Kapowski. She was a stupid bitch and I hated her face and her bangs and the fact that she was alive."

"I really thought it was going to work out between the two of you," Sandy mused. "You sent him all those fan letters and everything."

"And he never wrote me back," I said sadly. "Then they had to do the college-years series and ruin everything about *Saved By The Bell* that made it wonderful. It was like watching someone you know and love get hooked on heroin and you can't stop them."

We gave a moment of silence for *Saved By The Bell*. Rest in peace, Zack Morris.

"Anyway," Sandy said as I bit into a crouton. "You love him, and he obviously wants to bone you, so why not go for it."

"He does not," I grumbled with another blush. And then said, almost as an afterthought, "And I don't love him. I don't even know him."

He looked at me knowingly, but didn't call me out on it. "Well, you know what they say. When life hands you lemons—"

"You'll slice them to make lemonade, only to find you have miniscule little cuts on your hands and it causes it to sting really bad," I finished for him. "Oh, and lemon juice squirts in your eye and blinds you for like twenty minutes."

"You're like that donkey from Winnie the Pooh," he told me. "On crack."

"I'm a manic-depressive, drug-addicted donkey?" I asked, incredulous.

"If the tail fits," he snapped at me.

"Reality would be if Eeyore was on Paxil. No one could be depressed as much as he is for that long without needing antidepressants. Winnie the Pooh and Piglet probably staged an intervention at their house at one point."

"They didn't live together," Sandy said.

"Of course they did. They were life partners."

"Pooh was porking Piglet?"

"Brings new meaning to the sentence 'I ate ham for breakfast.'"

"I bet there's like an Easter egg on one of the DVDs," Sandy said, taking a drink of his tea. "A deleted scene that shows Eeyore jerking off to a photo of Pooh fucking Piglet while hanging himself with his tail in the closet."

We laughed quietly, horrified with ourselves for thinking such things.

And, of course, that was when it happened.

God. Hates. Me.

"What's so funny?" Vince asked as he appeared out of nowhere like some evil, dark, hot wizard. He had a grin on his face as he stood next to the table, looking so freaking awesome in his suspenders and tie. I wanted to snap one against his skin just to hear the sound it made, but somehow I refrained from doing so, only because I was still laughing at the thought of a beloved childhood character committing suicide when he spoke, and tried to distract myself by shoving more salad in my face at the same time. So, naturally, instead of being way cool and snapping his suspenders while letting him in on the joke and winking at him until he became putty in my hands, I inhaled sharply and a piece of raw spinach was sucked into my black hole of a mouth and lodged itself in my throat.

And I started to choke.

At first, it wasn't so bad. I thought I could still breathe around it and I made a noise that made me sound like an Ewok: "Urka. Urk. Urk." Sandy was looking up at Vince, staring at his mouth as if all the world's secrets lay there. I felt an outrageous flash of jealousy rip through me, but it was waylaid as my Ewok noises turned into full-fledged attempts to gasp in air, however futile they were. I became annoyed that I was dying and my best friend hadn't even noticed because he was making goo-goo eyes at the man who had a knack for showing up at the worst possible times.

I kicked Sandy under the table, who flashed an annoyed glance at me, as if *I* was the evil one here. But then, it must have sunk into his tiny little brain when he saw my skin color doing an impression of a Smurf orgy (blue everywhere, like Papa Smurf had just smurfed all over the other Smurfs). He started screeching that he didn't know CPR and wouldn't *someone just save his best friend in the world?*

I couldn't be bothered with trying to remind him that I needed the Heimlich maneuver, not CPR, because I was choking, not drowning. But his high-pitched damsel-in-distress wails brought attention to us from everyone in the damn restaurant, and I wanted to kick him in the nuts, but realized he'd taped them up enough that even that probably couldn't hurt him anymore. Even as I choked, I glared at everyone who worked in the restaurant, making sure that they knew that this was *their* fault for having a vegetarian place when we, as humans, were so obviously made to eat meat. I told myself if I died here, I would haunt this place and make it look like pork chops were raining down from the ceiling. I would be such an awesome ghost.

And then I felt everything go dark and my breath stopped and my heart thudded lightly in my chest. I saw a white light and went into it. My body died, but I ascended into heaven, where a group of shirtless and way-hot angels waited for me and wanted nothing more than to cater to my every whim. My favorite was an angel named Esteban Ortega who whispered dirty words in Spanish in my ear and who I called "*Papi.*" I was happy, happy at last, and that's where I stayed for all eternity, with a Latin angel and my ginormous penis. And a halo. And wings. And I also could make unlimited wishes.

The end.

Okay, I'm just fucking with you. I didn't die. That'd been a bummer way to end the story, don't you think? Gay people get happy endings too, Hollywood!

I was aware of my back getting pulled into a strong body, big arms wrapping around my waist. *Oh,* I thought, even as I choked. *This is nice.*

Then it stopped being nice when the hands attached to the big arms joined at my midsection and jerked into my stomach, pushing in and up. I could feel my eyes bulge out of my head, and warm lips near my ear saying, "C'mon, c'mon, c'mon," and then the hands thrust into me again. The action caused the remaining air in my body to expel out. The spinach that tried to kill me ejected from my mouth…

… and landed with a splat on the cheek of my best friend who was demanding that I be saved.

A hush fell over the room.

Sandy's cheek twitched. The spinach slid slightly down his face.

Arms around my waist. Heat against my back. Breath against my ear.

My heart rapid in my chest. Salad stuck in my teeth.

Then Sandy started screaming, clawing at his face to get what had ejected from my mouth off him. He didn't have a hard-core aversion to germs or anything like that, but I figured something that had once lodged in a throat and was now stuck to his face deserved a bit of hysterics. Hell, I'd have been shrieking had it been me, but since it wasn't, I was just staring at him like he was overreacting. "Really," I sniffed as he rubbed his cheek furiously with a napkin. "We're in public, Sandy."

He glared at me.

The people in the restaurant started going back to their own meals, the lunch theater starring the homosexuals now over.

"You okay?" our waitress asked. "Your color is coming back. Do I need to call for paramedics?"

I shook my head, feeling my face turn even redder. "I'm okay. Sorry for causing a scene. I will learn to chew my food before I come back here." *Not that I'm coming back to your vegetarian place of death ever again, you purveyor of killer spinach!*

She smiled. "You're lucky this gentleman was here and acted as he did. He doesn't seem to want to let go of you now." She winked and walked away.

And then.

Oh, boy.

And then. And *then* I realized who she was talking about, who I was still lying against, who still had his arms around me, rubbing one of his hands in a small circle on my stomach like he was trying to soothe me. And *then* I leaned back without any forethought and felt that broad chest against my back. A chuckle rose near my ear and my skin felt alight with little shocks of electricity.

And then I remembered *who* was behind me and who *I* was and stepped away quickly, keeping my head and eyes down, looking everywhere but at him. I heard him sigh quietly, sounding exasperated, but I thought I'd heard it wrong. After all, there were so many ways to interpret a sigh. He might have been sighing in relief, happy that he no longer had to have me pressed up against him like that. The jerk.

"Sorry," I mumbled to Sandy. "I didn't mean to project my throat spinach on your face."

"You better not have," he snapped at me, a little bit of Helena in his eyes. He dipped his napkin into my cup of water before dabbing it roughly across his cheek. "I wouldn't be able to continue this decades-long friendship any further had you done it on purpose."

I knew he was joking—kind of—but I was still mortified. "Sorry," I mumbled.

"It was an accident," Vince said, coming up behind me. He sounded almost angry, and Sandy and I both jerked our heads up at him. He squeezed my shoulder but didn't look down at me. "You don't need to be such a jerk," he told Sandy coldly.

"Ix-nay!" I hissed at him. "Ix-nay!" I didn't know why I resorted to Pig Latin right then. It just seemed like the thing to do.

He ignored me as he scowled at Sandy. "You should apologize."

Sandy's eyes narrowed. "Listen, pretty boy. You better back the fu—" He caught himself and closed his eyes, taking a deep breath. When he opened his eyes again, Helena was gone from them and he smiled weakly at me. "You okay, baby doll?"

I nodded, wondering what the fuck was going on that Vince was trying to be my knight in shining Versace while my best friend had backed down from a hissy fit when his alter ego had been looming heavily in his eyes. This was turning out to be a very weird Monday.

And, oddly, I couldn't help but notice how Vince's hand on my shoulder tightened at the words "baby doll."

"Okay," Sandy said, picking up his bag that was really a purse, but we pretended it wasn't. "I'll tell you what. I need to go get some fresh air before lunch is over, so I'm just going to start walking back to work now. You going to be okay?" A certain wickedness returned in the curve of his lips.

I nodded, unable to open my mouth to beg and scream for him to not leave me alone with a masturbatory fantasy (not that I'd gone that far… yet). I could tell when he saw the words I wasn't saying but ignored them regardless. He slid his man bag (*Your stupid purse!* I thought savagely since he was leaving me behind. *Your lady's purse, you big homo!*) over his shoulder and looked at Vince, still standing with his hand on my shoulder, the grip even tighter. "Thank you," he said quietly. "For helping my friend."

He nodded, a tentative smile on his face.

Then Helena returned in full force, rising up out of the dark. She stepped over, moving like smooth liquid, her hips rolling. The change was startling. "But," she said in a deep growl, "you do anything to hurt him? Sugar, I will tear you apart until your insides are on the outside. We understand each other?"

Vince's eyes widened just a bit, but he nodded, his jaw tightening. I wanted to ask which one of them was going to piss on me first, but then I realized two things: first, they probably wouldn't even hear me as they were too focused on each other; and two, I was not into watersports. Why would you let someone pee on you to get you off? That's so fucking gross!

Helena seemed to be appeased like a volcano god receiving a virgin sacrifice and went back to sleep. Sandy leaned in and kissed me on the cheek, lingering maybe just a little bit longer than normal. He pulled away with an audible smack of his lips, gave Vince one more look, and turned, walking away with a perfect swish to his hips.

And then I was alone with Mr. Yes Please himself. Me. Paul Auster. With Dimples.

I was just a bit nervous, to say the least.

Okay, okay. So. First things first. Aaaaaaaaaaaaaahhhhhhhh! Second thing: I should probably say "thank you" for saving my life. Say it and then follow it up with something funny like… okay. Spinach joke. Spinach joke. Shit. Um… Oh, I know! What do anal sex and spinach have in common? If you're forced to have either as a child, you won't want it as an adult. Holy fucking Christ. What the fuck is wrong with me? There is no way I can make a spinach/molesting joke! I am a monster. Think of something else. Think of anything else.

"Thank you," I mumbled, not able to think of anything else to say.

Vince looked at me. He was taller than me, maybe by an inch or two, so he had to angle his eyes down. His big brown eyes. His pretty, huge brown eyes that looked like chocolate. I realized I was standing far too close when I could feel his breath on my face and I could see my reflection in his irises. I had a deer-in-the-headlights look on my face, and apparently a little piece of spinach still on my lip. I looked away and not very discreetly wiped my face with my hand.

"What'd you say?" he asked.

I cleared my throat. "I said thank you," I tried again, a little louder. "You know. For helping me to live." *Oh, that didn't sound overtly dramatic. Like at all.* "Erm. What I meant to say was, you were pretty fast there. You know, with your hands." *Oh great. Now you're calling him a whore.* "Er. What I meant to say was you have chocolate eyes." *Shut up! Shut up!* "And do you know what anal sex and spinach have in common?" *For the love of God, close your fucking mouth!*

I closed my mouth.

He stared at me.

I took a step back and he dropped his hand. I wondered if I should inhale more spinach so I could actually choke to death so I'd be put out of my misery. It would be so much easier than standing here in front of him and having him think I was bursting from my cocoon as a mentally disabled giraffe. I turned to pick up my phone and wallet, wanting to get the hell out of there. I couldn't believe it'd gotten this far. I felt punchy and maybe my eyes burned a bit. I didn't know. I just wanted to leave.

"Paul," Vince said, his voice kind.

"What?" I grumbled.

"Where you going?"

"Back to work. I have work to do."

"Wanna have lunch with me?"

I would have your babies if you asked. "I'm kind of busy." That, and the fact that I suddenly couldn't get the image out of my head of that twinkie Eric grinding up against him or of Bear Dude grabbing a handful of his ass and Vince seeming to enjoy it while I hid in the shadows of my tower.

"Paul," he tried again.

"What?" I snapped at him. I was *way* outside my comfort zone. I didn't talk well with people I didn't know, and even worse, hot guys I didn't know. I felt awkward, and I'd already made an ass out of myself in front of him. In addition, my best friend had queened out and basically threatened to disembowel him if he hurt me, like we were dating or something. Talk about embarrassing. *He probably feels sorry for me and wants to make me his project.*

He looked kind of glum. "You don't have to if you don't want to," he said, almost pouting. He saw me watching and unbelievably, stuck out his bottom lip and sighed forlornly, playing the hurt up so well that Helena would have been proud.

"Oh, no," I told him. "You don't get to do stuff like that, looking the way you do. That's not fair."

He grinned. Dimples returned. I wanted to poke them. "And how do I look?" he asked.

I rolled my eyes. "I'm not going to feed your ego. Your obvious narcissism looks good enough for the both of us."

"My what?" he asked, his smile never fading, but a look of confusion coming over his eyes.

"Never mind," I muttered.

"You know," he said, turning serious, "there's a saying that once you save someone's life, that you're responsible for it. It's an old… African chant."

I gaped at him. "African?"

He nodded. "From Africa."

"That's a Chinese proverb. Not an African chant."

"What's Chinese?" he asked, further confused.

"What you said about saving someone's life. That's Chinese."

He shrugged. "I don't speak Asian. I want to go there, though. One day."

"To Asia?"

He nodded.

"Where in Asia?"

"The Asian places," he explained, dead serious. "I've always wondered if the fortune cookies taste different there."

Kinda what I thought. Very, very pretty, but not exactly bursting with brains. I didn't know if that made me feel better or not. "Fortune cookies," I said slowly.

He nodded. "You know, those cookies that have the little pieces of paper in them? Sometimes they just give you numbers for some reason, but other times you get ones that say things, like, 'Your beauty helps make the world go round.'"

"You got a fortune cookie that told you you're beautiful?"

He nodded. "It was kind of weird, but I just rolled with it. I seem to get those a lot for some reason."

"Maybe because you're beautiful?" I blurted out, unable to stop myself.

Vince grinned at me and blushed a little. So unfair. "You think I'm beautiful?"

I winced. "That wasn't what I meant to say."

"Oh, so you *don't* think that."

I blushed. "It's not... ugh. Shut up."

His smile widened before he narrowed his eyes and scowled toward the front of the restaurant. "Was that your boyfriend?" he growled.

The conversation felt like the equivalent of whiplash. "My what now?"

"That guy. Who kissed you. That you spit on. You seem to do that a lot, by the way. Was that your boyfriend?"

"*Sandy?*" I said incredulously. "No! Er. No. That's my best friend. You've seen him before. We're not dating. We're not together. I mean, we tried it once, but it didn't work out. I kissed him yesterday just to make sure, and there was nothing."

His scowl turned to me. "You kissed him yesterday?"

"Yeah. Dude, you know him already. You've seen him before."

"What?" He looked adorably confused again, and I hated myself for using words like *adorable* and *beautiful* to describe him. I was pretty sure I was about to flop my vagina on the table.

"That's Helena Handbasket."

"The drag queen?"

"Yeah."

"But… he looks so *little* as a man."

I shuddered. "Don't let him hear you say that. Helena will come out before you know it, and that bitch is fierce. This one time, some big leather daddy tried to start some shit with him, and then Helena came out to play, and the daddy ended up on his knees with a collar around his neck, apologizing to Sandy, who held him on a leash. They ended up dating for two weeks, but then it ended because Sandy figured out she wasn't meant to be a Dom."

He watched me for a moment, looking for what, I don't know. I couldn't read the expression on his face. I didn't know if he was still with me or if something I'd said had confused him. I felt like a jackass then, at least a little bit.

And then he spoke, and I understood that he wasn't confused per se, he was just still stuck on a point a few turns in the conversation back. "So *do* you have a boyfriend?" he asked. "Or a partner or whatever?"

I started getting nervous and shy again, but I allowed myself a brief moment to feel awesome about myself when I realized I'd been having a conversation with him for, like, five minutes. Even if I'd told a pedophile joke, it seemed to be going better than I ever thought it would. This, of course, caused me to shut down just a bit further.

I looked down at my feet. "No," I mumbled.

"Thank *God*," he said, sounding extraordinarily relieved. "Can I take you to dinner?"

Uh. What? "Uh. What?"

"Din-ner," he said slowly, as if I was stupid. "Can. I. Take. You. Out?"

I was starting to get defensive. "Why?"

His brow furrowed. "Because I want to. Don't you want to go with me?"

"Guys like you don't go out with guys like me."

He looked me up and down as if trying to figure out what I was talking about. I wasn't wearing my nicest dress clothes, but I thought I looked okay this morning. But standing next to him now made me realize I probably looked like a homeless albino who found these clothes in the sewers. "What's wrong with you?" he asked finally. "You sick or something?"

"Sick? What? I'm not sick."

His eyes widened, and he looked around quickly before leaning forward to whisper, "You *are* gay, right?" He was sort of pensive at this.

"Way gay," I reassured him. "Like, super gay. I fart and rainbows come out." *Oh, crap.*

He rocked his head back and laughed, a delicious sound that was deep and gravelly. I wanted to lick a line up his exposed throat, but I didn't think the rest of the restaurant wanted to see that. Besides, I didn't think he'd want it, either, even if he was presently confusing the shit out of me.

"Can you please ignore what I just said?" I asked desperately. "I don't fart. Ever."

He shook his head, wiping the tears from his eyes. "You said it, so it's out there, man. You are something else. I knew you would be, right when I first saw you."

"You did?" I squeaked, unsure if that was a good or bad thing.

He smiled a lazy smile that screamed insane possibilities. "So... dinner?"

And then it hit me, what this probably was, and I felt sick to my stomach. I couldn't believe I hadn't seen it before, or even thought of it, especially with the fact that he was at the club with Darren and his group, the biggest bunch of assholes in the history of the world. They were such pretentious pricks that I couldn't believe I'd forgotten he was there with that group to begin with.

"You're Freddie Prinze Junioring me, aren't you?" I accused him, slight anger in my voice.

"I don't even know what that means," he reassured me, not perturbed in the slightest.

I scowled at him. How could he *not* know? Then I realized that not everyone knows the things that go through my head, so I had to give him the benefit of the doubt. "Freddie Prinze Junior? The actor, probably the greatest one of his generation? He was in that movie *She's All That.*"

He shrugged. "Never seen it."

"Whatever. In the movie, he's a cool popular jockish dude who makes a bet with his cool popular jockish friends that he can turn the most unattractive girl in school into prom queen. He only asks her out because he's an asshole, at least at first. Then the girl goes through life-changing things for him and gets to go to prom with Freddie Prinze Junior, but she finds out about his bet and he realizes too late that that he loves her. She breaks up with him because he shouldn't have made the stupid bet to begin with!"

"I thought you were thirty?" he asked me, baffled.

Of *course* he would bring that up. "I *am* thirty," I said with a sneer.

"Then why do you want to go to prom?"

"*What* prom?" I asked, throwing my hands up in the air. What the fuck was he talking about? He was *so* missing the point.

"You're talking about going to the movies or to the prom with some girl," he said. "I don't even know what you're talking about. We can go to the movies, I guess. Sometimes I get headaches, though, sitting in the dark like that for a while. I can take some Tylenol before. That might help if you really want to go to the movies." He rubbed the back of his head with one of his big hands. "I don't know about prom, though. I'm probably too old to go. Why are you going with some girl?"

"You... you're...." I sputtered. "You're impossible!"

"No, impossible is understanding you sometimes. You always talk like this?"

"I talk just fine," I said.

He grinned. "You are pretty fine," he agreed.

"Did you make a bet with your friends?" I said as I ground my teeth together.

"About what?"

"To ask me out."

He shook his head. "Why would I bet them? I knew I was going to when I first saw you. I don't need anybody trying to bet me about it. I would have done it regardless. I'm *doing* it now."

"But Darren...."

"You know Darren?"

"I know *of* him."

"He's a great guy."

"Yeah, if you like bitchy barracudas with ridiculous egos."

"What's that?"

"What?"

"Barracudas."

"An evil fish with big teeth that eats your face off."

"Oh. So do you want to go to dinner with me?"

I took a step back. "I don't think that's a good idea."

Was he a little upset by that, or was it my imagination? "Why not?"

"I'm not…. You're…. Look, it just wouldn't work out, okay? You seem like a sweet"—*and oh so fine and nice and funny and I want to have a hard-core bone sesh with you and live forever in our Dream Castle*—"guy, but you're not really my type."

He rolled his eyes. "I'm *everyone's* type," he said. He winked and flexed his arms a bit.

My mouth went dry, but it was suddenly easier to take another step away. "And that's the problem," I told him quietly. "I have to get back to work." I started to walk away, only to be stopped by a hand gripping my arm. I turned to find him watching me intently.

"You may as well just give up now," he said.

"What do you mean?"

"You're going to go on a date with me. It's just easier if you say yes now."

"Cocky fucking bastard."

"Nah, I just see that you want to, but for some reason you're saying no."

"Maybe because I *don't* want to. You ever think of that?" I was such a liar.

He shrugged. "Maybe. But you do. And you will." And then, before I could stop him, he pulled me forward into a tight hug, my chin pressed against his shoulder, his lips near my ear. It was so unfair how fucking good he smelled. My stomach flip-flopped a little as he whispered in my ear. "You may as well just say yes. I saved your life, and that means you belong to me now. I'm totally going to Freddie Prinze Junior you so hard later." Then he let me go and walked toward the door.

"That's not what that means!" I shouted after him, causing people to stare at me like *I* was the ridiculous one. "You *don't* get to make it sound dirty and hot!"

He didn't even look back.

CHAPTER 5

Bicycles Are For Tree-Hugging Hippie Heterosexuals

"YOU said *what*?" Sandy asked me furiously when I returned from lunch.

Shit. I hadn't meant to say a damn thing. "I said no."

He looked at me like I was the stupidest person alive, which, to be fair, I probably was. I'd turned and run out of the restaurant with my tail between my legs, trying to protect my fragile ego.

"Are you out of your fucking *mind*?" he hissed at me. He looked absolutely livid.

"If you think he's so awesome, why don't *you* ask him out," I retorted.

"Because he doesn't want to make babies with *me*, you stupid idiot! *He asked you out and you said no.* I taught you better than that!"

"Go away."

"Oh, Paul. It probably would have been better for your sake had you not told me that."

That didn't sound ominous or anything. "What do you mean?" I asked warily.

Sandy glared at me. "It's become *painfully* obvious that you can no longer handle your own affairs. So from this point on, I'm going to do everything *for* you. You're going out with Vince."

"Knock it off."

"No. You had your chance to do this your way. It's not working. You're making things worse. Now I'm taking over."

"Sandy, I mean it."

"First order of business: What are you going to wear on your first date?"

"I will punch you in the balls, so help me God—"

"If he's taking you somewhere nice, then you should wear those gray slacks that make your butt look hot."

"By hot, you mean fat. Besides, I'm not *going*—"

"If it's going to be someplace casual, then you could probably go with jeans and that leather jacket I bought you for Christmas that you never wear."

"I wore it that one time at that thing we went to! Then someone asked what kind of motorcycle I rode and I told them I didn't have one, but I'd always wanted a Vespa—"

"And then we'll obviously need to figure out some kind of first-date etiquette. Do you hug him? Do you give him a rim job? Do you ride him? I don't want you to be out of your comfort zone. Or seem like a whore."

"*Ride* him? Did you smoke *meth* on your way back from lunch? You are out of your damn *mind*—"

"We'll figure it out. Now, do you want me to RSVP with him for you, or are you going to tell him yes?"

"We're through. I no longer want to be friends with you. My love for you has died like a dusty flower in the desert with no rain. I hate you."

"I'll give you until Wednesday."

"Fuck you."

"Until five o'clock on Wednesday. If you don't do it, I'll give him your phone number and tell him where you live."

I looked at him, scandalized. "You wouldn't *dare*."

"Bitch, please," he said with a smirk. "Who do you think you're talking to?"

"Sandy, I'm warning you."

"Oh, like I'm scared of you."

"You should be," I tried to say menacingly.

"That almost worked, but then I remembered how when we were eight, you cried because your mom wouldn't buy you the My Little Pony that had the little jewel thing on its ass."

I gasped. "Morning Star? He was so *pretty*."

"I can't believe there are male My Little Ponies. You, my friend, are a homo."

"Says the drag queen."

"Wednesday, Paul. Five o'clock."

"I will fuck you up, Sandy."

My work phone rang. "This is Paul." Oh, crap. "Mrs. Jackson. Mrs. *Jackson. Mrs. Jackson.*"

Sandy smirked at me.

Balls.

I DECIDED that for the rest of the day, I would ignore Sandy completely and pretend that Vince didn't exist. So, naturally, they were all I saw.

Word of Vince spread quickly through the small office, with all the little gossip whores whispering back and forth about how hot he was, and that rumor had it he was gay. I wanted to tell them of *course* he was gay, that no self-respecting man could look like him and *not* be gay, but that would mean acknowledging his existence, so I kept my mouth shut.

It didn't help that every time I saw him he was surrounded by adoring fans who seemed to be fawning all over him already. It didn't help that I couldn't stop myself from scowling as Brittany Ward, the female office slut, kept giggling and pushing her grossly huge breasts against his arm like sexual harassment wasn't a real problem in the American workplace. It didn't help that I couldn't stop myself from grinding my teeth when Tad Cook, the male office slut, kept giggling and finding some way to touch Vince on the arms, stroking his biceps. I figured it must come with having your name be something as pretentious as *Tad*, because, really? Who names their kid *Tad*?

But as much as I wished the ground would open up and swallow both of them whole into an underground river of lava, what made it worse was the fact that I even cared if the office sluts were trying to mark their territory. I pretended to ignore the grin on Vince's face. For all I knew, maybe he was bisexual and he'd have both Brittany and Tad at the same time (which did nothing to help my overactive imagination, and I quickly had to curtail those thoughts because even though I hated their stupid faces, the idea was still kind of hot. Except for the part with the vagina).

So I spent the rest of Monday in alternating states of anger, jealousy, disdain, horniness, and awkwardness, so much so that by the time five o'clock hit, I was ready to spread myself out like a buffet for Vince or murder him and hide his body underneath the floorboards in my house.

It was about that time I realized I might have been obsessing a bit much, and since I didn't want to end up boiling a rabbit in his house and screaming, "*Why won't you love me?*" as my mascara ran down my face, I decided to just push it all away and forget Vince completely.

"Won't even worry about it," I told Wheels that night as we sat on the couch watching *Man v. Food,* trying to make the all-important decision on whether I'd rather do the host Adam Richman, or eat the four-pound bacon cheeseburger he was currently stuffing in his face. I decided I'd do both at the same time and felt better.

Wheels huffed as he raised his eyes to mine, his head never leaving my thigh.

"Don't give me that look," I scolded him. Then Adam Richman swallowed a piece of bacon whole, and I finally understood the meaning of food porn. "I don't need you giving me any crap, either."

He sighed and growled a little growl at that back of his throat.

"You don't understand," I told him, scratching his ear. "What would he even see in a guy like me? I'm not going to be anyone's project. Even if he's not Freddie Prinze Junioring me, you *know* eventually he's gonna be all like, 'Hey, let's go to the gym and work out for six hours and totally get our cardio on.'"

Wheels barked.

"Right? That's why it'll never work out. I don't *want* to get my cardio on. I can't think of anything more awful than that aside from having a vasectomy while awake with no anesthesia. And even if I *did* want to go out with him—which I don't—soon, he'd get bored anyway and then we'd argue and break up and be all sad. Then we'd have to see each other *every day* because we *work* together, and by that time, he'd probably have Tad spread over his fucking desk making him squeal like a little bitch. God, I hate that fucking name!"

Wheels raised his head and gave a little howl.

"Amen!" I agreed. "Preach it, sister. So, it's decided, then. It's easier this way."

I swore Wheels rolled his eyes then, letting me know *nothing* is ever that easy, and even if it was, maybe it wasn't a good idea to settle for easy.

That life was too short to *settle* for easy and that maybe, just *maybe*, I should step out of my comfort zone for once in my fucking life.

Then I realized that this was my two-legged dog and that he probably didn't mean a damn thing at all. Either that, or he was psychic and could see that my downfall would occur the very next day and it would involve a pair of bike shorts.

God, I'm such a sucker for bike shorts.

WHEN my alarm went off the next morning, I woke with renewed determination. I let Wheels out, listening to his cart squeak as he went about his business. In the shower, when I wasn't singing at the top of my lungs, I practiced my speech to both Vince and Sandy, as they were almost the same. *I'm very flattered that you want to take me out/help me out. But I've decided that I don't need that right now/don't want your help. I'm asking that you respect that/fuck off before I cut you. So, while we can be friends, I think we should just keep it at that/never talk about this again, you stupid queen.*

The coffee was gurgling as I finished getting dressed, and I let Wheels back in the house. I poured the coffee in my travel mug, grabbed a granola bar (don't worry, it was one of those ones that are supposed to be healthy, but is really just covered in chocolate), and went out to face the day.

On my way to work, I sang along to Kelly Clarkson's "Miss Independent," completely agreeing with the music's timeless lesson, even if I looked like a raging fruit as I danced in my car. "That's right!" I shouted at the traffic light, waiting for it to change to green. "I don't need no fuckin' man tellin' me what to do!"

I forgot that my window was down until the woman in the car next to me shouted back, "Me either! Don't need no fuckin' man!"

I would have been beyond embarrassed, but I was feeling way too fucking good, so I shared a kindred moment with the woman, both of us grinning at each other like fools. I cranked up the stereo and we sang as loud as we possibly could until we missed that the light had turned green and the guy in the truck behind us began to honk and scream out his window, "Move your gay asses!"

I thought about flipping him off because I *was* Miss Independent, but then I saw he was in a Ford F350 and I was driving a Prius, and I liked my face shaped the way it was, so I just waved as sarcastically as I could. And if you think one cannot wave sarcastically, then you'd be wrong.

So there I was! Feeling good! Feeling *fine*! I pulled into work and I was going to make it after all! I'd made it thirty years, and I was gonna make it *another* thirty years! I parallel parked on the street better than I'd ever done before, and I was gonna fucking *rock* this motherfucking Tuesday! I looked at myself in the rearview mirror and grinned the biggest fucking grin. "Today is *your* day," I told myself. "Make it shine!"

I looked in my side mirror before opening the door and saw a bicyclist approaching, waiting until he passed. I think I told you that I'm an ass man, so seeing a guy in tight biker shorts seemed like another good start to my motherfucking Tuesday. His head was bowed, helmet on, sunglasses on his face, and he went by without looking at me, and I caught a glimpse of a hard-core ass, probably in the top ten I'd ever seen, maybe even top five. I looked back into the rearview mirror and grinned again, rolling my eyes. A boy can dream, right?

But no. *Oh* no. God wasn't done fucking with me, no, sir, he wasn't!

I got out of the car and walked across the street, looking up just in time to see the bicyclist pull up to the bike rack next to the building. And then everything went in slow motion.

Okay, so you remember the TV show *Baywatch*? How *everything* the beautiful people did on that show always seemed to be in slow motion, be it running down the beach or taking a shower like it was some soft-core pay-cable program? I would always watch it because of the abundance of man flesh, though I don't know if my twelve-year-old self completely understood that fact. I think, though, that I was very well in tune with the fact that I was far more interested in the slow-motion pecs versus the slow-motion tits. I wasn't a stupid boy by any stretch of the imagination. "Are you sure you should be watching this?" my mother had asked one time, frowning as Mitch climbed out of the pool, the fur on his chest dripping with water. "I like it for the stories," I replied, slightly slack-jawed.

So it was kind of like that. My very own soft-core pay-per-view show. The bicyclist stepped off his bike in super slow motion, and I could feel my heart thudding against my chest, the blooding roaring in my ears.

The long slow flex of his thighs in those bike shorts made my mouth go dry instantly. The hard curve of his ass pulled against the black spandex and all I wanted to do was fall to my knees and bow in exaltation. I would worship that ass.

And then, in even *slower* motion (it was like time was running *backward*), he lifted the helmet up and off, shaking his head back and forth, brown hair cascading like he was in some kind of fucking pornographic shampoo commercial. I wanted to rub my hands through the hair and scream out, "Yes, yes, yes!" like they used to do in those Herbal Essences ads that they discontinued because no one actually had an orgasm using the shampoo. This thought distracted me, just for a moment, wondering if the *real* reason those people always shouted in the commercials was because someone was actual going down on them and you just couldn't see it. Then I realized that all those commercials involved women and that would mean someone was munching carpet while the other was washing her hair, and I got kind of grossed out because vaginas have more folds than a pile of laundry.

Blargh.

"Paul?" the bicyclist called out, pulling me out of my Herbal Essences, vagina-induced reverie.

I focused again on that ass. "Hello," I mumbled, unsure about how the man I'd dubbed Favorite Ass Ever knew my name.

"Wow, is *this* all it took?" He chuckled. "My eyes are up here, sailor."

Okay, *that* totally ruined the moment, but it made me well aware that I was eye-raping him, which was then made all the more worse when I realized the bicyclist was *Vince*. I blushed furiously and tried to walk away, but it was like *one* of my feet was glued to the ground, because I could take *one* step, but I couldn't move any further. I was looking everywhere but at him, trying to focus on things like the big tree in the courtyard and the blue sky above and that cloud that looked like a penis going into a butt....

"Oh *God*," I moaned. "Not a sex cloud! Why would you do that to me!"

Vince got a funny look on his face as he looked up into the sky, taking off his sunglasses. "What's a sex cloud?"

"A product of high winds, humidity, and atmospheric conditions," I muttered. "Why are you riding your bike? Don't you have a car?"

He shrugged. "Yeah, but I *like* riding my bike. It helps with the ozone... and stuff."

"You're trying to avoid leaving a carbon footprint? And here I thought bicycles were just for tree-hugging hippie heterosexuals."

He eyed me seriously. "We all have to do our part to help avoid nocturnal emissions. The planet needs us."

I stared at him. "The planet needs us to avoid nocturnal emissions?"

He nodded. "Nocturnal emissions are the number one cause for the hole in the ozone."

"You're... you...." I sputtered. "You can't... adorable fucking... it's cheating, is what it is... bastard... ass... so much *ass*...."

He grinned and pressed a foot up near the seat of his bike, stretching out his leg so it was horizontal and then doing an obscene stretch that outlined his crotch so perfectly I wanted to run away screaming with my arms waving over my head.

"Work," I said weakly.

"Work?" he asked, quirking an eyebrow as he pressed down on his thigh. His mad-crazy, hot thigh.

"I have to work." Well, I had to work on *breathing*, because he switched to bring up his other leg, doing another stretch, bending down until his stomach was flat against his thigh, like he was folded in half.

"I'm pretty bendy," he said casually, his gaze never leaving mine, and what was I supposed to do with *that*?

I tried to remember the pep talk I'd given myself the night before. I tried to remember being Miss Independent while driving into work, sharing that moment of camaraderie with the woman in the car next to me because we didn't *need* no fuckin' man. But that seemed like a lifetime ago, because I was pretty sure I was getting an erection while standing outside my work, watching a man who was turning me inside out doing the most erotic version of Pilates I had ever seen (and that's saying a lot, because I once saw a porno disguised as a nude Pilates video. I tried to follow along on my own floor, but it's hard to do when you've got a boner).

"Bendy, huh?" I mumbled. "That's… swell."

"I like this office," he said, putting his foot back down on the ground before bringing one arm across his chest and grabbing his shoulder with his other hand, continuing to stretch. "You want to know why I like this office?"

"So… sweaty," I breathed, watching a little trail of sweat roll down his cheek.

"I like it," he said, switching to stretch his other shoulder, "because they've got a small gym here, downstairs. Didn't have one of those at the office in Phoenix. Do you know what's in the gym, Paul?"

"Free weights and an underserved sense of accomplishment?" I asked.

He shook his head slowly and walked around his bike until he was standing two feet in front of me. I tried to cover up my traitorous dick with my coffee cup, but I don't think it worked too well. It wasn't that big of a coffee cup, even if I didn't have a huge dong. "Showers that no one uses," he said in a low voice. "Ever." He took another step toward me, until I could feel the heat radiating off him in waves. Hot, sweaty manly man waves.

"Oh?" I managed to say, trying to force myself to take a step back, but unable to do so.

Biker Vince nodded, eyes glinting. "Except…." He bit his bottom lip, then let it go. "Except for me. I use them." He took another step, until his chest brushed against mine. He leaned in and I could feel his breath on my face and my lips parted and—

"Kelly Clarkson," I said.

He stopped, mere inches from my face. "What?" he asked, that adorable look of confusion on his face yet again.

"Don't need no man," I whispered. "She told me to be independent."

Must… resist… bike shorts….

"Who's Kelly Clarkson?" he asked, leaning back a little and frowning. "Is she a friend of yours? If you want, I can talk to her for you. Put her at ease."

"Nocturnal emissions are wet dreams!" I shouted at him and then ran around him and back up the stairs. I tripped, but that's cool. I meant to do it because it added more drama to my exit.

I didn't look back.

I TRIED to hide from him for the rest of the day. Supply closets are great places to try this out. I got bored after two minutes and started taking an unofficial inventory. We had 262 highlighters. That's a lot of highlighters. We were running out of envelopes. Someone really should have gotten on that.

Tad came in to the supply closet at some point midmorning, claiming he needed paper clips. I glared at him the whole time, wishing silently that he'd get herpes on his face, right on his perfectly plump lips. I wondered briefly if that was very wrong of me to think, but then he gave me this knowing little smirk and said, "Oh, *heyyyyy*, Vince," really loudly when he left the closet, so I didn't feel so bad about it. As a matter of fact, I also included in my wishes for him to have a burning sensation when he peed. And to get eaten by a shark while being set on fire on the surface of the sun.

Sandy found me sometime in the afternoon. "What the hell are you doing?" he hissed at me, shutting the door behind him. "Are you trying to get fired? I've been covering for you all day! I've had to tell management you have explosive bowel issues from eating Los Betos!"

"Don't you speak badly about Los Betos," I said with a scowl. "And why did you have to say it was *explosive*? Can't it just be normal?"

He waved his hand in dismissal. "Makes it sound more believable."

"Yeah, but people are going to be looking at me weird now."

"As opposed to when they find out you're hiding in here with Post-it Notes?"

"We need to order more of those. Almost out."

"Why are you in here?"

"Bike shorts," I muttered, my brain shorting again at the memory. "Ass in bike shorts."

His eyes widened slightly. "What? Who?"

Shut up, mouth, shut up, mouth! "Vince." Dammit!

Sandy grinned the biggest shit-eating grin in the history of the world. "*Really?*" he said gleefully. "That good?"

"The ass to end all asses," I said, unable to stop myself. "The Holy Grail of asses. If we lived in a world with fairies and elves, there would be epic quests to go get that ass. I wanted to bite it." *And* that's *not something I can unsay. Yeesh.*

Sandy started laughing so hard I thought he was going to pop a few blood vessels. He started to choke on his tongue, so I patted his back carefully a few times because I didn't think my employer would be appreciative of a dead drag queen in the supply closet. That has a tendency to look bad on a company.

Sandy got himself under control (sort of), wiping the tears from his eyes. "You're going to cave," he told me, still giving these wet-sounding chuckles. "You're so going to cave."

"I am not!" I crossed my arms, trying to look indignant, but probably looking petrified instead.

"Well, you have"—he looked down at his watch—"twenty-eight more hours before I do it for you. But it looks like you're making some headway."

"I don't want to be friends anymore," I told him seriously.

He sidled up to me, all slinky-like, bringing out some Helena in the roll of his hips. I tried to move away, but he backed me into the shelves against the wall. I was cornered. "Oh, sugar," he purred, dropping his chin on my shoulder, watching me with those big eyes, curling his hand into my hair. His breath felt hot on my ear. "You should know by now that you're stuck with me. For life. There's no way, come hell or high water, that you're ever going to escape me. I've got my claws in you, and I don't plan on letting go." He fisted my hair and gave it a little jerk.

I shivered lightly.

Then, when I knew things couldn't get any worse, things got worse.

The supply closet door opened and Vince walked in. And, of course, I knew immediately how it looked, me pressed up against the shelves, Sandy all but wrapped around me like he was getting ready to eat me whole. If I walked in on something like that, I'd have assumed the two people were about to play a game of Dick Up The Butt.

You could tell it took him a moment to take in what he was seeing. There was a blank look, then surprise, then recognition. Then came that scowl again, just like the one he'd given me yesterday when he'd asked if Sandy was my boyfriend.

Sandy knew *exactly* what was happening too, and pressed himself against me just a *tiny bit closer*, his gaze never leaving Vince. He curled his fingers through my hair again, pulling me toward him, giving me a lingering kiss on my cheek. I felt my face grow hot, but I didn't say a damn thing for fear of squeaking. I don't know of anyone who thinks squeaking is cool.

After what felt like a decade, Sandy (or was it Helena?) finally uncoiled himself from me with an evil smirk and sauntered his way slowly past Vince, whose scowl had only become more pronounced. He reached up and dragged his finger along Vince's shoulder, just a light touch, but noticeable. He moved past him and turned and glanced down at his ass, giving a low whistle.

"You weren't kidding, Paul," he said in that throaty Helena voice of his that almost drove me up the fucking wall. "Remember, you have until five tomorrow." Then he moved out the door, closing it behind him.

I could feel Vince's gaze on me, but I couldn't look at him for some reason. "What happens at five tomorrow?" he finally said, his voice neutral.

"The end of the Mayan calendar," I muttered.

"Isn't that supposed to be when the world ends?"

"Yeah."

"So the world might end tomorrow?"

Oh good Lord. "It's always possible." Because it *could*. For all I knew, right now, somewhere in space, a group of ragtag oil workers were trying to stop an asteroid from hitting and destroying the earth by drilling deep to place a nuke inside. They could fail. We could all die.

Damn you, Michael Bay!

"And he's not your boyfriend?" Vince asked, his voice tight.

I was getting whiplash again. "No."

"Good. Then he won't be pissed when I do this."

I was about to ask, *Do what?* But before I could, that fucker had moved quicker than I had seen anyone move before. One second he was near the door and the next he was standing right in front of me, his fingers going to the back of my head, his thumbs on my cheeks, and then his *mouth* was on mine. There was a bright flash and a *brzzzzzzzzzzzzzzzzaaaaaap!* as all the electrical charges in my brain went off at once. But then he started to *move* his lips over mine and my eyes started to flutter closed like I was some kind of goddamn teenage *girl*. And even though my synapses had fired off all at once, I was able to think, *I can't believe this is happening and this is not* even *a real thing and this. Is. Awesome!* Then it became even *more* awesome when he touched his tongue to my lips and I sighed, opening my mouth without even thinking about it. He was the cause, I was the effect. Action, reaction. And fuck if he wasn't getting a reaction out of me. He tasted me gently, gripping me tightly, and I couldn't move, I couldn't breathe. I either wanted to bring my hands up to grab him or push him away, I wasn't too sure.

And then it was over. That first kiss. That tentative moment when there's a connection like a gold thread stretching between two people, tenuous but hopeful. And it was done. Gone. Snapped. Nothing more than a memory.

Until he leaned in and did it again. And then stopped. And then kissed my forehead. For some reason, that put a lump in my throat.

"I told you," he whispered against my skin, "I get what I want. You better be ready, Paul."

And then he stepped away, winked at me, and walked out of the supply closet.

I stood there for a time, muttering to myself. "That's just... well, I *never*. I don't even... who does he think he is? Tasting like coffee and... bastard... this is my *work*... running out of Post-its and shit. I'll show *you* until five o'clock on Wednesday. I don't need no man. Fucking Kelly Clarkson. She ruins *everything*. It's not going to happen, Paul. Not going to happen."

But.

But....

Even *I* could not ignore that little teeny-tiny light that seemed to ignite within me like some kind of misplaced hope, a small ray of sunshine on an otherwise stormy day that maybe, just *maybe*—

"Oh sweat balls," I told the supply closet, close to panicking.

The highlighters did not reply.

"WHAT the hell am I going to do!" I cried at Wheels that night as we sat on the couch. *Man v. Food* was on again, but even Adam Richman eating the world's biggest hot dog didn't do anything for me (to be fair, it *was* a repeat; I remember watching that episode for the first time thinking, *Yeah, you take it. Take it all.* I might be a bit of a perv).

Wheels snorted, cocking his head at me from his spot on my thigh.

"That's all you have to say about it?" I scolded him. "That bastard *kissed* me! He wasn't supposed to do that! I could have gotten fired."

Wheels barked once, a soft sound followed by a guttural growl. He laid his head back on my thigh, his eyes never leaving me, calling me a fucking idiot in that way he did so well.

"I am not," I said, sulking slightly. "You don't understand. *Why* would he do something like that? *Why* is he trying to get my hopes up? Is this just some kind of fucking game to him?"

Wheels huffed and tried to roll on his side, away from me, so obviously disgusted with me that he didn't even want to look at me anymore. His wheels were too bulky for him to be able to lie comfortably on his side on the couch. I undid the harness that kept his little cart attached and removed it carefully. Once this was done, he huffed at me again as if to reiterate his point and rolled over, curling his front two paws up underneath him, his ear stretched out on my thigh.

"Oh, now you're going to ignore me?" I snapped at him. "What, gonna give me until *five o'clock* tomorrow to do whatever you say? You're just a fucking jerk too, you half dog."

He sighed.

I felt bad. "I didn't mean that," I said quietly. "I just don't think any of this is real." His bottom wiggled a bit, wagging his imaginary tail. I often wondered if dogs were like human amputees who could still feel ghosts of their limbs long after they'd been amputated. It always made me a little depressed to think about, because I couldn't stand the thought of

Wheels being uncomfortable in any way. "You forgive me?" I asked, scratching his head.

He rolled over and licked my hand just once, then grabbed ahold of it in his teeth. He applied a bit of pressure and shook his head back and forth once each way. *Don't be a fucking idiot, you fucker*, he was telling me (in my head, Wheels cursed with the best of them). *Fucking man up before your balls fall off and you and the Period Ghost have something in common. I don't need two wailing chicks in my house, so man the fuck up.*

"Dammit," I whispered.

I hated tomorrow already.

CHAPTER 6

Performing CPR Is Just One Tongue Away From Making Out

MY ALARM went off, but I was already awake. I hadn't slept much. Every time I closed my eyes, I would remember that kiss, the feel of his hands on my face, the shine in his eyes that made me feel warm even though I was sure it was all a fluke. Even the talking-to Wheels had given me the night before seemed somewhat of a distant memory and my resolve seemed a weaker.

I tried to get determined in the shower.

I tried to get determined in front of the mirror.

I tried (and almost succeeded) to get determined while brushing my teeth.

I tried (and failed spectacularly) to get determined while getting dressed.

I knew that Sandy wasn't just fucking around when he said he would give me until the end of the day or he'd do it for me. There are times when I think he's pulling my leg, but this was not one of them. I knew because of the gleam in his eye, the way Helena peeked out from inside. When Helena tells you she's going to do something, you can be sure as shit that it's going to get done. Helena doesn't believe in wasting time by just saying she'll do things. She likes to grab life (and muscle men) by the balls. And if there was ever a ball-grabbing moment for her, this was it.

I figured I'd have the rest of the day to work up my courage before five o'clock hit, so I had plenty of time. I stared at myself at the bathroom mirror for the sixteenth time. "You're cool," I told my reflection. Wheels barked at my feet in what had to be complete agreement. "You're hip. You're a badass. You don't take no prisoners. You're a go-getter. You see something you want? You *go get it*. Be suave. Be *smooooth*. Practice. Practice." I cocked my eyebrow at my reflection. "Hey, Vince," I said, dropping my voice a bit. "Let's go get physical. Oh fuck. Olivia Newton-

John? *Really*, Paul? *That's* the first thing you go to? Don't be such a homo! Try it again." I smiled at myself, trying to put a sexy curve to it. It looked like I was smelling something awful. "Hey, Vince," I said again. "You and I should go get some coffee." I tried to lick my lips seductively as I finished: "I like mine with extra *cream*." I ended up looking like I was licking my own face off.

Wheels howled quietly, then barked once, saying, *Yooooooooooouuuuuu suck!*

"Okay, I can do this. It's not like I've never asked out a guy before. Okay, I haven't, but I'm not even *asking* him out. He already asked *me* out, and even though I said no, I'm allowed to say yes now!" I glared at myself in the mirror. "Don't be such a pansy," I growled at Pansy Paul. I gave a sort of regular smile. "Hey, Vince. Fancy seeing you here. Oh goddammit! We *work* together, for Christ's sake! Hey, Vince, I decided to take you up on your offer of dinner. You're welcome. Ew. God, that sounded smarmy." I sucked in my stomach and puffed out my chest, lowering my voice. "Hey, Vince. Let's go work out and run on a treadmill for eighteen miles because that's so much fun to do." I gasped in air. I turned and looked at myself in the mirror. "Do I have a double chin?" I asked Wheels, frowning at my reflection. It didn't look like I did until I lowered my chin to my chest. Look up, single chin. Look down, double chin. Look up, single chin. *Okay, so always look up. Suck in the gut a little. Your ass looks pretty good. Not great, but not bad either. Maybe you should try some lunges. And* lunge! *And* lunge! *And—ow, my fucking thigh! Goddammit. Okay bring it on in. Bring it on in. And... pose! Not too shabby, Auster. Not too shabby indeed. Except for the fact that you are already sweating and your face is red and you always look down because you're shy, so you will always have a motherfucking double chin!*

My reflection stared sadly at me, shaking his head. Judgmental bastard.

There was nothing else I could do, I knew. Well, there was; I could have always gotten into my car and driven down to Mexico and changed my name to Esteban Mendez and opened up my own dusty bar in the tiny town of Xonoca. I look pretty good in a poncho, and I could have gotten a big sombrero and grown a sweet mustache and spent my days saying things like *Sí* and *Toda la cerveza se ha acabado, pero puede comerse algunos de estos tacos que hice. ¿Qué le pasó al Sr. Rodríguez? No ha sido el mismo hace que su esposa él dejó. He oído que ella era una puta bastante grande.* (Translated: I am all out of beer, but you might have some of these tacos I just made. What is up with Mr. Rodriguez? He hasn't been the same since his wife left. I heard she was quite the whore).

But I didn't. I didn't drive down to Xonoca to open my bar called Taco's Bell. I decided against that whole life because I had to go to work and face my motherfucking fears. To prove the point to myself, I turned on the stereo again and put in Celine Dion's cover of "All By Myself" and sat at the stop light, waiting for it to turn green. "Allllll byyyyyyyy myyyyyyyyyyyselllllllllllllf," I sang forlornly. "Don't wanna be, alllllll byyyyy—" And then I realized my windows were down *again* and the *same* woman from yesterday was sitting next to me. Except this time, she wasn't singing along, but rather staring at me with tears streaming down her face, her nose running. She looked positively *wrecked.*

"I don't want you to be all by yourself!" she cried at me when she saw me watching her. "You go *get* yourself a man! You deserve it so much!"

"I'm *trying*!" I shouted back, above Celine. "The motherfucker *kissed* me yesterday!" It felt good to share that.

"Where?" she called back.

"In the supply closet!"

"No! I meant where on your *body*?"

"What?"

"Did! He! Kiss! Your! Penis!" she screamed as she sobbed.

I gaped at her.

"Hey, *move* it, assholes!" A horn started to honk behind me. And it was the *same* motherfucking guy in the truck from yesterday. This time, I *did* flip him off because I wanted to continue the conversation with the strange lady in the car next to me to find out *why* her first thought would be that I got kissed on the cock instead of the mouth? But she had already pulled away, and Celine Dion was starting to grate on my nerves, and I was kind of worried the guy in the truck would follow me and rip off my testes, so I drove away rather quickly, trying to speed around a few cars to put some distance between me and the truck driver.

Twenty minutes later, after dealing with the police officer who pulled me over for speeding and weaving in and out of traffic to the point where the first thing he asked me was, "Sir, if you're drunk this early, then you've got a drinking problem," I pulled into my parking space on the side of the street. My hands were sweating, and I was breathing heavily. I looked myself in the rearview mirror, and my eyes were so wide, I'm pretty sure you could see parts of my brain poking through. "Calm down," I whispered hoarsely. "Just calm the fuck down, and everything will be okay. You've already had his tongue in your mouth. You can do this."

So without looking, I opened my car door.

And it was about that time that Vince Taylor was riding his bike past my car. Physics teaches us that when a moving force meets an immovable object, bad shit happens to hot people. I think Sir Isaac Newton said that. Or Sir Elton John. I don't know. I get my "Sirs" confused sometimes.

But, regardless, the moving force of Vince and his bike met the immoveable object of my opened car door. I heard him say, "Oh *bananas*," and then he crashed into the inside of the door, flipped up and over it, and landed on his back on the pavement on the other side. The front tire of his bike crumpled before the whole thing fell over onto the ground next to my car with a metallic clang.

Then it got really quiet.

I just stared.

I thought about closing the car door and just driving away, but knowing my luck, I would have run him over in the process, and I'd already had one brush with the law today. Plus, I worked for a *car* insurance company, and that sort of thing is frowned upon.

My next thought was I was happy he was at least wearing a helmet.

My third thought was how awful I was going to look in prison orange if he was dead.

My fourth thought was how sad I'd be if he was dead, and why didn't I just let him kiss my cock in the storage closet?

My fifth thought was that I had to save him, just like he saved me the day before. He was the one who sort of caused me to choke on spinach, and now I was sort of (read: completely) the reason he probably had splenic lacerations and contusions on his pretty, pretty behind.

I jumped out of the car and tried to close the door, but part of his bike got caught in it and I ended up closing the door on my leg. This caused me to trip over the bent tire and I fell, skinning my hands and a knee on the asphalt. I gritted my teeth against the sharp pain, realizing that whatever I was feeling, Vince had flipped *over* my fucking *car*, so I couldn't be bitchy about scrapes on my hands and dirty khakis (even though I was already bitching in my head).

Once I was able to disentangle myself from the stupid bike and got my leg out of my stupid car, I rushed around the door and saw Vince sprawled out near the front tire, on his back, eyes closed. He didn't move except to ooze little driblets of blood from his right arm and left leg. Little flecks of gravel were stuck in the blood trails.

Of course, to me, it looked like he was dead, and I was sure that I'd killed him, so I rushed over to him, trying to remember back to my *Baywatch* days and how they gave mouth-to-mouth resuscitation. I didn't even check to see if he *was* breathing, because I was convinced he *wasn't*. I figured that this was real life, so I probably shouldn't go in slow motion like they did on *Baywatch*. David Hasselhoff could save people, and so could I.

So I got down on my knees next to him, ignoring the obvious gaping flesh wound on my leg. I thought about chest compressions, but I didn't want to break any more of his ribs, and I was pretty sure his clavicle was probably already going to be pushing through his skin, and I really didn't want to see that. So I ignored the chest compressions and tilted his head back (something about avoid tongue blockage or some bullshit) and pressed my lips against his and gave him the gift of life.

"Breathe, dammit!" I whispered fiercely, taking another breath and pushing it into him. "Live, I say! Live!"

It took two or three breaths into him before I realized a tongue that was not my own was in my mouth each time I went back down, and that for all intents and purposes, I was making out with a man I'd hit with my car. Okay, well, semantics, it really should be that he hit *my* car, but whatever. When this hit me, I froze a little bit, my breath caught halfway between him and me, and then he brought the arm that wasn't bloody and gross up behind me, pressing the back of my head, holding me in place while he tangled his tongue over mine. He pulled away slightly to nibble on my bottom lip and groaned, though from pain or what, I don't know.

I opened my eyes to find his inches from my own. "Totally worth it," he whispered with a grin. Then he passed out.

It took me almost a full minute to call 911 because I just sat there, his taste still in my mouth.

"HELLO?" I said to the pretty black woman at the front desk at the hospital a couple hours later. I couldn't help but think that if this were a TV show, she'd be the sassy black nurse that always had something funny to say before dispensing pearls of wisdom.

She looked up at me and smiled. "Can I help you?"

"I hope so," I said nervously. "Um, I hit a man with my car and he was brought here? Okay, well, he technically hit me, but that is so beside the point."

She frowned slightly.

Which I took as a sign I should continue babbling. "I mean, who doesn't see a car door opening on the side of the street? And he had to have been going at least eighty miles an hour. Okay, well not *eighty*, but at least ten. I feel really bad, but he sort of deserved it for making me all weird and crazy over the past few days, right? I mean, I've only known him since *Saturday* and we've already made out twice and he can make me feel all twisted up already? What is *up* with that?"

She cocked her head at me.

"My dog gives me the same look," I told her. "You two could be related."

She gasped.

"Oh, crap," I said, the blood draining from my face. "That is *so* not what I meant! Oh, Jesus Christ! I'm *so* sorry. My dog is just a mutt. Er, not to say that *you're a* mutt or anything. Besides, mutts are boy dogs, I think. And you're obviously not a boy." I eyed her boobs, making everything that much worse. "*Very* obviously not a boy. Girl dogs are bitches, right? So you'd be a bitch and… oh my *God*, I didn't mean to say *that* either!"

She narrowed her eyes and crossed her arms over her chest, not saying a word.

"I'm not very good at talking to women," I admitted. "I'm gay, so your dangly parts scare me a bit. Uh, not that anything of yours is dangling or anything. Everything seems to be perky enough. Um. Perfectly perky. It even looks like you had work done, they are so pointy. And as you can tell, I don't have any social graces. This is why I like to deal with people over the phone, so I don't have to look at them when I speak. It makes life easier for me so I'm not sitting here calling you a bitch with really nice tatas."

She shook her head.

"Please," I said bleakly. "Please help me shut my mouth. I just need to know where Vince Taylor is. That's all. Please tell me and I will go so far away that you'll never see me again and I'll be nothing but a horrible memory for you by the time you get home to your cat."

She glared at me but clacked on her computer. Finally, "What's your relation?"

"Oh, uh. He's my… brother." *Quick thinking.*

She got a weird look on her face. "Your brother?"

I nodded. "My younger brother."

"And you've made out with him *twice* and only known him since Saturday?" she asked, looking like she was going to hit a button and have men in lab coats come carry me away.

Oh sweat balls. "Erm, we didn't know we were brothers? Long lost. It was awkward, for sure." I was sweating profusely. "Caused a big family drama. I think my mom will need therapy for the rest of her life."

"Are you sure she's the only one?"

"No, no. I'm pretty sure I will too once this is all over." I laughed and I sounded way crazy. "It's hard being attracted to your own brother. No… no other way around that."

"This is some Maury Povich shit up in here," she said. "Lord have *mercy.*"

I couldn't help but grin. "I *knew* you'd be the sassy black nurse."

"Now you racial profilin' me?" she huffed. "Just because I'm *black* doesn't mean I'm gonna be sassy, you hear me, cornbread brother lover?"

"Yes, ma'am."

"Now, if you done bullshittin' me, Mr. Taylor is in room 214. He'll be discharged in a bit."

I felt relieved. "Thank you. I'm sorry about everything I said."

She turned serious. "And," she said softly, "you need to make sure you get yourself some help. Nothing ever came from being in love with your brother."

"Pearls of wisdom," I said in awe. "You *are* the sassy black nurse—"

Her eyes flared. "Boy, I ain't no nurse. I am an *administrative professional*, and you best get your ass out of my face before I make you leave." She tapped her acrylic nails against the desk so loudly that each one sound like a gun shot. I couldn't help but notice how orange they were, and I knew I needed to leave before I told her I saw her as more of a magenta.

"Room 214?"

She nodded tightly.

I turned and walked away, feeling her eyes like daggers in my back. That was pretty much the reason right there why I don't like meeting new people. I tend to say things that others have a filter for, and I don't have the power to stop myself. It's like once I start, I can't stop until everyone involved is either mortified or ready to shoot pepper spray in my eyes because I've somehow made it seem like I'm either a serial rapist or a participant in an incestuous relationship with my long-lost brother. Sometimes I don't even know how these conversations get where they go, but it can't *all* just be me. Other people seem to bring out my crazy, which is why I didn't like speaking with pretty much anyone face to face.

Room 214 didn't take that long to find, even though I wished it had. The closer I got to it, the more nervous I got. Not only did I want to agree to go out with Vince, I'd now maimed him, and I didn't know if that was the best way to start a relationship. Then I started thinking about the word *relationship* and why my mind immediately went there, and that made me start to sweat even more. I was pretty sure I was sweating buckets by the time I reached room 214 (which, in my head, sounded slightly ominous, like a direct-to-DVD horror movie starring some eighties pseudo-icon who has not aged well. *Room 214: Check-In To Terror*). I thought about bypassing the room completely, but then I heard Vince's voice and I just couldn't. I tried not to think about what that meant.

You can do this, I said, psyching myself up. *Just go in there, and speak as little as possible.*

I knocked quietly on the partially opened door. It swung open almost immediately, a doctor standing on the other side. I was about to smile and introduce myself, but I was immediately distracted by the fact that Vince was sitting shirtless on the edge of the bed, wearing only his biker shorts.

It was right then that I believed in God.

Dear God, I thought. *Thank you for this bounty you have bestowed upon me. I will be your humble servant forever now because of this view. Love, Paul. P.S. He has a pierced* nipple?

He was lovely, completely and thoroughly. His tan skin reminded me of cinnamon, his strong chest covered in a smattering of curly hair that drifted down from his pecs to his stomach. My eyes stuttered on his right nipple for a moment, the small silver bar going through it flashing in the harsh fluorescent lighting overhead. I wondered what it would be like to tease it with my tongue and if he liked it to be twisted.

Then I realized I was in very real danger of popping wood in front of him and a doctor, so I thought of gross things like maggots and Mitt Romney and I was able to keep my errant dick under control.

Then I saw his abs, which weren't quite defined, but almost so, and even the thought of Mitt Romney laid out spread-eagled in front of me covered in offshore tax incentives couldn't keep the blood from flowing. Literally only four seconds had passed since the door opened, but I'd spent those entire four seconds ogling Vince like I wanted to eat him right then and there. Which to be fair, I kind of did. I glanced up to his face and caught the sly but tired grin that said he knew *exactly* what I was doing.

I blushed and looked away.

"You here for Vince?" the doctor asked cheerfully, oblivious to the fact that I'd been essentially eye-fucking his patient.

"Er. Yeah," I muttered.

"I'm Dr. Hal," the doc said, shaking my hand.

"Paul," I mumbled, looking down at the floor.

"He's the guy who put me in the hospital," Vince confided in the doctor.

"Oh!" Doc Hal said. "Well, this has got to be a bit awkward for the two of you. But it's a nice thought that you're coming here to check on him."

"We knew each other before this," Vince said, leaning back on his hands, the muscles in his stomach clenching slightly and awesomely. I shot him a scowl, but it fell from my face when I saw the bruising forming on his side, wrapping around to his back where I couldn't see it anymore. I felt awful. "I guess he didn't think there were any better ways to get my attention." He grinned at me again, and I didn't feel so awful after that.

Doc Hal frowned. "Why didn't he just ask you out?"

Vince shrugged. "Dunno. I asked him out a few days ago, and he kind of freaked out a bit, and then he choked on spinach, so I saved his life with some Heinrich maneuvering."

"Heimlich," I said. "It's *Heimlich*."

"Quick thinking," Doc Hal told him, ignoring me completely. "So he thanks you by hitting you with his car instead of going out with you? That's odd."

"Right? His life belongs to me now. It's an old Japanese idea."

"It's *Chinese!*" I said indignantly.

Vince rolled his eyes. "It's all Asia," he said. "I want to go there some day," he told the doc.

"Asia?" Doc Hal said, looking over Vince's charts. "Where at in Asia?"

I could tell this confused Vince, but he just shrugged and said, "All over." I didn't think he understood the concept of Asia as a continent yet.

"Ah. Well, Vince, you've got a moderate concussion, but your CT scans were clear, so you should be right as rain in a few days or so, thanks to the fact that you were wearing a helmet. Way to protect the ol' noggin. You're probably going to be a bit more sore the next couple of days, so I want you to take it easy. You'll need to stay awake for the next few hours, just to make sure no further symptoms manifest. You have a roommate who can watch over you for a while?"

He shook his head. "Live alone."

"Parents?"

He hesitated. "Out of town for the next couple of weeks."

"Friends?"

"No one I'd feel comfortable with."

"Well, then, I wonder who we could get to sit up with you for a while?"

And, of course, it was obvious where it was going from there. Both Doc Hal and Vince turned to me at the same time, and I tried to count the ceiling tiles while pointedly pretending I hadn't heard any part of the conversation.

No one said anything, and I knew it had become a contest of wills to see who would crack first, though I couldn't figure out why Doc Hal wanted to play. Maybe he saw how uncomfortable I was, or maybe he was a secret closet romantic who thought he was doing something sweet when all I wanted to do to *him* was wipe that knowing smirk off his face with some brass knuckles. But then I realized I didn't know where to *buy* brass knuckles, or even if those were real things anymore, so I sighed, resigned to my fate. "You guys totally planned this, didn't you?"

Doc Hal and Vince exchanged a look I couldn't quite place. "I don't know what you mean," Doc Hal said blandly. "Now, since you will be taking care of the man you injured, there are a few things you should know."

I winced. Vince chuckled. Bastard.

"You need to keep an eye out for any symptoms such as dizziness, dilated pupils, nausea. If those start to occur, it might be a good idea for him to get back here for further tests. I've given him a mild painkiller, but he'll need to stay awake for a few hours before he can sleep, so it's up to you to keep him up."

"I'm sure we can think of a few things," Vince said, waggling his eyebrows.

"None of that for the next day or so," Doc Hal admonished slightly.

Vince pouted.

"No sex," Doc Hal told me. "I'm not releasing him to you just so you can molest him in his weakened state."

"But... it's...." I sputtered. "It's *not*... I don't...."

"No buts," he said sternly, like I was trying to disagree with him.

"Wow," Vince said. "Maybe you should hit me with your car more often. Arguing with the doctor about sex with me? That's hot."

If looks could kill, Vince would have exploded in a blast of meat and blood given the way I glared at him. "I'm not arguing," I hissed at him. "I'm not going to have sex with you!"

"You can this weekend," Doc Hal said as if trying to soothe me. "He just needs some rest before he should try to get it up."

I was horrified. "What the hell is wrong with you?"

"You cleared from work the next few days?" Doc Hal asked him.

Vince looked at me.

I scowled at him.

He waited.

"Fine," I said. "Yes. I told them what happened and that you'd need a few days off. Everyone says they are thinking of you, and they called me a jerk for putting you in the hospital. Tad told me to tell you that he hopes you get better soon so he can take you in the supply closet next time. I fucking hate that guy so fucking much. He's such a little bitch."

"Paul and I made out in the supply closet," Vince told Doc Hal. "I think hitting me with his car was kind of his revenge. Or maybe foreplay. He might be into some kinky shit, I dunno."

"Like he needs to hit things with his car to get off?" Doc Hal asked, glancing at me. "That brings a whole new meaning to the word 'autoerotic'."

"Are you even *allowed* to say things like that?" I growled at the doctor.

"I don't get it," Vince said, sounding confused again.

"I spent twelve years going to medical school," Doc Hal said to me. "And I still have over a hundred grand in student loans. I'm allowed to say things like that because if I didn't have a sense of humor, I'd be sad."

"You're not funny," I retorted.

"I still don't get it," Vince said. "But now I'm really fucking tired." He looked at me, and I could see all the humor had fallen away. "Can we go home now?" he asked me quietly. His words seemed a bit slurred, whether from exhaustion or narcotics, I didn't know. All I knew was that my heart thumped a little beat in my chest at the sight of him like that. I tried to fight down the urge to wrap myself around him and shield him from everything and to take care of him forever.

Jesus, I'm such a fucking girl sometimes.

I looked to the doc, who nodded at me. "Yeah," I told Vince. "We can go."

He looked at me gratefully before looking down. "Don't have a shirt," he mumbled, as if suddenly embarrassed. "They cut off my cycle jersey 'cause it hurt too much to pull it off over my head."

"I can get you some scrubs," Doc Hal offered.

I shook my head. "Don't worry about it," I told him. I unbuttoned my dress shirt and took it off, almost but not quite self-conscious about only wearing the white T-shirt underneath. I walked over to Vince and hesitated for a moment, but then I found some bit of resolve buried deep in me and wrapped it around his shoulders.

He sighed softly and pressed his forehead against my shoulder as I fussed with the collar. I grazed his skin with my fingers and he was warm. I had to stop myself from going any further.

"Here's a scrip for some muscle relaxers," Doc Hal said. "Only have him take them if he absolutely needs them. He should try to stick to over-the-counter stuff if possible."

I nodded and took the scrip and shoved it in my pocket.

"Ready?" I asked Vince.

He moaned softly but nodded, and I helped him to his feet. With my arm around his shoulders, I steered him out.

CHAPTER 7
My Two-Legged Dog Is A Big, Fat Traitor

I WALKED him toward the car, though part of me wondered just how much he *really* needed to be hanging onto me like he was. He was acting like he could barely walk and kept leaning against me, his face going into my neck, brushing his lips against my skin every few steps. I tried to ignore the sassy black administrative professional as we walked by her desk, but she narrowed her eyes as she watched him "accidentally" kiss my neck again, and she shook her head as we passed by. I thought about saying something snarky to her ("I'm gonna have me a piece of my brother, sassy-face!"), but then Vince squeezed against me a little bit tighter and I forget about everything else as I focused on being able to put one foot in front of another.

I got him in the car slowly, carefully, and then walked around front and got in the driver's seat. I closed the door behind me and silence fell. It hit me then that this was the first time he and I had been alone, actually truly *alone*, that didn't involve supply closets or ambulances. I thought of about six or seven different things to say, each one involving some kind of apology for putting him in the hospital and also trying to make myself sound cool at the same time. But then the silence stretched into minutes and became awkward because I could feel his eyes on me as I stared straight ahead, gripping the steering wheel.

"So," I said.

"So," he said.

I cleared my throat and willed myself not to blush. I failed. "Your place? Or...."

"I want to go to your house," Vince said. I could hear the smile in his voice, but I didn't turn to him because I knew that his dimples, even if they weren't out in full force, would most likely cause me to do something sexually stupid. Like ask him if I could touch his penis. I didn't think that would be polite.

I squeaked. Or grunted all manly like. I don't know which, though if I had to place a bet on it, I'm sure I sounded like Mickey Mouse getting anal. "You do? Why?"

"You have to watch me, right?"

"Uh. That's what the doctor said."

"And you're shy and shit?"

I winced. "That's fun."

"What?"

"That my entire being can be reduced down to 'shy and shit'."

He waved his hand at me. "Well, you are. So I figure we go back to your house because you'd be more comfortable there."

I thought on this for a moment. "You're the one who's hurt, and you're thinking about what would make *me* comfortable?"

"What can I say? I'm pretty awesome."

I couldn't take it anymore and turned to look at him. Vince was pale and it looked like he was grimacing slightly, as though he was in pain. But even through all of that, he smiled quietly when I looked at him, and those dimples made an appearance, smacking me across the face. *Don't ask if you can touch his penis.* "Can I touch your...." *Oh sweat balls.*

"Touch my what?" he asked, cocking an eyebrow.

I blushed furiously. "That's not what I meant to say. You're going to be fine going to my house? You don't want your own bed or anything?"

"Why? Do *you* want my bed?"

"Vince."

"Yeah?"

"I'm trying to be serious here."

"Me too."

"You're hitting on me." And I have no fucking idea why.

"You're the one who wants to touch my something."

Christ. "My house it is, though you should be warned...."

"That sounds a little creepy. Do you have a sex dungeon in your house?" But his eyes didn't show he thought that idea was creepy. If anything, it looked like he'd be very happy if my house had a sex dungeon. I felt slightly disappointed that I hadn't invested in one. I didn't think it would add to property value, and it probably would be hard to explain to potential buyers if I ever had to move. That and the fact that my elderly swinger next-door neighbors would probably ask to use it regularly, and I didn't want old people having sex in my house. I'm kind of a prude like that.

"No," I said, kind of regretfully.

"Do you have dead bodies buried under your house?"

"No."

"Is your house haunted?"

"Er…."

"No fucking way!"

"Well, I don't know for *sure* it's haunted. This guy I—" I stopped abruptly.

"This guy you what?" He looked interested and weirdly jealous all at the same time. Or, rather, that's what I wanted to see. For all I knew, he was stoned and hallucinating that I had black balls hanging from my chin.

I sighed. "This guy I… *dated*… once said he was psychic and that I have a ghost in my house who is always on her period."

His nose wrinkled. "You have a ragging ghost in your house?"

I shrugged. "I've never seen her, but I put tampons out once just in case."

His eyes widened. "Did she take one?" he whispered excitedly.

I felt bad that I was going to ruin his joy of my fake period ghost. "No," I said, and his face fell. "But that doesn't mean she's not there!" Now all I wanted was to see the vaginal-bleeding ghost in my house just to make him happy again. What's a little spectral menstrual blood when a hot guy is smiling at you? "That's not what I wanted to warn you about, though."

"Then what?"

I took a deep breath. "I have a two-legged dog named Wheels who pretty much hates everyone in the world except for me. And Sandy. Sometimes he likes my mom, but most of the time he just shits in her shoes when she comes over. I don't know why he has anger issues. He's just really… *selective* about who he does and doesn't like. It doesn't mean there is anything wrong with you. It just means you're not good enough for my dog to like you." And that came out way wrong.

He stared at me. "You have a two-legged dog?"

"Yeah." I looked away.

"Named Wheels."

"Uh. Yeah. Because he has a wheeled cart attached to his butt that helps him get around. It seemed appropriate."

"And you think your house is haunted by a ghost on her period?"

"Well, no. *I* don't think so. That one guy did."

"But you put tampons out for her."

"I thought she might need them," I said defensively. "You don't know how much courage it took for me to go buy those things. I felt like an idiot when I had to ask a woman in the aisle the difference between the ones with applicators and the ones that looked like those bath toys we played with as kids that you'd drop them in the water and they'd expand into animal shapes. I told her I couldn't take it if it was going to blow up to look like a bloody duck-billed platypus. That would have been way too much for me to deal with."

"Paul?"

"Yeah?"

"Don't take this the wrong way."

I tried not to flinch. *Here it comes.*

Vince sighed. "I think I'm going to fall in love with you." He made it sound as if it was inevitable. And wonderful.

I choked on air. And my tongue. And my saliva. And my thoughts.

It took all that I had to turn back and look at him again, my heart thundering in my chest.

He was asleep, his head against the window. A soft little snore escaped from his mouth. I didn't think anyone died from going to sleep with a concussion no matter what doctors wanted us to think, so I let him be.

My hands shook as I started the car and headed for home.

WHEELS turned out to be the biggest traitor of all.

We got back to the house and I woke Vince gently, letting him know he had to wake up. His eyes fluttered open and he smiled at me as he awoke, and it was all I could do to keep from taking off my clothes right then and screaming, "Take me!" Somehow, I was able to restrain myself.

Barely.

I helped him out of the car, and he leaned on me far more than was necessary, but for some reason I let it slide. What can I say, I'm a nice guy.

I could hear Wheels even before we got to the front door, obviously overly confused and excited as to why I'd be back so early in the day. His thrilled yips made it sound like he was giving birth to a dog twice his size, and I knew if it went on, most likely his heart would explode

"He's a little dog, isn't he?" Vince asked as I fumbled with my keys. His arm went around my waist as he leaned in and nuzzled my neck. I cursed under my breath as I tried to put my car key in the lock on the door.

"Er. Yeah." I suddenly felt the need to defend my tiny dog. "Kind of. I was going to get a golden lab, but he was a jerk."

"The dog was a jerk?"

I almost dropped the keys. "Yeah. I guess. He thought he was better than everyone else. And he was mean to Wheels, so I picked Wheels over him instead."

"You picked your little dog as revenge to another dog?"

"Not *revenge*. Wheels needed a home." I finally found the right key and opened the door.

Wheels attempted to spin in circles when he saw me walk through the door, his cart rocking up onto one wheel as he turned. He spun three times before he stopped, becoming painfully aware that there was someone with me. He froze, glaring up at me as if I'd betrayed him completely.

"Don't you give me that look," I scolded him as I helped Vince through the door. "I don't have time to deal with you right now."

Vince started laughing quite hard. "*Ow!*" he said, holding his side as he huffed out laughter. "*Ow!*"

"What's so funny?"

"He doesn't have a *tail!*"

I scowled. "That's not his fault. He got hit by a car."

"He looks like he hates me already." He chuckled.

"You're laughing at him. You got hit by a car and I didn't laugh at you."

Vince smirked tiredly. "Nah. You just made out with me."

"I was trying to give you mouth to mouth!"

"Dude, I was still breathing."

"I panicked," I defended myself.

He squeezed me tighter. "You can panic on my tongue anytime."

I helped him to the couch rather than say anything in response. It seemed safer. Everything felt all topsy-turvy, and I didn't want to risk opening my mouth and making it worse. I tended to do that quite often, and this situation felt perilous.

I could hear Wheels following us, his toenails clacking on the tile, his wheels squeaking as he rolled behind us. He was sniffing in these short, tiny bursts, and I knew he was smelling Vince, trying to figure out who the fuck I'd brought into his house. I also wanted to sniff Vince repeatedly, but that was something I figured I'd better keep to myself. He wasn't cocaine, after all. Well, not that I did cocaine or anything. I'd seen *Scarface*. I knew what it did to people.

Vince groaned as I set him on the couch. I felt twinges of sympathy pain in my own ribs, but then I realized it was because he was still holding on to me, digging his fingers into my side. He was trying to pull me down onto the couch with him, and I didn't want to go there. *Not yet*, I thought before I could stop myself. *But wouldn't it be fun?*

I worked my way out of his grasp, and he grunted, knowing exactly what I was doing. He finally gave in and let go, settling back against the cushions. "You want something to drink?" I asked him, trying to keep from wringing my hands in front of me. "You can't take the muscle relaxers yet. We have to keep you up for a few hours to make sure you don't have brain damage."

"I don't have brain damage," he assured me.

"That remains to be seen," I said before I could stop myself.

He looked at me weird. "I could use a beer," he said finally.

I gaped at him. "It's eleven o'clock in the morning! On a *Wednesday*."

"I'm on vacation, apparently."

"You can have water. Or juice."

He scowled at me. "We should have gone to my house. That way I could have done whatever I wanted."

"Too late. You wanted to come here. Water or juice."

"Beer."

I waited.

He rolled his eyes as Wheels sniffed his leg, and I realized he was still in bike shorts and my shirt. That got me a little hot and bothered. "Water," he said finally. He leaned forward with a slight moan and looked down at Wheels, who froze again, looking up at him.

I left them to stare at each other, telling Vince to not touch the dog's cart because Wheels tended to freak out if anyone who wasn't me touched it. I clicked on the TV before I left, making sure it was loud enough that I wouldn't be overheard. As soon as I hit the kitchen, I whipped out my cell phone, hit speed dial, and started to sweat profusely.

"This is Sandy, how can I help you?" he said when he answered his work line.

"I am so fucked," I groaned into the phone.

"Paul." He didn't sound surprised to hear from me at all. "You know, I've been sitting here this morning, looking at your empty desk, wondering at just what point in your life you were taught that it was okay to hit hot men with your car. Where did I go wrong with you? Was it something I did? Do you have unresolved issues with your father?"

"I *didn't* hit him!" I whisper-shouted. "He hit my door!"

"Uh-huh. You don't think it was your subconscious acting out?"

"Now's not the time, Sanford," I growled at him.

He chuckled in my ear. "Why do you sound so freaked out, baby doll? You said earlier that he'd be fine. You're not going to get arrested or anything. I'll make sure a claim gets filed for you here and his bills will be taken care of. It's not a big deal. Nothing's broken, right?"

"No. Just a concussion and bruising."

"Then why do you sound like you're passing stones the size of watermelon?"

"He's sitting on my couch wearing nothing but bike shorts and my shirt."

There was a clattering noise through the line. A moment later, "Sorry. I dropped the phone. For a moment, I thought you said that Vince Taylor was sitting on your couch wearing your clothes."

"And bike shorts."

"And bike shorts. Yes."

"You can't forget the bike shorts." Nor would I. Ever. "He was the one that wanted to come over here," I said, as if that mattered somehow.

"Paul?"

"Yeah?"

"You know I love you, right?"

"Yeah."

"Don't take this the wrong way, okay?"

"Okay."

"Why the *fuck* are you on the phone with me?" he snarled quietly at me. "Are you out of your goddamn mind? You get your fucking ass back into the living room, and you sit down next to him and you take care of his every single whim, no matter what the fuck it is. Do you understand me?"

I replied with the only thing I could think of, the only thing that had been going through my head for the past thirty minutes. "I told him about Wheels, and he said he thinks he's going to fall in love with me."

Silence.

"Sandy?"

"He said that?" Sandy finally said. He sounded funny.

"Er. Yeah. Stupid, right?"

"It's just like your parents," he said in awe. He knew the story of how my parents met and this was probably freaking him out as much as it was me.

"What? No. *No.* I don't even want to talk about that right now."

"Paul?"

"Yeah?"

"I need you to listen to me, okay? You're going to do exactly what I say. Understood?"

"Yeah." This was why I'd called him. I needed someone I trusted to tell me what to do.

"You are going to go to your room. You are going to get those very expensive pajamas that I bought for you. The ones you never wear because you stupidly say they make your thighs look like sausage encased in plastic after it's been sitting out in the sun for two weeks. He's got to be uncomfortable still wearing those bike shorts."

"Okay," I said, trying to remember to breathe.

"Then you are going to sit with him all day and answer his every single beck and call. I don't care what he asks for. I don't care how uncomfortable it makes you. You are going to do *whatever* he asks because you hit him with your car and for *some* goddamn reason, he goes over to your house and tells you he could love you."

"Well, he told me he could love me first and *then* he came over to my house."

"Paul!"

"What!"

"Don't you sass me!"

"I'm *not!*"

"Pajamas!" Sandy hissed. "Anything he asks!"

I felt bad. "He already asked for a beer," I admitted. "I told him I'd get him a juice instead."

Sandy groaned as if I was the most insufferable thing on the planet. "Okay. From this point on, though. Okay?"

"What if he wants to fist me?"

Sandy snorted and tried to cover it up so he could still sound stern. "Has that come up?"

I'd meant it as a feeble attempt at a joke, but now I was worried. "No." But what if he did? How does one politely turn down a fisting? I appreciate the offer, but I don't want your arm up my butt. I like my intestines shaped the way they are.

"Paul, I'm going to tell you the same thing my drag mother told me when I was first starting out. 'Helena,' Vaguyna Muffman said, 'you can't worry about fisting until it actually happens. You'll live your life in fear and you'll never unclench your anus.'"

"May she rest in peace," I said, and we had a moment of silence for Vaguyna. She'd passed away a few years ago from cancer, and it had been hard on Sandy. When he quoted his drag mother, the one that'd taught him everything she knew about drag, you knew Sandy was serious.

"Is that all?" I asked him after a respectful amount of time had gone by.

He thought for a moment. "No. Because knowing you, you'll do exactly what I say, but you won't say anything for the whole day. So in addition to everything I've said already, you must learn seven new things about him. I will call you tomorrow after I get off work, and you will tell me those seven things you learned about Vince. And they can't be something stupid like he's pretty or he's nice. They have to be *real*."

"He *is* pretty, though," I muttered. "And nice. That should count as two."

"It doesn't. Seven new things, Paul. By tomorrow."

"This whole new deadline thing you've got going on?"

"Yeah?"

"I hate it and I hate your face," I said as savagely as possible.

Sandy wasn't fooled in the slightest. "You're welcome. Do you need to write any of what I said down or can you remember it?"

"I'm not going to do *anything* you said!" I swore.

After a time, he said, "Feel better now?"

"Bite me," I mumbled.

"That's going to be Vince's job." I could hear the smirk in his voice.

"You're a bitch."

"Seven things. By tomorrow."

"I'll see you in *hell*."

"I love you, baby doll."

"I love you too. Am I going to mess this up?" I gnawed on my thumbnail.

He didn't hesitate. "Possibly. But that's why you have me."

"I'm not going to make it to your show tonight." I felt bad about that.

"Paul, is this important to you?"

"I think so, though I really can't say why."

"Good. There will be other shows. Hundreds, possibly millions if I figure out how to live forever. I can survive one night without you, I think. You're always just cramping my style, anyway. Maybe tonight I can finally get laid." He didn't mean it, though. Not like that.

"Thank you," I said quietly.

"You're welcome. Now don't go trying to get *too* fucked. You did hit him with your car, after all. Boy needs to heal before putting his cock in your bum."

"The doctor said we can't have sex until the weekend," I said absently. Then I realized what I'd said. "Oh *sweat* balls."

Sandy sounded like he was going into apoplectic shock. "Apparently," he gasped as he hyperventilated, "you don't... need my help... at all! You've already thought... this one... through."

"I'm going to go now before I make it worse," I said.

"Don't think... that's... *possible*," Sandy said as he struggled to breathe. He sounded like he was dying. "Should have... recorded... this phone call. No one... will believe me. Need... record for... posterity. The world... must know... what happened."

I hung up the phone. "Fuck," I whispered.

I didn't stop to think, because if I did, I'd end up having a minor meltdown right here in my kitchen. Instead of turning into the Paul I knew, I pushed him away and turned into Semi-Confident Paul whose super powers included the capability to have light conversations without stuttering, and to not sweat and turn red at a moment's notice. Of course, this led to me wondering what kind of boots my superhero costume would have when I was Semi-Confident Paul, and whether or not I could pull off a cape. I liked to think I could.

I went back to the living room and Semi-Confident Paul turned into Shocked Paul, who then transformed into Big Puddle O'Goo Paul and lastly morphed into I Want To Eat You Like A Buffet Paul.

All four of my alter egos would have rocked a cape and boots.

Somehow, someway, Vince had gotten Wheels to turn into a big fat traitor, the Benedict Arnold of doggy-dom. My antisocial mutt had turned into the world's biggest slut in the five minutes I had been pretending to get juice.

I rounded the corner and found Wheels lying on his back on Vince's legs, his little car discarded next to Vince on the couch. The little whore had his two front paws pointed lazily to the ceiling, his head hanging off Vince's knees, his tongue lolling out of his mouth in that way he does when he's getting a *really* good stomach rub. Vince was smiling down at Wheels as he scratched his belly. His nub of an ass wiggled back and forth (Wheels, not Vince. I would have been a little weirded out had I come around the corner to find Vince was shaking his ass while touching my dog).

I was about to shout that my dog was the biggest skank in the history of the world when Vince caught me watching him and said with a grin, "I think he likes me. I always wished I could have a dog."

From there, Big Puddle O'Goo Paul wanted to find a female dog and go back in time to save Wheel's manhood from ever being snipped so there could be billions and billions of *puppies* that I could shower upon Vince because he *always wished he could have a dog.* He'd gotten past my own dog's defenses, which in turn shoved him right past my own. "That's… that's so special," I managed to say. "I'm surprised he let you touch his cart."

Vince reached up and grabbed Wheels by the face and started an ear massage, and Wheels made a sound like he was about to orgasm all over Vince. Unfortunately, that was not an image I could get out of my head and it made me a bit queasy. "He didn't mind," Vince said, oblivious that he had gotten to second base with my dog. "I just picked him up and he tried to lay in my lap. I told him I'd let him if I could take off his wheels 'cause I didn't want him to get hurt."

It was about that time that I noticed how the muscles in Vince's arms flexed against the shirt he wore as he massaged the dog's head. I remembered then that he was wearing *my* shirt, and for some reason, Big Puddle O'Goo Paul roared until he blew up into I Want To Eat You Like A Buffet Paul.

I Want To Eat You Like A Buffet Paul wanted to punt Wheels like a football out of the room so *he* could climb in Vince's lap and lie on his back and have Vince rub his face. I Want To Eat You Like A Buffet Paul didn't think it was fair that the stupid half dog got all up in Vince's lap without having to do a damn thing. I Want To Eat You Like A Buffet Paul was jealous of a dog and began to plot deviously to knock off said dog so there would never be any question again as to who belonged in that lap.

"You okay?" Vince asked me. "You've got a weird look on your face."

And that, ladies and gentleman, was when it really began.

CHAPTER 8
The Greatest List In The History Of The World

Seven Things I Learned About Vince Taylor:
A Perspective
By Paul Auster

1) Vince Taylor Is Comfortable With His Body (Dear Jesus God, That
Ass)

I did as Sandy told me, bringing in the pajamas he'd gotten me that he had sworn cost him at *least* $15,000 (no one can embellish like a drag queen). Vince smiled up at me as I handed him the pajamas, while I simultaneously took Wheels off his lap (and resisted the urge to hiss "bad dog"). Wheels glared up at me as I reattached his cart and sent him on his way. I turned to tell Vince where the bathroom was so he could change, only to find him standing at the other end of the couch, sliding his bike shorts down his mad crazy hot thighs, bending over slowly and in deep concentration as if trying to keep the pain at bay.

It was at that time I learned Vince liked to wear a black jock under his bike shorts. It was also at this time that I found out that I really enjoyed black jock straps. Like *intensely* enjoyed them. To the point that I was sure God himself had come down from heaven and said, "Here, my son, I've brought you a gift. Check out that sweet ass framed by black straps. You're welcome."

I didn't even bother to think on whether Vince was doing what he was doing on purpose, because I couldn't get a single coherent thought together (though, in retrospect, I am absolutely certain that Vince was a fan of *Baywatch* because he had the slow-motion thing down *pat*). All I could really focus on was that ass framed by the jock, the white skin even paler against the black fabric, and the light dusting of hair on his ass. He lifted one foot slowly as he bent forward and pulled his leg out of the shorts. Then he did the same with the other foot, bending forward *slooowly* to get the shorts off completely.

Once this master class on How To Give Someone An Erection By Doing Almost Nothing was completed, he stood up straight and lifted his arms carefully above him and leaned back slightly, stretching out what I'm sure were very sore muscles. My dress shirt rode up the front of the jock and the hair on his stomach was so dark that it looked like night. This, of course, led to the second thing I learned about him.

2)   Vince Taylor Is A Manipulative Bastard (And I Have No Self-Esteem)

Part of me wanted to do a little dance, possibly break out the Hammertime bit that I knew how to do really well (it's really about how fast you can move your feet and hips. Don't tell me you've never tried it because you'd be a big, fat liar, so just stop: Hammertime). That part of me wanted to dance because Vince Taylor was wearing *that* jock with *my* shirt and standing in *my* house doing this totally awesome pseudoyoga stretch that was obscene given the fact that his junk was practically visible.

At least I know he's circumcised now, I thought, somewhat relieved. I didn't have anything against uncircumcised penises, it was just that I'd never had one before, and I didn't want for my very first one to be with Vince, because I was pretty sure I couldn't handle anything new on top of everything already happening. Then it hit me that I actually *had* that thought, like I was going to get anywhere near his cock at some point in the future. I had to stop myself from running out of the room in sheer embarrassment.

But he knew. That smug bastard knew *exactly* what he was doing. I knew this because while I was ogling the magnificence that was the sight in front of me, he kept glancing at me out of the corner of his eye, making sure I was watching him do his thought-out, choreographed peep show. He stretched back even further, though a mild grimace shot across his face, as if the position pained him.

But then he decided to take it one step further, coming back up from his stretch. Probably one step too far, if what happened after was any indication.

He reached up and started to unbutton my dress shirt, starting with the bottom button, moving his hands slowly because he knew I was watching every single movement he made. The first button slid out and he spread the shirt a little, exposing the top of the jock and the hairs on his stomach. He rested his hands on his skin for a moment, gently tapping where the hair disappeared into the fabric.

Then he moved onto the second button, and undid it just as slow. Unfortunately, it brought back that doubt that had plagued me ever since I was eight years old and that jerk Brady Johnson (older, meaner, and just plain stupider) had called me a fat ass on the playground and had tried to rip my shirt off over my head to show everyone what he called my "big fat titties." That day, for the first time, I felt like I wasn't good enough, that I was somehow lesser than everyone else around me. The little voice inside my head was born that said I was gross and disgusting, and everyone who said something negative about me was right.

So watching Vince undress in my living room brought the voice back, loud and in charge. It had been quiet for a few days, maybe because I'd been floating in a state of suspended animation. But the voice reminded me of when I'd first seen Vince, surrounded by Darren and the other homo jocks at the club. It reminded me of how Vince had looked when that twinkie Eric had started to grind up on him like I wasn't even there, the jock friends looking on and grinning at him like they were part of some great, big secret club that the rest of us couldn't belong to. It reminded me that Vince did not push him away. It reminded me of that Bear Dude later in the night who grabbed a handful of his ass as he brought them closer together to pretend to dance when in actuality it was just fucking with their clothes on.

By then, Vince was to the third button, but his grimace had returned and that spark in his dark eyes had faded slowly. He was still the sexiest thing I'd ever seen, but he was tired, so very tired. Before I could stop myself, I moved until I was in front of him and batted his hands away carefully. He briefly looked surprised, but then just grateful, only a little bit of the former smugness returning.

My hands shook as the surreal act of unbuttoning my own shirt on another man washed over me. We didn't speak, and I tried to focus on my fingers, trying to be as quick as I could be without acting like I was ready to pounce on him and put my balls on his chin.

I was hyperaware of how he breathed, these low, shallow breaths through his nose that I could feel on my forehead when he exhaled. He smelled medicinal, as if the hospital had leached its way into him. But underneath, there was the scent of sweat and soap, nothing flashy, but still noticeable. His chest rose and fell underneath my hands as I undid the next to the last button. I almost stopped on the last one but I wanted to see the bar through his nipple again (and I *really* wanted to touch it).

The last button came undone and the shirt opened completely, the bar through his nipple only hinted at through the fabric of my shirt. We both were breathing heavier than we should have been, and the close proximity was doing nothing to help me. I wanted to turn my face up and press my mouth against his. I wanted to slide his shirt off the rest of the way and run my fingers through the hairs on his chest. I wanted to wrap my lips around that piercing and tug on it until he gasped and grabbed my head.

But it was too much. It was too fast. It wasn't real. It couldn't be real.

I blushed brightly and stepped away. I thought I heard him sigh, and he turned and put the pajamas on.

God, that fucking ass.

3) Vince Is A Big Baby When It Comes To Pain And Whines Incessantly

Oh Lord, does he.

And he gets grumpy too. Quickly. I couldn't help but think it had a little bit to do with me nixing his attempt at whatever he was trying to do. But an hour later, he was in full-on bitchy mode, especially when he started to nod off and I kept having to wake him up.

"You can't go to sleep yet," I said as I reached out to give him a little shake. We were both sitting on the couch, but at opposite ends, me trying to put as much distance as I possibly could between us without making it extraordinarily awkward. I didn't want him to sleep because I'd changed my mind and was sure he would die from the concussion the second he nodded off. "Still a few more hours."

He scowled at me as his eyes snapped open. "I'm not trying to sleep," he said with a growl. "I'm just making sure my eyes still close okay. You know, as a sign of brain damage. From when you hit me with your car."

I tried to keep from getting angry. "You ran into my car door," I said evenly. "From an insurance perspective, I'm pretty sure I can argue that you're at fault for this."

"You didn't maintain a proper lookout when exiting your vehicle," he retorted. "Everyone knows that I had the right of way."

"Maybe if you hadn't been riding so close to the cars, this wouldn't have happened."

"Maybe if you had looked before you opened your door, I wouldn't be almost dying."

I fought the urge to roll my eyes. "What happened to this being *totally worth it*?" I mocked, trying to mimic his deep voice. Instead, it came out sounding like I was an asshole.

"It was," he grumbled. "I would do it again if I had to."

What the fuck? "You'd run into my car door again? Why?"

He looked down at his hands. "I'm here, aren't I?"

And, of course, I started to sputter. "What… you can't say that… that's just… I… you… so damn *cute*… why… just *why*…."

So, after that, at least for a moment, I was a bit more lenient. I let him nod off for a few minutes before I woke him up, just to make sure his pupils weren't dilated and he could remember my name and answer a simple question. I asked him who the vice president was and he looked at me like I was out of my goddamned mind. "How the hell am I supposed to know that?" he grumped at me. "I didn't vote." So, instead, I asked him to count to five. When he started counting out of order and slurring his words, I got freaked out. Then he grinned and winked at me and said, "Just kidding." At that moment, I gave very serious consideration to making his concussion much, much worse, but then he whined a little bit in the back of his throat and sounded so much like Wheels when he was hungry that I crumbled completely.

Manipulative bastard.

So, of course, when I finally told him he *could* go to sleep and stay asleep, he wasn't tired. I listened to him bitch and moan on my couch about how much his back hurt and how much his ass hurt and, wow, wouldn't it be nice if there was someone who would be willing to give him a massage? He'd sure like a massage, he said, to ease his sore muscles. He wondered aloud if there was anyone in his immediate vicinity who would be willing to provide such a massage; perhaps a certain individual feeling guilty about something? Perhaps that guilt extended from causing a certain accident to happen? It was entirely possible, he hypothesized, that should a person feel guilty about such an accident that caused injury, an easy atonement would be offering to give said injured person a rub down.

It took six minutes of me grinding my teeth before I got up and went into the kitchen, telling him I'd get him some more juice. While I did this, I also ground up two of the muscle relaxers into the juice and brought it out to him, not feeling guilty in the slightest (about the secret-drugging thing; I still felt like crap that he hit my car). I stood next to him as he drank it down, smacking his lips, telling me how much he loved pulp in orange juice.

It was twenty minutes later that I found out that, regardless of whatever else he was, Vince was a lightweight who got stoned very, very easily. We were sitting on the couch watching *Animal Planet* ("I could wrestle an alligator," he told me confidently) when I felt eyes on me. I looked over at him and saw the loopiest grin on his face.

"What?" I asked.

"You're awesome," he said, a slight slur to his words. This time, the slur sounded real.

"Uh. Thanks?"

"You're welcome. How come…." He got distracted by something on the ceiling. "Whoa."

"Oh boy."

He looked back at me, trying to widen his eyes. "You poisoned me!" he said, trying to be stern, but his lips kept quirking into a smile.

"I did not!" I said indignantly, even though I sort of did.

"You made me high!"

"You need to go to sleep."

He tried to point a finger at me, but it kept going off in other directions, like he was trying to dance with one hand. "What'd you give me?" he asked, very interested in his hand. "Crack?"

"You think I gave you *crack*?"

"Maybe."

"Is there anything about me that screams crack?"

He grinned as he swayed. "Your butt crack," he whispered before dissolving into giggles.

"Oh Jesus Christ," I muttered. "You are going to be so embarrassed when you wake up tomorrow."

"Why?"

"Because you're giggling like a five-year-old girl."

"I am not. I'm all man."

"So you've tried to show me."

"Hey," he said

"Hey, what?"

"Why won't you... oh, man, the room is like all twisty."

I started to get a little concerned. For my couch. "Are you going to throw up?"

He shuddered. "I sure as shit hope not. I hate throwing up. I hate being sick. I hate being hurt. My back really hurts." Now he started to pout. The effect was unnerving.

"I'm sorry," I sighed.

"My bike's all busted."

"I'll buy you a new one."

"Maybe that bike had a special meaning. Maybe it belonged to my late grandfather and it's the only piece of him I have left."

Ouch. "Did it?"

"Did what? Your ceiling is pretty."

"Did the bike belong to your late grandfather and is it the only piece of him you have left?"

He snorted. "What are you talking about? I got that bike from the bike shop over on Speedway. Can I tell you something?"

"You would anyway."

He leaned toward me and almost fell off the couch. Once he righted himself, he said, "I like wearing your clothes. They smell like you."

My face burned. "That's... cool."

Vince frowned. "How come you won't go on a date with me? I'll treat you so good. Better than anyone ever."

I sighed. "Can we not talk about this now? It's almost five. You should get some sleep."

"Answer the question and I'll go to sleep."

"It just wouldn't work, okay?"

He watched me for a moment. Then, quietly, "Is it because I'm not smart enough?"

I snapped my gaze to his. "What?"

He looked away. "I know I'm not the smartest person in the world," he said, picking at a loose thread on my pajamas he wore. "My dad told me once that it's a good thing I look like I do because it's the only thing that'll get me through life."

"Your dad said that to you?" I asked him, keeping my voice even and trying to keep the anger from my face. This was the first time he'd really mentioned his dad, and already I wanted to find out where his father lived so I could kick him in the balls.

Vince shrugged. "Yeah, but he's right, you know. I can be pretty dumb sometimes. It's how I am. I know I look all right. That helps me, I think. But... you know. That's all people can see sometimes."

"I think you're fine just the way you are," I told him honestly. "And you know what? Fuck your dad. You're totally smart."

He looked astonished. "Wow, if you knew my dad, you wouldn't say that. He can be kind of scary when he wants to be."

I tried to show more confidence than I actually felt. "I'd say the same thing to his face."

"Whoa," Vince said softly, his eyes starting to glaze over. "You're pretty awesome, Paul."

"Sure, Vince."

"Why don't you believe me?" he asked, suddenly sounding coherent.

"About what?"

"That I want to take you out."

"I don't know."

"Don't do that."

"What?"

He looked aggrieved. "Don't try to dodge the question. You always do that."

"You're stoned, Vince. You don't know what you're talking about."

"Only because *you* drugged me."

"Guilt trips don't work on me."

"I'm at your house wearing your pajamas. Guilt trips work on you very well."

"Bastard."

"I'm going to take you out on a date," he said, as if that was that.

I couldn't take it anymore. "Why? Why do you keep pushing for this?"

He looked me in the eye. "Because," he said, "I like you."

I almost felt like bursting into song. I couldn't look away. "Vince… people like you don't go for people like me."

He frowned. "You've said that before. What do you mean?"

I gestured between the two of us. "Look at me. Look at *you*. You're… pretty. I'm… not."

Before I could stop him, he captured my hand in his and brought it to his lips, kissing my fingers gently. Then, he used my own words against me. "I think you're fine," he said, "just the way you are. And besides, I think you're *very* pretty."

And then he leaned his head back on the couch and closed his eyes, holding my hand. Every now and then, his thumb would brush over my palm. I didn't know what to say, so I said nothing. It seemed safer.

Finally, he opened his eyes. They looked bloodshot. He was a little pale. "Fuck, I'm tired," he muttered.

Without allowing myself any time to think (because otherwise I would overthink and never, ever take a single chance) I tugged on his hand, pulling him down. He came easily, stretched out along the couch, groaning slightly due to the twinges I'm sure he felt. A few warning bells went off in my head, but they were silenced the minute his head hit my leg. He sighed contentedly as he rubbed his forehead against my legs as if trying to mark me with his scent. He looked up at me and I looked down at him. Neither of us said anything.

4) He Has The Softest Hair Ever

I curled my fingers through it as he drifted off to sleep. He hummed softly as I scratched along his scalp. He fell asleep and I started to. We stayed that way for hours. I didn't move.

I didn't want to.

5)   Vince Has No Problem With Germs And Is Curious About Tampons

I woke up a while later. It was dark outside, and my legs were asleep. I looked down at my lap. Vince was still curled up against me, his face pointed toward my stomach, snoring softly, one of his hands curled into my shirt like he wanted to be tethered to me. I watched him for a long time, wondering just what the fuck I was getting myself into. This was turning out to be the weirdest week of my life, and I didn't know if I wanted it to stop. For now we were in this little bubble, and it was only me and him, and nothing else mattered, at least for the moment. I brushed my hand through his hair again. Then I realized I was watching him sleep and how creepy that really was. Some people might have thought it was romantic. I thought it was one step away from putting him in a hole in my basement, telling him to rub the lotion on his skin or else he'll get the hose again.

Besides, my legs were starting to cramp.

"Hey," I said quietly, shaking him.

Nothing.

"Vince," I said a little louder.

Nothing.

"I'll suck your dick if you wake up right now." *I did not just say that.*

"I'm awake," he said rather quickly, opening his eyes.

I scowled at him. "That's cheating."

He smirked as he stretched. "You already promised. You can't back down now."

"Get off me. Your head weighs like thirty pounds."

"The human head only weights eight pounds," he scoffed as he sat up.

I stared at him.

"What?" he said defensively. "I may not be smart, but I *do* know some things."

"And one of those things is how much a person's head weighs?" I asked.

"You didn't know that, did you?" he asked, sounding weirdly shy.

I did (I don't know why), but it seemed important for some reason that I didn't let him know. "Nope. I sure didn't."

He looked inordinately pleased. "Stick with me, kid. I'll teach you some stuff."

I somehow resisted the urge to roll my eyes. "Are you hungry?"

He shook his head. "Those pills kinda messed with my stomach a bit." He tried to send me a meaningful look to make me feel guilty. He failed. Miserably.

"I'm not going to feel bad about that," I told him. "You needed to sleep."

"You realize, though," he said, "that I'll never be able to take a drink from you again without worrying that you're trying to drug me."

"Good," I said.

"Great comeback. Can I take a shower?"

My mouth went dry. "Uh."

He leered at me. "You can join me if you want."

"That's okay. I'll take Wheels outside and you can... take a shower."

"Naked," Vince said, arching an eyebrow.

"Naked," I agreed weakly. "Most people do it that way."

"And you could do it with me."

I don't know where it came from, but I decided to play back. "Tell you what," I said, leaning closer to him. His breathing picked up as my lips almost grazed his ear. "If you can stand without grimacing, groaning, or showing you're in any kind of pain, I'll get in the shower with you." I moved just a fraction of an inch closer. "Naked."

"You *will*? No joking?"

"No joking."

"Oh, man. You should *not* have said that. You're going to be *so* naked in like two minutes."

"If you say so." I sat back and waited.

To be fair, he did try very damn hard, which could have meant he wanted me really bad. Which I still didn't quite understand. He sat there for a moment taking deep breaths in and then letting them out slowly. A look of supreme concentration came over his face, and for a brief moment, I thought he was going to make it. My mind wandered to the thought of that nipple piercing again, and I wanted to know what it would look like when it was wet. Then he shot up from the couch quickly, groaning as he did so, his face contorting in pain. He gasped when he stood upright, wrapping an arm around his side. He looked almost stricken when he glanced over at me.

"I can try it again," he said through gritted teeth.

I shook my head as I stood. "You're an idiot," I told him, though there was no heat behind my words.

That didn't stop him from flinching away. I cursed softly when I realized what I'd said. "I didn't mean it like that," I said. "I'm sorry. I just don't want you to hurt yourself."

He nodded tightly but didn't speak. I wanted to find everyone in the world who had ever insulted his intelligence and punch them in the face. It was a weird feeling to have.

I sighed. "C'mon. I'll show you where the shower is. The hot water will feel good on you. I'll get the guest room ready and you can go to bed when you're done."

I tried not to think of the naked man in my bathroom as I stood outside with Wheels while he did his business. "What the fuck am I doing?" I asked him softly. Wheels didn't answer, deciding to take a shit instead. I wondered if that was answer enough.

After letting him chase a lizard for a few minutes (there's something inherently funny about seeing my half dog going up on one wheel as he tears around in circles—it's like he's performing daredevil tricks!) he followed me inside and went immediately for his food bowl, acting like the little boy he was and scarfing down his kibble like it was the first time he'd eaten in years.

The shower was still running and I could hear Vince singing horribly off-key to himself. At least I knew he hadn't fallen and died in my shower, which I was eternally grateful for. I quickly made up the guest room (and by made up, I mean I pulled the covers back on the bed and sniffed the sheets to make sure they didn't smell like ass or dog—they didn't).

The shower turned off and I heard a thump followed by some muffled cursing. I hovered near the bathroom door, unsure of what to do. Finally, I knocked. "You okay?" I asked.

"Yeah," he grumbled. "Just hit my elbow against the wall."

"You probably shouldn't do that."

"Har, har."

"Drugs wore off, huh?"

"Yeah. Sorry you couldn't have your way with me before then."

It was easier, for some reason, talking to him through the door. "What makes you think I didn't?"

There was a pause. "I still have spunk in my junk," he finally said.

"You're like a dirty Dr. Seuss."

"I'll do you on the grass. I'll do you during mass."

"No thanks. I think I'll take a pass." *Dammit! Stop rhyming!*

He snorted. "You just want a piece of my ass."

"Wow. That's thirty seconds of my life I'll never get back."

"Your fault."

"Don't even try to blame that one on me."

The lock on the door clicked.

"I'm not going to try and bust in there," I said, somewhat annoyed.

"Oh, I know," he said. "Even though I wanted you to, you didn't."

"Then why'd you lock the door?"

"Because I'm going to use your toothbrush and I knew you'd probably freak out."

I glared at the door. "Don't you dare. That's disgusting!"

"I've had my tongue in your mouth. Same diff."

I blushed, even though he couldn't see me. "I will break this fucking door down!" A six-year-old Girl Scout would have sounded more threatening than I did.

"See, I knew you'd freak out." He started laughing. "Pink? *Really?* Your toothbrush is *pink*? Oh my God! Even your toothbrush is a homo!"

"My dentist gave that to me!" I shouted at him, as if that made it special.

"Toothpaste," he muttered. "Where is the toothpaste?"

"Vince, I will punch your face off," I warned him.

"Found the toothpaste. Oh, and I found the tampons too. Why is there one missing?"

Oh, crap. "I… uh."

"Did you *use* one?"

"What? No! I just wanted to see what they looked like!"

"Dude. Paul. Gross."

Then silence, for a moment.

"What are you doing?" I asked him.

"Opening a tampon. I want to see what they look like too."

"Oh. This is the weirdest conversation of my life."

"Why is there a *string* on it?" he asked, sounding baffled.

I waited.

"Wait… is that how they… pull it…? Oh, *gross!*"

"You better not have thrown it!"

"Sure did. Didn't see where it went. That's just wrong. Reason number 6,432 I'm glad I'm a dude."

"That's a lot of reasons."

No answer.

"What are you doing?"

"Brushin' ma teef," he said as if he had a mouthful.

"You *bastard*," I growled.

I heard him spit into the sink. "My teeth feel clean. And a whole lot gayer."

The lock clicked. The door opened. Shirtless Vince stood before me, droplets of water on his chest and shoulders. I stared as a single drop of water clung to the bar through his nipple. I wanted to taste it. My pajama pants were slung low on his waist. He had that totally hot V thing that buff guys have going on right above the waistband. But I could also see the bruising on his back and sides, spreading more than it'd been at the hospital. The colors were also darker—blues, greens, and purples. His skin was rife with darkening colors.

"I'm minty fresh," he told me with a smile.

"How… how about that," I muttered. "Does it hurt?" I pointed at the bruises.

He turned slowly so I could see how far they spread on his back, along with shallow scrapes and gashes along his shoulder blades where he'd landed on the ground. "Fuck," I said succinctly. "I'm so fucking sorry."

He shrugged. "Wasn't your fault," he said. "I should have watched where I was going." He took a step forward and started to crowd me. I took a step back, flustered yet again.

"I made up the guest room for you," I said, looking at my feet, double chin be damned. I pointed to the door behind me. Then I said the rest as I'd planned. It came out in a rush. "I have to go to work in the morning, but you can stay here if you want and I can take you home when I get off work, it's no big deal, okay with me."

He hesitated. "You sure?"

I nodded, refusing to meet his eyes. "Yeah. Unless you have somewhere to be? Or unless you want to go home. Maybe you do. I don't know. I just thought you'd like to sleep in or something. Or maybe I can just come home at lunch and take you then. It doesn't matter to me, so whatever you want to—"

"Paul."

"Yeah?"

I felt a hand on my chin and he lifted up my face. Before I knew what was happening, minty lips brushed against mine, just a scrape before they were gone. "That sounds okay. Thank you for taking care of me."

My face was red yet again. "I did hit you, after all," I said apologetically, my face still in his hands. I couldn't take the closeness to him anymore without doing something stupid, so I stepped away and moved down the hall. "Good night," I said without turning around. I closed my bedroom door behind me.

And, of course, two hours later, I was still wide awake as I stared up at the ceiling, cursing my own lameness, wondering at what point in my life my testicles had been removed. "I'm a eunuch," I muttered. "I'm a hairless, no-balled eunuch. I should put up missing posters to see if anyone can return my manhood. Because it's gone. It's lost. I am a walking vagina."

There was a knock at my door. Wheels lifted his head. I watched the door warily. "Yeah?"

"Paul? You awake?" He sounded nervous. Odd.

"Probably why I said 'yeah.'"

"Oh yeah. Can I come in?"

I sighed and stared at the ceiling. "Okay."

The door opened, and he stood in the doorway. My eyes were adjusted to the dark, and I could see him scratching his stomach, looking everywhere except at me. "Everything all right?" I asked him.

He shrugged but still wouldn't look at me. "Couldn't sleep," he muttered.

"Do you need the muscle relaxers again?"

He shook his head. "Don't like feeling fuzzy. It doesn't hurt too much. Shower helped."

"Oh. Okay. So… what's up?"

He sighed. "I…." He stopped and rubbed his hands over his face. "Look, I usually don't sleep very well, okay? Never have."

"You slept fine earlier today," I reminded him. "Though it was probably just the drugs."

He nodded and started gnawing on his thumbnail. "Wasn't just that," he mumbled.

"Well, what was it?"

"It was you," he said defiantly, as if expecting me to contradict him.

"Me?" I squeaked and then coughed. "Me?" I said again, my voice far deeper, sounding like I was doing an impression of Darth Vader. I wanted to tell Vince I was his father, but I didn't think we were quite up to role-playing yet.

"Yeah."

I considered his words. "So… you're saying I put you to sleep. That's… comforting."

He scowled at me. "I wish you wouldn't do that."

"What?"

"Twist my words. Make it something they're not. Make you sound bad. Stop it."

"Yes, sir," I said, feeling properly rebuked.

"Oh, I like that." He grinned, waggling his eyebrows at me, some of his smugness returning. Then it faded almost immediately. "I just... I think I sleep better. You know. With you."

Oh, man. What a fucking line. That's so not going to work on me.

I waited.

He squirmed.

I sighed... and lifted up the comforter on my bed.

He looked relieved as he walked over and climbed into the bed, lying on his side to avoid putting any pressure on his back. And so he could look straight at me.

"You're used to getting your way, aren't you?" I asked, bemused. Wheels took the opportunity to drag himself between us, where he laid down with a mighty huff.

Vince shrugged. "I guess. That's not what this is about, though."

"Oh? Then what is it about?"

"Sleep, Paul. I'm not going to have sex with you tonight, so stop asking."

I was too speechless to think of anything coherent to say in retort. By the time my brain started functioning again, he sighed that happy sound and closed his eyes. But before he drifted off completely, he reached out and grabbed my hand, curling it into his own. And then he slept.

6)   Vince Likes To Send Text Messages and Go Through My Shit

What r u doing?

Who is this?

U can't tell? How disappointing

You spell out disappointing but you can't spell out the word "you"?

U text like u talk. That's special

I don't remember giving you my number, Vince

Ha! U DO know who this is. Oh happy day!

What can I say; I'm psychic

So

??

What r u doing?

Working

Guess what I'm doing?

What?

Going thru ur stuff

What?!?! Vince!! PERSONAL SPACE

U have a lot of movies

I like movies

Yeah, and they're all action movies

So? What's wrong with that?

Nothing. I just thought u'd have more girly stuff

GIRLY STUFF?!?!

Yeah. Like chick flicks. U know

And why would you think I have chick flicks?

Becuz. Ur Paul. Float like a butterfly, sting like a unicorn ;)

I'm going to hit you with my car for real this time

o_O ← that's the face I'm making at u

You don't want to know the face I'm making at you

Sex face? >_<

No. Not sex face

Blowjob face? *o*

That looks dirty. Stop it

I know. I'm going in ur room to look in ur drawers

Vince! So help me God, I will hart you

U'll hart me? I hart u 2!

HURT. I WILL HURT YOU

Text threats are illegal. Look up the penal code

That's not a real thing

I know. I just like saying penal. SEX FACE >_<

I am going to tell management that you're faking your injuries

Nah. U won't. What's ur middle name?

What the hell? Do you have ADD?

No. Do u have SUBTRACTION? Haha, get it??

Yes, Vince. I get it

I need my own TV show

No one would watch it

Middle name?

James

So ur Paul James Auster? That's pretty hot

No, it's not. What is yours?

U'll laugh at me

What? No I won't

Everyone does

I'm not everyone, Vince

Fine. It's Melody

Your name is Vincent Melody Taylor?

Yes. Melody was my grandmother's name. I had no choice

I see

Ur laughing at me, aren't u?

Yes. So hard. I'm going to tell everyone. Especially Tad

Why don't u like him? Tad's nice

If by nice, you mean a plague-ridden whore then yes. He's nice

U don't need to be jealous. I only have eyes for u (That's a song!)

Oh, please. I'm not jealous (I'm well aware that's a song)

U have a lot of argyle socks, Paul

I like socks. Get out of my drawers!!!

Yeah, but u REALLY like them. Like fetish like them

I don't have fetishes

U could open up an argyle sock and sex store. Call it Sock 'N Cock

Don't joke about that. It's my dream. Not the cock part

I believe u can fly. I believe u can touch the sky

Do not threaten me with R. Kelly song lyrics. I'm offended

He likes watersports

I don't want to know how you know that

Do u?

What?

Like watersports?

Are you asking me if I like to get peed on?

Yes

No, Vince. I don't like to get peed on

That's good to know. I've never peed on anyone except myself in the shower

You share way too much

I'd pee on u if u got stung by a jellyfish

How charming. We live in the desert

Yeah, but when we go on vacation in Asia. They eat jellyfish there

That's disgusting

U could eat one and get stung and then I'd pee in ur mouth

You are so fucking gross. I'm not going to Asia with you

Yeah, u will. U just don't know it yet. Is that ur parents in the picture?

Are you still in my room!?!?!

Yeah. They look nice

I guess. They're kind of weird

I like weird. I can't wait to meet them

You want to meet my parents?

Sure. When?

That wasn't an invitation

Oh

Why?

Why what?

Why do you want to meet my parents?

Because they look nice

Vince?

Yeah?

Are your parents nice?

I guess. Don't really talk to them all that much. They've got better
things to do

Oh. That sucks

Eh. It's okay. Who needs em, right?

Yeah. Maybe. My grandma lives in Tucson too

Oh? That's cool. My grandparents are all dead

She has a homophobic parrot named Johnny Depp

Please tell me ur not joking

Not joking

Paul?

What?

That. Is. AMAZING

Wait until it screams that it doesn't want you to rape it

LOLOLOLOL

I'M NOT JOKING

That's so awesome. I'll go with u next time. I want to see it

Uh, okay?

Hey, what's in this box under ur bed?

STAY OUT OF THAT BOX!!!!!!!

OMFG. U HAVE SEX TOYS?!?!?!?! LMAOOOOO

VINCE!!!!!

THIS DILDO IS HUGE!!!!!!!!!!!!!! And it's BLACK!!! LOLOLOL

I hate everything about you

Do u use these!?!?! That is so fucking hot. Grrrrr

No. I don't use them. I didn't even know they were there

Ur a liar. Here. Hold on

What?

Did u get that pic I just sent?

You mean the one of you with your mouth on a black dildo?

Yeah

No, Vince. I didn't

It took u long enough to respond. U go into the bathroom and jerk it?

NO I DIDN'T!!!

U did too! And u know what face u made?

Let me guess. Sex face?

SEX FACE!! >_<

Put the sex toys away!!!

I did. I'm looking to see if u have a diary

What?!?! Vince, knock it off!

U seem like the type. I want to see if u wrote about me

I don't have a diary

Dear Diary: Vince is sooooo awesome!

I DON'T HAVE A DIARY.

Dear Diary: I think about Vince when I use the black dildo on my butthole

I do NOT!

Really? Why not? I'm using it and thinking of u right now

Shut up. You are not

Want a pic?

I am not having text sex with you while I am at work!!!

So u'd have it with me when ur NOT at work? Score!

Are you really using the dildo?

No. Wheels and I are reading ur diary

I DON'T HAVE A DIARY!!!!!

Dear Diary: I hope Vince asks me out on a date. He's so DREAMY

You already did. I said no. And dreamy? REALLY????

Dear Diary: Vince asked me out on a date and I said yes!!!

Oh, you are so fucking clever

U'll see. U just wait.

7)   Vince Prefers the "Wear You Down" Method Of Seduction

That night, I pulled into his apartment complex. "Here you are," I said.

"Here I am," he replied. He made no move to get out of my car.

"You sure you'll be okay?"

"I'll be fine. All alone. By myself."

"That's a shame."

"So."

"This is where you open the door and get out of my car."

"Let's go do something tomorrow night. It's Friday."

"I know what day it is."

"Just as friends."

I arched an eyebrow at him. "Just as friends?"

He smiled and those dimples were out in full force. "Just as friends."

I wasn't fooled. "You're totally thinking in your head that it's a date, aren't you?"

He nodded, not even looking remotely guilty. As a matter of fact, his smile widened.

"Vince…."

"One date, Paul. One date. If you hate it, I'll never ask you out ever again."

"Ever?"

"Ever." He paused, considering. "Or until next Tuesday, whichever comes first."

"You think you're so cute, don't you?"

"Do *you* think I'm cute?"

"Fuck off," I grumbled.

"So?"

I sighed. "Fine. Tomorrow."

Vince beamed at me and my heart skipped a couple of beats.

"But I'm not going to have fun," I warned him, already feeling nervous about it.

He rolled his eyes. "Sure you will. And then I'll get to ask you out again for a second date. And then on the date after *that*, you'll show me what you do with those sex toys." He grinned an evil grin at me.

"Get out of my car," I said, absolutely mortified.

"See you tomorrow for our date," he said, leaning forward and brushing his lips across mine before I could stop him. And then he was gone.

Five minutes later as I drove home, I received my billionth text of the day.

Miss u already. SEX FACE >_<

And I smiled because it's hard to be mad at someone who misses you when you're apart.

CHAPTER 9
First Date Jitters: The Only Thing I'll Be Blowing Is Chunks

"WHY are you nervous?" Sandy asked. "You've already made out with him at work and at home, seen him almost naked, slept in the same bed, and spent an entire day with him in your lap. What could you possibly be nervous about?"

"I don't know!" I wailed, tearing through my closet trying to find that one outfit that would say, *Hi, my name is Paul. I'm confident, sexy, and I am not sweating gross buckets under my armpits and at the back of my knees.* So far, I was without any luck as every piece of clothing I put on either made me look like an obese rhinoceros or a Vietnamese hooker. Sandy said he couldn't quite see the Vietnamese hooker, but I assured him that I looked like my name was Pham Dao Lin and I worked at a brothel called the Lotus Flower where I offered hand jobs to men with rubber glove fetishes.

"Well," he said, frowning at a pair of chaps that came from my wannabe-cowboy-BDSM days, "I would give you a Xanax, but chances are you'd pass out and drown in the soup appetizer. I don't know if Vince would think that's attractive. Or maybe he's got some really weird kink and would think you're really hot with minestrone dripping off your face."

"Oh God," I moaned. "What if he *does* have weird kinks? What if he wants to put things up my pee-hole while he makes me dress up as Sailor Moon?"

Sandy stared at me. "What the fuck have you been watching?"

"I accidentally googled the word *kink*," I told him, finding a pair of Crocs in the back of my closet. I didn't know where those came from because I was pretty sure I wasn't a lesbian who owned a bookstore in Ohio. "I thought I could find some slightly sexy things to do just in case... you know." I couldn't look at him.

"Uh-huh. And what did you find?"

"So many things," I muttered. "There are some seriously fucked-up people in the world. Then I started to get turned on and that scared the crap out of me, so I looked up regular porn like normal people."

"Thank God for regular porn," Sandy said. "Baby doll, please understand that I love you with all of my heart. I really, really do. But we need to take you shopping in the worst way. I'm pretty sure I just found corduroy, and I'm seriously reconsidering our friendship."

"Hey, it made a comeback," I said. "In the nineties."

He waited.

"The early nineties."

He waited some more.

"Okay, in March of 1992. But you know I have a hard time throwing anything away."

He sighed. "I know. But I also know I'm going to turn on the TV one day and find you starring in an episode of *Hoarders,* and I'll wonder if I could have done more to save you. By then, I'll most likely be super famous and living in a palace with a harem of Iranian men who lick my balls whenever I ask, and you'll be here with your piles and piles of corduroy. I'll think fondly of you, but your memory would most likely be accompanied with mild disdain."

"I hope your dreams crash and burn," I hissed at him.

He probably wasn't even listening. "Okay, you've got thirty minutes before he gets here. Go get in the shower, and I'll figure out what you're going to wear."

"This was probably the worst idea I've ever had," I said, looking around at the disaster that was now my room. "Why the hell did I say yes?"

"Because he was wearing a black jock strap while standing in your living room and you did absolutely nothing about it and this is God's way of punishing you," Sandy said. "You must be the only gay boy in the world that would have been able to resist that. If I were you, I'd give serious thought as to what you can do to rectify that situation."

"It was really hard," I admitted.

"I bet it was," he said with a smirk.

"Not like that."

"Uh-huh."

"It was so black."

"How big was his cock?"

"Sandy!"

"What? If I'm spending my Friday night digging through a closet that, if I didn't know you I would have assumed belonged to a fifty-four-year-old Russian woman who works in a steel mill, then you can sure as shit give me some details!"

"It looked big," I allowed. "And his nipple is pierced."

Sandy made the sign of the cross over his chest. "Sweet Jesus. Baby doll, you know I've always been in your corner and I'm rooting for you now, but if you mess this up in any way, shape, or form, I can't promise you that Helena isn't going to swoop in and take him for her own."

"You tell that bitch he's mine," I snapped at him.

Sandy grinned. "Territorial, hmm? Go shower while I sort through this mess. You have twenty-six minutes."

I ran out of my room, tripping on a discarded pair of jeans (stonewashed, no less; why the hell was my closet an interdimensional portal to the previous century?) and almost running into the wall. I grinned sheepishly at Sandy, who just shook his head and muttered something I couldn't quite make out but sounded suspiciously like "he better love you."

I hadn't actually spoken to Vince since I'd dropped him off at his house the day before. He had texted me a few times today, telling me a knock-knock joke that I still didn't get and telling me he'd pick me up at my house at seven. I had asked him where we were going, and he told me not to worry about it, which, of course, made me worry about it even more. I told him it was important because I needed to know what to wear. He told me I could wear absolutely nothing and that would be okay. Then he started to try and get me to have text sex with him again and I told him that I had to go to a meeting, when in reality I was sitting at my desk, trying to figure out how to get rid of my boner. Speaking to customers on the phone when I had an erection was not the best part of my day.

I was only in the shower for a few minutes, almost slipping and falling when Sandy leaned into the bathroom and shouted over the water, "Do you need to trim your bush?" I screamed at him to get the fuck out of my bathroom and that *no*, my bush was perfectly *fine*. I heard him chuckling to himself as he went back to my bedroom, and I glanced down just to make sure my pubes didn't look like they were Rastafarian. They didn't, and I breathed a sigh of relief. I didn't think I would be able to put a razor near my junk with how my hands were shaking, and asking Sandy to do it seemed to be stretching the boundaries of our friendship. Friendship should never be about asking your friend to hold your balls out of the way so you can shave your taint.

By the time I was done in the shower, I had worked myself back up into a mini freak-out. I wiped away the foggy condensation from the mirror and stared at my wide-eyed reflection. My eyes looked blown out, like I was witnessing something so shocking that I'd never be the same. And, to be fair, I was getting ready for a date with the hottest man I'd ever seen, so it wasn't too much of a stretch.

"What am I doing?" I whispered to myself.

Reflection Paul didn't respond except to grimace at me like he was nauseated. Which he just might have been. I know I was.

Then I made the mistake of trying to do my hair. And, of course, every time I ran my fingers through it to smooth it out and let it do what it normally did *every day*, it would start sticking up in random spots. I would smooth down one and another tuft would pop up as if my very *follicles* were mocking me. I scowled at my hair as I squashed it down with both my hands and then it was sticking up *everywhere*, and Sandy must have heard the sharp buzz of the hair clippers and figured I wasn't trimming my pubes and was able to stop me before I shaved my head.

He made me sit on the toilet, removing anything sharp from my immediate vicinity, nodding slowly as I babbled at him how my hair was out to destroy me. He put his hand on my chin and made me look up at him, eyeing my hair with an empirical look. He turned and dug through my cabinet and wouldn't answer me when I asked him what he was doing. Then he whirled around and assaulted me. Well, *I* said he was assaulting me, and *he* said he was just applying some kind of gunky, pasty crap that he'd found on one of my shelves. I told him in a very clear voice that I didn't *like* gunky, pasty crap in my hair because I was now thirty, not some douchey twenty-year-old who thought I was better than everyone else. He responded that he was well aware I was thirty because parts of my hair were falling out while he was trying to style it. It took him five minutes to calm me down after that, telling me to just *breathe*, that he was just *joking*. I called him the evilest bitch who ever existed, and he preened at what he considered a compliment. I told him our friendship wouldn't continue on past tonight and that I was pretty sure there was a special place in hell for him. He smiled at me and made me stand to look in the mirror. And somehow, someway, he'd been able to make my plain, old, boring hair look like it was the greatest thing that ever existed. It had this trendy, spikey, faux-hawky thing going on.

"Holy shit," I whispered.

"Right?" he grinned. "Stylish. He's not going to know what hit him. Now, let's go get you dressed. We don't have that much time left after your meltdown."

"That wasn't my fault. You told me I was going *bald*!"

He didn't even bother responding, instead grabbing my hand and then pulling me back to my bedroom, which was still somewhat of a disaster area. "Now," he said, "I couldn't find any sexy underwear, so this will have to do." He threw a pair of black boxer briefs at me.

"Sexy underwear?" I asked, somewhat bewildered. "Sandy, what about me suggests to you that I would wear sexy underwear?"

"*Everyone* should have at least one pair of sexy underwear," he replied, as if that was totally obvious. He turned away.

"Why?" I asked as I dropped the towel and slipped on the boxers. "And what the hell is sexy underwear?"

"Like, skimpy briefs."

"Gross. I don't want to wear that. Well, okay. I would if they had like X-Men or Transformers on them, but that makes it sound like I'm a pedophile, so I think I'll just stick with the underwear I have." I snapped them up and Sandy turned back around, giving me a critical look up and down. You want to know what it means to be self-conscious? Try being slightly overweight and standing in nothing but black underwear while your best friend, who is the skinniest person in the world, stares at your crotch as if it holds the secrets of the universe.

"Your penis looks good in those," he said finally, giving me a nod of approval.

"Oh joy," I muttered. "It's a good thing that's what I was going for. Penis fashion is all the rage these days."

"Judging from your wardrobe, you wouldn't know fashion if it fucked your mouth and came on your face," Sandy said with a glare. "I didn't realize how appalling the state of your closet had gotten. This'll all be rectified very shortly, so you may as well accept that now."

"*You're* gonna be rectified," I snapped lamely.

"Ouch," he said. "Put these on." He tossed me a pair of jeans he'd bought for me on a trip to Austin two summers ago. I'd never worn them because I always thought the ass pockets looked like they'd been bedazzled. And not in a good way. Well, come to think of it, I don't know if there *is* a good way for something to be bedazzled.

But Sandy had that "don't fuck with me" look in his eye, so I put the pants on without protest. They had a button fly, too, which I always found tedious and completely ridiculous. Sandy must have seen the reaction on my face because he huffed to himself. "Button flies are delicious," he said sternly. "There's nothing hotter than going up to a guy and using one hand to rip them open before going down on him."

"That's not going to happen," I assured him as I sucked in my gut inconspicuously so I could finish buttoning up. "I have too much self-respect to let someone go down on me on the first date."

He found this hilarious and laughed until I was sure he was going to choke on his tongue. I crossed my arms against my chest, trying to look intimidating, only to realize I was standing shirtless in a pair of shiny designer jeans and my nonsexy underwear.

"Is this the entire outfit?" I grumbled at him.

He wiped his eyes. "It could be, if you wanted. I'm sure Vince would appreciate the view."

I poked my stomach and watched it dimple. "I highly doubt he wants to see what happens when you eat too many burritos from Los Betos. Am I allowed to complain that I'm having a fat day when I'm always fat?"

Sandy clucked his tongue. "You're not fat," he said seriously. "You've got some padding. There's a difference. It means that you can get fucked pretty damn hard."

"I'm not going to have sex with him!"

"Why not?"

"I have principles."

"Fuck your principles. Put this shirt on."

He tossed me a fire-red button-down collared shirt that I hadn't seen in forever since it had shrunk a bit in the wash and I didn't feel comfortable wearing it out in public. I thought about protesting, but it wouldn't have mattered. I slid it on and buttoned it up. Sandy then came over and straightened the collar and rolled the sleeves up my forearms. I tried to take shallow breaths to avoid having the shirt explode like I was Bruce Banner and I'd just gotten very, very angry.

Sandy stopped fussing and took a step back, looking me up and down. He let out a low whistle, causing me to blush. "You clean up nice, Auster," he growled, a little bit of Helena slinking through. "You're gonna get balled." He grabbed me by the hand and pulled me in front of the mirror.

Reflection Paul looked moderately resigned for a split second, but then his eyes widened and his jaw dropped. "Holy crap," I said. For some reason, I looked *good*. Like, way *good*.

"Told you," Sandy said smugly.

"I look *ripped*," I breathed, starting to flex my forearms in the mirror. "Ish."

"Er, let's not go that far," Sandy said, pulling me away from the mirror, lest I became betwixt by my reflection and started macking on the glass. "And don't do that in front of Vince either."

He pulled me into the bathroom and spritzed me three times with my cologne and was about to open his mouth to say something when the doorbell rang. Wheels starting barking like we were under attack, his little cart squeaking as he rode the ramp down my bed and tore into the hallway.

"Oh sweat balls," I whispered, starting to panic

"Now's not the time to freak out," Sandy warned me. "Paul. Paul!"

"What if he realizes just how boring I am?" I said, ignoring him. "What if we're sitting there, trying to have a conversation, and it just peters out into nothing because we can't think of a single thing to say to each other? An awkward silence will fall where we'll just look at each other and he'll wonder just what the hell he was thinking asking me out on a date and then he'll do the whole 'Oh, sorry. Looks like my neighbor just texted me and my apartment was destroyed by a turbine that fell off a plane, so I need to take you home and, oh, by the way, I'm moving to

Alaska tomorrow, so we won't be able to see each other again.' But *no*, because we *work* together, I'll have to see him every *day*, and then that motherfucker *Tad* will be all like, 'Oh, hey, Vince! I heard about that god-awful date you were forced to go on with Paul where he didn't even wear sexy underwear and had jeans that made his ass look like a disco ball! I'm all tight and hot and perky, so you and I should go fuck on Paul's desk and laugh at him while you put your dick up my butt.' God, I hate Tad so fucking much, that stupid little whore!"

Then I realized I was talking to myself. I heard the front door open and Sandy exclaimed, "Vince!" quite loudly. "How lovely it is to see you again. How are you feeling? I certainly hope you haven't gotten hit by any more cars!"

I ground my teeth together, planning intricate revenge plots that would end with Sandy framed for the murder of an English baroness.

"Hey, Sandy," Vince said cheerfully, and my traitorous heart stumbled in my chest.

"You'll have to bear with us a moment," Sandy said loudly. "Paul's in the bathroom talking to himself in the mirror about sexy underwear and plane turbines."

"Plane turbines?" Vince asked, sounding adorably confused. "I have a lot of pairs of sexy underwear."

Of course he did.

"He's worried a turbine will fall on your apartment, the poor thing," Sandy said, raising his voice even louder.

I gripped the countertop tightly, trying to remember that Sandy and I had been friends for more than twenty years and that someone somewhere would miss him if he was buried in the desert in an unmarked grave.

"I think I have renter's insurance," Vince said. "But I don't know if that covers planes."

"I'm sure it does," Sandy said smoothly. "Paul? Oh, Paul? Are you done talking to yourself? You have a guest!"

You can do this. You can do this. You can do this.

If this were a movie, this would have been the point where some cheesy-ass song would play as I walked down the hallway into the living room. The music would swell, blaring something about kissing or loving or fucking or some other romantic bullshit, and then Vince would see me for the first time, a grin growing on his face, a hint of lust blooming in his eyes like fire, all because of me. I'd walk into the living room and all the rest would fade out around him and he would only have eyes for me. Sandy would disappear, my house would disappear, the *world* would disappear, and he'd breathe my name because I was the hottest thing he'd ever seen. And, of course, I *would* be the hottest thing he'd ever seen, and he wouldn't even be able to remember a time he didn't know me because I'd be his whole fucking world. The music would reach its screeching chorus and he'd step toward me and murmur, "Fuck the date, let's just go to bed so I can do naughty things to your butt," and then we'd live happily ever after.

The end.

Okay, but that's not the end. Because that's not what happened.

What happened was I was halfway down the hall when Wheels heard me coming and started yipping excitedly. After all, his three most favorite people in all the world were standing under the same roof for the first time ever and the *universe* needed to know about it! "Daddy!" he was barking at me as his claws scrabbled along the tile, his wheels squeaking. "Daddy! I'm coming to you because I'm so excited I could just *shit!*"

And me, of course, being wrapped in my own neurosis, didn't see him until the last second, when he was right under the foot I was about to step down on. And as my foot fell and I heard his happy little bark, I could already see the headlines: *Gay Man Distracted By First Date Steps on Two-Legged Dog and Kills Him* and *Canine Lovers Everywhere Demand Dog Killer's Testicles* and *The Christian Right Says, "This Is Why Gay People Are Evil; They Kill Handicapped Dogs To Satisfy Their Immoral Lust."*

So at the very last second, I launched my foot forward with a squawk, the heel of my foot sliding along the right wheel of his cart. Naturally, this made me lose my balance, and I went forward, stumbling to the end of the hall, then careening into the living room and smashing into the far wall. But it was okay! Instead of the obvious solution of stopping my forward momentum by pressing my hands against the wall, I took the extremely radical approach of stopping myself with my face. Into the wall.

Silence fell over the room.

Then: "Sandy?" I asked, my face still pressed against the wall. My nose and right cheek hurt like a son of a bitch, but I wasn't bleeding. Not yet.

"Yes, Paul?" He sounded somewhat shocked, but like he was also trying very hard to keep from laughing, a breathless sound that reminded me why having a best friend was never a good thing.

"Will you do me a favor?"

"Yes, Paul."

"Will you look up the nearest Taiwanese restaurant for me?"

"Of course, Paul. Can I ask why?"

"You may. I'd like to see if they would buy my dog."

"Wheels, Paul? You want to sell your dog?"

"Yes, Sandy. To a Taiwanese restaurant. So they may cook him and serve him to a table of four. I may even give him up for free."

"Table of four. Got it."

"Sandy?"

"Yes, Paul?"

"Did you both see me trip and smash into the wall?"

"Yes, Paul."

"Has Vince run screaming yet?"

"No, Paul."

"Would you tell him it's okay to do so now? I'd like to take the rest of the night to die of embarrassment and look up recipes for the Taiwanese restaurant. I'm thinking something with cayenne pepper. I feel it would complement the taste of mutt on the palate."

I didn't even hear Vince approach, didn't even notice him until he was right up on me, pressing up against my back, putting his arms around my waist, holding me close. "You okay?" Vince murmured in my ear.

"Sure," I said. "I just wanted to teach this wall a lesson by headbutting it. It's always giving me dirty looks and I just got sick of it. Thought it was time to man up, you know?"

He chuckled near my ear, his lips *almost* on my skin. "Anything broken?"

"Aside from my pride? Nope. Nope. Everything else seems to be just peachy."

"Why don't you turn around and let me make sure?"

"I'd really rather not do that. I think it may be better if you leave and go to the U of A."

"The college?"

"Yeah."

"Why?"

"Because I need to see if you can find a physicist there and ask him how long it will be before time travel is invented. Because I *really* would like to travel back in time to when this house was being built so I could have stopped the builders from putting up a wall here, and then I would travel back to right now and instead of being face-planted against the wall, it would have looked like I was showing off some really sweet dance moves in a long hallway."

Vince snorted in my ear, which I found to be rather gross, and yet was okay with him doing it anyway. He turned me around in his arms, and even though I tried to avoid looking at him, he wasn't having any of it. He gripped my chin and forced me to look up, inspecting my nose and cheek. They throbbed a bit, and I felt my face heat up under his careful gaze. I was proud of the fact there were no tears in my eyes, even though such a facial smash deserved them. I was manly, after all, I reminded myself; manly men didn't cry after getting tripped by their two-legged dog and running into a wall with their face.

Vince poked my cheek. "Ow!" I snapped at him.

He shrugged. "Doesn't look like it's broken. Nose, either. Probably will get a black eye, though."

"Oh, thank you, Dr. Taylor," I said, rolling my eyes.

He grinned at me, dimples exploding like fireworks. "Did you notice how I didn't laugh, even though it was pretty funny?"

I glared at him and then heard a choking sound. I looked over to where Sandy stood in the middle of the living room. He had his hand over his mouth, squeezing tightly, tears streaming down his face as his body shook.

I stepped away from Vince and his hands fell to his sides. I pointed at Sandy, who I was pretty sure was going to burst at any moment. "You can go home now," I scolded.

He nodded once and grabbed his keys off the coffee table. He almost made it completely out my door before he couldn't hold it in anymore and starting howling with laughter, the sound ringing back to us as he closed the door.

"This can't possibly be a good way to start things," I muttered.

CHAPTER 10
I Hate Waiters Named Santiago and I Really Hate YouTube

VINCE tried to say we could just stay in, but I told him that it was probably a good idea if we went out, given that I wanted to pretend Wheels was a soccer ball and I needed to score a basket. Vince then told me that it was a soccer *goal* and not a *basket* and that's why those announcers always screamed, *"Goooooooaaaaaaallllll!"* I cocked an eyebrow at him and he just rolled his eyes at me.

There was silence in the car that was almost uncomfortable, but I was distracted by the fact that my face was slightly throbbing. I wondered if I would actually get a black eye or not and if it would be believable if I told people in the office on Monday that it was from the fight I'd gotten in over the weekend, where I took on a gang on the south side with nothing but my fists.

"Don't keep touching it," Vince told me as he drove. "You're going to make it worse if you keep poking your face."

"I'm making sure I don't have nerve damage," I said, poking myself again, feeling the burn. "I may have smashed all my nerves to death, and I want to make sure I don't get droopy-eye."

"It's going to bruise," he warned.

"Maybe it's my penance for hurting you. Like some kind of divine retribution for causing pain and misery and giving you two days off from work in a row where you did nothing but text me the whole time."

"You liked it when I texted you," he said, sure of himself.

"It was pretty annoying," I said.

"Then why'd you keep responding?"

I poked my cheek instead of answering him. It hurt. A lot.

Instead of arguing with me further, he took my poking hand in his and held it, intertwining our fingers together, effectively shutting me up, an action I thought impossible. I suppose I could have used my other hand to poke my face, but it didn't seem all that important anymore.

And since I wasn't allowed to distract myself by poking my war wounds, I began to get nervous again, realizing not only was I *on* the date I'd been dreading/hoping for, but he was already holding my *hand*. This immediately caused me to start sweating, which made my hand clammy, and I was pretty sure that Vince was getting drenched, but he held on anyway, regardless of the fact that my body was leaking all over him, and not in the good way.

He took me down to Fourth Avenue, near where the gay bar was, and I let myself reminisce that this was where we'd first laid eyes on each other... six days prior. I rolled my eyes at my own mushiness, which hurt my cheek quite a bit. Then I started to sweat some more.

He parked near a little street café called Poco's and asked if it was all right. I'd never been there before. It looked cute and I hadn't heard any news stories of rats being found in the food, so I figured it would be okay. I didn't share any of those thoughts, though. I just smiled widely and said this was one of my favorite places ever. I felt bad that I was building the beginning of our relationship on lies, but I figured it was just about a restaurant, so Jesus would forgive me. Then I got stuck on the word *relationship* and blanched at my audacity to think such a thing, which caused my hands to sweat even more. I'm pretty sure anyone walking by me would have thought I'd just climbed out of a pool. Luckily, Vince had dropped my hand by that point (probably to discreetly wipe his hand off on his shirt in disgust and to wish he had an industrial-sized bottle of hand sanitizer), so I didn't have to worry about getting him any more wet then he already was.

We were seated almost immediately at a table near the sidewalk where we could see people walking by. Before I could open my mouth and find out exactly what would fall out, we were assaulted (yes, assaulted!) by what had to be the world's most attractive waiter. He was all skinny and tall with eyelashes that looked like they had to be fake and eyes so green that you would have thought they were made of emeralds. His hair was dark and his skin was a lovely mocha color, like he bathed nude on a beach in the Dominican Republic, his lithe body and tawny muscles browned by the sun. He was wearing a red collared shirt, much like the one I wore, but he looked far better than I ever could. In a nutshell, he was fucking gorgeous, and I was dressed like a waiter at the café. Fan-fucking-tastic.

And of course, when he saw Vince, you would have thought he was going to flop his dick out on the table, crawl into Vince's lap, and rut against him right in front of me.

"Good evening," he purred at Vince, ignoring me completely. "My name is Santiago, and it will be my pleasure to... *serve* you tonight." He looked Vince up and down, and I had an urge to call 911 for the eye-rape I was witnessing. It didn't help that Santiago had an accent that made you want to either stab him or touch his balls. Guess which one I wanted to do?

Vince grinned up at him, though part of me realized he was oblivious to Santiago's (who *names* their kids like this?) blatant "come fuck me" gaze. The other, more impractical, part of me wanted to punch Santiago in the back of the head and then throw a glass of water in Vince's face for even considering looking so attractive in public. I was able to choke this part down. Barely.

"Hey, Santiago," Vince said. "We're going to need some time to decide."

"Oh, of course!" Santiago gushed. "If you need any help with the menu"—*or getting your cock sucked* was the clear implication—"please don't hesitate to flag me down, because I'm here for *you*. I'm sure I could see those arms from a distance, though." He winked and dragged his fingers along Vince's bicep. I eyed the tight polo shirt Vince was wearing, his arms straining against the sleeves, his chest hard against the fabric. I could even see the outline of his nipple piercing. I'm sure Santiago could too, because his gaze strayed over Vince's chest and stopped exactly where the bar was poking through. He didn't lift his fingers from Vince's arm.

"Can we get some bread and some butter up in here?" I blurted out, sounding way fatter than I actually was. "I'm *hungry*."

Santiago looked startled, as if he was only then aware of my presence at the table. When he saw me, a grimace came over his face like he smelled something awful. But then he twisted his lips into what I'm sure he thought was a professional smile, but was absolutely sardonic. "Of course, sir," he said politely. "I shall get you some bread and butter. Lots and lots and lots of butter." He turned back to Vince and the smile turned dazzling again. "And you, sir? I can get you *anything* you want while you wait for your"—he glanced back at me—"father's bread."

"Father?" I repeated, outraged.

Vince didn't get the dig. "That's not my father," he said to Santiago. "That's Paul."

"Oh!" Santiago said, as if that explained everything. "So he's your accountant or something?"

Vince's brow furrowed. "He's not an accountant. We work together."

Relief spread over Santiago's face. "Do you?" he asked, his voice again a purr. "Well, that certainly is good news. I'll be right back with your coworker's loaf of bread that he really seems to want, and then maybe you and I can get to know each other a bit better." He winked and walked away, his hips doing enough of a roll to put Helena Handbasket to shame.

"Wow," Vince said. "He sure seemed interested in you. I wonder if I should be jealous at all." He looked at me with a pretty smile.

"I don't think it was me," I said, trying to keep the bitterness out of my voice. "In case you didn't notice, he was practically fucking you right in front of me."

Vince laughed. "What? You're so full of shit. He was just being nice."

"He was rubbing all over you!"

Vince shrugged. "I didn't even notice. I was too busy watching you."

My eyes bulged. "What... you can't say shit... like that... so unfair... I don't even...."

"You're so cute when you sputter, you know that?" Vince said, reaching over to take my hand on top of the table. I thought about pulling it away, but his hand was warm and it seemed awfully rude to not allow him the comfort of my touch.

Santiago chose this moment to walk back to the table, and I knew the moment he saw our hands joined because he almost tripped and fell right into Vince's lap. Vince didn't even look up at him; he sat there, rubbing his thumb over the back of my hand. Santiago scowled at him, then looked at me with a dark smirk. "What happened to your face?" he asked me. "You look like you got punched in the eye."

I blushed and mumbled something incoherent, looking down at our joined hands.

Vince took that as his cue. "Me and Paul are into some pretty kinky shit," he told Santiago, whispering loudly. "You should see the bite marks on my ass. Nobody gives it to me like my boyfriend."

I don't know who was more shocked at Vince's pronouncement, me or Santiago. While Santiago was probably more focused on the kinky-sex aspect of it, all I could hear in my head was the word *boyfriend, boyfriend, boyfriend* over and over again. I tightened my grip on Vince's hand and I'm pretty sure I almost broke three of his fingers by the slight wince he gave.

"*Boyfriend?*" Santiago asked in a low voice, sounding incredulous.

"*Boyfriend?*" I asked, high-pitched and slightly hysterical.

Vince shrugged and smiled at me.

I didn't even notice Santiago leaving because I was staring at Vince like he'd made the most insane statement in the history of the English language, which, to be fair, he pretty much had. Granted, I did maybe spend a second or two at the thought of putting bite marks on his ass (I mean, come on; who wouldn't?) but I couldn't seem to wrap my mind around the word *boyfriend.* As sad as it might seem, I couldn't think of a time when anyone had actually called me that before, nor did I think there was anyone *I* had thought of that way. The last guy I'd dated (the psychic psycho, for those keeping track) turned out to be batshit crazy. I didn't do the *boyfriend* thing. I was fucking Paul Auster. It didn't happen to me.

But Vince continued to smile at me and he continued to hold my hand. He looked like he was going to say something further, but he stopped himself. He was obviously waiting for me to say something, *anything*, but since it *was* me, I let the silence drag on, making things even more awkward than they were before. Finally, I said the only thing I could think of.

"You're really not Freddie Prinze Junioring me?" I asked faintly.

"Only if you want me to," he said with a wink. I still didn't think he understood the concept of being Freddie Prinze Juniored. He made it into something dirty and that was not helping the situation in the slightest.

"You're the weirdest person I know," I told him. "And Santiago is probably going to put pubes in my food."

Vince rocked his head back and laughed. "I'll make sure your food is pube free."

My eyes burned a bit. No one had ever said that to me about pubes before. Part of me still wanted to believe he was pulling my leg, that this was all going to end badly. But that little hopeful part that had grown out of nowhere, that little light flickering way down in the dark, got brighter, and I latched onto it, hopeful for something I couldn't quite name.

And then Vince had to go and ruin it by asking seven words that I should never be asked, given my history of being incapable of holding any kind of intelligent conversation with a hot guy, even if he'd just essentially proclaimed he was my boyfriend. I wanted to stay in the afterglow of the moment, staring deeply into each other's eyes as if to communicate with each other's souls without speaking or some such bullshit. I couldn't make a jackass of myself if I didn't speak (well, that's not *entirely* true, since I'd proven earlier that I was perfectly capable of being a jackass by simply trying to walk down a hallway).

But Vince must have realized that we couldn't spend the rest of our lives just staring at each other, so he made it all that much worse. "So, Paul," he said as he leaned forward, "tell me more about yourself."

"Excuse me?" I squeaked.

"Well, I know a few things about you. But since you're my boyfriend now, I obviously need to know more. I don't know if I can get by on just knowing you like black dildos and action movies."

"Keep your fucking voice down," I hissed at him, looking around to see if Santiago was listening in, trying to eavesdrop for the intel he could use to tear me away from Vince like some Victorian heroine. I saw the top of his perfectly manufactured head through the window near the kitchen, and I wondered if he was pulling out his pubes one by one in preparation for when we ordered. "I told you that dildo wasn't mine! I'm holding it… for a friend."

"You're watching a dildo for a friend?" he asked in disbelief.

"Yes! My friend…." *Think of a name, think of a name!* I looked down at the table. "My friend… Salt. Cup. Straw. Table. My friend Saltcup Strawtable. He's Indonesian." I was building a relationship on lies, all *lies*.

Vince waited with a smirk on his face.

"Fine," I growled at him. "It's mine, okay? I tried to use it once, but it was too big, so I put it in the box under my bed and left it there. It felt like it was going to tear me in half."

"We'll just have to try it out again," he said, his voice going all husky.

Synapses fired. Fireworks across the sky. Angels sang. Jesus clapped politely.

"Sure," I managed to say.

"What about the other ones in there? Blackie wasn't the only dick in the box."

"No comment."

He smirked. "So what else?" he asked. "I want to know everything." He leaned forward again.

And there it was, folks. One of those defining moments. This was the beginning, the start of something that I thought could quite possibly be amazing if it turned out to be real. I'd been alive for *thirty years*. There was *thirty years* of history that he could get to know. I glanced into the café again and saw Santiago scowling at me, and I knew I needed to make it something badass. Sexy. Dangerous. I could have told him about the time Sandy and I had gone to Hawaii and went snorkeling and that I'd thought I was going to get eaten by a shark (conveniently leaving out the fact that the "shark" turned out to be a rock). Or I could've told him something heartfelt. Sweet. Kind. I could've told him about how I sometimes volunteered at Wingspan, which helps GLBTQ youth in Tucson who are going through a tough time with their family or friends or school. I could've told him about how I dreamed of quitting my job and one day traveling across Europe. Or that I wanted to learn to speak Italian. Or that I was still kind of scared of the dark some of the time. Or any other number of things that had happened in the past thirty years that made me who I was.

But no.

Of course not.

My subconscious hijacked my mouth and made me say the one thing I didn't want to say at all. My deepest shame. My darkest moment.

"Last year I fell into the hippopotamus exhibit at the zoo." *Oh sweat balls!*

He twitched his lips as he stared at me. "I'm sorry. You did *what*?"

"What's good to eat here?" I grabbed the menu and put it in front of my face.

"Paul," he said, sounding like he was choking.

"Yes, Vince?" I muttered.

"Did you say that you fell into the hippopotamus exhibit at the zoo?"

"No. I said I once had a problem with my hypothalamus gland and it caused me to get the flu. You really need to get your hearing checked. I'm thinking of having a salad."

"Are you guys ready to order?" Santiago asked as he appeared at the table, sounding extremely put out.

"I think," Vince said as he gasped, "that we're going to need more time."

"Why is your face all red?" Santiago asked. "Did the accountant say something stupid? I've heard that accountants can be really boring lays." He turned to me. "Are you a really boring lay?"

"Be gone, you he-bitch!" I growled at him.

Santiago rolled his eyes at me and scowled before walking away.

I hazarded a glance at Vince. He was on his phone, looking like he was going to explode.

"What are you doing?" I asked suspiciously. "You better not be texting anyone right now!"

"I'm not," he said, tears streaming down his face as he laughed. "I'm looking you up online. There has to be a news story about this."

I made a grab for his phone. "Don't you dare!"

"There's a YouTube video?" he said, pulling the phone away, just out of my reach. "With a *million* hits? Oh my God, you're famous!" He squinted. "Wait. The user who uploaded it was DancingQueenSandy? No. Fucking. Way." I made a play for his phone again and he looked up and glared at me. "You stay on your side of the table," he told me. "This might be the most important thing to have ever happened anywhere."

"That's bullshit! What about *Jesus* being born? Or the advent of nuclear physics? Or gay-for-pay porn stars?"

He shook his head. "None of those even compare to this."

"Remember how I said I didn't use that black dildo?" I said desperately. "I lied. I use it all the time. As a matter of fact, I used it right before you came over. I laid on my back and shoved that whole fucking thing up my ass as I moaned your name and pretended it was you. How about we get out of here and I show you how I do it?"

He licked his lips as he glanced up at me. "Yeah. That's… that's quite a thought. But we both know this is going to happen, so it might as well happen now." He raised his finger and started to lower it to the touch screen on his phone.

"You play that video," I warned him, "and I swear to God I'm going to break up with you. You told me I was your boyfriend seven minutes and twenty-six seconds ago. It'll be the quickest relationship of your life."

"Gonna press it," he said, lowering his finger even further, grinning at me.

"I'll suck your cock right now under the table if you don't!" I shouted.

That got his attention, and he jerked his hand away from the phone. Unfortunately, it hit his glass filled with water and knocked it all over me. Water splashed up into my face, and only then did I realize it was filled with at least nine billion lemons. "My eyes!" I screeched. "I'm *blind*!"

"I'm *so* sorry!" Vince said, even though he didn't sound sorry in the slightest. "Here, have a napkin. Have a bunch." I felt a handful of napkins press into my hands and I grabbed them and started rubbing them over my face, which immediately hurt my nose and cheek.

"You can't say stuff like that," Vince scolded.

"Obviously," I snapped at him. "I'll never say that I'm going to suck your cock again because apparently you throw citric *acid* in my face!"

And then I heard a tinny voice coming from his direction. Sandy said, *"Paul, back up just a little bit so I can get the whole area behind you."*

"Like this?" I heard myself say.

"You're watching the video?" I yelled at him, still unable to see. I knew right then what it must have felt like to be Helen Keller. Well, except for the deaf part. Whatever. We were both American heroes for what we had to put up with.

"Well, yeah," he said as if I was stupid. "You *fell*. Into a *hippo* exhibit. Of *course* I'm going to watch it."

"Can you stand up on that metal part?" Sandy asked as the video resumed. I tried to place a curse on Vince so that his face would melt, but then I remembered I didn't know any curses and that curses weren't a real thing, unless you were me and had lemon water thrown at your eyes.

"Probably. Give me a second. You know what? I don't really understand the point of hippos."

"They are definitely God's mysteries. They're pretty ugly too. Not so high, Paul. You'll fall in. Be careful."

"I won't fall in. I know how to keep my balance. I'm not that big of an idiot. Have a little—Waaaaaaaaaaaauuuuuughhhhh!"

A great splash.

Sandy screaming: *"Paul! Paul! Oh my God! Someone save my friend! He's dying! Oh Saint Janet Jackson, Ms. Jackson if you're nasty! He's drowning in fetid hippo water!"*

"Sandy!"

"Paul!"

"The hippos are going to eat me! They're going to eat me because I look so big and delicious! I don't want to die!"

A helpful bystander: *"I think hippos are herbivores."*

The zoo tour guide: *"Actually, they're omnivores. What you also might not know is that hippos are responsible for more human deaths in Africa than any other animal. They can sometimes even resort to cannibalism."*

The tour group: *"Ohhhhhhhhh."*

Sandy, shrieking: *"You're standing there giving a lecture on* hippos? *Are you out of your fucking* mind! *My friend is going to be eaten!"*

Me, in the background: *"Pretty sure a hippo just shit in the water! I'd really like to get out of here now! Hello? Somebody?"*

Tour guide: *"Sir, please stop kicking and flailing your hands! You are attracting the hippos to you! Take a deep breath and calm down!"*

Me: *"You fucking calm down! If I get eaten, I swear to Christ I will sue your asses off!"*

Sandy, murmuring: *"He won't sue you. At least I don't think he will. Love those shorts, by the way."*

Tour guide, grinning: *"Yeah? I always thought they were too short, but we're required to wear them. Gives me a pretty good tan, though."*

Helena, purring: *"Oh? And how high does that tan go, Mr. Zoo Man?"*

Tour guide, voice husky: *"Pretty high up. I like to lay out sometimes with the zebras when no one's looking. Naked. My name's Jerry, by the way."*

Me, splashing loudly: *"Sandy! Oh God, Sandy! I think I got some of the hippo shit water in my mouth! Call the fire department! Call the army! Send big guns! I don't want to die! There are still so many things I need to do! I always wanted to learn to line dance!"*

Helena, ignoring me completely: *"Jerry, huh? That's a hot name."*

Jerry, the bastard: *"Yeah? What's say we get out of here later and you can show me how hot it can be?"*

Helena: *"Oh, Jerry. You can't even begin to imagine the things my tongue can do. I'm going to wrap my lips around your—"*

Me, screaming: *"Are you* flirting? *Seriously?* Oh my fucking God, Sandy! I will fucking murder you! The hippos are getting in the water! Get laid another fucking time!"*

Jerry: *"Guess I better go rescue your friend. Wait for me here?"*

Helena, sighing: *"My hero. I'll count the seconds until your return. Paul? Paul! Jerry's going to come down and save you! Isn't he just so awesome?"*

Me, outraged: *"Jerry? Jerry? You're already on a first-name* basis? *You fucking whore! This is all your fault!"*

Sandy, returning: *"Paul, Jerry says you need to keep quiet so the hippos don't eat you. I'd listen to him since he is obviously a consummate professional."*

Me: *"Fuck Jerry! Fuck hippopotamuses! Fuck the fucking zoo!"*

Sandy, smirking: *"Paul, there's a piece of hippo shit floating near your mouth."*

Me: *"Aaaaaaaaaaaaaahhhhhhhhhhhh!"*

The video ended.

"Paul?" Vince said, his voice neutral.

"Yes, Vince?" I still hid behind the napkins even though my eyes were no longer filled with lemon water.

"Remember when you were taking me home from the hospital a few days ago and you thought I was just really stoned and you were talking about your period ghost and I said I thought I was going to fall in love with you?"

I thought he hadn't even remembered saying that. "Yes, Vince, I remember." And I did. It wasn't something I thought I was ever going to forget. Not for as long as I lived. I was pretty sure he was going to retract that comment pretty damn quickly.

He took a deep breath. "Well, I'm pretty sure I'm about halfway there now."

I lowered the napkins from my face and stared at him. He looked uncharacteristically flustered and couldn't quite meet my eyes. His cheeks pinked a bit. "You just watched a YouTube video of me falling into a hippo exhibit at the zoo and swallowing hippo-shit water and now you're halfway to being in love with me after knowing me for only a few days?"

He nodded. "Sounds about right."

"Oh sweat balls," I said. But I reached out and grabbed his hand.

He grinned and squeezed my hand back.

And that would be a great place to end the first date, right? That declaration, the knowledge that I'd swam with hippos, that Santiago might or might not have put pubes in the food that would come later. It's magical! It's wonderful! So very, very romantic! Nothing could make it better!

Nope.

"Paul!" my mother shouted from behind me on the street. "Yoo-hoo! Paul, dear! It's me, your mother! Your father is with me too! Paul! Oh, for heaven's sakes, Larry, I don't think he can hear me. I'm practically screaming his name. Maybe he's going deaf."

"You aren't *practically* doing anything," my father said mildly. "I'm pretty sure they can hear you down in Mexico."

"Lawrence Auster," she scolded. "What a mean thing to say."

"Just… ignore them," I ground out to Vince.

"Are they your parents?" he asked, looking over my shoulder. "They look like that picture you have in your bedroom."

"When I say so, get ready to run, okay?" I whispered harshly. "On three."

"What? We're not running."

"One—"

"Yoo-hoo, Paul!"

"Two—"

Vince waved over my shoulder at my parents.

"Three!" I got up and started running, but Vince didn't let go of my hand. Apparently his muscles were quite real and Vince was just a tad bit stronger than me. I only made it two steps toward the exit before I was jerked back to the table. Vince spun me around neatly so that I landed on his lap, my back to his chest. To give him credit, he didn't even cry out in massive pain as my bulk landed on him, surely crushing him to dust, especially given how sore he still must have been. I was too shocked at this sudden turn of events to even feel remotely sorry, given that he was a traitor along the lines of my dog.

"You can't run away from your parents," he admonished lightly. "It's rude."

"I don't want to be your boyfriend anymore," I told him, quite sure of myself.

He rolled his eyes. "Yes, you do. I make you so fucking happy."

"Gross. You do not," I mumbled, doing my damnedest to ignore that little glowing light in me.

Matty and Larry Auster were very curious by this sudden turn of events, watching the two of us closely as they walked up the sidewalk toward us. I tried to move off Vince's lap, but he wrapped his arm around my waist and gripped me tightly, his point very clear. It probably didn't help things when I wiggled in his lap to get more comfortable and felt his dick against my ass. He groaned just once, and it was quiet, but it was enough to make me freeze as his cock hardened while my parents were standing two feet away.

"Paul," Dad said in greeting, looking amused. "Nice to see you, son."

"Dad," I managed to say. "Mom."

My mother's eyes sparkled. "Paul, what a surprise this is!"

"Oh no. Not a surprise. I'm pretty sure this is God fucking with me," I told her.

"Language!" my father frowned.

"Sorry," I said, even though I wasn't sorry in the slightest.

"Hello," my mother said over my shoulder. "I'm Matty Auster, and this is my husband, Larry. We're Paul's parents."

"Nice to meet you," Vince said cheerfully. He very smartly extended the hand that was not wrapped around my waist, knowing that if he let go I would use that time to escape. To exact my revenge, I flexed my ass against his lap and felt him shudder underneath me. To his credit, his voice was only a little tight when he shook my parents' hands and said hello. "I'm Paul's boyfriend, Vince Taylor," he said, squeezing me again.

Goddammit.

"Boyfriend?" Dad said, sounding perplexed. "Paul, you never mentioned anything about a boyfriend."

"It's a new thing," I said as I blushed.

"At least fifteen minutes now," Vince agreed.

"Fifteen minutes?" Mom said. "That's fifteen minutes longer than anyone else."

"Mom!" I hissed.

"Well, it's true, dear. You don't normally have boyfriends, though for the life of me I can't understand why. I think you'd make the perfect partner to a nice man."

"Oh, he does," Vince said.

"What happened to that guy that Sandy said you spit on last weekend?" Dad asked. "I thought you were going to try and get with that?"

I groaned. "Dad? Do me a favor. Never say 'get with that' ever again. You've just fried my brain. And you guys really need to stop talking to Sandy."

Dad looked over at Mom. "How else am I supposed to say it?"

Mom shrugged. "Maybe you were supposed to say 'make love to.' You know Paul is secretly a romantic at heart. Once you get past that icy cold exterior it's like his insides are made of marshmallow fluff. You remember those letters we found that he'd written to Zack Morris from *Saved By The Bell*? I'd never read such beautiful love poems. Paul has such as sweet way with words."

"Oh right," Dad said. "How did that one go? 'Hark! And behold/Your love is but my soul/Us together would be like the greatest art/I would give you the world and my heart/How I wish I knew thee well/Oh, Zack Morris! From *Saved By The Bell*.'"

"I didn't write that," I told Vince hastily as he laughed at me. "That was my twin brother named Toby who died under suspicious circumstances when we were twelve. My parents deny he ever existed, but he's the one that wrote love poems to fictional characters."

"Paul, really," my mother sniffed. "You didn't have a twin brother. My uterus wouldn't have survived another one of you coming out."

"See?" I whispered to Vince. "I told you."

"You wanted to make love to that guy you spit on?" Vince said, sounding positively gleeful. "And you already told your parents about it?"

Of *course* he was still stuck on that. "I never said those words!"

"I'm the guy he spit on," he told my parents.

"Technically, I spit on the twinkie barback," I reminded him.

"It was meant for me," he said, absolutely sure.

"Oh, that is so lovely!" my mother said, her eyes brimming with tears.

"Certainly an interesting beginning," Dad said.

Apparently, Vince had no problem with meeting parents because he wouldn't shut the fuck up. "This is our first real date, even though I consider it our second, or maybe our third."

"Your first date?" my mother exclaimed. "How wonderful! And you brought him—"

"Are you guys *finally* ready to order yet?" Santiago interrupted.

"My wife was talking," Dad told him sternly. "It's not polite to interrupt, young man."

Santiago rolled his eyes. "All I want to do is my job."

"We're not ready," Vince told him as Santiago glared at me sitting on his lap. "I'll let you know, okay?"

"Whatever," the waiter said, spinning on his heels and going back inside.

"Well, he was a rude little bitch, wasn't he?" my mother said. I grinned at her.

"Language!" Dad snapped at her, but I could see his mouth quirking at the sides.

"He was trying to get in Vince's pants," I told them, only because I tell them pretty much everything. Well, some things.

My mother narrowed her eyes as she glared inside the restaurant. "Is that *so*? He looked like the type. Little floozy. I hope you saw right through that, Vince." Her voice was hard, as if daring him to contradict her.

"I did," Vince assured her. "I have a one-man heart."

Oh Jesus Christ.

"That is so sweet," my mother said, wiping her eyes.

"Why do you have a black eye?" my father asked me suspiciously, reaching over to turn my face so he could see it better. I'd totally forgotten about it.

"Dear," my mother whispered loudly. "Isn't it obvious? Vince is the Dominant and Paul is his submissive. Look how Vince is holding onto him like he owns him. It was probably just from a rough scene in Vince's playroom. Vince may have made him pretend to be a pony, like on that one HBO show that we watched. You remember? Where that one man put that bit in the other man's mouth and made him wear a saddle? We promised ourselves we'd always support Paul with whatever he chose to be. It just so happens he's kinky. We'll support him no matter what."

My father nodded as if this made complete sense. "You a pony, son?" he asked me.

I tried to keep from screaming. "No, Dad. I'm not a pony."

"I don't like horses that much," Vince said, obviously not understanding at all. "They scare me a bit. I don't like the noises they make."

"It was Wheels," I explained. "He tripped me and I hit the wall."

"With your face?" Mom asked sympathetically. "You do have hands, you know."

"I'll keep that in mind for next time," I promised her.

"He does that a lot," Mom told Vince. "He's always been a bit klutzy. This one time, he was trying to walk down the stairs, chew gum, and talk on the phone at the same time. Ended up with a broken arm." She shook her head. "He always runs into things or falls down. It would be endearing if it wasn't so painful. And expensive."

"I'm nowhere near that bad," I muttered, glancing at my dad for help.

He took the hint. "Matty, I think we should leave these boys to their date," Dad said. "I'm sure they don't want us hanging around. Besides, we'll be late for our own reservations."

Mom leaned over and kissed his cheek. "You're absolutely right, my love. You may wine and dine me, and then maybe we can get out the spurs."

"Oh. My. God," I groaned.

"Giddyup," my dad said, grinning at her.

"Oh, Vince!" she said. "Before I forget. We are having a get-together tomorrow for Paul's birthday at his nana's house. You *must* be there. I won't take no for an answer."

"Is that the one with the homophobic parrot?" he asked me.

"Yeah," I sighed. "You don't need to go. It's not that big of a deal."

"Are you kidding me? You bet your ass I'll be there."

"Language," my father scolded him lightly.

Mom clapped her hands together. "Wonderful. Maybe I should get your phone number so we could—"

"Mom. Stop it."

"Oh, you're right, dear. I'm sorry. You're on a date now. I can get it tomorrow, Vince. After all, I'm sure I'll want to talk to my future son-in-law on the phone at some point."

"Mom!"

"Time to go, Matty," Dad told her gently.

She leaned in to kiss me as my father shook Vince's hand. Then they reversed and my dad shook my hand as she kissed Vince on the cheek. He looked surprised, just for a moment, bringing his hand to touch where her lips had been. I wondered at it but didn't ask.

"I'm sorry," I said, unable to think of anything else to say.

He arched an eyebrow. "About what?"

"Them. My parents. I told you they were weird."

"I thought they were okay," he said. And it looked like he meant it.

"Oh."

"You want to get out of here?" he asked suddenly, looking thoughtful,

"Uh, sure." I wasn't hungry anymore.

"Good. I want to take you somewhere."

"Don't you want to wait and say good-bye to Santiago first?" I teased him.

He shook his head and stood, holding out his hand.

Surprising even myself, I didn't hesitate.

WE WENT to the park and sat on a set of swings in the dark. He was like a kid, trying to go as high as he possibly could and laughing when I told him he needed to be careful because I wasn't going to take care of him if he fell off the swings and became paralyzed. I already had one handicapped animal to look after.

"Would you get me my own set of wheels?" he asked.

"With streamers hanging off," I threatened.

He laughed and grabbed my hand, pulling me toward the center of the park to a little stretch of grass away from the lights and the traffic. And away from where anyone could hear us scream. "You know," I told him, "this is probably a perfect spot to get raped and then murdered by a homeless person with a hook for a hand. I don't know if that's the best first-date memory to have. I like my blood on the inside of me."

"I'll protect you from the murdering homeless rapist with hook hands," he promised. "I have really big muscles." He lowered himself to the grass and lay on his back, staring up at me. He patted the area beside him. I looked around, sure there'd be some hobo wanking it behind a cactus, but it looked like we were alone.

I tried to lie on the ground next to him, but he wouldn't have it, so I found myself with my head on his stomach, our bodies making a T shape. It took a bit of getting used to at first, but then I allowed myself to focus on every breath he took in and every breath he let out. I rose and fell with him. It felt surreal.

I was quiet for a time until he started twisting his fingers in my hair lazily, and I made an embarrassing little moan in the back of my throat that caused him to chuckle, a sound I felt before I heard. It rumbled against my ear and I felt it down to my toes.

"What?" I asked.

"I like the noises you make," he said, a smile in his voice.

"Um. That's good to know. But I'd rather you didn't hear all the sounds that come from my body. And I wish I hadn't just said that."

He laughed. "I'm sure I'll hear them all."

I didn't even know how to begin to take that.

Silence, for a time.

Vince sighed, tugging gently on my hair. "Do you know constellations?"

"Some. My dad showed me when I was a kid."

"Oh."

"Do you?"

"Nah. My dad didn't have time for that." He tried to laugh it off. It didn't work.

I waited to see if he would say more. He didn't. "You know Orion's Belt?" I asked him.

I felt him shrug, which I took to mean no. I moved off his stomach and onto my back, pressing our heads almost together. I took his hand in mine and pointed out three bright stars with our fingers. "Alnitak," I said for the first star. "Alnilam," for the second. And, "Mintaka," for the third. "My dad said Orion was a great hunter, the son of Poseidon, the sea god. He could supposedly walk on the waves because of that. He once went hunting with the goddess Artemis and her mother Leto. For some reason, during the hunt, he said he was going to kill every creature on the planet. Mother Earth hated him for this and sent a giant scorpion to kill him. And it did. The goddesses then asked Zeus to place him in the stars. Zeus agreed, and as a memorial to Orion's death, he also added the scorpion to the sky as well." I took his hand and moved south, tracing over the other constellation. "And that is where Orion and Scorpius are still locked in battle." I lowered our hands but I didn't let go. He placed my hand on his chest. His heartbeat was soft.

A moment later, he turned his head toward me. Our noses almost touched. His dark eyes searched mine. I waited.

"You're so smart," he whispered finally.

I flushed. "Nah. Just something my dad taught me. I liked the story, so I remembered it. That's all." I didn't look away. I couldn't.

He reached out and touched my cheek. "That's not all."

We watched each other quietly until I finally worked up the courage to ask what I'd been thinking for hours. "Vince?"

"Yeah?"

"Is this for real?"

"What?"

"You know." I swallowed. "You and me."

No hesitation. "It is."

"Okay."

He watched me. "If you need me to, I'll tell you every day it's real."

"Okay."

"It's real."

"Okay."

"Paul?"

"Yeah?"

"I'm going to kiss you now."

"Oh?"

"Yes."

"Okay. Just make sure you—"

And then he kissed me.

CHAPTER 11
The GPS In My Prius Wants To Murder Me

"YOU laid out and watched the stars and then he kissed you?" Sandy asked as we drove in my car the next day. "I love it, but I also think I threw up a little bit in my mouth. And got cavities from all the sweetness. And then threw up again just to say I did. It's precious, like I expect a crack whore with a heart of gold would be."

"Thank you for that ringing endorsement," I said, trying not to get mad at the GPS on my dashboard that was trying to convince me to drive off the road and into a ditch. For some reason, my GPS (appropriately nicknamed That Damn Bitch) hated me and tended to get more sarcastic when it had to recalculate. I'm not joking either. There's nothing like hearing the female robotic voice say "Recalculating... recalculating," when you can also hear the implied "dumbass" you just *know* she wants to say.

"Turn left in thirty feet," That Damn Bitch said.

"We're on a bridge!" I scowled at her.

"I think you're the only person in the world that has a homicidal GPS," Sandy observed. "What the hell did you do to That Damn Bitch to make her hate you?"

"I didn't do anything!" I said, slightly offended. "She came with the car and she was already pissed off when I got it. I try not to use her that much, but I don't know where the fuck this stupid bike shop is. In case you haven't noticed, I'm not the bike-riding type."

"Recalculating," That Damn Bitch snapped at me.

"Fuck off," I told her.

"What happens when you and Vince get married and he wants to go on a bike-riding tour of Asia for your honeymoon?" Sandy asked.

I glared at him. "Do I even need to tell you how many things are wrong with what you just said? I'm going to anyway. At least sixteen things."

Sandy laughed. "You say that *now*, but I bet if this were a movie, there'd be an ironic flash cut one year into the future that would show you huffing and puffing up a hill on a bike in the Hainan Province in China wearing an 'I just got husband-fucked grin' on your face while Vince is riding ahead of you screaming about how much he loves you and Asia."

"None of what you said is going to be a real thing," I assured him. "And I wouldn't huff and puff. I'd be riding the bicycle magnificently. Wearing a kimono that would flow gently in the breeze."

"I wouldn't go that far. And kimonos are Japanese."

I waved my hand in dismissal. "It's all Asia."

Sandy stared at me. "Oh my God, you're already starting to talk like him."

Crap. "Shut up."

"Paul's got a boyfriend," he sang.

I blushed, unable to stop myself.

"You have arrived at your destination," That Damn Bitch said.

"We're in the middle of the freeway!" I shouted at her.

"Recalculating," she growled.

"She just wanted us to stop so we'd get hit by a tractor-trailer," I muttered.

"Maybe you should see if your psychic ex-boyfriend knows any mediums so we can see if your car is haunted too."

"Ugh, like the period ghost took over my GPS? I'm not going to put a tampon in the tailpipe. I'm pretty sure that wouldn't be good for the ozone. Might have one of Vince's nocturnal emissions."

Sandy giggled. "Or maybe it's a whole *new* ghost, one that died on a lonely and dusty stretch of road when her jealous lover killed her in a fit of rage. Now she tries to exact her revenge by going after men who remind her of her killer."

"And I remind her of her straight, jealous boyfriend?"

"Lover," Sandy corrects me. "She had a boyfriend, too, but in the end, she decided she wouldn't leave him for the jealous lover, which caused him to murder her. It's all really hypothetically tragic."

"And now she's hypothetically haunting my Prius?"

He sighed forlornly. "She's waiting until the moment when you finally listen to her and drive off the edge of a cliff so she can move on to her next victim."

"If I die, I'm coming back to haunt you."

"Or," he said, "you'll get reincarnated as the makeup tape I use to hold my junk back when I'm performing."

I grimaced. "I really could have done without that thought."

"Well, don't die, then."

"You hear that, That Damn Bitch? You can't murder me because I don't want to be ball tape."

"Please make a U-turn," That Damn Bitch said.

Sandy stared at the GPS. "Isn't she supposed to say to make a U-turn when it's safe to do so?"

I shook my head. "She used to say that, but for some reason she stopped. I thought it was a malfunction at first, but now I know she just wants me to die."

He looked out the window, a slight frown on his face.

"Are you okay with this?" I asked him suddenly, before I could stop myself.

He looked surprised. "Going to the bike store? I told you I was. I wouldn't be going if I didn't have to. I'm a big girl, Paul. I know how to say *no*. Or, *please don't stop, Daddy*."

I grinned at him. "I love you, you know?"

He smiled sweetly at me. "I know, baby doll. And I love you."

"I wasn't talking about the bike store, though."

"Oh?"

"I was talking about… you know." *This is so stupid.*

"What?" He looked perplexed.

"Me and Vince."

Sandy cocked his head at me. "What *about* you and Vince?"

"That we're... you know."

"In lurve?"

"Gross. Shut up. No. That we're... dating. Or whatever."

"Paul, are you trying to ask me if I'm mad that you have a boyfriend?"

"It sounds so stupid when you say it like that."

"But that's what you're asking?"

"Yes."

He reached over and grabbed my hand, holding it gently. It felt safe. Comfortable. Like he was my home. "Sugar, I am over the moon for you," he said quietly. "If there is anyone I know that deserves happiness, it's you. You are the bestest friend I've ever had, and if someone else finally gets to see what I get to see, then you will never find me jealous of him for taking up some of your time. But know this: if he hurts you in any way, shape, or form, no one will ever be able to find his body. You get me?" A bit of Helena flashed in his eyes.

I squeezed his hand. "I get you. And I'm not going to let things change. Things will be just like they've always been."

Sandy's smile took on a melancholic curve. "Everything changes sometime."

"Not us," I insisted. "I won't let that happen. It'll still be you and me against the world."

"And Vince."

"No. Not *and* Vince. You've been here practically my whole life. I've known Vince a few days." *Even though it feels like so much longer,* was the thing that went unsaid. We both heard it, but didn't address it.

"But it's been the best few days of your life," he said, no recrimination in his voice.

I didn't know how to respond to that, because it was true. And I hated it. Sort of.

He knew me too well. "Right, Paul?"

I shrugged.

He sighed like he was a bit annoyed which, to be fair, he probably was. "Honey, just when I start to think you can accept things and move forward with them, you have these idiotic little notions in your head that you're not good enough, that you don't deserve to be happy like everyone else."

"I don't think like that," I replied weakly, but we both knew it was a lie.

He didn't call me on it. He didn't have to. "And whether or not you can admit it," he continued, "you've smiled more this past week than you have at any point that I can remember."

"You must have mistaken smiling for looks of frustration, bewilderment, and full-on horror."

"Hey, Paul?"

"Yeah?"

"I'm going to say a word," Sandy said. "Just react how you normally would, okay?"

I glanced warily at him. "Cracker Jack psychology. Fun."

"Ready?"

I nodded.

"Vince," he said.

I smiled widely; I couldn't stop it if I'd tried. "Oh, goddammit!"

He smirked at me but didn't say anything in response.

"Finding alternate route," That Damn Bitch said succinctly.

THE bike store smelled like rubber and sweat and good health. I hated it.

"Can I help you?" the cheery little woman asked as we walked in. She had to be just under five feet tall, but she was ripped, and I thought it was possible she could kick my ass in a fight. Then I wondered why my first thought was that I was going to fight this woman, and I just chalked it up to me being weird. As usual.

"Hi, I'm looking for a bike," I said.

"Well, you came to the right place!" she said with a chuckle.

"Oh, really?" I asked her. "I wouldn't have guessed since the sign outside says 'Bike Shop'."

"Forgive my friend," Sandy said smoothly as the bike chick stared at me oddly. "He's not normally so rude. He's just a little flustered.

Wonderful, exciting things are happening in his life, and he doesn't know how to deal with them quite yet."

"Oh?" she said, recovering slightly. She looked me up and down. "Have you decided to make some healthy lifestyle choices and become a bike rider?"

Before I could scratch her eyes out, Sandy spoke for me again. "The bike is for someone else."

"My *boyfriend*," I said, quite loudly, sure she would also be a homophobe and wanting to stick it to her good. "I hit him with my car and broke his other bike." *Oh sweat balls.*

She narrowed her eyes slightly. "Is that so?"

"It was an accident," Sandy said. "Look, this probably wasn't the best way to start this. Hi, I'm Sandy, and this is Paul. We're here to look at bikes." He shook her hand, but I didn't, because I had convinced myself the little biker chick was evil since she thought my "lifestyle choices" included shoving my face with lard. I didn't want her evil to rub off on me in case I became a weed-smoking hippie who went to music festivals in a skirt made of hemp.

"I'm Jenny, and I think I can help you," she told us, but really speaking only to Sandy. I had a tendency to alienate people with my mouth. You'd think I wouldn't have been let out into public as much as I was. "It's probably a good idea if I knew what kind of bike you're looking to replace."

Sandy looked at me. "What?" I asked him.

"What kind of bike was it?"

"What do you mean? It was a bike." How hard was that to understand?

Jenny looked at me with bemusement. "There are many kinds, Paul. Was it a mountain bike? A road bike? Touring bike? Racing? Time trial? Triathlon? Track? BMX? Freight? Roadster? Cyclocross?"

"It was blue," I said hastily, not even remotely impressed by her listing off bicycles. "I think. Maybe a little bit gray."

"Were the tires thin or thick?"

"Paul's a size queen," Sandy said. "That's probably not the best question to ask him."

I glared at Sandy before looking back at Jenny. "Does it really matter what kind it was? I just want to get him a new bike."

Jenny nodded. "It's very important. It's almost like a way of life. The type of bike a person has can define who they are."

"I don't think that's a real thing," I told her. "I don't have a bike and I know who I am."

"Who are you, Paul?" she asked me, looking as if she was trying to peer into my immortal soul. I wondered briefly if bike-riding hippies had some kind of Wiccan voodoo magic that they ascribed to.

"I just want a bike," I assured her. "Not to be defined."

"Hmm," Jenny said. I didn't know what that meant.

"Did you take a picture of the bike?" Sandy asked. "That could have made this easier."

"Of course I did," I scoffed.

"Well, then show it to her."

"Well, after I took the picture, I accidentally deleted it while trying to download an app that allows you to take pictures of guys and then tells you if they're a top or a bottom."

Sandy looked interested. "Smart phones are way smart," he said astutely. "Does it work?"

I shook my head. "I think it's broken. I took a picture of myself with it and it told me that I was asexual. I didn't even know it could do that. Wait. What if it was insulting me?"

"Technology hates you for some reason," Sandy said. "Maybe you should get a shack in the wilderness in Montana and live off the grid."

I tried to picture that. "Would I have to grow a beard? I don't know if I can, and even if I could, if it's something I could pull off."

"No, I don't think you'd need a beard. But one of these days your toaster is going to become sentient and stab you. I just think it would be easier if you didn't rely so much on technology."

"But what would I do in my Montana wilderness shack? I can't just live in the middle of nowhere without being able to provide for myself."

Sandy thought for a moment. "You could always start a small business that only a crazy person would have. Like making earmuffs for cats."

I frowned. "But wouldn't I need a small business model that included some kind of online plan? I don't think if I'm living in a shack in the middle of nowhere that people would come buy my Cat-Muffs, no matter how good they were."

"Man," Sandy mused. "Technology is a vicious circle. You can't escape it, no matter what you do. Even if I were to take care of the Internet side of it for you, how would I tell you about the orders that you have? I can't call you on the phone because it might try and electrocute you. But I like the name Cat-Muffs."

I grinned. "I thought you would. I even thought of a jingle already."

"Lay it on me, baby doll."

"If your cat is cold and its life is tough," I sang, "all you need are Paul's Cat-Muffs."

"Testify!" Sandy exclaimed, throwing his hands in the air.

"So, are you guys going to buy a bike or something?" Jenny asked.

"That's why we're here," I reminded her.

"I just wanted to make sure," she said. "It sounded like you were about to make a foray into domestic terrorism."

I scowled. "How are Cat-Muffs domestic terrorism?"

"I think they're amazing," Sandy said, just as baffled.

"Most people who live in the middle of nowhere in a shack are looking to blow something up," she explained.

"Do I *look* like I want to blow something up?"

"You probably shouldn't answer that," Sandy interrupted. "Paul, why don't we just look around at the bikes and see what we see?"

It was probably better than nothing, though I was sure I wasn't going to be able to find the right one. There literally had to be at least eight trillion different bikes in the shop, each with a different sized frame and tread. I saw one that I thought was perfect, but Sandy said he didn't think Vince would appreciate a pink bike with streamers and a basket on the front that had butterflies on it. "Besides, that bike is for eight-year-old girls," he said, pointing to a sign next to the bike that said, *Perfect for eight-year-old girls!*

"What is this world coming to?" I sighed. "Little boys are going to fall into these predetermined gender roles and never be able to choose the bike they want to ride? We haven't come as far as we like to think we have."

"His dad bought him a butch bike when he was a kid," Sandy told Jenny. "He's never been the same since. You should ask him how he knew he was gay."

Obviously unable to stop herself, she asked, "How did you know you were gay?"

"I was eight years old when I realized that my G.I. Joe and Optimus Prime were more than friends," I told her. "Theirs was a forbidden love that dared not speak its name."

"Optimus Prime is a robot," Jenny said. "Humans and robots can't be in love."

"Oh," Sandy groaned. "You shouldn't have said that."

"Blasphemy!" I hissed at her.

"It's true!" she insisted.

"I hope you never have children," I snapped. "Obviously you'd want to destroy their imaginations."

She was indignant. "I have two kids."

"Is your last name Dream Killer?"

"It's Lopez."

My eyes went wide. "Your name is Jennifer Lopez?"

"I go by Jenny," she assured me.

When was I ever going to get this chance again? "I'm not fooled by the rocks that you got because you're still, you're still Jenny from the block."

She rolled her eyes. "Like I've never heard that one before."

"It's not every day you meet someone named Jennifer Lopez," I tell Sandy.

"I would be more impressed if her name was Gwyneth Paltrow," he replied.

"Because she's an ice queen?" I glanced at Jenny. "That's not a very nice thing to say right in front of her, even if her kids are probably dead inside because she won't let their Optimus Prime ever know love outside of his species."

"Can I please sell you a bike?" Jenny begged me.

"I don't know what kind of bike Vince had," I admitted.

"Vince? Vince Taylor?"

I was startled. "Yeah. How'd you know?"

She laughed. "I don't know why I didn't make the connection to begin with. You're Paul Auster!"

"It's like you're famous," Sandy whispered. "See if she'll let you sign her boobies with a Sharpie."

I ignored him. "Do I want to know how you know my last name?" I asked Jenny.

She grinned. "Vince told me all about you. And I have to say, he was right on the money."

I groaned. "I really didn't want to know."

She patted my arm. "You know he adores you, right?"

"I've known him for a *week*. Well, almost a week. I'm still unclear as to what day counts as the first one."

"What's that have to do with anything?"

"He doesn't know me well enough to adore anything about me."

She shook her head. "Since when does that matter? What he *does* know is enough for him. That should be enough for you."

"I'm sorry. I didn't see that this was a bike shop *and* relationship counseling all in one. Unless I missed the sign out front that listed your credentials."

"Do you need a therapist already?" she asked, concerned.

"Yes, but not for what you think," Sandy said.

"That's not funny."

Jenny clapped her hands together. "But this makes my job *so* much easier. He called on Thursday to let us know he needed to order a new bike. I thought it was going to take a couple of weeks, but I called our other store and they already had his bike there, so I had it delivered over here. I was going to call him today to have him come pick it up."

I was relieved. "So I can just pay for it and take it with us? I brought some bungee cables so I can put it in the back of my car."

"You can." She called out to the other chick working in the shop, who went to the back and brought up an almost exact replica of what I remembered Vince's bike looking like. I was absolutely convinced that I was probably the best boyfriend of the history of boyfriends who had struck their *own* boyfriends with their car door and sent them to the hospital. Then I got hung up on the fact that I was using the word *boyfriend* three times in a single thought, and I got this goofy smile on my face that I couldn't seem to get rid of. I grinned at Sandy and Jenny and let them see just how happy I was.

Jenny laughed as she went to the front desk. "I can see why he likes you. There's something about you, Paul. In all the years I've known him, I don't think I've ever seen him this happy before. It looks like you two have got a good thing going."

I flushed as she typed something into the computer. "He's pretty okay," I allowed.

"I bet he is," she said with a smile. "Okay, that'll be $1,976.25."

"The fuck you talking about!" I shouted at her.

She recoiled as if I'd slapped her. Everyone in the store stared at me.

"Sorry," I said quickly. "I was just startled. I thought you said that bike was over nineteen hundred dollars."

She nodded slowly. "It is?"

"For a *bike*? I didn't put that much down when I bought my *car*!"

"It's a 2012 Diamondback Podium 3 road bike," she said as if that explained everything.

"I bought a *Prius*," I said as if that made everything better.

"These things can be expensive."

"Is it made of *blood* diamonds?" I asked incredulously. "Did children forced to work in deep, dark mines dig up the diamonds with their bare, bleeding hands?"

"Paul's very… *particular*… when it comes to money," Sandy said.

"That makes me sound cheap," I growled at him.

He shrugged. "You just screamed at this woman about the price of a bike. You sort of are."

"I am *not*. I just want to know why a *bicycle* has any right to cost this much. You know, I bet those poor blood-diamond children have never even *seen* a bicycle before, and here we are exploiting them just so we can ride in luxury!"

"You're not doing any riding," Sandy reminded me. "Well, not of the bicycle variety." He winked at Jenny. "Paul prefers the reverse cowgirl position."

Jenny smirked. "I sure hope Vince knows this about him. I think that'll make his day."

"I wouldn't be sad if either of you were kidnapped by Serbian nationalists," I said, grinding my teeth.

"Are you going to buy this bike or not?" Sandy asked. "And if you are, can you please be my sugar daddy too? I like blood diamonds. Lots and lots of blood diamonds. As a matter of fact, I want a tiara made of nothing but."

"This will probably guarantee you all the reverse cowgirl you want," Jenny said. "I know if someone bought this for me, I'd let them tear my vagina apart."

Sandy and I both stared at her, horrified.

She glared at us. "Oh, you two can talk about getting it up the butt, but I can't talk about my vagina? Men. So typical."

"We're *gay*," Sandy said. "Paul, give her your credit card so we can leave before she starts using words like *clitoris* and *cervix*. What is the service industry coming to?"

"No."

"Paul."

"*No.*"

"Paul."

Before I could respond by running out of the shop, Sandy moved quickly and snatched my wallet out of my back pocket like he was some Cockney thief out of a Dickens novel. I made a grab for him but ended up almost plowing into an innocent bystander who was checking out the pretty bike with the streamers and basket. Before I could recover and apologize profusely, Jenny already had my credit card in her hand and had run it through the machine. She handed the card back to Sandy, who put it back in the wallet and then handed it back to me. I grabbed it out of his hands and held it to my chest. "My precious," I snarled at the both of them.

"And I just need you to sign right here," Jenny said.

"You can go fuck yourself."

Sandy stepped forward and forged my signature. "That's a federal crime," I told him. "Punishable by three to five years in a minimum-security prison. You'll get passed around like condiments at a barbeque."

"My hole is already quivering," he said.

Jenny grimaced. "I can't talk about my vagina, but you can talk about your asshole quivering?"

We both glanced at her. "Uh, *yeah*," Sandy said. "We're *gay*." He shot me a look that said, *What is up with this chick?*

I didn't give him the satisfaction of a response because I was pretty sure he was now my mortal enemy.

"Vince is going to go through the roof when he sees this," Jenny said. "Cyclists go through withdrawal if we can't get a ride in."

"Yes, I'm sure it's just awful," I said. "I don't know how you guys survive."

Either she didn't hear the sarcasm or she'd already found a way to be able to ignore it. "I just want Vince to be happy," she said. "We love him here, and were so happy when he moved back to Tucson. He's been coming in here since he was fifteen years old, and it's nice to see him home again. I just wish it was under better circumstances. It's got to be hard on him, given his dad and all."

"His dad?" I asked. "What does his dad have to do with anything?"

She didn't understand my confusion. "His dad," she said again. "You know, the mayor of Tucson?"

Oh. Fuck. "His dad is Andrew Taylor?"

"The *Republican*?" Sandy said, sounding a little gut-punched.

Jenny's eyes widened. "You didn't know?"

"I've only known him a week!" I tried to think back as to what he'd said about his parents, but I could only remember a couple of off-the-cuff remarks about his dad that made me think they didn't have that great of a relationship. That must have been an understatement when your own father was essentially a political homophobe who publicly decried passing gay civil-rights laws, saying they were unconstitutional. I remembered hearing a few years back that he had a gay son and thought how shitty it must have been to know that your own dad didn't believe you should have the same rights as everyone else.

She started to backpedal. "It's not that big of a deal," she stammered. "They don't talk that much. Not anymore."

"Then why'd he come back to Tucson?" I asked. "What circumstances were you talking about?"

She looked away. "It's not my place, Paul. You should hear it from Vince. Though you only have to turn on the news to know."

"Oh, Jesus," Sandy whispered.

"What?" I asked, looking back at him.

He looked miserable. "It's his mom," he said. "It's been in the news for a while now."

"What has?" I racked my brain, trying to remember anything I might have heard, but nothing came to mind.

"Paul, she has cancer," he said. "They tried to keep it quiet, but it got out. She has cancer, and she's dying."

CHAPTER 12

I'm Sorry About Your Mom. Here, Have A Bike.

PLASMA cell leukemia. Apparently it's a rare type of cancer involving white blood cells called plasma cells. It's extraordinarily aggressive and results from Kahler's disease, in which the infected white blood cells accumulate in the bone marrow where they interfere with the production of normal blood cells.

Or, at least that's what Wikipedia told me on my phone as Sandy drove us home.

"That's what he's probably doing today," I said as we neared my house. "He told me that he had to go visit someone and that he'd call me later."

Sandy just nodded.

Lori Taylor came out publicly with her fight against cancer last year, but only after it somehow leaked to the press. She had smiled in an interview with the local media, laughing off the rumors of her failing health, her husband by her side. She looked healthy, if a bit thin. She did admit that while traditional avenues like chemotherapy hadn't given the results they'd hoped for, she was optimistic about her chances and would continue to fight as best she could. She looked so much like her son when she laughed that I had to look away from the screen on my phone to be able to hold myself together.

I remember one question catching my attention. The reporter said, "There was a bit of a public fallout with your son, who is openly gay. How is he doing with all of this?"

They were good, the both of them, his mother and father. Nothing was given away that they didn't want anyone to see. "Vincent has always been strong-headed," his father said. "But he knows that this is a time for family and that any other issues we may have are not as important as this."

"He's a good son," Lori added, patting her husband's hand.

The latest reports I could find were from five weeks ago, when inquiries were made into her health. The mayor's office released a statement asking for respect and privacy during the difficult time, and once any further information was known, it would be released.

"Let him come to you with this," Sandy told me before he left. I stood at the door to his car, looking down at him. "He obviously didn't bring it up for a reason, so it wouldn't be good to say anything. You might put him on the defensive." Vince and I were going to meet up with Sandy at the bar after we finished at Nana's house so that I could help him with the show. Vince had also said he wanted me to meet some of his friends and asked to meet mine. I didn't have it in my pathetic heart to tell him he'd met Sandy and Wheels, and that was pretty much it.

"Yeah," I muttered. "We haven't really had the time yet for the whole 'my dad's a fascist prick and my mom is dying' heart-to-heart yet. I was hoping that we could do that next week."

Sandy reached out his car window to grab my hand. "You need to be careful with this," he told me quietly. "I'm not saying this to be an ass, but you already sound like you're making it about you. You can't do that, Paul. Not with this. This is obviously a contentious situation as it is, and it's got to be hurting him quite a bit. You can't get pissed at him for this. You can't. Do you understand me?"

And as much as I sort of hated him right then, I knew he was right. I didn't feel a bit of indignation that Vince hadn't told me who his jerk of a dad was. It wasn't like he'd lied to me, and it wasn't as if he'd held anything from me... not exactly. I had to remind myself again that we'd only known each other a week (well, a week that we'd *seen* each other, five days since we'd first spoken). It felt like much longer.

"I know," I sighed. "It just sucks. I'm still sort of pissed, but only because I feel like I *should* be mad, not that I actually am. Anything that I'm feeling has got to be a billion times worse for him." I didn't know how much longer I would last without talking to Vince about it, not knowing what I did now. All I wanted to do right then was chew him out a little bit, then hug him until all the problems of his world went away and left him alone. It was an odd feeling, this protective one. I didn't know what to do with it, and it was twisting me up.

"Is he coming here?" Sandy asked.

I shook my head. "He's supposed to meet us at Nana's house."

"Just take it easy on him, okay?"

"You sure you don't want to go? I could use a little help with this. I feel like I'm going to open my mouth and say the wrong thing. Which, to be honest, isn't really a new thing for me. This just seems like it's worse, though."

"I gotta get ready for the show tonight, baby doll. You'll be fine. The best thing for you to do is to be a supportive partner and let him come to you with this."

I snorted. "Partner. Jesus Christ. This has been the weirdest week of my life."

Sandy grinned at me. "You told him about *your* parents yet?"

"No! And I've already warned them to keep their mouths shut! I don't need him finding out that Mom and Dad got married a week after they met. That'll put ideas into his head that I don't want to be in there. For fuck's sake, he's already told me he's halfway in love with me. I am *not* going to end up like my parents."

"You mean having a loving marriage thirty-five years later? Yes, Paul. That sounds freaking awful. I don't know how you'd survive. The social ramifications alone would destroy you."

"You know what I meant," I said with a scowl.

"Apparently I don't. Maybe you should try and beat their time instead. You've still got a few hours left."

I gaped at him. "You... crazy... the fuck you talking about... I don't even...."

He squeezed my hand tightly. "Breathe, Paul. Just take a breath."

"Yeah, that's *exactly* what I need. Getting married would solve *all* our problems."

"And what, might I ask, do you and Vince have problems over?"

I opened my mouth to speak... and nothing came out. Not a single damn thing. I couldn't think of a *fucking* thing. "Oh *shit*," I whispered.

"Sounds like a little bit of love to me," Sandy said, laughing.

"Or it could just be the first week of a relationship," I snapped at him, trying to calm my thundering heartbeat. "It's called the honeymoon phase. There *shouldn't* be any problems at this point. That'd be a problem itself if there *was*."

Sandy's eyes flashed and Helena came forward. "I know you think sometimes that you don't deserve to be happy. I've done my best to try and make you see otherwise, to show you that you're fine just the way you are. But I can only do so much. Vince can only do so much. You have to do the rest yourself. And I swear on everything that I have that if you fuck this up because of some misplaced sense of pride, I will never let you forget it. You do *not* get to let Vince walk away from you. You do *not* get to push him away. You get me?"

"I get you," I said, even though I was more worried then about what I'd do to fuck it up.

"Give me a kiss, sugar," Helena purred. I did. "I'll see you tonight, okay? You tell that fabulous boyfriend of yours that he may come up to the dressing room with you when you arrive."

I was shocked. Helena *never* let anyone else up into the room aside from Charlie and me. Even the bar owner, Mike, had to steer clear or face Helena's wrath. The fact that Vince had already shot past so many people's defenses was knocking me off-center.

"You sure?" I asked, starting to sweat a bit.

"Positive," she said with a grin. She threw her car into reverse. "Kisses," she said. And then she was gone.

ON THE drive over to Nana's house, I debated whether to tell my parents about Vince's mom and dad, but in the end, I decided not to. I didn't want anything to be said until I could talk to Vince on my own, and I didn't want him to be uncomfortable, especially given how uncomfortable this situation was already going to be. I had tried to warn him that Nana could be pretty... *blunt*, but I didn't think he was taking my warnings seriously, especially after meeting my parents and practically worshipping the ground they walked on. I felt a bit guilty after thinking that, given what I knew now about his own parents. I knew Mom and Dad liked him quite a bit, even after just one short meeting, but I didn't want that to turn to pity if Vince didn't need it.

Of course, best-laid plans and all that.

"You ride a bike over here, son?" Dad asked as he opened the door at Nana's house.

I pushed past him, wheeling the bike inside. "No. It's...." *Shit, I haven't told them I hit Vince with my car.* "It's a... present. For Vince."

Dad grinned as he shut the door. "Wow. Maybe I should find myself a boyfriend too. Apparently the gay boys give each other nice things."

"I heard that," my mother said from the kitchen. "You go find yourself a nice man, Larry. Let me know how that works out for you."

"Your mom thinks that if I was gay, I'd be a bottom," he whispered to me.

"The fact that you're sharing this with me does not bode well for how tonight is going to go," I told him. "I've been here for two minutes, Dad. You think we could wait until at least dessert before we have to have this conversation and show Vince just how dysfunctional we really are? I'd like to lead him in with a false sense of security before ripping it all away to reveal the dark underbelly of the Auster family."

"Of course," he said cheerfully. "Oh, and your mother wanted to know if you are going to be allowed to eat at the table with the rest of us, or if your master is going to make you sit at his feet and stare at the floor and feed you by hand." He glanced over his shoulder then leaned in closer to me and lowered his voice. "We haven't told Nana about that side of you, so I just wanted to ask if you could keep the pony sounds to a minimum. We're not stifling you, and we want you to be who you are, always, but I don't want Nana to get worried when you start neighing when Vince hands you a sugar cube or piece of apple."

"I can't believe you guys think I *do* that. Dad, I'm not a fucking pony! Vince is not my master! He's my *boyfriend*."

"Language," my father said.

"Sorry," I grumbled. And I was. If there was one thing my father asked for, it was that we watched our mouths. He was of the opinion that cursing added nothing to a conversation. I didn't fucking agree with that in the slightest, but it was fucking important to him, so I fucking did it. Fucking shit balls. "I'll be sitting at the table like everyone else."

"Is that Paul?" I heard Nana shout from the living room.

"Yes, Nana. It's me."

"Johnny Depp! You hear that? Paul is here!"

"Ass-wrangler!" Johnny Depp squawked. "Don't touch me!"

"This is so not going to go well," I muttered. I wheeled the bike down the hall and hid it in one of the bedrooms before going back out to the living room.

My nana, Gigi, sat in her old lounge chair, her feet propped up on a bright green ottoman that clashed horribly with her bright purple recliner. Ever since I was a kid, she'd always had a thing for vivid colors, not caring if they went well with each other or not. She used to tell me that she was a little bit color-blind, and the bright colors helped her see them clearly. It wasn't until years later that I learned that one cannot be "a little bit color-blind" and that she was essentially full of shit. Some might think that she was batshit crazy, and given that her cat used to eat out of her mouth, she just might have been, but she was also my nana: a hard-core woman fiercely protective of her family. Unfortunately, she included Johnny Depp as part of her family and told me once that it was just good-natured ribbing and that the bird wasn't really homophobic. I didn't believe that one in the slightest. The bird hated homosexuals.

"Paulie!" she grinned at me toothlessly. Her white, curly hair shot off from her head in odd directions. She was a short, squat woman with a kind, wrinkled face and eyes that showed a sharp intelligence that had yet to fade.

"Fairy!" Johnny Depp told me. He sat in a large cage in the corner, his gorgeous plumage hiding his evil, beating heart. He glared at me as I entered the room, clicking his claws against the wooden beam as he moved closer. "Don't put your finger in my bum!"

Nana cackled.

I hadn't heard that one before. "Are you teaching him new things?" I said as I kissed her cheek. "I told you that it can't be healthy for an animal to be so hateful."

"I didn't teach him a thing," she said, grabbing and squeezing my hand. "He seems to think of these things on his own."

"You're so full of shit," I told her.

"Larry!" she called out.

"What?"

"Your son is using foul language around me!"

"Language," my father scolded from the kitchen.

"Paul touched penises with a neighbor's dog," Johnny Depp said.

"Oh Jesus," I groaned. "Nana, can we put him in another room, at least until we leave? Or better yet, can I flush him down the toilet?"

"Killing animals is a sign that you could be a serial killer," she told me. "I saw that on the news. You kill animals, you grow up to kill hookers."

"I don't want to kill anyone," I told her. "Especially not hookers. I just don't want that bird to be around tonight. Or alive."

"Paul's a homo!" Johnny Depp told the room. "Homo, homo, homo."

"What happened to your face?" she asked me, concerned about my black eye. She pulled me down until I sat next to her on the arm of the recliner.

"I was mobbed because I'm so famous. They wanted my hot body as I was trying to escape. Men were trying to rip off my clothes and I got an elbow to the eye."

She nodded sympathetically. "You tripped and fell again?"

I sighed. "Into the wall with my face. Wheels got under my feet, and I didn't want him to die, so I stepped on his wheel instead and face-punched the wall."

"See? I knew you wouldn't want to kill hookers. Not if you got beat up to avoid killing Wheels. How many grandmothers can say that about their grandchildren?"

"I think you're seriously overestimating the number of serial killers out in the world."

"Is the young man coming over to meet me a serial killer?" She reached out with a gnarled hand and patted my knee. "I overheard Larry and Matty talking. Why did they say you're a pony?"

Goddammit. "I think you misheard them, Nana. They were probably talking about how I planted peonies at my house." Lying to your grandmother is okay if it has to do with sadomasochistic sex. Trust me on that.

"You full of shit, Paul?" she asked me.

"Dad!" I shouted. "Nana's cursing in here."

"Language!" he called back.

"Paul's a cock-monger," Johnny Depp muttered.

"He's not a serial killer," I assured her. "At least I don't think he is. He doesn't have a mean bone in his body, so I am pretty sure he wouldn't go after a hooker. I don't think he knows any hookers, so that's a good thing, just to be safe."

"His name?"

"Vince Melody Taylor," I said with a grin.

"Melody?" She giggled. "Oh. Is he a floater like you?"

"Nancy-boy?" Johnny Depp asked.

I rolled my eyes. "No, Nana. He's not a floater. He's a manly man. Apparently Melody is a family name." And the thought of his family again sent a pang across my chest. I tried to keep it from my face, but Nana's too quick and too perceptive; she always has been.

"What's wrong?" she asked. "Do I need to knock him down to size for you?"

I gave a fake laugh. It almost sounded real. "Nah. Nothing to do with him. He's actually...." I stopped myself.

"Actually what?"

If not to her, then who? "Amazing," I told her quietly. "I don't know what the hell he's thinking being with me. He's not the smartest guy in the world, but he makes up for it, Nana. He does. He's got this heart that just... I don't know. He sees the world differently than anyone else I know. He chooses to see the good in people. He's persistent, he's sure of himself. He knows what he wants and he goes for it." I looked down at my hands. "He's everything I'm not. And that confuses me."

She smiled sweetly at me and reached up to cup my face. "Paul, I'm going to tell you this once and only once, okay?"

I nodded at my beautiful grandmother.

She slapped me upside my head. For being such an old little thing, she had freakish strength. I thought she might have made a deal with the devil to be the strongest old lady to have ever existed. "If you spout any of that bullshit to me ever again, I will tan your hide, you hear me? You need to get over yourself and stop being a whiny little bitch. If he sees something in you that the rest of us have seen for years, then God almighty, you better be giving it as good as you get."

"Ow," I mumbled.

She rolled her eyes. "Don't be such a baby. There's too many other people in the world who want nothing more than to kick you when you're down. Don't you dare do that job for them."

"You were talking to Sandy too, weren't you?" I accused her.

"Of course I was," she said. "He's family. And if he didn't tell me what was going on, I wouldn't be hearing about it at all since you keep all this to yourself."

I chewed on my thumbnail. "But what if he's Freddie Prinze Junioring me?"

"I don't even know what the hell you're talking about," she snapped. "Maybe instead of making up words, you should focus on pleasing your man. Your old nana knows a thing or two about that, you can be sure."

"There are times in my life I wish I didn't understand English," I told her. "Hearing you say that is one of those times."

"Is he handsome?" she asked with a smirk.

I blushed, unable to stop myself. "Quite hideous, to be honest."

"Uh-huh. That's why you look like a tomato right now. I can't wait to meet this young man if he's got you all up in knots after only a few days. After all, you know what happened with your parents after a wee—"

"No chance in hell," I said. "And I'd appreciate if that was never mentioned to him. Ever."

"Wow. You were sure quick to protest *that* one."

"Nana, you don't understand. He's already convinced that he's halfway in lo—"

The doorbell rang, cutting me off.

"Oh sweat balls," I moaned. "This will be the second I'll remember later on as the moment before the shit hit the fan."

"Language," my father shouted from the kitchen.

"Go get the door," Nana said.

"Butthole bitch," Johnny Depp said.

"You stay out of this," I warned the bird. He eyed me warily through the bars on his cage. "For some reason, Vince wants to see you, but I swear to God if you keep up the whole time we're here, I will put you in the washing machine."

"Dick-lips," he responded.

"Bastard," I hissed at him, moving past the cage.

I took a deep breath once I reached the door and sent up a little prayer to God for tonight to not be the social abortion of the season. I opened the door.

God, he was so fucking handsome.

I could see the slight nervousness on his face as I opened the door, as if he was unsure who'd be on the other side and was fretting about it. But as soon as he saw it was me, that look faded and a brilliant smile bloomed on his face, dimples out in full force. He was so fucking *happy* to see me that it almost knocked me flat. I didn't think I'd ever had anyone look at me like that. It was disconcerting. It was terrifying. It was fucking awesome.

"Hi," he said, almost shyly, stepping into the door and kissing me sweetly.

"Hey," I said roughly. "Thanks for coming over."

He shrugged. "Your mom invited me. I couldn't say no to that."

And what about your mom, Vince? What's going on with her?

"You may end up regretting that sooner than you think," I muttered to him. Only then did I notice his arms were full. "What's all this?"

He blushed. He fucking blushed. It was so unfair. I blushed and I looked like I had third-degree burns spreading over my body. He blushed and it made him hotter. "Just thought I should bring something for your folks and your nana." He shuffled his feet. "Also got you a birthday present, even though your birthday has already passed. I felt bad that I missed it."

"You... come in here all... so awesome and I can't even... so unfair...."

He looked up and grinned. "You're sputtering," he murmured. "That usually means I've done something good. It's nothing big. Just flowers for your mom and Nana, and some scotch for your dad because he looks like he'd like it."

I shook my head. "You're so fucking weird."

"Yeah. But you think I'm awesome."

"Did you have a good day?" I asked, trying to keep my voice level as I closed the door behind him.

I thought he stiffened slightly, but it was gone before I could be sure it was there. "It was fine," he said.

"Oh. That's good." Only then did I notice slightly dark circles around his eyes. "You okay? You look tired." I felt bad. "Look, we don't have to do this now if you're not feeling it. Trust me, my family can be exhausting like you wouldn't believe. Maybe we should—"

"It's fine, Paul," he said with an exasperated smile. "I just haven't been sleeping well."

"Is it your back? Still sore?"

"Yeah. A little bit."

"Are you sure you—"

"Paul!" Nana shouted from the living room.

I groaned. "Here we go," I whispered. "Yeah?" I shouted back.

"Quit trying to get fresh with your young man in the hallway and bring his ass in here so I can meet him!"

"Language!" my father yelled from the kitchen. "Hi, Vince!"

"Hi, Larry!" Vince called back.

"Hi, Vince!"

"Hello, Matty!"

"Paul's a fudge packer!"

Vince's eyes bulged.

"Johnny Depp," I sighed. "I told you. This is going to be bad. He hates everyone and all he does is say horrid things. I would feel bad, but *you* wanted to see this. I only ask that if you feel like screaming and running in the opposite direction you give me plenty of notice so that I can start looking for a new country to live in so that I may die in embarrassment around people who don't speak the same language I do."

"This will probably be the most magical day ever," he assured me.

"You say that now. I'll ask that you remember that in two hours when you're trying to find the best way to file a restraining order against us, or if you're looking up support groups after being verbally raped by a parrot."

"Hi, my name is Vince," he intoned. "Paul's homophobic parrot touched me in my no-no place."

"You're a natural," I sighed. "Let's get this over with."

He followed me down the hall and into the living room, where Nana was waiting expectantly in her chair. She'd put on her glasses, smoothed down her hair, and sat with her hands in her lap. If one saw her like this, they'd think her a sweet, demure little old lady. Too bad the façade was all a lie. I knew the steel-trap mind and tiger's claws that were buried underneath. If Gigi didn't like him, she'd tear him to shreds piece by piece. I'd seen her do it before and there was little one can do to stop it.

So imagine my surprise when she saw him for the first time and her face lit up in a wide smile. Imagine my surprise when she pushed herself up from her recliner with a very unladylike grunt and practically shoved me out of the way. It was good to know where her loyalties lay, even without having ever seen him before today.

"You must be Vince!" she beamed at him. "I'm Paul's grandmother. You may call me Gigi or Nana, whatever you wish. It's quite lovely to meet you."

He smiled down at the little woman. "I got these for you," he said, handing her a beautiful bouquet of summer flowers.

Nana giggled. She fucking *giggled* as she took the flowers from him. She *never* giggled about *anything*. If she found something to be funny, she had this low, raucous laugh that sounded whiskey smooth. But this? This was a high-pitched giggle of a little girl who was suddenly and without warning pleased beyond comparison. "So pretty," she said, inhaling her flowers deeply. "And the flowers are too." She winked at him.

Oh. Oh, so gross.

"Nana," I groaned.

"Oh, hush, you," she told me. "It's not every day that I get a piece of eye candy of his caliber walking into my house. The cable repair man came the other day, but I'm pretty sure he either had gout or the plague because he was not attractive. Let an old lady enjoy the sights."

"That's *my* boyfriend you're talking about," I reminded her. "Not some piece of meat."

"Paul is pretty much in love with me," Vince told her. "He gets kind of defensive around me."

"You must be out of your damn mind," I growled at him, trying to keep from bursting into flames. "Because that would be the only excuse that'd make any sense for saying something like that."

"Ignore him," Nana said. "He thinks too much for his own good. Let me give you a tour of my house, and I will show you all the most embarrassing photographs of Paul that I have. There's one of him dressed up as a slutty Snow White for Halloween when he was sixteen that I think you'll just positively adore. Paul?"

"Yes, oh destroyer of any future potential relationship I may have?"

"Be a dear and take these lovely flowers Vince gave me and put them in water. It looks as if he's gotten some for your mother as well, so take those to her. Is that scotch, dear boy? Oh, Larry will just *love* it. And what's in this bag?"

"That's for Paul," Vince said. "I think I'll just hold on to it while you show me Paul as a Disney princess whore. He'd probably try to open it without permission."

"Oh, you're absolutely right. He would always try to open the corners of his Christmas presents when he was a kid. He thought he was being all sneaky about it, but the little screams he would give when he'd see them were a dead giveaway. It was like having a tiny shrieking Christmas monkey. Speaking of Christmas, you simply must be here this year. I won't take no for an answer."

"Christmas is seven months away," I reminded her, trying to keep my cool.

She glared at me. "I *know* what month it is, Paul. I'm not so old that I've slid from my mental faculties and need to wear diapers."

"And that image will never leave my head," I said.

She shoved the flowers and the scotch into my hands before hooking her arm through Vince's and leading him around the living room. Their first stop was in front of Johnny Depp and I smirked, waiting for the incarnate of evil to start spewing vitriol left and right at my grandmother's insistence. I didn't think she actually *taught* Johnny Depp to say those things, but she certainly didn't stop him either. Gigi wasn't homophobic in the slightest. Just her bird.

But, of course, that's not how things went. At all. I didn't know what the fuck Vince had done, if he was some kind of cyborg sent from the future that had the power to make everyone literally roll over and expose their bellies to him like he was the greatest thing to have ever existed. Yes, I thought he was pretty dang rad, but Jesus *Christ*, Johnny Depp? Johnny Depp, the most hateful bird alive?

Johnny Depp *adored* him.

My grandmother pulled Vince up to the cage, and I could see the parrot eyeing him. I waited for the bird to call him a turd-burglar or some such nonsense when all of a sudden, Johnny Depp whistled like he was some New York City construction worker and a hot piece of ass had just walked by. It was a low sound, a *lecherous* sound, and I almost walked over to choke the life out of the damn parrot for hitting on my boyfriend, because that's *exactly* what he was doing.

He shuffled over on his bar to get as close to Vince as he could. "He's very pretty," Vince said, and Johnny Depp gave a little chattering sound like he was *pleased* with the compliment, like he *understood* what Vince had said. He mewled at Vince and stuck his beak through the bars, clicking his tongue. Vince reached up and stroked between his eyes and the bird fucking *sighed* in pleasure. "Pretty," Johnny Depp said. "So pretty." He clicked his tongue again.

"You're like some weird, gay Dr. Dolittle," I accused him.

"You just have to be nice to animals, Paul," he said. "They know when you don't like them."

"Yeah, because they're so smart like that," I said with a sneer.

Johnny Depp reared up and looked over at me. "Paul's a lady-boy," he said. He turned back to Vince. "Pretty. Pretty, pretty."

"You two should get a room," I said snidely.

"I see what you mean about getting defensive," Nana said. "Paul, it's a *bird*. Really, you'd think you wouldn't get jealous over a *bird*."

"Paul pretty much loves me, I guess," Vince said with a wink.

I scowled at the both of them and went to the kitchen.

And walked in on my parents making out. "Aughhhh!" I cried. "My eyes! It's like I stared at an eclipse even though all the warnings told me not to!"

"Oh please," my mother said. "You act like parents can't be intimate, Paul. You weren't immaculately conceived, you know. Your father put his pe—"

"Let's pretend the conversation ended right there, okay?" I interrupted. "Here, Vince got you flowers and got Dad scotch, which, with how this has been going after only five minutes, I'm pretty sure we should break into now so that I am numb for when the rest happens."

My mother gushed over the flowers and Dad grinned over his bottle. "What are you worried about, Paul?" Mom asked as she pulled a vase from underneath the sink. "Everyone will be on their best behavior. It's not like we're savages, you know. Believe it or not, we *do* know how to keep our pants on."

"And I appreciate that more than I could ever say," I told her. "I wouldn't know how to explain that to him if you didn't."

"Sassy boy," she said fondly.

We were interrupted by a loud shout of laughter coming from the hallway. Vince sounded like he was dying.

"Slutty Snow White?" Dad asked, opening the bottle to his scotch and sniffing.

"Slutty Snow White," I admitted. "Remind me again why I decided to wear that?"

"Because you and Sandy wanted to see if you could find seven men to be your dwarves," Mom said. "I reminded you that it's never a good idea to go looking for seven different guys when I was pretty sure you couldn't handle more than two." She sniffed and wiped her eyes. "You grew up so fast."

"Wow, did I have a delusional childhood."

"No more than most kids," she said.

"I'm pretty sure most sixteen-years-olds don't dress in drag and look for a seven-man gang bang," I pointed out.

"Language!" My father warned.

I heard the bedroom door open down the hall and Vince's laugh suddenly cut off. "Oh shit," I breathed.

"What?"

"The bike."

Dad cocked his head. "You didn't want him to find it?"

"I don't know," I muttered. "I just—"

Vince walked swiftly into the kitchen. "Matty, Larry," he said in greeting. "Can I borrow Paul for a minute?"

My parents looked highly amused. I couldn't look at Vince, the tightness in his voice making me think I'd done something wrong. "Go ahead," Mom said. "We'll be ready to eat in ten minutes or so, so take your time."

"Thank you," he said, grabbing my hand and jerking me out of the kitchen. They chuckled behind me as Vince dragged me down the hallway to the front door. His grip was biting into my wrist, but I didn't dare shake him loose. He looked tense in front of me. He opened the front door, which I then snagged to close behind us after we went through.

He paused for a moment on the front stoop, snapping his head left then right. He must have decided right because he jerked me in that direction, going around the side of Nana's little house, away from the street and anyone's view of us. As soon as we'd cleared the corner, he roughly pushed me up against the side of the house, bringing his hands up to frame my face. He was breathing heavily when he said, "That bike in there."

"What about it?" I panted, squirming in his grip. I was harder than I'd ever been in my entire fucking life. I was also a little bit worried, given the way he was looking at me, his eyes narrowed but alight with something I hadn't yet seen in him. It was like fire. It was like he was burning up from the inside and it was all for me.

"Is it for me?" He brushed his fingers through my hair, digging into my scalp.

"Yeah. You needed a new one, 'cause I broke your other one, and Jenny at the bike store said that it was the one you—"

He cut me off in a very effective way. As soon as the last word came out, he bent in and kissed me deeply, pressing me up against the side of the house with his body, his fingers curling in around me. There was no shyness here, no gentle insistence, no sweet hesitation. The moment his mouth was on mine, he pushed his tongue through my lips, clashing our teeth together. The groan I gave came from nowhere, and he bit my bottom lip, pulling it between his teeth as he ground against me. Our groins rubbed together, and I could feel how hard his cock was, pressed up against mine. He gasped at the touch but pressed harder, the heady sensation almost too much for the both of us to handle. I had a very dim sense that I was being rutted against on the side of my nana's house with her and my parents only feet away, but it didn't seem important to me in the slightest.

What *was* important was how he moved his lips from mine to trail along my jaw. His thumbs went to my chin and lifted my head until he nuzzled into my neck, his tongue trailing along my skin, his teeth scraping hotly, his breath moist against me. "All this," I groaned, "because of a fucking bike?"

He growled against me. "No one's ever done something like that for me before," he said, sounding snappish. He used his foot to kick apart my legs, then pressed his knee up against my crotch. My dick thought this a fine idea as I ground against him. Beyond fine. Amazing, even.

"I'll keep that in mind for the future," I said as he found my ear with his mouth. It was about that time I realized all I wanted to do was take this man home, throw him on my bed, and ride him until I exploded. These were not normal Paul thoughts. This was not normal Paul. Normal Paul had fled. This was horny, *slutty* Paul who wanted to fuck and fuck some more. My hands scrabbled for his jeans as he sucked on my ear lobe. I gripped his dick through his pants and marveled at the fact that even if it *was* horny, slutty Paul doing this, it was still *me*.

"I'm going to do so many, *many* things to you tonight," he whispered harshly in my ear. "You're not going to be able to walk right for a fucking week, you get me? You don't get to say no. Not now. Not ever again."

"Jesus *Christ*," I muttered as I realized I was all but humping his leg like a dog in heat. "We gotta stop. We gotta—Oh *balls*," I said as I found that ass, that perfectly perfect glorious ass. I grabbed as much of it as I could. His breath was getting more ragged in my ear, a little whine escaping from his throat as he continued assaulting my neck. "Vince. *Vince*! We gotta stop." I squeezed once more before dropping my hands.

"Why?" he moaned, causing me to very seriously consider coming right then and there.

"Because we still have to have dinner with my fucking *parents*. I don't want to do that sitting in my own spunk. And besides, having sex at my grandma's house is not one of the things I wanted to do before I die."

He pressed his knee to my dick again, that cruel, vicious bastard. "Not even if it's with me?" he whispered, causing goose bumps to break out on my neck.

"Not even," I managed to say, even if it was a total and complete fucking lie. I gathered up all my resolve and pushed him off, leaning against the wall to catch my breath. He eyed me like I was some kind of prey as he wiped the back of his hand over his mouth. I tried to keep my eyes at an appropriate level, but I figured since I was pretty much damned already, it couldn't hurt, so I glanced down at his dick and saw the very clear outline through his pants. I swallowed thickly, trying to keep from looking like I was drooling.

"You keep looking at me like that," he said hoarsely, "and I'm not going to give a fuck where we're at. I'll do you right here."

I couldn't help it. I grinned at him. "That doesn't sound like much of a threat."

His eyes searched mine. "You didn't have to do that, Paul," he said finally. His voice was soft. "It means so much to me, and thank you, but you didn't have to do it."

I knew he was talking about the bike. I shrugged. "Even if I didn't have to, I wanted to. Okay? You're... you...." I shook my head and looked down at my feet.

"Paul," he said sharply. "Look at me." He didn't move. He didn't force me with his hands to do so.

I took a deep breath. And looked up at him.

"What were you going to say?"

Fuck. "You... you mean a lot to me, okay? I don't know when that happened or why or how or what the fuck I'm doing, but I just want to make you happy. All the time, I want you happy. That's all I want. I don't know what you're doing to me, but I don't want it to stop and I just want... fuck. I just want you, okay?"

The smile he gave me was beautiful. He moved forward, and while the kiss he gave me then wasn't as ferocious as the ones before, I felt it all the more because of the sweetness it held.

"This doesn't mean I'm going on bike rides with you," I warned him when he pulled away.

Vince just laughed.

THE rest of dinner went okay. Nana smirked at the two of us when we went back inside, asking me with a sparkle in her eye what had happened to my lips? I told her that I couldn't possibly know what she was talking about, that Vince had just needed to show me the tread on his tires to see if I thought he needed to get new ones so he wouldn't pop a tire on the freeway, flip his car, and die in a fiery explosion. My grandmother assured me she didn't understand the euphemisms of today's youth, but if I was going to be treading tires, I'd better make sure I was careful and wrapped up my tire gauge. We both gaped at her as she cackled.

The thing that stood out the most was how comfortable the rest of dinner went, aside from Johnny Depp screeching, "Pretty, pretty," from the living room, trying to call Vince back in so that he could show off his plumage. I told Vince this, and he said that I did the same thing to him. I scowled at him as my parents laughed at me.

But… the weirdness never came. The nervousness that I'd felt previously didn't return. My family was attempting to be on their best behavior, though a few things slipped through that I would have rather Vince never learned about me for as long as we lived ("When he was six, he told us he wanted to grow up to be a Charlie's Angel" and "Larry, tell Vince about the time you caught Paul practicing kissing with his stuffed bear. You'll like this, Vince. Paul was seventeen at the time…."). But aside from those few excruciating moments, the thing that stuck out the most was the bright-eyed look on his face when my parents asked him questions, when they included him in on conversations that were about our family. I was dreading the moment when any of them would bring up *his* family, but for some reason, it didn't happen, which confused the fuck out of me. Normally, Mom, Dad, and Nana are so fucking nosy that it was awkward, but none of them took the obvious ins I would have expected.

Toward the end is when it sort of went downhill.

"So how did you two meet?" Vince asked my mom and dad.

Of course, I was sipping a glass of wine right at that moment and proceeded to choke on that and my tongue. Mom and Dad smiled fondly at each other while I did a great imitation of someone dying from lack of oxygen. Vince, however, knew of my propensity to choke in his general vicinity and got up immediately to try and put me in another Heimlich maneuver. I shook my head at him as I gasped in air, hoping my face wasn't as purple as I expected it was.

"You okay?" he asked me worriedly.

I nodded. "Just fine."

"I saved Paul's life the other day," he told my family, and I almost started choking again. "It gets me a bit worried when he starts hacking like that."

Six eyebrows went up. "You did what?" my mother asked.

"He was choking to death in a restaurant," Vince explained.

"I was not!" I said.

"On like a burrito or something."

"It was *spinach*."

"Anyway, he would have died had I not done the hemorrhoid maneuver."

"Heimlich. It's Heimlich."

He waved his hand at me. "It's all the same thing."

"You almost died?" Dad said, sounding astonished.

I rolled my eyes. "No. Vince is being overdramatic. I was *fine*." I knew what my parents were thinking about, and I didn't want them to say a damn word.

"He wasn't breathing," Vince told them. "So I maneuvered him and he spat the burrito onto Sandy's face. And then he could breathe again. Then I asked him out on a date and he said no."

"I had just almost *died*," I said. "You just shocked me, is all."

"I thought he was being overdramatic," Nana said.

"He almost died," Vince said again. "So his life became mine, because once you save someone's life, they belong to you."

Dad nodded. "It's an old Chinese proverb."

"In Asia," Vince agreed. "Then Paul hit me with his car."

"*What?*" they all said.

"I didn't *hit* him with my car," I said. "He ran into my door on his bike."

"And flipped over the door and landed on my back," he said. "Then he saved my life by pretending to give me mouth-to-mouth, but really he was just making out with me."

"He wasn't breathing and you were trying to give him tongue?" my mom asked me. "Paul, I taught you better than that." She shook her head as if disappointed in me.

"I was *not*! I thought he was *dead*!"

"Were you wearing a helmet?" Dad asked him sternly.

"Yes, sir. I always ride with one."

"Good. So Paul hit you with a car and made out with you afterwards? What happened then?"

"Oh, for fuck sakes," I muttered.

"Language," Dad said.

"Well, my back hurt pretty bad," Vince explained. "Paul must have been so worried about me because he called an ambulance after he got done making out with me and I had to go to the hospital."

"You poor dear," Nana said, patting his hand and shooting me a glare.

"I didn't do it on purpose!" I snapped at her.

"Paul's a butt pirate!" Johnny Depp screamed.

"It's okay, Johnny Depp," Vince called out.

"Pretty. Pretty!"

"So I had to go the hospital, where they told me I had a concussion and bruises, and even the doctor thought Paul should go out with me."

"Well, if the *doctor* said so," Nana said. "I know I *always* do what my doctor says. They *do* go to medical school for, like, sixteen years."

"So then Paul took me back to his house and kept me there and took care of me."

"I should hope so," Mom said. "He *did* hit you with his car."

"It's like I'm not even here," I said into my hands.

"So he saved my life and I saved his, and I sort of figured we belonged to each other," Vince said, smiling fondly at me as if I hadn't said a single thing.

"You weren't dying," I told him.

"You thought I was. Otherwise, your tongue probably wouldn't have been in my mouth."

"You put *your* tongue in *my* mouth."

He shrugged. "Does it matter who did what where? What matters is that I got you."

"Aww," Nana said.

"It was meant to be," Mom said, eyes brimming.

"That's pretty swell," Dad said gruffly. "So Paul didn't tell you how me and his mom met? That's surprising, given the similarities."

"Who wants pie?" I asked loudly. "Seems like a perfect time for pie! I couldn't imagine an even better time to have everyone except for Vince go into the kitchen, where we will not be raising our voices in any way, shape, or form. Just a normal family discussion about pie."

"Pie can wait," Mom said absently.

"Similarities?" Vince asked.

"I have an announcement to make," I said desperately. "I have decided to become a Wiccan and you should now all call me Heaven Moonstorm."

No one even blinked. I put my face in my hands and waited for it to be over.

"A little over thirty-five years ago," Dad said as he reached out and grabbed Mom's hand, "I was seated at a restaurant in what used to be downtown Tucson. I was there with some buddies from school. I was a freshman at the U of A then."

"A very handsome one," Mom said, smiling at him, as she always did when he reached this part.

From there, I'm sure you can figure out the rest. It's actually deceptively simple yet decisively beautiful. It's also so completely unrealistic and illogical that it doesn't seem like real life, like something that would really work.

Dad's eating with friends and inhales something wrong and starts to choke. Mom just happens to be passing by at the time and stops him from choking by performing this new trick she'd heard about on the news, the Heimlich maneuver. Dad lives, all is well. They smile at each other, instantly enamored. But then Mom has to go, she can't be late, and he doesn't get her name. She's a student, he knows, just the same as he, but he doesn't know where to start looking. No one seems to know her name.

The next day, he's walking through a parking lot when she backs her old Volkswagen out of a parking space and up and over his foot, breaking three of his toes. She's hysterical, apologizing profusely, but he doesn't really hear it because even before he learns her name, he knows that he's in love with her completely and fully in a way he never thought possible. He's not a stupid man, nor is he a foolish one. He doesn't have the propensity to daydream about things that could never happen. He's rational. He's solid. He's sound.

But all of that goes out the window when he says, "What's your name?"

"Matilda," she says through her tears. "But everyone calls me Matty."

"Well, Matty," he says with a grimace. "I'd appreciate a ride to the hospital, if you don't mind. And I also think I might just be in love with you."

She's shocked right out of her tears and laughs such a bright sound that my father's heart is shredded.

A week later, they were married.

"Didn't your parents freak out?" Vince asked when my dad finished.

He shrugged. "A bit. They thought we were high."

"I figured they'd smoked some grass," Nana agreed. "When Matty came to not only introduce a guy I'd never heard of before but also to tell me they were getting married, I figured they were stoned off their asses."

"Language," my father said with a frown.

"Were you?" Vince asked.

"Not in the slightest," Mom said.

"That wasn't until the honeymoon," Dad said, eyebrows waggling.

"You brought this on yourself," I muttered to Vince.

He ignored me. He seemed focused, solely focused, on the two of them with such intensity I didn't think I wanted to know what was going on in his head. Though, from his expression, I had a pretty good idea. I didn't know how I felt about that. "And you both knew?" he asked. "You just knew?"

They nodded. "It hasn't always been easy," Mom said. "But nothing worth having ever really is."

And then Vince looked at me.

And, of course, I looked away.

WHEN someone says to you that they didn't mean to eavesdrop, chances are they probably did.

That being said, I totally didn't mean to eavesdrop. Seriously.

Vince was helping Mom in the kitchen while Dad and I sat with Nan in the backyard, shooting the shit. I protested initially, but Mom shooed us out of the kitchen, latching on to Vince and pulling him along with her. I looked to Dad for help, but he already had wrapped his arm around my neck and we trailed after Nana.

I tried not to think about what my mother was saying to Vince, but I feared the worst. That, any minute now, he'd come outside and tell me that it was so over, that my family was fucking nuts and he didn't know what he saw in me in the first place, and actually, he *hadn't* seen anything, he was actually just Freddy Prinze Junioring me.

I hate my imagination sometimes.

So, after ten minutes, I made the excuse I had to use the restroom. Both Nana and Dad rolled their eyes, but no one tried to stop me. I really did have to piss, but I figured I could also intervene in case Mom was going a little overboard.

But I shouldn't have worried. When I entered the house, I heard them laughing and talking about nothing of consequence while they did the dishes and put the food away, and I didn't want to disturb them if necessary, so I bypassed the kitchen and used the restroom at the other end of the house. It wasn't until I came back that I stopped, only because my mother said my name.

"Paul doesn't know, does he?" she asked him.

Ah hell.

"Know what?" He sounded confused.

"Who you are."

There was silence then, and it lasted long enough to become uncomfortable. I was about to walk into the kitchen when Vince spoke. "I don't know what you're… shit. You recognized me?"

"Your name sounded familiar," Mom said. "And you look like your dad. Larry met him once, a few years ago. When we met you yesterday, it wasn't that hard to put it together."

"Ah. No. Paul doesn't know."

"Okay." After a moment: "I'm sorry about your mother."

He sighed. "Yeah. Me too."

"Is that why you moved back? So you could be near… when? You know what, forgive me for being so rude. It's none of my business."

"It's okay. I just... it feels... weird... to talk about it."

"Why?"

"Because I haven't been good with my parents for a while." He sounded angry, the first time I'd ever heard him like that. It tore at me, like little claws against my skin. "If you know who I am, then you know that my parents didn't want anything to do with me back then. The election year is not the best time to come out when your father is a Republican running for office. Apparently it causes a *disruption* to the campaign."

"Well, that's some bullshit if you ask me," Mom said fiercely.

Vince snorted. "Language."

"So you moved back because she's sick?"

"Yeah. She's... she's in hospice care over at UMC. She was moved there a couple of weeks ago. It's supposed to be all hush-hush, given that no one wants to read about something so depressing on the news." The last part came out bitter.

"When was the last time you saw her?"

"Today."

Oh fucking hell, Vince.

"How did that go?"

"I told her and my dad about Paul."

My heart skipped a few beats in my chest.

"Did you?" Mom sounded pleased. "And what did they say?"

"That it's not possible to fall for someone so quickly. That life doesn't quite work that way."

"Do you believe that?"

"I don't know," he whispered. "I just...."

"What?" Mom asked kindly.

He was hesitant. "When you saw Larry for the first time... did you know?"

"Know that I'd be spending the rest of my life with him?"

"Yeah."

"No. No, I didn't. It was unrealistic. It wasn't possible. I forgot about him almost as soon as I'd left the restaurant."

"Oh." It was such a disappointed sound that my breath caught in my throat.

My mom continued: "But I knew the second time. When I ran over his foot."

"You did?" There was hope there, now.

"I did. To be honest, I was so freaked out that I didn't recognize him as the guy from the restaurant. All I could think about was how much Nana was going to kick my ass when she found out."

"But then?"

"But then I got so close to his face that I saw him." I could hear the smile in her voice. "I saw him for what he truly was. A beautiful, kind, loving man, and it took my breath away. So, while I may have not known then that it would be a lifetime, I at least knew I *wanted* it to be. Right then, I knew."

"Paul's...."

"Paul's not easy, Vince. He never has been. He's never had the confidence you have. He's never had the bravado. He's always been quiet. And shy. And a bit of a loner. But he is brave. He is oh so brave. Even though we tried to stop it as much as we could, he still got picked on for how he looked. How he acted. How he dressed. Other than Sandy, no one really knew what to make of him. He was too gay for the straight boys, too quiet for the girls. Sandy came along, this fierce little diva of a boy, and took him under his wing. I don't... I don't know what would have happened to him without Sandy. As much as a mother wants to be there for her son, as much as she wants to take away all the little hurts until everything is better again, there's no way I could have done it completely. Nor could his father. It took someone like Sandy to bring him out of his shell. He's gotten better. So much better than he used to be."

"He's the bravest person I know," Vince said without a trace of irony. "And he's kind. Do you know how kind your son is?"

Mom laughed. "I might know a thing or two about that. But he's humble about it, Vince. He doesn't want people making a big deal out of those little acts that he does. He wants them to be known, but not necessarily acknowledged."

"Why doesn't he know what he's worth? Can't he see he's worth more than all the rest of us combined?"

My eyes burned and I wanted to leave, but I couldn't. My feet felt stuck to the floor. He couldn't have been talking about me. He couldn't have been meaning me. He'd gotten me confused with someone else. He wasn't thinking right. He couldn't have meant me.

"I don't think he knows," my mother said slowly, "because other than us, I don't think there's been anyone to tell him."

"I will. I promise. I promise I will. Every day."

"Vince?"

"Yeah?"

"Do you care for my son?"

There was no hesitation. "With my whole heart."

"Why haven't you told him about your parents?"

He sighed again. "I didn't want to freak him out. I didn't want to have to lay all my crap on him all at once. There's something… there's something peaceful about being near him. It calms me down. It clears my head. With him, I don't have to worry about all the other bullshit that's going on. I don't have to wonder why I'm not smart enough, or why I'm not good enough. Paul doesn't care about that stuff. I'm not smart, Matty. I know that. I say dumb stuff sometimes, and most of the time, I don't know what I'm talking about. I don't even understand what Paul says half the time, but it doesn't matter to me because it doesn't matter to him. I think he likes me just the way I am, and I've never had that before. Not really. I don't have to be anyone else but myself with Paul, and I think that's okay with him."

No one had ever said such things about me before, not even Sandy. I didn't know how to take his words, because the sum of those parts made a picture of the complete faith he had in me. Or, at least that he *almost* had in me. He hadn't told me about his parents.

And as if my Mom knew that I was there and knew what I was thinking, she said, "You're going to need to tell him very soon."

"I know," he said quietly. "But I don't know how to."

"How long does she have?"

"A week. Maybe a little less."

"Oh, sweetheart. Is she in pain?"

He sniffed. "A bit. The meds help mostly. But she's aware. Her eyes are brighter than I've seen them in a long time. She's conscious and talking, which is more than I could have asked for. That may go away soon, but at least I'm able to hear her voice while I can, even if I don't agree with what she's saying all the time."

There was movement then, and I knew my mother had gone to him. It should have been me. It should have been me telling him that everything was going to be all right, whispering words of solace and peace in his ear. It should have been me, but I couldn't do it. I didn't know how.

"You'll have to tell him, Vince," my mom finally murmured. "You have to make sure he knows before he finds out some other way."

"I just don't want to drop all of this on him. I don't want him to see this shit if he doesn't have to. I want him to be my escape from all of it. I don't want to have to worry when I'm with him."

"And what happens when you can't escape it anymore?"

"I don't know."

"Just… think about it, okay? And if you need to talk, you let me know. Don't let Paul tell you that you can't call me. He needs to get used to you and me talking, don't you think?"

Vince laughed quietly. "How can any of this be real?" he said with bemused wonder.

Mom was quiet for a moment before answering. "Because sometimes it's about letting go of what your mind tells you and following what your heart shows you instead. That's how you know it will always be real."

CHAPTER 13
The Lair of the Queen, An Audience With The Homo Jock King

"DARLINGS," Helena purred when we arrived in her dressing room. "How lovely it is to see you here."

Vince looked around in awe, as if he'd never been inside a drag queen's sanctuary before. Then I realized he probably hadn't, because most people are not invited into the inner lair of a queen while she prepares to greet her subjects. From how she was dressed already, it appeared she'd already taped her cock and balls, so I was at least grateful for that. I didn't think I was ready for Vince to see my best friend turning from Sandy to Helena by grunting with his hands shoved down his spandex.

"Hi, Helena," Vince said somewhat shyly.

I rolled my eyes. "Dude. You know her."

"Yeah, but she's *Helena* now. I only know *him* as *Sandy*. There's a big difference."

Helena chuckled deeply. "Oh, sugar," she said to Vince. "It's so nice to finally meet a big strapping man such as yourself who understands the distinction." She trailed a gloved hand around his neck and kissed him on the cheek. He blushed brightly, but a smile grew on his face. For some reason, I felt like tackling a drag queen right then and there so she'd take her grubby fucking hands off my man.

I cleared my throat as they gazed lovingly into each other's eyes. "Do you guys want to go ahead and fuck and get it over with? I can definitely go sit with Daddy Charlie and allow you guys to have some time alone. I'll warn you, though, Vince. Sandy's balls have already been taped, so his erection will hurt."

"Don't listen to him," Helena said, her lips right near Vince's ear. "Paul's just jealous because all the boys think I'm pretty. Do you think I'm pretty, Vince?"

"Yes, ma'am," he said. "But I don't think I'm going to be able to look at you the same when we go to work on Monday. Oh, and I think Paul is prettier than you. No offense."

Helena laughed.

"Gross," I muttered even though I wanted to grin and break dance. Then I realized that doing somersaults on the floor is not considered break dancing, so I did nothing.

"Who's your daddy?" Vince asked me suspiciously.

"Uh, you are?" I said, bewildered. Were we at this stage already? I didn't know the etiquette of the proper response to answering such a question this early in the relationship.

He snorted. "Thanks. I think that might be hot. Sort of. I meant who's Daddy Charlie?"

"That'd be me," Charlie said as huffed up the stairs behind us. "And you are?" Then he saw who was asking, and he widened his eyes and started laughing. "Looks like Paul certainly had an interesting week," he said to Helena.

"He most certainly has. I told you at the show on Wednesday that our little Paulie was going to be just *full* of surprises. Turns out that Vince has an ass to die for and Paul just couldn't resist following it around everywhere." She winked at me. "Isn't that right, baby doll?"

Of course I sputtered. "I *didn't*… I don't even know… you hush your mouth… bike shorts… he was wearing *bike* shorts…."

Helena and Charlie shared a knowing look. "Our little boy is growing up so fast," Helena sniffed.

"I knew you liked my ass," Vince told me smugly.

"I got over it quickly," I lied through my teeth.

"I want to see what's got our Paul so twisted up in knots," Charlie said.

Vince immediately dropped his hand to the button on his jeans. Charlie and Helena grinned lecherously before I stepped in. "I don't think that's quite necessary," I said with a glare. "And do you just take off your pants for *anybody*?" I growled at Vince.

"Only for people who ask nicely," he said.

"You're a big, fat whore."

He leaned in and kissed me. "Not a very nice thing to say to your boyfriend."

"Blech."

"You got five minutes," Charlie said to Helena.

"You coming down to the floor tonight, sugar?" she asked me. "I promise I won't pull you on stage this time."

"He'll be down there," Vince said. "He's got to meet Darren tonight. He doesn't get to hide up here."

Helena beamed at Vince. "Oh, baby doll. How I adore you right now."

"I'm glad people talk about me like I'm not even here," I grumbled to Charlie.

"Boy, you lost the right to think for yourself over your shenanigans last weekend. You're lucky you weren't here on Wednesday when Helena told me what you were up to. I was planning on an ass beating that you'd never forget."

I grinned at him. "You promise, Daddy?"

He snorted. "Don't tempt me, boy. You're lucky Vince is up here right now with you. I wouldn't have believed you otherwise and your pants would be around your ankles and your butt would be smarting something awful."

"Did you guys used to date or something?" Vince asked. He was trying to keep his voice even, but I could hear the strain behind it. The smile had faded from his face, and he glanced between the two of us as if he could see something no one else could.

Charlie grinned evilly. "Oh, am I going to like *you*."

"Don't you encourage him," I scolded Charlie. "You're gonna end up getting me in trouble for something I haven't even done."

"Paul likes to be spanked," he told Vince.

"I do not!"

"Just take your big old hand and bring it down on that ass. It'll get nice and pink and he'll squeal for you like a little bitch. Give him some nice coloring to match his wall-face bruise."

"A home, Charlie. Remember that. I will put you in a home. With leaky roofs and an all-female nursing staff."

"They're just messing with you, sugar," Helena said to Vince. "Paul doesn't do stuff like spanking. His idea of kink is having a gang bang with six black guys who have names like D'Wayne and The Dominator."

"You guys are the poster children for why people shouldn't have friends," I muttered.

"That explains the big black dildo under his bed," Vince said thoughtfully.

Shocked silence. Helena slowly turned to me, eyes flashing. I glared at my traitorous boyfriend quickly before schooling my face. "That explains the big *what*, Paul?"

"I have no idea what he's talking about." I pretended I had something on my hands worth staring at intently.

"Boy, you holding out on us?" Charlie asked. He had this annoying little gleam in his eye.

"Paul has a box full of dongs under his bed," Vince explained, obviously proud of himself for being the world's biggest jerk. "I read in his diary that he uses them all the time and thinks about me."

"I don't think this is working out between us," I told him. "You and I want different things. It's not me, it's you."

"After our third date, Paul said I could use them on him," he told a rapt Helena and Charlie. "I have the whole conversation saved from when he texted me. Tonight is considered our third date. He's going to make so much sex face, it'll freeze that way."

"This isn't our third date!" I said with a scowl. And then, as an afterthought, "And I didn't say you could use them on me."

"Hospital, Santiago and the park, dinner with your parents, then gay bar," he counted off. "And yes, you did say I could use them on you. You were practically drooling when I told you that."

"The hospital wasn't a date!"

He shrugged. "I got to first base with you. I consider that a date."

"None of what is coming out of Vince's mouth is true," I growled. "Who are you going to believe? I mean, *really*?"

"I can't believe you write in a *diary*," Charlie guffawed.

"I can't believe you have sex toys!" Helena grinned. "My baby is all growed up and he's turned into a silicone slut!"

Vince walked over and stood in front of me. I glared at him as he kissed the tip of my nose. "I'm pretty funny," he said.

"Not even in the slightest," I pouted.

"You coming down with me?"

"Er. Argh."

"I'll take that as a yes."

"Vince...."

"Paul...."

"I'm not really the *meet*-people type. I'm more the... Quasimodo in the bell tower kind of guy."

"I don't know what that means."

"It means he's being a whiny little bitch," Charlie said.

I sighed. "Thanks, Daddy. That's exactly what I meant."

"Then let me say it a different way," Vince said. "Instead of asking you, I'm telling you. You *are* coming down to meet my friends." He paused and then broke. "Right?"

He looked at me with such earnestness I couldn't say no. I had a feeling that was going to be a common event. "Yeah, I'm going down. Just give me a few minutes, okay?"

You would have thought I'd gifted him another bicycle with the way he attacked my face. I almost forgot that we had an audience as he sucked on my tongue. I was finally able to break away before I jacked him off in front of an old man and a drag queen. There gets to be a certain point where once you get going, you just can't stop, and he'd brought me close there twice in four hours. "You gonna let me stay the night at your house tonight?" he whispered in my ear, flicking his tongue out and grazing it just once.

I didn't even allow myself time to think. "Yeah."

"Good answer," he said, giving me another dirty kiss before backing away.

Helena and Charlie stared at me.

"What?" I tried to ask defiantly, knowing I was beet red.

Charlie shrugged and spoke for the both of them. "Diaries, dildos, and making out with a hot guy who apparently is now your boyfriend? Who are you and what have you done with Paul?"

"I don't have a diary," I said weakly.

"Can friends borrow dildos?" Helena asked Charlie. "Or is that a sex toy no-no?"

"As long as it's cleaned, I don't see the problem."

"I want the big black one," she told me. "But clean it first."

"So gross," I shuddered.

"It's showtime, girlie," Charlie said. "Get your pretty ass in gear."

"Walk me down the stairs?" she asked Vince, batting her fake eyelashes at him.

"Sure." He glanced back at me. "I'll give you five minutes. If you're not down there, I'm coming to get you and making you go down."

"I'm a grown-up," I snapped at him. "I'll come down when I damn well please."

"Five minutes, Paul." He grabbed Helena's hand and led her toward the door.

"You sure know how to work him already," I heard her say. "You got to grab him by the balls if you want to get him to do something."

"Oh, I plan to," was his reply.

The door closed behind them.

"Fuck," I whispered.

Charlie burst out laughing. "Boy, you surprise the royal hell out of me sometimes. I didn't think you had it in you."

"I don't know if I do," I said truthfully. "Vince kind of wore me down until I couldn't say no anymore."

"Yeah, I bet that was *such* a hardship on you, looking as he does. It's a good thing you decided to hit him with your car."

"I *didn't*! He ran into *my* door!" When were people going to believe me?

"Uh-huh. You should have just asked him out if you wanted to get his attention."

"I didn't want his attention."

"Bullshit. You're just as head over heels as he is. The difference is you hide it better underneath all the remarkable bluster you have sometimes. But since I'm your daddy, you can't bullshit me. I've known you for far too long to get fooled by you, Paul Auster. Vince may not see it yet, but you can't pull the wool over my eyes."

I sputtered at him for a good minute or two until he went over to his perch on the balcony to man the spotlight and the camera. I took my usual place beside him, but this time, instead of watching Helena, I immediately searched for Vince. It didn't take long to find him standing with the same jocky boys he'd been with the week before. I shouldn't have been surprised to see him standing next to Darren Mayne. And I probably shouldn't have been surprised to see Darren wrap his arm around his shoulder, his mouth close to Vince's ear as he said something to him. The drag show hadn't yet started, but it was noisy enough that I couldn't make out what was being said. All I knew is that Darren seemed to be standing *way* too fucking close to Vince, and Vince was doing absolutely nothing to push him away.

Darren Mayne. What a lot of people might not realize is that gay bars are exactly like high school, in that there are cliques. Tucson isn't big enough to have multiple gay bars to cater to specific groups of homos. Instead, they all converge on this one place. Sometimes they mingle with one another, but mostly they stick to themselves within their own groups.

You've got your bears, your Muscle Maries. You've got the twinks, the ravers, the leather crowd. You've got the models, the lesbians (who, to be fair, have their own subgroups, but since I don't have a vagina, I'm not privy to them). There are the queens, the transsexuals, and those random guys who just like wearing skirts. There are daddies and their boys, masters and their slaves. You've got the older and the younger, the middle age. There's even a small group that comes out every now and then consisting of married couples with children, though they're usually exhausted and leave by nine o'clock.

And then you've got the jocks, of which Darren Mayne is the king. I'd never spoken to Darren before, aside from the usual, "Sorry, sir, I totally didn't mean to be breathing your air even though you seem like a big asshole," that I would mumble under my breath every time we passed each other. There were a couple of times we'd pass each other and he'd catch my eye and I'd be convinced that he was about to say something, but either he thought better of it or it was my imagination. I didn't know what possible thing Darren Mayne would have to say to *me,* so I figured it was always me misinterpreting.

But regardless, he was the king of the jocky gays, his little muscled boys around him like they'd just walked off one of those gay college porn sites that I've never, *ever* subscribed to (you know, the ones where the cookie-cutter hairless toned frat boys sit next to each other on a random couch and go through the cringe-worthy banter with the camera man who tries to convince the audience that the two dudes both have girlfriends and that they've *never* tried anything before with another guy, only to watch them proceed to fuck like bunnies. Very, very *experienced* bunnies at that).

Darren himself was probably around the same age as Vince, which put him slightly younger than me. And of course he had great blond hair that did whatever he wanted it to do. A killer body that looked like he spent every waking moment in the gym. He had a smile that could make your insides feel a bit loose and a great laugh, from the one time I'd actually heard it. I'd always heard that he was a bit of a slut (those jocky college boys tended to be like that), but he was never cruel, at least that I could see, and even more, he was always at Helena's shows. Thinking back on it, I couldn't remember the last time he *hadn't* been there on a Wednesday or a Saturday, grinning at her while slipping her fives and tens rather than the usual one-dollar bills she got for tips.

But now I hated his stupid fucking face because he was standing way too fucking close to my fucking boyfriend who wasn't doing a fucking thing to move back. They looked awfully chummy standing next to each other, their muscles bunching together like they were going to be sitting on some couch in their near future, talking about how their girlfriends didn't know they were there, that they'd never really thought about doing anything with another guy, and then deep-throating each other like they'd been sucking cock all their lives.

And, of course, right then was the moment Vince obviously chose to say something about me, because he pointed up toward the balcony and they both glanced my way. I'm pretty sure they saw me with my crazy "I want to murder you because I'm weirdly jealous" face going on. I attempted to school it quickly and looked away, but not before I saw the flicker of confusion go across Vince's face and the amused little smile on Darren's. The fucker.

Ever-watching, Charlie hadn't missed this exchange at all. "Give him a *little* credit," he chided me. "I'm pretty sure he's not bored with you yet."

"Or maybe I'm the other woman," I said forlornly. "Or maybe he and Darren have been together for twelve years and I was meant to be a present for Darren's birthday and we're going to have a threesome and then they'll throw me to the curb like a box of unwanted newborn kittens before they go back to their lives, where they're planning on adopting a Croatian baby named Braslav."

"Sometimes I wonder if you should be on medication," Charlie said. "It can't be healthy to have you thinking all by yourself without some kind of pharmaceutical intervention."

The DJ proceeded to announce Helena, and Charlie trained the spotlight on the curtains while flicking on the video camera. Before she started, he leaned over to me and said, "You're being summoned."

I looked down and saw Vince crooking a finger at me. I thought about shaking my head, but Charlie must have known that I was acting a bit stupid because he kicked my stool and knocked me over. I almost fell to the floor, but instead gracefully stumbled, making it sound like an obese herd of elephants had just been spooked by lions and was trampling up on the balcony to get away. People below looked up as if they expected the roof to come caving down on them, which, to be fair, it probably almost did. Charlie didn't even have the common decency to look slightly repentant, instead just smirking and waving me away.

So I started toward the Stairs Of Doom which would lead me to one of the most horrifying experiences of any young gay man's life: meeting the friends of the new boyfriend. By the time I had reached the halfway point, I'd convinced myself that not only were Darren and Vince butt buddies, but that they had orgies all the time with all the jocky pretending-to-be-straight-to-be-slightly-more-appealing boys and I *really* was getting Freddie Prinze Juniored and this was going to be the moment that I would stand in the middle of the dance floor, the period ghost up on the balcony, and blood would rain down on top of me like I was Carrie at the prom. Then they would all point and laugh at me, and Vince would be at the front, getting handed money by Darren because *he* won their bet and then they would start blowing each other and Darren would have the world's biggest cock and I would sit there and watch, having been menstruated on all over my head.

Pretty much convinced meeting new people was the worst idea ever in my current state, I decided to make a run for the exit as soon as I passed through the door. I would tell Vince later that I saw a robbery in progress and attempted to thwart it, only to end up being kidnapped and held against my will in an Islamic prison, which would be the reason he wouldn't hear from me for a few days. Plan set, I opened the door.

Vince stood on the other side.

"Oh sweat balls," I muttered, looking longingly at the front of the bar.

"Going somewhere?" he asked, slightly amused.

"No, dear," I said. "Just coming down to see you like I promised. I'm super excited about meeting Darren."

"Good," he said cheerfully, grabbing my arm. "Glad to hear you are so ready for this."

"I was being *sarcastic*," I snapped at him, trying to pull from his grasp as he weaved his way through the crowd. Helena did her patented backward cartwheel look-how-special-I-am move, and the crowd roared around me. Please. If only they knew how long it took her to perfect that and how much I had to help and how much of *her* sweat I got on me, they wouldn't be cheering. They would be fleeing in terror.

I tried to relay to the people we were passing that I was being forced somewhere against my will in hopes that one would step in and save me. However, apparently Good Samaritan laws do not apply in gay clubs as no one stepped forward to risk their life for me.

I smashed into the back of Vince when he came to a sudden stop in front of me. I thought about burying my face in his back and hiding behind him but figured he didn't want his friends to know he was dating the world's most gaping vagina, so I steeled my balls a bit and looked up at him when he brought me to his side, dropping his arm on my shoulder. He leaned over and nuzzled my neck. "It'll be fine," he said for only me to hear. "You'll see."

Somehow, I managed to keep my eyes from rolling. I put on my best smile, preparing to relay to the group that I was just *thrilled* to meet them all, when I realized it was only Darren standing in front of me. The rest of Vince's jock posse was gone, as if they'd never been there at all. I could only think about Darren with his arm wrapped around Vince's shoulders, like he thought he had every right to be there. I thought I had every right to make him live the rest of his life as an amputee.

"Paul," Vince said above the music. "This is Darren. Darren, this is my boyfriend, Paul."

I held out my hand and Darren looked at it for a moment as if deciding whether I had scabies and running chances in his head of getting it himself if he touched me. It was about to get awkward when he reached out and shook my hand. "Nice to meet you," I mumbled.

"What?" he said, raising his voice.

Hurray. This is weird already. "I said nice to meet you!" And of course, as I shouted this as loud as I could to be heard, there was a pause in the music and my voice echoed over the silent club like I was some screeching capuchin monkey who had just discovered masturbation. Everyone in the club (and most likely on Earth) turned to look at me.

"That was my distant acquaintance Paul, everyone!" Helena said into the mic. The music picked up again and she rolled back into her routine.

Vince chuckled quietly in my ear. "Still haven't found that time machine yet," he said. "I'll keep a list for you of all the things you'll want to undo."

I glared at him.

"Nice to meet you too," Darren said, smirking at me like I was the funniest piece of shit he'd ever seen. "I wish I could say I'd heard a lot about you, but that would be a lie."

Oh, there goes the chance for the three-way. Maybe they're a monogamous couple and Vince just sprung this on him out of the blue. "Oh!" I said back loudly. "That's... I don't know what that is."

"No, it's fine," he said, as if trying to reassure me there was a chance it could have been *not* fine. "I'm just surprised that Vince jumped into this so... quickly."

"That's what *I* told him."

"It's a good thing I don't listen to either one of you," Vince said happily. "God knows where I'd be then."

I rolled my eyes right as Darren did, and I felt a strange kinship with him, at least for a second, that we could both be exasperated by Vince. Darren caught my eye for a moment and a small smile formed on his face. It was either genuine or calculating, and since I didn't know him, I couldn't tell which. The next words out of his mouth didn't bode well for the latter. "Hey, Vince. Why don't you go buy us a round of drinks. I'll keep Paul company here."

Don't leave. Don't leave. Don't leave.

"Sure! Paul, what do you want?"

To not be left here with the Homo Jock King. "SKYY vodka cranberry is fine. With a lime."

"And I'll have a beer," Darren said, obviously way manlier than me. "No lime."

Asshole.

"Be right back." Vince leaned in and kissed me briefly, then took off through the crowd.

Darren and I sized each other up for a moment, and I realized only then just how big he was. Vince and I were almost the same height, but Darren had to have at least three inches on me. He was also very *wide*, built like a tree trunk. A very intimidating tree trunk with pale-blue eyes that were more shrewd than I cared for. He was all hard lines and planes, and I felt soft and squishy inside *and* out standing next to him.

He looked away for a moment to watch Helena perform a complicated series of kicks and twists, as if he knew her routine and when that part was coming up. Helena had worked months on getting it just right, and it was a sight to behold. His eyes softened a little bit as he watched, and I had this strange moment where I wondered if he liked what he was watching before the look disappeared and he turned back to me.

"So," he said.

"So," I replied.

"You and Vince, huh?"

"Yeah, I guess."

He moved closer to me so we could hear each other above the music. I wanted to take a step back to keep space between us, but he wouldn't allow it, crowding me near the wall. "I've never known Vince to have a boyfriend," he said.

"Oh? That's... cool." *With the reception I'm getting from you, I wonder why.*

"And then he disappears for a few days and comes back with bruises and the biggest grin on his face."

"I'm not abusive," I said stupidly.

He laughed, but he didn't sound like he thought it was funny. "Didn't say you were. Though I'd appreciate it if you didn't hit him with your car again."

"I *didn't*—" It was no use. Forever I would be defined as *that* guy. "Fine. I won't ever hit him with my car again. Next time I want to get his attention, I'll ask him for it."

"Vince isn't smart," he said suddenly. "Not like I am and not like I'm assuming you are."

This caused unbidden fury to roil through me. "He's perfectly smart," I growled at him. "You better not be calling him an idiot."

Darren seemed amused as he held up his hands to placate me. "I'm not," he said. "I'm just saying... he doesn't think like most people. He needs to have people watch out for him, otherwise he ends up getting hurt. He hasn't had that a lot in his life."

"And you're saying you think I'm going to hurt him? No offense, but you don't know me and I'd really like to tell you to go fuck yourself." *And, um. I'd really like to take that back but I'm trying to be intimidating here. So, sorry. Didn't really mean it.*

"You've got some balls, don't you?" I couldn't tell if that impressed him or pissed him off.

"Last time I checked."

"What do you want from him?"

This baffled me. "What? What are you talking about? I don't want anything from him. He's the one that came after *me*."

"If you don't want anything, then why are you here?"

This pissed me off even more. I was tired of getting questioned. I was tired of doubting myself. But you know what? Out of all of it, I was tired of having it sound like I wasn't good enough, like I didn't deserve to breathe the same air as the homo jock royalty, that I didn't deserve to have Vince come after me like he did. I'd had enough.

"Look," I said with a scowl. "You don't know me. I sure as shit don't know you. But I *do* know I don't have to explain a goddamn thing to you. So you can stand there and look all badass and like a big, fat fucking jerk, but you're not going to chase me away. I'm sorry if you want to fuck him, but you can't because he's *mine*. He picked *me,* and sure as shit, I'm not going to back down just because you're having this little bitch fit of yours. Go bench press a llama, you fucking 'roid queen, and stop being an asshole." I quickly reviewed my words and thought it went quite well (except for the llama thing. And the part where I insulted him. And the part where I sounded slightly douchey).

His eyes went comically wide. "Do you talk to Vince like that?" he asked.

"He was annoying for a little bit," I admitted. "I thought he was trying to play a joke on me by asking me out so much."

Darren shook his head. "Vince doesn't do shit like that, Paul."

"Well, I know that *now*." And I did. For the most part.

"Look, I don't think you understand. Vince doesn't pursue *anyone*. Usually, it's all these shitty fucking guys trying to get up on his nuts for a good fuck, then dropping him as soon as they're done using him. He tries not to get his hopes up anytime someone new comes along, but he keeps getting shat on, and I fucking hate it. They like how he looks, they like how his body moves, but they don't like it when he talks because of the dumb shit he says."

"I like it when he talks," I said. Which was weird, because I didn't know when that started happening.

"Good, because you're the first thing he's been excited about for a long time," Darren says. "And I have no problem telling you that if you fuck this up, I will break you in half."

"Really?" I asked as I caught him glancing over at Helena again. "You do that and I won't introduce you to a certain drag queen you seem to be eyeing."

He stiffened. "Go fuck yourself," he rumbled at me, not meeting my eyes.

Oh, Sandy's going to shit himself silly. "I don't want to hurt him," I said seriously. "I promise you that. But…."

"But what?"

I shook my head. "Never mind. It doesn't matter."

"Of course it matters. You wouldn't have said it if it didn't. Don't be a dick, Paul. What is it?"

I hesitated. "You've known Vince a long time?"

He eyed me warily. "You could say that."

I wanted to know what he meant, but didn't ask. "You know his… parents?"

"Uh. You could say that."

"I know who they are."

He hung his head. "He said he hadn't told you. That you hadn't figured it out."

"He didn't. But I know."

"You can't be mad at him for that."

"I'm not. I... will he tell me? When it happens? You know, with his mom?"

Darren watched me for a moment before answering, as if trying to gauge my sincerity and trying to choose his words before speaking. "He trusts you," he finally said. "I don't know how it happened or why it happened so fast, but he does. I think he will. He's not going to let you think it'll hurt him, but it will. Maybe not destroy him, because there's too much bad shit between them. But it's still going to hurt. He's going to need you, I think. He'll need me too, but I think you're going to be the one he leans on. If you let him."

"Okay." I hoped he was right.

"Hey, Paul? You're okay, you know that?" He was looking at me with something that bordered on respect. Homo jocks were so confusing. They were supposed to be pounding beers and twinks, not talking to me.

But he was right, so I nodded. "I am pretty awesome."

He laughed, glancing over at the bar to check on Vince. His eyes hardened quickly and the smile slid from his face. I followed his line of sight and saw Vince up against the bar, drinks in front of him, another guy bent over near him to speak in his ear. I bristled immediately when I saw it was hottie Bear Dude from last weekend, the one that had been grinding up against Vince on the dance floor. Bear Dude was trying to get pretty chummy with Vince again, crowding up against him, his hand on Vince's bicep, squeezing it tightly so that I could see the dimples in Vince's skin. It was a possessive grip, and the man's stance screamed *mine*. I tensed, not able to stop the flood of doubt washing over me.

"Wait," Darren breathed next to me. "Just watch."

I didn't want to watch. I wanted to push my way through the bar and piss in a circle around Vince so that everyone else stayed the fuck away from him. My skin crawled a bit when Vince laughed at something Bear Dude said, and Bear Dude leaned back, smirking at him as if in victory. Bear Dude nodded his head toward the door, wanting Vince to leave with him. Vince shook his head and pointed back to where we stood and said something in return. This appeared to piss Bear Dude off because he frowned at Vince and tugged on his arm. Vince took a step back and shook his head again. Bear Dude turned and left.

Vince must have felt us watching him because he glanced over our way and saw us staring at him. His gaze immediately went to me, and he jerked his head in the direction Bear Dude had disappeared and rolled his eyes. Then he brought his hand up to the side of his head and made a pistol shape and committed fake suicide, blowing his imaginary brains out and collapsing on the top of the bar. Then he rose up and winked at me. He picked up our drinks and started moving out back to us. Through his little performance, not once had he looked guilty, like he'd been caught doing something wrong.

"He's different," Darren said near my ear. "He's not like you or me, or anyone else for that matter."

"His mime skills are obviously going to waste in the insurance industry," I said, unable to think clearly.

Darren cuffed the back of my head as if he'd been doing it for years. "Don't be a jerk," he scolded me. "You know as well as I do that the thought of doing anything with that guy never even crossed his mind. He doesn't think like that. Remember that, Paul. Remember that and he'll give you everything."

"Why haven't you gone after him then, if he's so great?" I asked, honestly curious.

Darren's eyes went instantly dark. "That doesn't matter," he muttered and looked away.

But it did. In the end, it did.

CHAPTER 14
I Am So Fucking Screwed (Figuratively And Literally)

WE DIDN'T stay long at the bar. There was something odd building in the air around Vince and me, sort of like a strange static charge that caused the hairs on the back of my neck to stand on end and the palms of my hands to feel itchy. Vince kept shooting these hot little glances over at me, catching my eyes for longer and longer while I tried to maintain a conversation with Darren. I tried not to flush under his gaze, but it became more and more impossible as he watched me for longer periods of time.

And then the touching began.

At first it was nothing major. Just his hand at the base of my spine, his thumb pressing slightly to let me know it was there. A bit of brief pressure, the scrape of a thumbnail through the shirt I wore, and then it was gone.

The second time it happened, he waited until I started to take a drink of the cocktail he'd gotten for me. Again he put his hand on my lower back, but this time, he pointed his fingers down toward my ass, the angle of his arm slightly awkward. I felt the tip of his middle finger lift the hem of my shirt and graze against the skin of my back. I choked on my drink, cranberry juice dripping down my chin. I mumbled an apology as I used my arm to wipe my face. Vince dropped his hand, and I refused to look at him. Darren didn't seem to notice.

And on it went. There would be a grip on my arm as Vince tugged me to the back patio, biting his fingers into my skin, part of me relishing the pressure, another part wanting it to stop immediately before I sprouted wood right then.

He would slide his hand down my arm when it became impossible to walk side by side, slipping fingertips along my forearm, my wrist, my palm until his fingers would catch mine, pressing our hands together as he led me through the crowd.

We reached the patio outside, and conversations were happening all around us, voices running together until they were just a wall of noise that I couldn't separate into single words. Vince kept glancing back at me as he pushed his way through the crowd, a little smile on his face, his eyes narrowed with something I couldn't quite place. I didn't know where Darren had gone, only that he was no longer with us, and I didn't know where Helena was, only that her show was over and the people around us moved and swayed and danced and writhed.

Vince found a dark little corner, near a set of stacked chairs, away from the crowd, away from the noise. It only took him a moment before he had me pressed up against the wall, putting his hands on either side of my head, standing so close that I could feel his breath on my face, but no part of his body touching mine. I tried to control my breathing so it wouldn't seem like I was panting, but that was exactly what I was doing.

I opened my mouth to speak—to say what, I didn't know—but it came out as a croak, a low noise that sounded as if I groaned. Vince quirked his lips, trying to become a smile, and I became fascinated by his lower lip, how full it looked, how it had tasted in my mouth, how plump it had felt as I rolled it between my teeth. His tongue came out, a flash of pink against a darker red, wetting his lips. I saw the hint of teeth, strong and white. He shifted his right hand slightly behind my head, scraping his fingers along the brick of the building, the sound like a roar in my ears.

I opened my mouth again. "So," I said.

"So," he said, his voice deeper than I'd heard it before, like a rasp.

I swallowed thickly. I couldn't think of anything else to say. I felt like I *should* say something, *anything* to fill the charged silence between us, but nothing came to mind, and I was afraid if I started babbling, I'd never be able to stop. I tended to do that when I was drunk, nervous, or turned on out of my fucking mind, and I was two out of three, which did not bode well for coherent conversation.

Fortunately for me (I think), Vince didn't seem to be in the mood to talk. I could feel the heat of his body so close to mine, but I didn't push for those last few inches that would have him pressed against me. It was already a warm night, and I felt sweat trickle down the back of my neck into the collar of my shirt.

He leaned forward then, still pressing his hands against the wall. He went to the side, his cheek barely scraping against mine, the grate of his stubble against my smooth cheek. His breath was on my ear, but he didn't take it further, just stayed there, breathing in and out. Then he pressed his nose against my neck and breathed me in. Our shoulders knocked together, his chest against mine as he breathed in, separating as he exhaled.

He found the patch of skin under my ear that drives me up the fucking wall. I stifled the groan that threatened to rise but could do nothing about the way my jaw grew tight, the way my blood thrummed just under the surface. He sucked on the skin, hard enough that I knew it'd leave a mark. I should have been somewhat horrified that I was a thirty-year-old man receiving a hickey in the back of a gay club while people milled only feet away, but I couldn't be bothered. I was too far gone under the sensation of his lips latched onto my neck, the scrape of his teeth, the press of his tongue. He leaned back and inspected his work, looking darkly pleased with himself. He took his left hand and rubbed his thumb over the mark, the slight burn growing stronger with the caress.

I'd never been so fucking hard in my life. His systematic breakdown of all my defenses was leaving me somewhat breathless. I was never one for public displays of any kind of affection, and the fact that he had me pressed up against a wall for everyone to see caused my stomach to twist. But even that emotion was overrun by the hot pleasure I was taking from him, the perverse idea that everyone was watching him fuck with my head, that they could all see my arousal. My dilated pupils. The quick breaths. The shaking of my hands. The way I craned my neck to give him better access to study his mark. I wanted everyone to see. I wanted everyone to know.

Keeping his right hand behind my head, he took his left and gripped my face, his palm against my chin, his fingers splayed out across my face. He squeezed gently and leaned forward and kissed me. I tried to respond to the touch, but he pulled away. Then he kissed me again and pulled away. And again.

And it was about that time that I realized that I wanted to fuck. I wanted to fuck like I'd never fucked before, and I wanted to do it now. I was done with gentle touches and wicked games. I couldn't help but snarl in his hand. I reached out and gripped his waist, spinning us until we'd traded places, his back against the wall, me standing in front of him. But I wasn't some fucking jerk who dragged out foreplay. Forgetting where I was and *who* I was, I pressed up against him, grinding my dick into his, marveling at the fact that he was just as hard as I was. He moaned, but I caught it in a kiss, letting it cross into me as I sucked on his tongue, chasing it with my own. If I wasn't careful, I was going to shoot right there in my jeans, something I'd never done before.

"Wanna get out of here?" I asked as I pulled away from his mouth.

"Why, Paul," he laughed, sounding out of breath, "I don't know what kind of boy you take me for."

Feeling daring, I said, "One who is about to get very, very lucky."

He grinned. "Oh? Is that so?"

"That is so."

"Well, far be it for me to say no to getting lucky."

"You don't seem like the type to say no to that." I winced inwardly as I realized how that sounded. Calling someone a slut is not sexy talk. I had a feeling that it was about to get awkward.

He arched an eyebrow. "Is that your way of seducing me? Compliments?"

"That's not really what I meant to say." The sexiness was leaving very quickly. "What I meant to say was that I like being pressed up against you."

He chuckled. "Do you?"

I scowled. "You're mocking me, aren't you?"

"Sort of." He leaned in and kissed me again, really just a peck. Like we were friends. The sexiness was almost gone.

"That's great," I sighed, starting to take a step back.

But he stopped me before I could. He grabbed me around my waist and pulled me back into him until were pressed together head to toe. Being almost the same height had its advantages, especially when I could tell he still had a hard dick. "Tell you what we're going to do," he said, his forehead against mine, a wicked curl to his lips. "We're going to leave here. We're going to go back to my apartment since it's closer. And then I'm going to fuck you through the mattress. Or through the wall. I haven't decided yet. Maybe we'll do both. That sound okay with you, Paul?"

And the sexiness returned rather quickly with that pronouncement, and I spoke before I could think. "That sounds awesome. Let's go do that—"

"Paul Auster, hiding in a corner pressing against some sexy man? As I live and breathe, I never thought I'd see the day."

"Oh sweat balls," I groaned, not wanting to turn around and see Helena's smirk.

"If either one of your hands is down the other's pants, I ask that you refrain from continuing your jack-off sesh, at least for the moment. Afterwards, you may continue with my blessing. And my participation, if necessary. I'm sure Vince has always wanted to try the queen-sized version."

Vince chuckled as I growled. "No jack-off sesh," he said. "Not yet."

Once I was sure I wouldn't stab anyone in the thigh with my erection, I turned and glared at Helena, who watched me with undisguised amusement, a red riding crop in one hand, slapping it against the other. She was dressed for her rodeo dominatrix routine, complete with these killer black thigh boots that zipped up the sides and had spurs and sparkly fringe. She gave me a quick once-over before her eyes landed on my neck. "Paul? Darling?"

"Yes?"

"You seem to have a hickey."

I blushed, lifting my hand to cover the spot. "That's not a hickey," I told her. "I burned myself on my hair curler trying to curl my neck hairs before we came out."

"It's a hickey," Vince assured her. "I gave it to him."

She eyed him. "Did you now? Impressive, considering I don't think Paul's ever had a hickey in his life. Disrupts his perfectly ordered world. My, oh my. The tongues shall be wagging at work on Monday."

Showing up to work on Monday with a hickey on my neck was not the best idea in the world, until I thought about that slut Tad seeing it. Then it felt like a badge of honor and I wanted Vince to give them to me all over my face until it looked like I had been beaten by tiny fists.

"You boys taking off soon?" she asked with a knowing look.

"We're getting out of here now," Vince said, stepping away from the wall and grabbing my hand. "I still have to give Paul his birthday present."

"Is that what they call it nowadays?" Helena asked. "Hopefully your present is big and wrapped."

"Are you really giving me a safe-sex lecture disguised as innuendo?" I asked incredulously.

"Aren't I fabulous?" She reached out and rubbed the riding crop against my face, then dragged it along Vince's. "I just want to make sure my baby dolls are playing it safe. Did you know that, if need be, you could slice open a sandwich baggie to use as a dental dam?"

I gaped at her. "Please don't ever say anything like that to me ever again."

"Do you like to get rimmed, Vince?"

"Please don't answer that question in public," I begged him.

"You know, for someone who was just rutting against a wall, you are somewhat of a prude, sugar."

"Sometimes," Vince said with a shrug. "Depends on who is doing it." Then he gave me a meaningful glance that could not be interpreted in any other way other than he would be totally okay if I tongued his butt. When one receives such a visual cue, one either runs with it or opens and closes ones mouth like a fish dying on dry land. Guess which one I did.

He leaned in and kissed me with his filthy, filthy mouth. "I'm going to go find Darren and say good-bye," he said. "Be right back."

Helena and I watched him go because it was such an awesome view. "Baby doll, I do believe you're going to get plowed like a field around planting time," she observed succinctly. "Gonna get seeded, that's for damn sure."

"Farming metaphors are not attractive," I snapped at her.

"Don't be jealous of my wit."

"I don't think jealous is the right word."

"You okay, sugar?"

"Yes. No. Fuck! I don't know!" Now that Vince was out of my sight, I was starting to panic a bit. "We're about to go have sex!"

Helena grinned at me. "Usually that's a cause for celebration. Or, at the very least, a modicum of happiness."

"What if he wants to do it with the lights on?" I asked her, the scenarios turning horrifically in my mind. "With my shirt off?"

"Pretty sure that's what sex is."

"Have you *seen* my naked body?"

"A few times."

"And have you seen *his*? Wait, don't answer that."

"I can imagine what it looks like." She licked her lips. "And I have a very active imagination."

I glared at her. "Then you know he's all big and hot and ripped and muscular and sexy and hot."

"That's quite a list of adjectives."

"And then there's me."

"Do you want some more adjectives? How about neurotic?"

"I'm being serious! He's going to want to get naked and when he does, he'll be all like, 'Oh, hey, look at me. I just came from the gym and my abs are so rock hard and perfect and I have thighs of steel.' And then *I'll* get naked and be all like, 'Oh hey, look at me. I just came from Denny's and I look like I swallowed a baby.'"

"Well, if you are already thinking about swallowing babies, at least you're on the right track," she pointed out. Like a jerk.

"Helena!"

"Paul!"

"You're not helping."

"What do you want me to do?" she snapped. "I suppose I could say that Vince probably has a pretty good idea what you look like under there and he wants you anyway. I could tell you it doesn't matter what you look like under there because you're perfect just the way you are. I could tell you that out of everyone in the world, Vince has chosen you to fall in love with, though sometimes I wonder if it's going to be worth it for him in the end, given how you're doing nothing but bitching and moaning and trying to find ways to talk yourself out of the good that is right in front of you. I could tell you all of that, but then I would just be repeating myself because I've told you that *time* and *time* again. So, instead, I'll just tell you to get over yourself before you fuck up the best thing that has ever happened to you and go get fucking laid. You get me?"

"Dude," I said in awe. "You are like a fucking Amazonian princess right now."

She was pleased. "Really? I was trying to be pretty scary."

"I was very scared. Like, quaking in my boots scared. And I'm not even wearing boots."

"Good."

"I'm scared. For real."

She sighed. "Don't be. You're going to rock his world. Just make sure to watch your teeth around his balls."

I was scandalized and I let it show, but I had run out of excuses. "Will you let Wheels out for me tonight?" I asked in a quiet voice.

She leaned over and gave me a sticky kiss on my cheek. "Of course, baby doll. I'll just take him home with me, how about that?"

"Okay."

"Stop looking like you're going to your death. Think about his penis in your man pussy and smile, for fuck's sake."

Before I could even think of a retort, the crowd parted and Vince walked through like he was some hot version of Moses.

"You ready?" he asked me with a grin.

I nodded.

"I was just telling Paul here that he needs to press against your taint right before you come," Helena said. "It'll make you jizz that much harder. So make sure you let him know right before you blow so he can push it real good."

"And that's our cue to leave," I said, grabbing Vince by the hand and pulling him away.

"I'll make sure he does it and let you know what happens," he called back to her, which caused me to almost trip and fall flat on my face.

"Have fun getting dicked, Paul!" she shouted as loud as she could. Everyone around us stopped talking to each other and started clapping as I pushed my way through toward the rear exit. Wolf whistles followed us, and a few people reached down and swatted our asses as we walked by. I kept my head down, my eyes at the ground in front of me, refusing to look up as apparently Helena was the Queen Bitch of the world and felt the need to announce my business to everyone (though, a small, quiet part of me didn't have a problem with reminding me that I'd literally just been almost fucking Vince up against the wall like I was a bitch in heat. I hated that small, quiet part).

We got outside and onto the street before I looked up again.

"You ready?" Vince asked. He pulled my hand up and kissed my knuckles.

Since running screaming in the opposite direction seemed off the table, I nodded.

WE DIDN'T say much on the way back to his apartment. I didn't know what he was thinking, and I didn't want to ruin anything by saying something stupid, so I kept my mouth shut. I tried to turn off my brain so I couldn't even think, but that was easier said than done. So instead, I focused on his hand still holding onto mine and the warm desert air flowing through my hair from the rolled-down window.

His apartment was more of a condo, really, with big picture windows at the front that exposed the living room. I'd only been inside briefly, earlier today, when I'd followed him so he could put his new bike in a back bedroom before we left for the bar. It was sparsely set up, just a couch and a flat screen in the living room, boxes still piled up in a corner that he hadn't gotten around to unpacking yet. I'd made fun of him for living that way until he reminded me that it was hard to bend over and unpack things after you'd been hit by a car. I'd looked for photos, but had seen none. His parents weren't anywhere that I had seen.

I wondered about Vince then, how that would affect the evening's calisthenics, if it was even still going that far. Then I remembered I still had a black eye and a reddened nose from my wall face-punch the day before and didn't think that could be remotely attractive. Helena's warning voice shot through my head and I pushed her away.

Vince let me in through the front door and closed it after we'd walked through. He leaned against it, crossing his arms over his chest. And watched. And waited.

I didn't know what to do, so I tried to mirror his stance up against the opposite wall, but I almost fell down while trying to stand still for, like, two seconds. Vince didn't say a thing. I patted my hands against my thighs. Vince quirked an eyebrow. I tried to name all fifty states in alphabetical order. Vince uncrossed his arms. *Alabama, Alaska, Arizona, Arkansas.* Vince stood up straight. *Delaware, Florida, Georgia.* He brought his big hands to the hem of his shirt and pulled it up, revealing miles and miles of hard, brown skin. The silver bar through his nipple caught the low light and flashed at me. *Illinois, Indiana. Iowa.* He pulled the shirt up and over his head, dropping it to the floor. *Uh. Kentucky? Washington. No. Wait. Uh. Nigeria?* Vince ran his hands down his chest, pausing to tweak his own pierced nipple, twisting it lazily before tracing his fingers over his stomach and down to the button on his jeans.

Portland... is a city. Okay. Uh. New Hampshire. New Jersey. New Mexico. Nipple. Nipple? Nipple is not a state. He flexed his arms as he hooked his thumbs into his jeans and leaned back against the door. I could still see the bruises on his sides, but they only added to his appeal, the pretty colors not yet faded into a mottled green. I wanted to map out the whole of them with my tongue.

"You want to come over here?" he asked, his voice husky.

"Oklahoma," I blurted. "Oregon. Pennsylvania. Rhode Island."

He looked confused.

"States," I muttered at him. "Just listing off states."

"C'mere," he said, ignoring my supreme weirdness.

I went. Somehow, I went.

And when I reached him, he raised his hands from his own lap and hooked them into my back pockets, pulling me flush against him like we'd been at the bar. Except now, there wasn't a shitload of people around and an annoying drag queen whose voice I couldn't seem to get out of my head, hearing her advice about using sandwich baggies as dental dams. Did Vince want that? Was I supposed to rim him? I'd never done that before. Did I need a baggie before I attempted it? How would he even feel anything besides a baggie going up his butt? What if it got stuck? What if it fell in? What if we had to go to the hospital and I had to explain why he had a sandwich baggie in his anus? What if I had to—

He kissed me, slowly. Surely. He must have seen the sheer amount of crazy going on behind my eyes and found the only way he knew to shut it up. Very effective, that man.

The kiss started out slow, a tentative touch that rolled into something bigger and stronger. Soon, I was chasing after his tongue with mine and running my hands up his sides as he laughed quietly into my mouth, my touch tickling him. He squeezed my ass through my jeans and I finally got my dirty wish when I gently touched his piercing. He arched into my hand, and I took that as an invitation. I didn't want to hurt him, but I didn't want to be easy on him either. I rolled the little ball at the end of the bar between my fingers, getting a good grip on it before I twisted the piercing. He gasped into my mouth, a little whine following from the back of his throat.

"That's good," he groaned, pushing into me. "That's real good. Do it again. Please, do it again."

I did, tilting my head back as he kissed along my jaw, trailing his tongue to my neck, biting over the bruise he'd left earlier. I wanted to tell him to mark me, that it was okay to mark me all over, but I couldn't seem to find my words. My balls felt heavy, my cock a hard line of lovely pain begging to be released.

Vince reached between us, pushing me back a little so he could palm my dick. He hooked his other arm around my neck and pulled me back for another sloppy kiss, our teeth clacking together as he pressed my lips back against my gums. He rubbed his hand over my length, up and down, the friction causing my eyes to roll back into my head. My knees buckled slightly, and I wanted to sag against him, but the pressure he had against my cock was too good and I wanted it to go on and on.

"Stop," I gasped trying to pull away. "I'm gonna come. Stop."

He didn't. He jerked me closer as he jerked me off, his lips against my ear. "Maybe I want you to come right here," he whispered. "Maybe I want you to come in your jeans right now. You ever think of that? Maybe I want you to come right here for me, and then I'll clean you up with my tongue. You want to come, Paul?"

Motherfucker had a dirty fucking mouth. And yes, yes, I did want to come very badly, but I wanted it to be while he was fucking me. I knew he was getting off on getting me off, but I thought I was a lot further along than he was. I needed to even us up a bit, bring him closer, push me back a little further.

So I squirmed out of his grasp and dropped to my knees in front of him, fumbling with the front of his jeans. Button fly. Helena was right; there was something delicious about giving it a single pull and having all the buttons come undone in a row. I opened up the fly and saw black briefs underneath and finally understood the meaning of sexy underwear. I couldn't decide if they were better than the jock or not.

Vince put his hands in my hair as I mouthed his dick through the cotton of his briefs, groaning as the heat of my mouth smothered him. I could feel the pulse of him under my tongue, and I pulled back the briefs, his dick smacking me in the cheek. I pulled his furry balls out and set the waistband of his briefs underneath them as I licked the underside of his cock to the tip, capturing it in my mouth. I looked up at him as I hollowed my cheeks. He was panting as he stared down at me, and he brushed his hand across my brow before rocking his head back and starting to thrust into my mouth.

I let him fuck my face because he seemed to enjoy the control. He held my head still and pushed himself to the back of my throat. I breathed through my nose as he pulled out and pushed back in. I felt slightly trashy being on my knees and letting him fuck me like this, but the look on his face when he figured out I could deep throat without any problems was priceless.

Soon enough, he started to grunt and I gripped his ass, suddenly wanting him to come down my throat. He knocked my hands away and pulled out, a string of spit falling onto my chin. He reached down and brushed his thumb over my lips as I lay panting against his thigh. "That...," he said hoarsely. "Jesus Christ, how the fuck did you learn to do that?"

I buried my face, unable to stop myself from blushing. "Good?"

"Good?" He was incredulous. "Paul, that was... I've never...." A little shudder rolled through him as I started to stroke him lazily. He let me go at it for a minute before he grabbed my hands. "Up. Get up. Bedroom." He pulled me up and I stood in front of him while he kicked off his shoes and wiggled out of his jeans and underwear. He stepped out of them and left them on the floor, standing completely ass-naked in front of me. His chest was heaving, his dick swinging out in front of him. He was fucking gorgeous, all of him, every piece and part. He grabbed my hand again and pulled me down the hall. My gaze never left his butt as he walked in front of me.

He was perfect. Everything about him was perfect.

And as we got closer to the bedroom, I realized how not perfect *I* was. My skin was pasty. My stomach was slightly flabby. I didn't have a muscled ass. I didn't have the biggest dick. I didn't have a built chest or a strong back. My body didn't make the V shapes his did. I was more shaped like a W. He was hard lines, chiseled flesh, bronzed skin. I was a marshmallow melting in a cup of cocoa.

The shakes started in my shins, of all places. Each step I took, I could feel my legs trembling until it worked its way up my thighs and past my groin, where it settled in my stomach like so much poison. I felt weak. Sweaty. Gross. Vince didn't seem to notice, but then he was a man on a mission.

Vince's bedroom was just as sparse as the rest of the house. An expensive-looking bed sat in the middle, unmade, the white sheets and comforter in disarray. He turned and closed the door behind us. I didn't know why—he lived alone.

He turned to me, his cock against my clothed thigh as he pushed me against the closed door. He started rubbing himself against me, and never even in my wildest imagination could I have ever thought something like that would happen. My frayed nerves quieted momentarily as a surge of lust shot through me at the idea of me being fully clothed and him naked. It made me feel stronger. Braver.

He attacked my mouth again and made this happy little sound as his tongue found mine. I tentatively reached my hands up and pressed them against his back, the skin warm and strong under my fingers. His piercing scraped against the fabric on my shirt and it was like a line of fire across my chest.

Then he put his hands on the hem of my shirt and started to pull it up. I panicked and grabbed his hands, forcing him to stop. He pulled away from me, a surprised look on his face.

"You okay?" he asked.

I nodded. "Yeah."

He tried to move his hands, but I wouldn't let him.

"Paul?"

"Yeah."

"What's wrong?"

"I just…."

He kissed me, his nose rubbing against mine. "You scared?" he whispered.

I let out a shaky breath. "You could say that."

"We don't have to do anything you don't want to. I would never rush you."

"I know." I couldn't help but sound annoyed.

"Then what is it?"

"You."

"Me?"

I struggled for words that wouldn't make me sound insane. "You… look at you. You're fucking perfect. Every inch of you is perfect."

He smiled shyly, looking away. "You like the way I look?"

"Yes," I said roughly. "Yes. I like the way you look." I gripped him tighter.

"I'm not going to hurt you," he said quietly. He leaned forward, still caught by my hands, and kissed my shoulder. "It's real, okay? I promise you it's real."

I was embarrassed by the way my eyes burned, and I looked away. He kissed his way up my shoulder, biting gently into the tendon and muscle near the base of my neck. He dragged his tongue up until his nose bumped my jaw. And then he kissed me again. During the moments it took him to complete this simple action, he never tried to move his hands from my hold on him, and he never tried to push until there was more that I couldn't give. He waited. He waited until I would either let him continue or push him away. And if I *did* push him away, if I *did* say no, I knew that he wouldn't judge me, he wouldn't snap at me harshly. He would accept it as he had so far and wait until I made the decision for myself.

And what, really, was I waiting for? The only thing between him and me was *me*. I could get it over with now instead of wondering forever what could have happened.

He must have seen he had calmed me down when I met his eyes again because when he kissed me, it was instantly a dirty thing, nibbling on my bottom lip with his teeth, stretching it slightly then chasing it again as he let go. Through it all, his eyes remained open and on mine, so close to each other that I could make out myself in the reflection.

This wasn't going to be an easy thing. There wasn't going to be some miraculous fix. I was still scared shitless, but I was tired of being that way. I was tired of waiting. I was tired of wondering. I didn't want to do that anymore, at least not with him.

I let go of his hands.

He kept them at his sides for a moment, as if making sure I wouldn't grab them again or push him away from me. He widened his eyes imperceptibly when I reached out and grasped his waist. Then his eyes fluttered closed as I kneaded the skin.

Vince's erection had started to flag, but perked up again at the attention. He started his movements against me, and I rocked with him, pulling him flush with my body as he humped my leg.

"I'm going to take your shirt off now," he said to me.

I froze.

He waited, but when I didn't move to stop him, he reached for the hem and pulled it up. His hands found the skin of my back and he rubbed upward gently, just a whisper of his nails on my skin causing my nipples to harden and goose bumps to prickle along my arms. He pushed my shirt up until we were chest to chest, then wrapped his strong arms around me. My bare stomach pressed against his. He looked me in the eyes and then slid the shirt up and over my head, dropping it to the floor once my arms were cleared.

I'd never felt more exposed in front of another person before, and I had to fight down the urge to shove him out of the way and run out of the room. As it stood, I couldn't decide what to do with my arms, either crossing them over my chest or folding them around my stomach. I felt my face start to burn as I looked toward the floor between us, ignoring his cock and focusing on my feet. I wasn't ashamed of myself, just… I didn't think I could compare. We'd never talked about any of his past boyfriends, and from what little I knew it was more of a string of one-offs that hadn't manifested into anything more, but given how Vince had looked at that twinkie Eric and Bear Dude, I didn't understand how he could look at me the same.

As if he could hear my thoughts, he said, "Look at me."

I shook my head.

"Paul."

I looked up at him. Somehow. Someway.

There was no pity in his eyes. There was no disgust. There was no hesitation. There was only hunger as he watched me, a flared lust that almost knocked me flat as his gaze traveled the length of my exposed torso. I tried to take a step back, to put some distance between him and myself, but I was against the door. I could feel his cock jutting out against my thigh.

Before I could speak, he dropped his hand to the fly of my jeans and with an expert flick of his wrist, the buttons came undone. Without stopping, he reached in past my nonsexy underwear and circled his hand around my dick, giving a sharp pull. I throbbed in his hand and laid my head back against the door, trying to clear my thoughts to be able to say something, to do *something*.

His lips came to my exposed neck as he jerked me off against the door. "I want to fuck you," he murmured into my skin. "Can I fuck you, Paul?"

"Yeah," I said hoarsely.

He let me go and left me near the door, going to the bare nightstand next to his bed. I felt bereft at the loss of his touch, the room a tad cold. I'm sure I looked ridiculous standing there, shirtless, with my dick hanging out of my unbuttoned jeans, watching the way his ass moved in the soft light coming in through the single window. He glanced back at me, a lazy smile on his face as he waved his hand at the bed. He flicked on a lamp near his bed and started rooting around in his drawer.

I reached back and put my hand on the doorknob and gave it an experimental tug. I needed the reassurance that it was there, that I could leave if I needed to. The knob twisted in my hand. I could leave. I could leave.

But then Vince found what he was looking for in the drawer and set it near the pillow, flopped down on the bed, and looked over at me. He gave his dick a gentle tug as he watched me. "You coming?" he asked.

I almost choked. "You keep jerking off like that, probably."

"That's the idea, yeah?"

"I guess."

"Paul?"

"Yeah?"

"It's real."

"Okay."

"We don't have to do anything if you don't want."

"So you said."

"But...."

"But?"

He dropped his hand to his side and looked uncharacteristically unsure. "Do you?" he asked. "Want? I know I'm not...."

I shook my head. "You don't get to say you're *not* anything."

"Then neither do you."

"That's not... you can't do that... you smarmy, sexy bastard... how do you even... I just...."

He groaned. "You can't sputter at me if you're not planning to let me do dirty things to you. It's not fair."

I took a deep breath. "Okay."

"Yeah?"

"Yeah."

He patted the bed next to him.

I gathered what little courage I had and slunk over to the bed. If he wanted me as much as he said he did (and if him jerking off as he watched me was any indication, he wanted me a lot), then I wanted to give him a little show of it before I climbed onto the bed. So I took what I considered to be a reasonably sexy step toward him, my slightly bedazzled jeans hanging low on my hips. According to the speed of his hand on his cock, the next step I took was even sexier, and I threw a little roll in my hips for good measure. *I can't believe I'm doing this!* I thought. *Me! Paul Auster. This is like some James Bond shit. Well, if James Bond was an overweight American homosexual in bedazzled jeans.*

It was because I was focusing on my sexy walk—to make up for my lack of sexy everything else—that I did not see the pair of shoes on the floor near the edge of the bed. I had started to let my pants drop as I took another step. My left foot caught the sole of a shoe lying on its side, causing me to stumble. My pants had dropped down to my knees, and since they were my bedazzled jeans, they were tighter than what I normally wore. That being the case, they restricted any kind of graceful movement, such as when one trips over a discarded shoe. So while I might have been able to correct myself while partially wearing normal pants, the power of the bedazzled jeans halfway down my legs gave no such room for correction.

I tripped and fell with a supremely unsexy squawk (sounding eerily like Johnny Depp, so much so that I thought about yelling out, "Paul's a fairy queen!"), and my face bounced off the edge of the bed. His mattress must have been the springiest I'd ever encountered, or my head must have weighed more than the eight pounds he claimed it should, because the force of the bounce propelled me back up until I tipped over the opposite way, landing on my back at the foot of his bed, staring up at the ceiling. My pants were at my shins, my cock and balls were just doing their own thing out in the open, and I was wishing that a megavolcano would rise up in the middle of Tucson and drown us all instantly in lava so I wouldn't have to face what was coming.

A face peered over the bed at me, eyes wide, laughter stifled.

"Before you say anything," I told Vince, "just know that I did that on purpose. There's nothing that says, 'Hey, come fuck me' like tripping awkwardly and falling to the floor."

"Your face," he giggled. He *giggled*!

"Yes."

"It bounced off the *bed*."

"I was there. I remember that part clearly."

"It was good up to that point."

"Was it?"

"Yes, but then it got *awesome*."

"I'm glad my attempts at seduction were so amusing."

"If that was what you were attempting, I can't wait to see what happens when you actually succeed."

I sighed. "I'm pretty sure that'll defy all logic and the world will explode."

"Paul?"

"Yeah?"

He disappeared for a moment, then returned, and in one smooth, fluid motion, he slid off the bed and landed on top of me, sliding his naked body up mine. My dick, which had previously died of embarrassment, was resur-erected, glory be to God. Vince moved his hips against mine, propping him himself up with his hands on either side of my head. He filled my vision until he was all I could see. I knew I could hide by closing my eyes, but I didn't want to. I couldn't find the strength to look away.

"Paul," he said again, his voice deeper as our groins rubbed together.

"Yeah."

"Remember how yesterday you showed me the hippo video on YouTube, and I told you I was halfway in love with you?"

"I didn't show you jack shit, but yeah. I remember." It was all I could think about. It was all I could hear, repeated in my head over and over again.

He leaned down on his strong arms and kissed me, eyes opened. "I'm pretty sure I'm about three-fourths of the way there now."

I stared at him. "Vince...."

He smiled. It was beautiful. "Paul."

I shook my head, but my gaze never left his. "It's not possible. If anything, it's just infatuation, though I still don't get it. You can't feel like that for someone so quickly. It's not realistic."

"And yet it's there anyway," he said, kissing me again. "You'll see." He laid himself against me, resting his full weight on me. He reached up with his hands and brushed them over my cheeks. I kissed the palm of his right hand because it seemed like the right thing to do. And because I wanted to.

"I don't...."

He silenced me with a finger. "It doesn't matter now."

I nodded even though I thought it mattered the most.

Using his feet, he kicked off my jeans the rest of the way, leaving them discarded under his bed. He let go of my face and reached out of my vision. Something *snicked* near my ear and he rose up off me, pressing his knees between my legs on the floor, spreading them out gently. The soft hairs of his thighs rubbed against mine as his hand went between us. I lifted my hips in the air, so very self-conscious but unable to stop. He slid wet fingers over my cock to my balls and then behind them. He pressed them against me, and the initial intrusion caused me to bite my bottom lip to keep from moaning.

"Okay?" he asked.

"Yeah. Yes. More. Please."

And he did. Moments later, his dick was sheathed in rubber and pressed against my entrance. The carpet scraped against my back, but not once did either of us suggest getting back on the bed. We were fine, we knew, right where we were.

"Paul," he said roughly as he breached me.

"Vince," I groaned, rocking my head back. It burned like so much fire, but I didn't want it to stop. I pushed back against him until his thighs pressed against my ass. He undulated on top of me as he latched his teeth onto my neck below my jaw.

It wasn't going to last long; I don't think it was meant to. We'd gotten each other too worked up at the bar, our nerves tender and frayed. Too many things were flitting through me that hadn't been there a week before, and I was overwhelmed, like I was being consumed completely.

Sweat formed between us, my cock trapped against his stomach as he slid into me, creating a delicious friction that I didn't want to push away. I felt fluid and slippery, and he growled against my neck, his breath light and quick as his hips snapped back and forth.

"I'm going," I whispered.

"Go," he panted.

I did, shooting between us. Moments later, I felt him stiffen against me, pressing his hips forward again, and he stayed there, a breathy sigh falling out of his mouth that formed my name as his body shook. He kissed my cheek. My chin. My eyes. My nose. And then he found my lips again, and I kissed him for all I was worth, because that little light inside me had exploded into a blinding sun.

IT WAS never an option that I was going home that night. As soon as we both stopped shaking and started feeling congealed, he pulled me up and dragged me into the shower with him, which, if you've never showered with Vince Taylor, you're missing out on quite the experience. He does this thing with the shower gel and his finger in my—

You know what? Never mind. That's probably not the best thing to share. Let's just say that I was clean. Inside and out.

Okay, fine: he put it in my butt, and I made a weird squeaking noise that rebounded around the shower stall. Fun.

After, he made me stand in front of him while he dried me off, taking his time as he got to my legs, kissing my flaccid cock as he rubbed the towel over my shins. I blushed furiously at this and at the attention he gave, but he just laughed and did it again.

He made me use his toothbrush, though I balked at first. He reminded me that he'd used mine, and he was pretty sure that since we just fucked, we were past sharing any kind of germs. Then I made the mistake of telling him that I would do it, but when he rimmed me for the first time, I wasn't going to use the same toothbrush as him. As soon as the words fell out of my mouth, I wanted to take them back, because I hadn't meant to say that in the slightest. He wouldn't let me brush my teeth until I repeated myself, demanding that I say it verbatim. When I did, an evil gleam formed in his eyes, and I accidentally used half a tube of Crest in one squeeze, getting toothpaste all over my hand and the counter, which, to be fair, looked oddly sexual, causing Vince to get all growly again.

"Bed," he said, not even allowing me to pretend to look for my jeans as he pushed me back into the bedroom. I found it slightly odd that I didn't even try to leave, or make some excuse about *anything* so that I could slink out and go home to lie in my own bed and wonder if the last couple of hours had been nothing more than a hard-core wet dream. I found it even *more* odd when the fact that I was staying gave me a sense of relief. I chose not to look into that too closely.

Then I remembered something as I pulled on my nonsexy underwear. I hated sleeping naked, especially since I'd be sleeping next to my version of a walking orgasm. "Hey, what happened to my present?"

I climbed onto the bed, testing out the mattress with my hands and legs instead of my face this time. When I didn't get a response, I glanced over at him to find him looking down at his hands. "What's wrong?"

He shrugged. "It's stupid now."

"Huh?"

He wouldn't look at me. "You went out and bought me a freaking bike. My present isn't that great. You probably won't even like it. It was pretty dumb."

"Dude. Stop being a labia. I bought you a bike because you didn't watch where you were going and crashed yours into my car. I felt sorry for you, and that's the only reason you got a new bike. You're lucky you didn't get the one I originally picked out for you. Let's just say you probably would have needed to have pigtails when you rode it."

He snorted. "It probably would have been cheaper."

"You think? You should have seen the look on my face when the little midget friend of yours, Jennifer Lopez, told me it was a billion dollars. I think I probably can't ever go back there because everyone will know me as that guy who shit himself in the bike store. So yes, I want my fucking present. I've *earned* my fucking present. Go get it."

He rolled his eyes, but I could see the small smile on his face. "Bossy bastard," he mumbled and walked out of the room. I pulled up the comforter and did a really lame thing by putting my face down on the pillow and inhaling deeply, delighted that it smelled like him. I figured I was either a sappy romantic or a creepy stalker. Then I decided (though it did not stop me) that sniffing pillows is never romantic, just creepy. Or maybe creepily romantic to the point where soon, I'd probably want a lock of his hair that I could put on the shrine I'd make to him that I'd hide in the back of my closet that I'd take out on alternating Tuesdays to light candles to while I made out with a picture of him with the lips cut out. Yeesh.

He came back into the room, refusing to look at me as he clutched a large flat envelope to his chest. "You don't have to like it," he mumbled. "If you don't, it's not going to hurt my feelings at all."

And that was bullshit, and I knew it as soon as he said it. He *wanted* me to like his gift, and he was *nervous* about giving it to me. I felt a bit weird seeing him act like that; there was this syrupy, queasy feeling in the pit of my stomach that made me want to get out of the bed and wrap myself around him and protect him from all the stupid shit in the world. Once again, I marveled at the fact that I'd known the man in front of me for only a week, had heard his voice for the first time only five days before. I pushed the thought of my parents and their quickie marriage out of my head (because, really, not only was it a frightening thought, but I didn't want to think about my parents while my ass still felt stretched and I was sitting half naked in my boyfriend's bed; sort of killed the mood that way).

"Can't decide if I like it if you're not going to give it to me," I told him lightly, like I was talking to a skittish animal. He clutched at the envelope a bit more tightly, scrunching it up against his chest. He looked horrified that it had gotten wrinkled and quickly smoothed it back down again, worrying his bottom lip a bit. "Vince."

He sighed and crawled into the bed next to me, sitting up against the headboard, his long body stretched out next to mine. It was all I could do to not reach out and rub my hands along his stomach.

He handed over the envelope, still without looking at me. He started gnawing on a fingernail, tapping his other hand nervously against his chest. I was curious as to the contents of the envelope that had gotten him so keyed up. I wondered if I'd open it to find something evil, like he was actually trying to blackmail me, and I would find photographs inside of myself in some kind of compromising position with hookers and a pile of cocaine (never mind the fact that I didn't know any hookers and did not own a pile of cocaine). Then I realized I didn't hold any kind of political office, but his *father* did, and then I wondered if it would be photographs of his *father* with hookers and cocaine and that Vince needed my help to bring down the corrupt Tucsonan government because Vince really worked for the FBI and then we'd have to go on the run and there'd be gunfights and explosions and sex on sun-drenched private beaches where we'd be in hiding for the rest of our lives....

I opened the envelope, half expecting the damning photos to fall out. Instead, there was a piece of paper and a photograph printed off the computer of the night sky with a specific star circled. I read through the letter, unable to speak because my breath was caught in my chest.

"I just thought that you'd like it," Vince said, glancing over at me out of the corner of his eye. "You knew so much about the constellations that I thought it'd be cool if you had a star named after you, so I went online and found out you could do that! It was only twenty-five dollars and I don't think you actually own the star, but it's called Paul James Auster now, and it's the only one in the whole universe with that name. I tried to get one as close to Orion's Belt as I could. Well, I tried to see if I could get one of the stars in Orion's Belt, but then I remembered those were already named and somebody probably already owned them. I tried to find online who did so I could see if they wanted to sell them, but even after looking for three hours, I couldn't find it, so I just got you a different one instead. But if you don't like it, I'll just keep it for me and then I'll have a star named Paul, and I think that'd be okay, too, so don't—"

"Vince." My voice was rough.

"Yeah?"

"You did this for me?"

He shrugged. "Guess so. You know, for your birthday. And because I think you're awesome. So… happy birthday."

"This is the nicest thing anyone has ever done for me," I told him truthfully. "Thank you."

"Yeah?"

"Yeah."

And then he beamed at me, full force, dimples and all, and I gave a little yelp as I rolled over onto his chest, kissing the ever-fucking life out of him. He gave a startled grunt but opened up quickly enough, and there was nothing more glorious than his mouth on mine right at that moment, frantic and messy. That little light in my chest exploded into a shining array of fireworks across a night sky, blues and greens, reds and yellows, like the grand finale of some spectacular.

And later, as his breathing evened out and he fell asleep against me, his face buried in my neck, I realized it for what it was.

A star? I thought. *Could there have been anything more ridiculously awesome than that? I mean, who does shit like that? Not to mention he's apparently three-quarters of the way in love with me after seeing me trip while my junk flopped about. I don't even want to know what has to happen for him to be all the way in love with me. Not that I want that. At all. In any way, shape, or form. Not even a little bit. Not even the smallest inkling. Not even if I'm already in love with him myself, and—*

My eyes widened. No. No *fucking* way.

"Oh sweat balls," I whispered as Vince slept on.

And that's when I made the decision to do a very stupid thing.

Love blows like that, sometimes.

CHAPTER 15

Red Leader, Red Leader: The Whale Has Breached

"ARE you sure you want to do this?" Sandy asked me the next day.

I sighed. "No. But I have to."

"Actually, you don't," he reminded me. "And I still don't get *why* you're doing this."

"Because he named a star after me and I'm pretty sure I love him and I hate everything about that because it makes me feel all sticky and sweet and gross, like I just snorted a line of Pixy Stix powder cut with rainbows and bunnies." I sounded slightly hysterical, which, to be fair, I probably was. I hadn't slept at all the night before, and when Vince had woken the next morning, a grin forming on his face as he saw me watching him, my heart started thudding like a bongo drum against my chest, and I was sure, absolutely *sure*, he'd be able to see every single one of my thoughts on my face and he'd *know*.

I had almost convinced myself not to follow through with my plan until after breakfast when he said he wanted to go into work for a couple of hours to catch up so when he returned on Monday, he wouldn't be buried under e-mails and paperwork. I'd cursed him mentally, only because he'd given me the perfect opportunity to do what I didn't want to do. I even went so far as to offer to drive him to work, but he'd waved me off, saying he would call me when he was done and would come over.

So I immediately called Sandy when I got home, babbling about how I was in love, constellations, and how I was pretty sure I was about to lie my way into a hospital so that I could go meet his mother behind his back, just so I could tell her how epically amazing her son was. Sandy immediately dropped whatever (or whoever) he was doing and picked me up, stopping to get a garish bouquet of flowers on the way as part of our cover. I'd almost convinced myself that there was a point to doing this, but it still felt a bit off.

"So you gonna to tell me why?" Sandy asked again, looking back at the hospital entrance.

I looked at myself in the rearview mirror, wondering if I should have worn a mustache as part of my disguise. As it was, I was wearing a newsboy cap, mirrored sunglasses that took up half my face, and the collar of my coat was flipped up around my neck. Either it was the greatest disguise in the history of mankind or the police would be called as soon as we walked in the hospital, given how I looked like I was probably going to be doing something lewd in public.

"Because," I said to Sandy. "I don't want the moment to go by where I'll never get to say a thing to her. She needs to hear from someone how badass her son is before she goes. And I think he's the most badass out of everyone, so why shouldn't it be me?"

Sandy snorted. "I think this will be the moment we'll look back on in the future as the time that Paul went batshit insane for love."

"Gross," I moaned. "Do not use that word around me."

"Batshit?"

"No. The other word. But where do you think that term came from? Did someone eat batshit once and go nuts?"

"Insane?"

"No, but that's kind of how I feel right now. The other word."

"Love?"

I groaned again. "I think I'm going to be sick. Clichéd emotional vomiting is definitely in my future."

"It's like your parents all over again."

"There's got to be something wrong with the way children are raised in my family," I said, shaking my head. "How can shit like this keep happening?"

"What about Nana Gigi?"

"Well, to hear it *her* way, she fell in love seven times and she has seven ex-husbands."

Sandy looked wistful. "That lady knows how to live. I hope when I'm her age, I'll still be as vivacious as always and talk about *my* seven ex-husbands."

"To have seven ex-husbands, you first need to have one," I reminded him.

He dismissed me with a wave of his hand. "Trust me, no one can handle me *and* Helena."

I thought about Darren and the way he'd been watching Helena perform, but I pushed it away. Other things to focus on now. If this didn't blow up in my face like I certainly expected it to, I'd make sure that Helena knew the Homo Jock King wanted to lick her ball sac. Or whatever Darren wanted to do. "Okay, so let's go over the plan again."

He looked baffled. "There was a *plan*? First I'm hearing about it. I distinctly remember you shrieking into your phone, telling me I needed to get my ass over to your house because you'd made a big mistake and wanted to marry Vince and have his babies forever and ever, but before you could give him your soul, you needed my help in breaking into the hospital to see the dying first lady of Tucson to receive her blessing so that you could live the rest of your life with your future husband and what will most likely be an ethnically diverse rainbow of children from such far-flung countries as Sudan and Iceland."

I gaped at him in horror. "I never said *anything* like that!"

"Semantics. And you should really flip down the collar to your coat. It's not 1987, and even if it *was*, you'd still look ridiculous. No one is going to recognize you by your neck. And where did you get those sunglasses? They look like a pair of mine that I lost under a suspicious set of circumstances last year and, at the time, you said you had no idea where they went."

"Yeah, I stole them," I admitted, not feeling bad in the slightest. "I didn't have the heart to tell you that when you wore them, it looked like you were trying to do a really awful impression of Tom Cruise from *Top Gun.*"

"Gayest movie ever," Sandy declared rightfully. "Anytime you do any kind of slow-motion scene involving men playing volleyball almost naked automatically puts your film in the pantheon of homoeroticism. And poor Val Kilmer. What happened to him? He used to be so attractive! Now he looks like a live-action version of Gollum."

"He aged, I guess," I said, putting down my collar because it was not 1987.

"Yeah, but his version of aging was like he got fast-forwarded sixty years. If that ever happens to me, I expect you to tell me and then drive me home after I get extensive plastic surgery."

"Ew," I muttered. "You're not that vapid. For the most part."

"Neither was Val Kilmer, and look what happened to him."

We offered a moment of silence for Val Kilmer because Sandy had a good point.

"So what is the plan?" Sandy demanded. "And the flowers must be part of it. I didn't spend thirty-five bucks on flowers not to have them in our diabolical scheme."

"They're very pretty," I assured him.

"Thank you. The guy at the flower shop called it a 'summer bouquet'. He was adorable. I almost asked him what kind of bouquet he'd recommend if I wanted to ask a guy selling flowers what it would take for me to sit on his face, but somehow, I was able to resist the urge. This seemed to be more important."

I rolled my eyes. "I thank you that you were able to hold yourself back from sitting on the flower guy's face. I know it must have been so hard for you."

"No, but it *could* have been hard."

"Puns? Really? That's what you've settled for? I don't think the flower guy would've gone for that."

"Oh, so you've been in love for twelve hours, and now you're suddenly the expert?"

"Don't use that word!"

"Love, love, Paul's in love!"

"Shut your face, you damaged queen!"

He stuck his tongue out at me. "Make me, lover boy. You better let me perform at the wedding. If you don't, our friendship is over."

I was hurt. "Of *course* you would perform at the wedding. Who else would I get—Oh, for *fuck's* sake! I'm not getting fucking married! You tricked me, you scandalous bitch!"

He smirked evilly at me. "I guess we know what *you're* thinking about."

"Can we talk about this later?"

"You bet your sweet ass we will. I see it more of a fall wedding, with leaves and centerpieces shaped like autumn squash—"

"Sandy!"

"Paul!"

"Focus! How are we going to get in?"

"Okay, okay. Let me think." He frowned and tapped a finger to the side of his head. "So, we don't know what room she's in, only that she's in hospice care. And since you won't go the easy route and just *ask* Vince, we need to find her first. We'll have to ask someone if they know where she's at."

"Why would they tell us? Isn't it supposed to be secret? They won't let us in to see the First Lady of Tucson if we just ask."

"Two things: one, I don't know if 'First Lady of Tucson' is a real thing. I just said that because it almost makes her sound like a princess, and that makes me happy because it makes me think that when you get married to Vince, it will almost be like a royal wedding since he would be the son of a princess."

"And the second thing?" I asked warily.

"Hmmm?"

"The second thing? You said there were two things."

"I did? Oh. Sorry. I forgot. I got distracted by the idea of a royal wedding. How dashing would Vince be in a uniform?"

"So dashing," I said dreamily. After a moment, I shook my head, clearing my brain of images of Vince in a blue uniform with a sword and scabbard attached to his hip. "We're off track again."

"It was your fault that time," he said. "Anyway, so since we have to incorporate the flowers somehow—"

"We don't *have* to incorporate the flowers at *all*—"

"You shut your face! We *do* and we *will*. So, since we *will* be using the flowers, and that is *nonnegotiable*, we can say that we are there to deliver the flowers to the First Lady."

"Won't they think we're like paparazzi or something?"

"Well, *you,* maybe, but that's why I'll be the one asking."

"Wait. Why would they think *I* was paparazzi and not you? I feel like I should be offended."

"You're thinking too much about it," he said, patting my arm. "I was born to act. You'll just look more believable if you stood off to the side away from me like a scene extra."

"Hey, I can act! I was in a play once. I was the best thing about the whole show."

"I know. You were eight. It was about the four food groups. You played a block of cheese and had to sing a song about calcium. Your mom spent four weeks on the costume and it made you look like you were an orange dice. You cried after the first show because you had to pee so bad and they couldn't figure out how to get you out of your cheesy prison."

I smiled, remembering. "I brought the house down with my last line, though. 'Give me dairy or give me osteoporosis!' It was my greatest role."

"And that's why you won't be playing the role of flower-delivery guy," he said. "You can be Stand Off In The Corner guy."

"Fine, but what about the Secret Service?"

"The what now?"

"The Secret Service. Won't they be guarding the First Lady's room?"

"I don't think we really understand how local politics work."

I shrugged. "I just go into the voting booth and vote for the Democrats. If there is more than one, I go for the one whose name I like better. That was really hard once when there was one guy named Diego Valdez and the other one was Rocco Cordova."

Sandy paused for a moment. "You went with Rocco, didn't you?"

I grinned. "Yeah, only because I made up a song that got stuck in my head. 'Hey, it's Rocco! Sucking my cock-o!'"

"How are we not famous?" he asked, seriously baffled.

"The world isn't ready for us."

"So, Secret Service? No Secret Service?"

I shrugged. "I have a feeling we're going to wing it once we get inside. The best thing I can think is that if someone pulls a gun on us, we should probably run."

"I'm pretty sure we're going to jail today," Sandy said. "It's a good thing you're in love with the mayor's son. Hopefully that means we can get out quicker."

"I really wish you'd stop using that word," I said with a scowl. "It's like you're rubbing it in now."

"What do you think sounds better? Paul Taylor or Vince Auster? Eh, now that I say it out loud, Paul Taylor makes it sound like you own a big-and-tall clothing store for single women above the age of fifty. Vince Auster sounds much more refined. He should get your name."

"Duly noted," I ground out.

He ignored me. "We doing this?"

"It's go time," I said, only because I always wanted to say something like that.

"Hands in, then," he barked at me. He held his hand out and I put mine on top of his. "The usual on three! Ready! One! Two! Three!"

"Rock out with our cocks out!" we shouted at each other.

The game was on.

AND the game turned out to be much easier than we thought it would be. I was almost disappointed at the lack of Secret Service agents second-guessing whether we were paparazzi and the complete lack of the necessity for me to use my acting skills that I'd honed while playing the difficult role as Chuckie Cheddar Cheese.

We walked into the hospice entrance and glanced around quietly. No one appeared suspicious of a skinny guy carrying flowers and a husky guy wearing sunglasses indoors. I certainly didn't see anyone speaking into their watch and saying things like, "Red leader, red leader, the whale has breached. Repeat: the whale has breached."

Sandy pointed to a corner that he apparently wanted me to go stand in like I was a four-year-old child who wasn't capable of speaking on my own. Then I thought of the last time I'd been in the hospital and had called the sassy black nurse (I still don't know what an "administrative professional" is) a bitch and a dog and convinced her I was way into incest, so I figured it was probably for the best. But just to show my individuality and the fact that I *wouldn't* be bossed around, I stood in a different corner than the one Sandy told me to. He rolled his eyes at me.

I was shocked when he walked over to me only a moment later and said, "Room 214."

"What? How did you get that?"

He looked a little surprised himself. "I changed the story at the last second and said I was dropping these off on Vince's behalf. The nurse gave it to me right away with this sort of faraway look in her eye like she wanted to climb Vince like a tree house. Competition is always healthy, I guess."

"I'll fucking cut her," I snarled.

"Easy there, Mrs. Jackson. The good news is they said his mom is having a good day today, whatever that means. The mayor apparently is going to be here this afternoon, so there shouldn't be anyone up there."

"Well, there hasn't been any Secret Service, at least from what I can tell."

"Gee, you're such a good lookout."

"Shut up, Sandy."

We started following the signs that led up a flight of stairs to the second floor and off to a quiet section of the hospital, which was the hospice wing. It seemed muted somehow, a shade darker than the rest of the hospital. People spoke in hushed tones, and no one paid us any mind.

"Are you sure you want to do this?" Sandy asked quietly. "Maybe you should just talk to Vince first."

I shook my head, resolute. "No, we're here. If she's able, I'd like to talk to her. At the very least to let her know that Vince is going to be in good hands, even after she's gone."

Sandy stopped me by grabbing my hand, the flowers in his other. I glanced back at him, curious about the guarded expression on his face. "What?" I asked him.

"You need to think about what you just said," he told me, his voice a-tremble. "If you're planning on telling a dying woman that you're going to take care of her son after she's gone, then you sure as shit better plan on doing it. If you don't, even I don't think I could forgive you for that, Paul."

I knew he was thinking about his own parents, and the bright anger in his eyes did little to calm me. "Sandy…."

"No, Paul. You do this and that's it. He's yours. No second-guessing yourself. No flip-flopping. No angst for the sake of it. You do this, you stand by it. It's not fair to anyone if you don't, but especially that woman in there. She may not like the fact that her son is gay, she may be ridiculous enough to hate him for it, but you don't get to go in there and make promises you don't intend to keep."

I looked down the hall and could see room 214 a few doors down. And I knew that Sandy was right. If I did this, I had to be in for it completely. This couldn't be some half-assed thing. This couldn't be something that I would pull back from weeks or months down the road. If I did this, I needed to do it right.

And I'll be honest, I almost turned around and walked out. I almost retraced our steps until I was standing outside the hospital in the bright sunlight and breathing in air that didn't smell like sickness and death. I almost walked back to get into the car and drive away and forget that I ever even came to this place. Maybe Vince would have told me about his mom, maybe he wouldn't have. Maybe I wouldn't know the day she died. Maybe Vince would suddenly say that he needed to go out of town when in actuality he would be going to her funeral.

Or maybe he would tell me everything. Maybe he would tell me everything that night. I didn't know if it had anything to do with trust, but with how much flack I'd given him over the past week, how fickle and flighty I'd seemed, I could see why he didn't think I could handle this being dumped in my lap. Maybe it was the very *real* fact that regardless of how he felt about me, regardless of what he thought he saw in me, we'd only known each other for *days*. Not years. Not weeks. Not even *two* weeks. *Days.* Maybe my parents had met almost the same way. Maybe they'd known that they loved each other right away, and maybe it had worked for them, but it was still fantastical. It was still a fairy tale. Things like that didn't happen. There was no such thing as love at first sight.

And, of course, that brought the doubts along with it. That maybe, just *maybe* the only reason he'd latched onto me the way he had was *because* his mother was dying, because he was losing someone who meant a lot to him and was transferring all of what he felt about her over to me. Once he'd gotten over his grief, he'd realize how mistaken he was about me, of *course* he'd have never gone for someone like me, it was all just a phase, an awkward dream, a lapse in judgment that wouldn't have worked out in the long run.

I opened my mouth to tell Sandy that he was right, that we should leave. Instead, I said, "I know. And I'm going to do it anyway."

He watched me closely, as if trying to gauge my sincerity. I don't know what he saw in me, but it must have been enough. He handed the flowers over to me and leaned in and kissed my cheek. We both ignored the brightness in his eyes. "Good," he said roughly. "I'm going to go see if I can find some coffee or something. Call me when you're done."

"You're not going with me?" I asked, slightly panicked.

He shook his head. "This isn't about me, baby doll. Besides, dealing with one stranger is easier than two. Just... be kind, okay? You don't know what she's going through. She may have been a shit to her son, but that doesn't mean she's not suffering enough as it is. Okay?"

I nodded, unsure of what else to say.

"All right, then. You go do this thing and then we'll get out of here, maybe go get your man and take him out to lunch. I think I need to get to know the guy who turned my best friend upside down so quickly." He kissed me again and he left.

Before I could give myself time to think (read: time to run away), I turned back toward room 214 and walked over. I knocked on the door.

"Yes?" a voice said, much stronger than I'd thought it would be. "Come in."

I pushed my sunglasses up on my head, took a deep breath and opened the door.

CHAPTER 16

I Brought You A Healthy Dose Of Awkwardness. Get Well Soon!

WHAT hit me first was how much Vince looked like Lori Taylor.

Obviously, there were some minor dissimilarities; her nose was a bit sharper, her chin a bit weaker. Her skin was paler and her eyes were a slightly different shade of brown. But other than that? She was all Vince. There was Vince in the curiosity in her eyes. There was Vince in the slight, tentative curve to her mouth. Her hair was gone, her head wrapped in a pretty blue scarf. Her frame was thin and there were shadows around her eyes, almost like bruises.

But even with that, even with the evidence of her illness etched across her skin in the thinness of her cheeks and arms, there was still strength there. There was still knowledge. There was a sense that while she'd been beaten down, she was not gone yet. Even without knowing a thing about her, I knew she was a fighter, and even though she was losing the fight, she was giving it all she could. I admired her for it, but part of me also hated her for it given that if she had that much tenacity, how much of Vince's life had she made a living hell after he'd come out? What did she do to him that made him flinch every time his parents were mentioned?

I had pity, yes. I had sympathy. I had concern. But I also had anger. And resentment. I was mad that she could even consider, even *entertain* the idea of thinking of someone as beautiful as her son as deserving of her scorn. I remembered back, seeing her on the news, standing next to her husband, waving out to the crowd shortly after he'd won the election. It was a narrow victory. Vince had been nowhere in sight. This fueled me, though I knew it shouldn't. I couldn't help but wonder if he'd been watching the same thing that day. What had he been thinking? What had to have been going through his head?

"Hello," she said evenly. "Haven't seen you here before."

"No," I said. "I guess you wouldn't have."

"Are those for me?" she asked, pointing to the flowers.

"Yes, ma'am."

"They're lovely. Can you put them near the window? They should do fine there with the sunlight that comes in during the afternoon."

I did as I was told, not sure of what to say. I fiddled with the flowers more than I should have, trying to stop my hands from shaking as I processed what I wanted to say. It didn't seem right to launch into some kind of tirade. I didn't want to upset her and make things any worse. Someone dying in a hospital does not need the added stress of a tyrannical speech that'll benefit no one, even if it would get things off my chest.

"You're not a flower-delivery man, are you," she said in such a way that was not a question.

"No, ma'am," I said, glancing at her shyly. She was pretty. So pretty. Even with how much had been taken from her, she was beautiful.

Lori didn't look angry or confused, merely inquisitive. "You're not one of my husband's staffers. I'd have seen you before, unless he's hired someone new out of the blue. Which could always be a possibility. Lord knows he doesn't tell me everything. But that doesn't seem quite right either."

"I don't work for your husband," I said. "I—"

"And," she said, overriding me, "you're obviously not a reporter because you'd have been a bit more aggressive by now, asking questions, snapping photographs, inquiring about the cancer or what I thought about my husband's support of cutting health-care benefits and how ironic it is that I am where I am now."

I was embarrassed. "How are you feeling?" I asked. "That should have been the first thing out of my mouth. I sometimes forget my manners, your majesty. Er. Your grace? First Lady Taylor? Man, I don't even know what to call you. Your highness? No, that would be if you were a queen. Well, not that you *couldn't* be a queen, because you totally could. From what I've seen of you on TV, you've got the whole parade-float princess wave thing down pat. You know, elbow, elbow, wrist, wrist, that whole thing." I demonstrated for her in case she didn't know. I was surprised I didn't spontaneously combust given how flaming I was being. I dropped my arm immediately and tucked my hands behind me so that I wouldn't feel the need to princess wave at her anymore. Probably not the best way to start things.

"Well," she said. "If you're not a staffer, and you don't deliver flowers, and you're not a reporter, and you obviously know who I am, then there's only one person you *can* be." She said this last with a small smile on her face.

Uh-oh. "And. Uh. Who is that?"

"You must be Paul. Paul Auster, I think it was?"

I groaned. "The fact that you know who I am after two minutes of me walking into the room and telling you how to wave while rambling at you does not bode well for this conversation."

She surprised me when she laughed. "Vince was right on the money about you."

"That's the second time I've heard that from someone who knows him, and I still don't know how I feel about that. I've really got to stop him from trying to describe me to people. With the description he gives, I probably sound like some awkward tentacle-monster trying to fight Godzilla for control over Tokyo." Thankfully, I was able to stop right there and not demonstrate what said tentacle monster from Tokyo would sound like, even though I desperately wanted to growl and snarl and howl as I stomped across the room, pretending to chase away tiny Asian people as I destroyed their beloved city. I figured Vince's mom wouldn't appreciate live theater in her room, even if I had once performed as a block of cheese.

"No tentacle monster," she assured me. "Just... different. He said you say whatever's in your head and you can't hide how you feel."

"Oh?"

"Yes. And even though you're nervous, I can tell you're also a little bit angry with me."

"Ah. No. No, ma'am. Ah, you see—"

"Lori," she said. "Or you can still call me 'your majesty', if you like. I think I quite enjoy the sound of that."

"Lori—er, your majesty, I just... I don't even... I'm not *mad*... I just don't...."

"Oh! He said you sputtered, as well. He seemed to like it when you do that. I can see why."

I sighed. "Why aren't you evil? You are supposed to be evil and I'm supposed to come in here and tell you to renounce your ways before you die so that there are no regrets. Everything about you should be evil, and you're not and I don't like that. I had this whole… *thing* planned—okay, well, not really *planned*; more like I was going to wing it—but you're sort of ruining it right now."

She smiled, though it looked forced. "Is that so? *Now* who's the tentacle monster? I should wonder what Vince has told you about us. About me. If it would make you feel better, you can still wing it and I'll listen."

I shook my head. "It kind of takes the bite out of a scolding when you ask for one. And he hasn't told me about you. At all. He thinks I don't know who his parents are."

"And yet here you are."

"Here I am," I agreed.

"How? Or maybe why is the better question."

I shrugged. "I don't know that it matters, really. Does it? I mean, it wouldn't change the fact that I'm still here. It wouldn't change the fact that I overheard Vince talking with my mom after she found out who he was, telling her that he didn't want to put all this on me because he wanted to keep it separate. It wouldn't change the fact that Darren thought he'd need me more than anyone after you go. It won't change anything."

She watched me for a moment without speaking. Then: "You're certainly an odd fellow, aren't you?"

"I guess, your grace. Do you hate your son?"

Her answer was instant. "No. Never. I never have."

"Does his dad?"

This time she hesitated. "Hate is a strong word," she said slowly. "I don't think my husband is capable of hate in any form."

"From someone on the opposite side of his argument," I said bitterly, "I see that differently than you do, I guess."

"Isn't that the way for the opposite of every argument?" she asked with no trace of sarcasm.

"That's not fair. Most arguments aren't about lesser rights for certain parts of the population. I'm not here to try and change your mind about that, no matter what you believe."

"And yet, I never said what I believe in." She had me there. "But if not that, then what *are* you here to try and change my mind about?"

"Vince."

"What about Vince?"

"He needs to know you love him. He needs to know you care. I don't care if you have to lie through your teeth to do it, you need to tell him everything is okay, that it doesn't matter in the end because you love him just the way he is." My voice wanted to crack, but I wouldn't let it. I pushed away the burn in my eyes.

Lori looked away from me, toward the flowers that were starting to get some sun. "Doesn't he know that?" she asked me quietly.

"How could he!" I exploded. "You and your husband all but disowned him publicly! I didn't even know him then, but I remember it. I remember how angry I was at the two of you, how awful that must have been for him. To know that your parents didn't think you deserved to be treated like everyone else? For God's sake, Mrs. Taylor, your husband voted *against* hate-crime legislation, knowing it would protect his *son*. How fucked up is that? Don't you know what that could do to a person?"

"Do *you* know?" she asked. "What that could do to a person? I'm not trying to be facetious, Paul. I'm asking for my own peace of mind."

"I don't know. Maybe. Maybe not as bad as others. Yeah, I got made fun of a lot in school, and maybe I got beat up a couple of times, but you know what I was able to do? I was able to come home to my family that didn't give a shit who I would grow up loving. I was able to have my dad teach me how to fight back, and not because he thought his son was a pansy, but because his son *was* a pansy who wanted to *fight back*. I was able to come home and sit on a chair while my mother kneeled before me, wiping the blood from a cut on my forehead where Donnie Craig's fist had hit me. I got to see the anger in their eyes, but it was never directed toward me. It was directed at everyone who thought they could hurt me. It was directed at anyone who thought I was something less than what I was. My parents never made me feel like I was something I wasn't. They never tried to change me or break me down. They loved me for who I was, and I never questioned that." By the time I finished, I was breathing heavily, curling my hands tightly at my sides, trying to keep my voice soft so as not to yell at a woman who was dying in the bed in front of me. But even so, it was a battle I almost lost.

"And do you think I don't love my son?" she asked, her eyes bright. "Do you think I don't care for him, that I don't worry about him every second of every single day?"

"If you do, you've certainly got a weird way of showing it."

To this, she said nothing.

"Look, I didn't come here to attack you," I said, feeling uncomfortable. "Not really. Nor did I want to make you feel bad. I... I don't know. I just want you to see Vince the way *I* see him. I just don't want you to have any regrets. And I certainly don't want *him* not to know how his own mother feels before he won't be able to find out anymore. It wouldn't be fair to either of you."

She looked away, and I wondered if I'd gone too far. I wondered if I even should have been in this hospital room. The more I thought about it, the more duplicitous it seemed, like I was going behind Vince's back, meddling in affairs that weren't mine. I tried to justify it to myself by saying I was doing this for Vince, and that if he really felt about me the way he did, then he'd understand, or he'd have brought up his parents already, consequences be damned. But this felt like transference, and it didn't feel right.

I took a step back, sure that the conversation was over, sure that if she *did* speak again, it'd be to tell me to get the hell out of her hospital room, to never come back here again, and that she'd make sure Vince knew what I'd done and how I'd gone about it. Wildly, I thought that maybe I'd never even make it out the door, because the Secret Service would barge in and I'd be arrested and thrown into Guantanamo with terrorists, never to see the light of day again except for a window the size of a book ten feet above my cot in the prison cell where I'd spend the rest of my life. The First Lady of Tucson would have her revenge because I couldn't keep my mouth shut or my face out of someone else's business.

And she did speak. But what she said was not what I expected.

I was about to turn and make a run for it when she said, "Vince died when he was nine. Did you know that?"

"No. I didn't." I looked up at her. She was staring at the flowers, the sun encroaching on them further.

"We lived in a house over on the west side of town. It was a nice house. A big house, with a garden and a pool. Andrew hadn't yet considered running for any kind of office, but he made good money with his construction business. I was a teacher, but we wanted to get pregnant again and were talking about having me stay home permanently. Vince was always an independent child, but it'd seemed lately that he'd become even more so, and I missed having a baby in the house. I missed the way they sounded, the way they smelled. I missed the little laughter and holding them in my arms."

She sighed and looked down at her hands. "So we decided to have another baby, decided to try before we were too old to have another, and everything was going to be perfect and wonderful. I wanted a little girl. Andrew wanted another boy. Vince couldn't care less either way as long as it didn't interfere with *his* life. He was very blunt as a child. Very straightforward. No-nonsense. He was never the smartest kid, and he's not the smartest adult, but you'd always hear the truth from him, no matter how abrasive it could be."

"Yeah," I said quietly. "I've noticed that."

She smiled to herself. "I figured you would. That's the difference between Vince and most people. He doesn't beat around the bush about things, but only because I don't think he knows how. He's singularly driven at times, if there is something he wants. Oh, he doesn't step on others to get it; no, I think that would hurt him if he tried. He… he just knows what he wants, and he goes for it, and the only consequences he doesn't worry about are those that could happen to his own self.

"One day, when he was nine and we were trying to have another baby, Andrew and I were upstairs and… well, you know. We were *trying*. Vince had been playing outside with his friends all morning and wasn't expected back in until lunch, which would have still been an hour away." Her voice was getting quieter, rougher. I wanted to tell her she didn't have to say anymore, but I couldn't find the strength to speak.

"After Andrew and I had finished, I went downstairs to make a cup of tea. I'd decided that I wanted the mug I'd used that morning instead of getting a new one. Had I not done that, I would not have walked over to the dishwasher. I would have not looked out the window. I would not have seen Vince floating facedown in the middle of the pool, the water around him red."

She said she remembered screaming for her husband, the tea mug falling to the floor and shattering. She would find out later from Vince's friends that he'd gone out back to get his squirt gun he'd left by the pool the previous day. He wouldn't be able to tell her exactly what happened, but from the size of the bump on his head, it seemed he'd slipped on the wet surface around the pool and hit his skull on the edge of the pool before falling in. She'd jumped into the pool and flipped him over. Andrew had followed her in, and they'd dragged him to the edge, then lifted him out of the water.

"He was blue," she said. "He was blue, his little lips and little face. I was screaming and Andrew was yelling at me to go call for help, but I was just *screaming*. I couldn't stop because it seemed that every single part of him was *blue* and he wasn't breathing. I knew then, I knew he was dead and that I'd never see him again. So I just screamed."

But eventually she had stopped and run inside, only after Andrew had started CPR, pressing on his chest so hard she was afraid he was going to break Vince's ribs. She'd babbled into the phone and then dropped it back onto the counter. She couldn't imagine, she said, staying on the phone and listening to the irritatingly calm operator. She thought she'd go insane if she had to, so she dropped the phone and ran out to her husband, who was slamming his fists onto Vince's chest. She tried to stop him, she tried to hold his arm back, but he knocked her down and hit Vince again.

"Do you know what happened then, Paul?" she asked me.

I shook my head, though I had an idea.

"Vince took in this great, gasping breath. His back arched off the ground like he was seizing, but he was *breathing*. He vomited up so much water at that point that I thought he was going to drown all over again, but one thing I learned as a mother is that if your child is crying, your child can breathe, and he was *crying*. I never thought that sound could mean happiness, that it could fill me with joy, but it could. It did. He cried and I cried, but only because I knew how close it'd been. Only because I knew how much I could have lost." She fell silent and watched the sunlit flowers.

"Why did you tell me this?" I asked her.

"Because," she said. "Because I needed you to know that I love my son. Regardless of my actions or the actions of my husband, we love our son. We almost went insane that day when we thought we'd lost him. I don't know that we would've survived had he died. No parent should ever have to outlive their child. So I need you to know that we love him in our hearts more than we could ever show."

"It's not good enough," I said, flinching at my own words.

"Oh?" She looked up at me, but there was no recrimination in her eyes. "And how do you figure that?"

"Because I doubt you've ever said to him what you're saying to me."

And this time, she *did* react. I could see it in her eyes, could see it in the way her skeletal-like hands made skeletal-like fists. "You don't have any idea how hard it is, do you? Being a parent? Especially when you're in the public eye, such as Andrew and I are. Politics tend to govern your lives when it's your job."

I shook my head. "Doesn't matter. That's not an excuse. As a matter of fact, that should have prevented both of you from ever acting as you did. If you're responsible enough to become a parent, then you should be responsible enough to accept your kid no matter how they turn out. It doesn't matter if they're disabled or gay or not as smart as others or green or black or blue or whatever the hell they turn out to be. You have them, you love them. Always. Being a parent isn't about getting to pick and choose what you want your kid to be. Being a parent means protecting your kid from anything that could ever harm him. Being a parent means you shelter, but you also make them stronger so one day they can stand on their own. How old was Vince when he came out to you? To his dad?"

"Sixteen," she whispered.

"And what was your reaction?"

"Anger. Indifference. We didn't understand. We didn't…."

"That's right. You didn't."

She looked up at me, tears in her eyes, but not yet falling. "He came in here yesterday and told us about you. You know what I noticed, Paul? You know what I saw in him the most?"

"No."

"Happiness. It was such a bright thing, such a fierce thing. He was so proud that he was able to find someone like you, that you belonged to him. I've never seen him so sure about anything in his life."

How many more times did I need to hear that before I started to believe it? "Trust me, I'm not that great," I told her honestly. "He was just talking me up. For whatever reason, he does that, though I don't know why. I tend to trip and run into things like dogs and walls. I can't control my mouth and end up saying things that make situations far more awkward then they really need to be. And I'm pretty sure that my ancestors once owned slaves and we've never made reparations for that, so my family is probably cursed by some ancient form of African voodoo magic. So… you know." And then, almost as an afterthought, "And it's only been a week."

"You know, for someone who talks highly about the worth of another, you don't seem to know your own," she said.

I tried to stop myself from rolling my eyes, but I didn't succeed. "I know you're probably filled with a bunch of medicine right now, but I hope you're not so high that you think you're a fortune cookie."

She laughed. "I like you, Paul."

"You do?" I asked, surprised. "I've broken into your hospital room, chewed you out as I criticized your parenting skills, all the while reminding you that you probably only have a few days left to live and demanding that you do things the way *I* want you to. And then you say you *like* me? If I were you, I'd probably hate my guts and get the Secret Service in here to take me away and throw my body in a ditch near the Mexican border. If you do that, I ask that you tell them to make it quick because I think I'd be a big baby under torture. It's probably why I could never be a spy."

"And that's the only reason?"

"I can act," I said with a scowl. "I played a block of cheese once, you know."

"Paul?"

"Yeah?"

"Do you care for my son?"

"More than I thought possible," I confessed. "I tried to fight it. Honestly. My parents...."

She waited.

I pushed forward. "They married a week after they met. And the way they met was weirdly mirroring how Vince and I met, and it's just so damn implausible and it doesn't make sense. It's like the universe is trying to shove your son down my throat and I'm trying to show I don't have a gag reflex, and now that I think about it, I really wish I hadn't just said that to you. That your son goes down my throat, not that I don't have a gag reflex." I blushed furiously. "Er. Both, actually. Look, can you please not think about me having sex with your son? It'd really make my day. Where is that fucking time machine when you need it?"

She grinned at me. "I don't think I'll get that image out of my head for as long as I live."

I choked on my tongue. "Did you just make a *dying* joke?" I asked in awe.

"Too soon?" she asked, arching her eyebrow and looking so much like Vince that I wanted to see him so badly right that second I almost hurt.

"Well, at least we know that regardless of whatever else you could have been, a comedian would have been one thing."

"Is he going to be hurt, after I'm gone?"

I frowned. "You're his mother. It doesn't matter what happened before. He's still going to lose you. Yes. It's going to hurt him."

She nodded. "Then I need you to promise me something."

"What?"

"That you'll take care of him. That you won't let him hurt for too long before you make him smile again. I am asking that you watch over my son, Paul. To make sure that he will come out of this okay."

I started to backpedal. "What about his dad? Or Darren? Or anyone else who has known him longer than I have? What if we decide we hate each other next week? What if he decides he *hates* me like an hour from now? He doesn't know I'm here. I'm pretty sure this constitutes as lying. Already."

"My husband won't understand," she said sadly. "And maybe that's my fault. I've sided with him for far too long. I've put his career ahead of things that I should not have ignored. I thought it was for the best, but I was wrong. Hindsight is a dangerous thing, especially this close to the end."

"What about Darren?" I asked desperately. "He's got to be able to do more."

Her eyes hardened. "Darren," she said slowly. "There's something you should know about Darren. He and Vince are—"

"Paul?" A surprised voice. A confused voice. A hurt voice.

I closed my eyes. *Oh, fuck.*

"What are you doing here?" Vince asked. "Mom, what's going on?"

"Paul was kind enough to stop by and bring me flowers," Lori said lightly, her skin going a little paler than it was before. She knew as well as I did that we'd been caught. "Wasn't that just sweet of him?"

Vince pushed past me until he was standing in between me and his mother, as if he was protecting one of us from the other, though I couldn't say which one was which. I know which one I hoped, but it immediately made me feel like an ass, so I pushed it away. This wasn't supposed to be about me.

"How did you know she was here?" he snapped at me. He looked angry, the first time I'd ever seen it. His eyes were narrowed, nostrils flaring. His chest rose and fell rapidly, his arms tense at his side.

"I was unaware that I couldn't have visitors," Lori said from behind him.

"The girl from the bike store," I told him honestly. "She mentioned your mom was sick and who your parents were. I wanted to come see her before there wasn't a chance to. That's all."

"That was days ago," he said, taking a step toward me. "Why didn't you say anything before then?"

I was on the defensive, though I didn't want to be. Going on the defensive meant I felt I had done something wrong, and maybe I had, but I needed to find a way to stand my ground. "Why didn't you just tell me who your parents were?" I asked him. "Jesus, Vince. You've met my whole fucking family already. For fuck's sake. You told my *mom* about your parents. Why wouldn't you tell *me* anything about yours?"

His eyes grew wary. "She told you about that?"

"No. She didn't. I was on my way back in to rescue you and heard you talking to her. Don't you try and blame her for anything, Vince. She didn't do anything wrong."

"I want you to go, Paul," he told me coldly. Somehow, his tone hurt more than his anger. He sounded like he was talking to a complete stranger.

"Vince, you need to calm down," his mother scolded. "Paul didn't do a damn thing wrong. If anything, this should show you how much he cares about you."

"Vince—"

"I can't see you right now. Please." His voice broke as he took a step back. "You shouldn't have come here. You shouldn't have gone behind my back."

"I just wanted to make sure she saw you as I do," I said helplessly. "I didn't know what else to do."

He laughed, but there was no humor in it. "I guess I shouldn't have expected you to. You were right, after all. We've only known each other a few days. You said it over and over and I didn't listen, so how could you possibly understand why this would hurt me?"

"The only way I'll know is if you tell me." I stood, rooted in my spot.

"Go away, Paul. Please." He reached up and wiped his eyes furiously. That hurt more than I ever thought it would, to see him upset and not able to do anything about it. Worse, being the *cause* of it, though I didn't understand why. "I don't want you here."

And that broke my trance, my reluctance. Those five simple words were enough to bring me back to my senses. I nodded at him, wondering how I could have possibly allowed him past my defenses, how I could have thought this would have worked. Being in love after days was stupid. It was foolish. It wasn't love. It couldn't be, not really. Love at first sight was a sweet thought, a romantic notion, but it wasn't real. Removed from the situation, I'd see that. I'd know. I'd see clearly. He didn't want me here to help him through whatever he was going through, and who was I to argue with him about that? He'd made himself very clear.

"I'm sorry," I said, but not to him, to his mother. I looked over his shoulder into her wet eyes. She shook her head at me, but I ignored it. "I'm sorry for what you're going through, and I'm sorry I won't be able to promise you anything. I wish… I wish I could have gotten to know you better. You seem like a very nice lady, and my heart breaks for your family." I turned my gaze to Vince, just for a moment. *And for you. Somehow, you've gotten past all my defenses and you almost made me believe. My heart breaks for you most of all.*

I turned and walked away.

CHAPTER 17

Interventions: Not Just For Addicts And Hoarders Anymore

"GO AWAY," I moaned from underneath my blanket as Sandy pounded on my bedroom door. "The light, it burns! I'm all alone and it *burns*."

"I *knew* I shouldn't have let you go into the bedroom!" he said through the door. "You open it right this minute or I swear to God I will break it down."

"You weigh, like, twenty pounds," I reminded him. "The only thing you'll be breaking is the idea that you could break down anything. Now go away and let me wallow in my own pity. Or you could go out and buy me six boxes of Ding Dongs so that I can eat them all at once and drown myself in chocolate while I decide if I'm going to go find Christ as a monk in the Himalayas or if I'm going to turn straight."

"I'll buy you so many Ding Dongs," he said soothingly. "Just open the door and we'll go get them together. I promise. I'll eat them with you and then we'll go to Los Betos and I'll buy you the biggest burrito your face has ever seen. Or if you decide to turn straight, I'll find you so many girls and all the vagina you can eat. We may need to get you a couple of practice girls first just to make sure you're doing it right. Or we could just go get a cantaloupe and cut it, and you can practice on that while we look up technique on the Internet."

"You want me to perform cunnilingus on a *cantaloupe*? It's like you don't even know me at all!"

He pounded on the door again. "Open this door!"

"No! It's all your fault! I *told* you!"

"*What*? It was *your* idea to go!"

"No, not that. When we were ten years old! I *told* you then! You *promised* me!"

"Are you doing lines of coke in there or something? What are you talking about?"

"The *promise!*" I bellowed at him. "When we were ten and I accidentally told Billy Harvey that I had a crush on him and he ran away screaming, I made you promise me to never let me think of ideas on my own ever again, and *furthermore*, if I *did* think of ideas on my own, you were *never* to let me act on them."

"Oh, yeah," he said. Then he chuckled. "I saved you on that one, though. It turns out Billy Harvey wasn't that great of a fuck. He had a small penis. Even at sixteen, I knew the difference."

I glared at the door. "You had *sex* with him? You do *everyone*! I can't wait until it's your birthday because I'm going to buy a sign for your front yard that says, 'Sandy lives here and blows everything that moves.'"

"If you open the door, I'll blow you," he promised.

"I don't want your love," I said dramatically. "Ha, I bet I'm the only person in the free world that's ever said *that* to you."

"Open this door!"

"Alllllll by myyyyyyselllllf," I sang forlornly. "Don't wanna be, alllllllll byyyyyy myyyy—"

Something slammed into the door. "Ow," Sandy muttered. "When did you replace the doors with sheets of steel?"

I rolled my eyes. "They're not. They're oak. Maybe that's like your kryptonite. Or maybe you're just a tiny, tiny man."

"Oak? So if I was a superhero, all anyone would have to do is bring a log of oak to a fight and I'd lose? That sounds supremely lame."

"Or, like, what would happen if your arch-nemeses lured you into the middle of an oak forest in the middle of fall? He would stand above you cackling as the orange leaves fell from the trees and you writhed in pain on the forest floor."

"What would my superhero name be? The Oak Diva? Got Wood? Lincoln Log?"

I considered. "Got Wood works, only because it's kitschy. But you can't be named after your weakness. It'd be too easy to kill you. Duh."

"And what would my superpower be?"

That one was harder. "Insatiable dance moves," I finally decided. "You can woo anyone with the magic roll of your hips." I started getting excited at the idea, already picturing the superhero costume in my head, complete with bitchin' thigh-high boots. "And then you could have a catch phrase that'd be all like—Wait a minute... you're trying to distract me!"

He sounded bewildered. "'Wait a minute you're trying to distract me' would be my catch-phrase? That sounds kind of dumb."

"No, you bastard! You're trying to distract me from the fact that you totally helped me fuck up everything!"

He snorted. "I didn't do jack."

"I knew this was a bad idea. I knew I should have never gotten involved with him in the first place. Stupid shit like this always happens. It's fucking ridiculous."

He groaned. "Are you really going to have an 'I feel so bad for myself' bitch fest? *Really?*"

"I'm allowed," I said. "I think. While it was possibly the shortest relationship on record, it burned pretty brightly."

"Who said it's over?"

"You didn't see the look on his face, Sandy," I said quietly. "I don't even really know why he got so mad, but he was. He didn't want me there, he made that much clear."

"That doesn't mean you guys broke up," he pointed out. "It could mean just what he said: that he didn't want you there."

"Yeah?" I sniffed.

"Yeah. Why don't you open the door now?"

"Yeah, I'm not going to do that."

"What?"

"Apparently your superpower is deviousness because I can see *right through you*! Trying to act like you're on my side and shit and then make me open the door so you can bite my head off like a gigantic praying mantis! I won't be your dinner, Sandy! I fucking won't!"

"That's it," he growled. "I'm calling Matty and Larry."

"You wouldn't *dare*."

"*And* Nana. And yes I would, you just watch me."

"I'm calling your bluff."

"I'm dialing my phone! That noise? That's me pressing the buttons!" I could hear the loud tones of a number being dialed. "You better come out before I tell your mom that you're pouting in your room because you and your boyfriend had a fight! You know what she'll do, Paul."

"Go to hell!"

"Hi, Matty? I'm good, sugar, thank you. Hey, you won't *believe* what Paul is doing right now." His voice faded as he walked down the hall.

I quickly looked to my window to make my escape, only to remember I'd put stylish safety bars on the outside after I'd moved in so no one could break in and rape me in the middle of the night. I cursed my intent to keep myself pure because I could not escape from my prison now. I was pretty sure I could take down Sandy if I tried, but then I remembered what he looked like as Helena and that was one fierce bitch and I didn't think it would be good for my already bruised ego to get knocked flat on my ass by a man who weighed forty pounds less than I did.

I just couldn't seem to get the look on Vince's face out of my head, like I'd betrayed him somehow by going in and seeing his mom. Lori had been right when she talked about how much hindsight sucked. Granted, hers was a bit more profound, what with a lifetime of regret, and mine made it sound like I was a thirteen-year-old girl since I was pining after my weeklong relationship.

But I still couldn't get him out of my head. I couldn't shake the feeling that I should have opened my mouth the night before and said aloud what I'd thought when I'd looked at the star he'd named after me. I should have told him then that I knew about his mom and dad, how he was going to regret it for the rest of his life if he didn't spend every waking moment with her until she was gone. I should have told him to put the past behind him and to just let it be until it was no more. It's easier to be angry at someone when they're gone, not when they're still here and suffering. He could have hated her then. He didn't need to now.

But she didn't seem like someone to be hated. She didn't seem like the wicked bitch I thought she'd be, the stereotypical bigot who didn't love her son because of who he was. Granted, it sounded like she'd put her husband's political aspirations ahead of her own family. That was a different kind of negligence. Indifference might not have the connotations of hate, but it could hurt just as badly.

I must have been lost in my thoughts a while, because the next thing I knew, there were the murmur of voices outside my door. I rolled my eyes and tried to shut them out.

There was another pounding on the door, this one a little lighter than Sandy's egregious wailing. "Paul?" Nana called sweetly. "We're here for your intervention. I brought you Ding Dongs *and* Los Betos."

"Oh, for heaven's sake," Mom said. "You can't tell him we're here for an intervention and then try to bribe him with food. He's not going to fall for that. We tried that when he was a kid, and he locked himself in his room until we promised to get Zack Morris from *Saved By The Bell* to come to his birthday party. He didn't believe it then, either. He said that if that was true, we'd put the food near the floor and blow on it so he could smell the burritos through the crack in the door."

Yeah, yeah. I was a fat kid. So what. I liked food. Bite me.

"And Zack still never came to the birthday party," I retorted through the door. "That's probably one of the reasons I'm so messed up today."

"Your father tried to dress up like him for you," Mom said.

"He dressed like Screech! No one likes Screech. All the kids at my party thought he was a homeless clown! And I don't smell Los Betos, you liars!"

"Oh, he's a smart one," Nana said, obviously sounding impressed. "You don't fall for the bait unless you have proof of life."

"I don't think that's quite what that means," Dad said. "And a homeless clown? Really, Paul? I never made fun of *you* when you dressed up like an orange dice for that play you were in."

"I *told* you," Sandy crowed.

"He was so wonderful in that," my mother said tearfully. "What was his famous line, Larry? You know, the one that everyone was quoting?"

"Give me dairy," everyone said, "or give me osteoporosis!"

"This can't possibly be healthy," I muttered.

"Is he going to open the door?" Sandy asked. "I tried to break it down, but he must have changed his doors to some kind of unbreakable metal."

"Or you could just eat more," Mom scolded him. "I saw you, like, three days ago and I swear you've lost at least thirty-eight pounds."

"It's all the crack I smoke," he explained. "I don't have time to eat because I'm too busy thinking crack thoughts."

"What are crack thoughts?" Nana asked.

"Oh, things like the government is going to come steal my babies."

"You don't have babies," Dad said, obviously frowning. "Unless I missed something and you adopted that Croatian baby that Paul wanted."

"I don't have babies," Sandy said. "But crack makes you think crazy things. That's why Whitney said crack is whack, God rest her soul."

"You shouldn't be smoking crack," my dad said sternly. "First Paul's a pony, and now you're smoking crack and having the government steal your babies? Who is Whitney? Is that your dealer?"

"Whitney Houston," Mom said. "You know, dear. She was that singer who sang that song you like that Helena performed."

"'Hit Me Baby, One More Time?'"

"That's Britney, dear."

"'Dirty?'"

"That was Christina."

"Umbrella?"

"And that was Rihanna. Larry, you're embarrassing yourself. You have a gay *son*, for God's sake. How can you not know your divas?" Mom sounded affronted. "Paul? Paul! If you can hear me, don't listen to your father! He obviously doesn't know his ass from his elbow!"

"Language," Dad scolded. "And I know my divas. I know them very well. What about that Woman Goo-Goo that Helena performs like?"

"That's Lady Gaga," Sandy sighed. "Did you really look at me and think I was Woman Goo-Goo? I don't know how I feel about that. I just might be offended."

"Your hair was very pretty," Dad deflected.

"Thank you, sugar," Helena purred. "You need to come back and see me sometime. I sure do miss you when you're not around."

"Oh, you," Dad giggled, obviously blushing.

"Oh *Christ*," I gagged.

"Language!"

"Dear, as much as I love you flirting with Sandy in front of me— Sandy, you should know Larry would most likely be a bottom, so I don't know really what you two would do together aside from bumping bums—we're here for Paul."

"That's right," Nana said. "He's obviously very depressed, and this is a cry for attention. I don't want him to go all emo and cut himself."

"I'm not going to cut myself," I said.

"Paul could never be a cutter," Mom said. "He's too much of a baby when it comes to pain. He'd go the Sylvia Plath route and stick his head in a gas oven like a real lady."

"Bull," Dad said. "He'd take sleeping pills and then choke on his own vomit."

"You're both wrong," Sandy said. "He'd get drunk on gin and fall asleep smoking Virginia Slim 120s and accidentally set the bed on fire."

"For some reason, I don't think the best way to start an intervention is by discussing the best way for the person you are intervening on to kill themselves," I told them. "That person might take it the wrong way."

"Mary J. Blige," Dad exclaimed. "She's another diva! She did that song 'No More Drama'. I think that was my favorite costume you had, Sandy."

"Oh, baby doll," Helena exclaimed. "I love it as well."

"That's such an apt song for right now," Nana said.

"If you start singing it, I'm going to lose it," I growled at her.

She sniffed. "I'll have you know that I was considered quite the singer back in my day. I didn't even have to show my breasts like all the young women do now. What happened to talent for talent's sake? Now if you want to be famous, it's about how much meat is on your dress or how much nipple you are willing to show."

"It's a tragedy," Dad agreed. "I don't know why we have to live in a time with meat nipples or whatever you said."

"Shall we get started?" Mom asked. "I have a feeling if we don't start now, we'll never get this done, and Paul will waste away in there because his pride won't allow him to give in."

"My body will just suck up its fat stores," I reminded them. "Maybe it'll be a good idea for me to stay in here. When I finally come out in a week, I could go into modeling and forget this week ever happened when I'm walking the runway in Milan."

"You'll have to change your name," Sandy said. "Paul doesn't sound like a modeling name."

"Well, *I* think Paul is a handsome name," Mom said. "I picked it, after all. But I could see how Sandy could be right. Maybe you should change your name to Gregorio?"

"Or Tunus?" Dad said.

"Or Talon?" Nana added.

"Ooooo," they all breathed.

"Talon is a good one," Sandy said. "Okay, let's get started."

"What are you guys doing?" I demanded through the door as something started to scrape on the other side.

"None of your business," Mom said. "Go back to pouting."

"I *wasn't* pouting!"

"Dear, remember that little pouting face he would get whenever he didn't get something he wanted? I always thought that he looked like a little cherub with those cheeks, even if it was the most annoying thing on the planet."

"Yes," Dad said, "but you fell for it every time."

"That's because I'm a good mother."

"You are pretty good," I agreed. "Most of the time. Right now is not one of those times."

The scraping continued until I realized that they were unscrewing the hinges from the door so they could take it off its frame. "I'm going to call the police and tell them you're breaking in!"

Sandy snorted. "If you do, can you make sure the fire department comes too? I am pretty sure I am owed some eye candy after having to put up with these shenanigans. And tell them I want the fireman to look exactly like the fireman calendar you had in 1999."

"Mr. October," we both groaned. Mr. October had been the most drool-worthy man ever to walk the face of the earth. My teenage fantasies of him (he who I had named Rodrigo) had included everything from him saving me from dragons (I was on a bit of a fantasy kick there for a while) to he and I being spies and falling madly in love on an undercover assignment, only to be betrayed by a mole higher up and being torn apart (no worries, though; the fantasy continued and after the betrayal, we were reunited three years later in a fiery passion on a beach in his homeland of Italy).

"I want firemen too," I said. "Maybe I'll just call them anyway."

"I thought we were doing this because you were in love with someone already?" Nana asked. "I don't think your parents raised you to be a whore."

"Language!" Dad barked.

"I think he might try to beat our record," Mom said.

"I've known him longer than a week," I said for some damn reason.

"Yes, but you didn't actually *talk* to him the first time until Monday, right?"

"I don't think I told you that, so the fact that you know kind of creeps me out."

"I have spies everywhere," Mom said, cackling.

"She really does," Dad said.

"Sandy is your spy, isn't he?"

"You bet he is," Mom said.

"No firemen for Sandy!" I decreed.

"You're going to make me a spinster," he muttered.

"And that should do it," Dad said. "You know, you kids today with your fancy iPads and iPhones and iTunes and iPods. None of those would have helped you here. Maybe I should market this as the iScrewdriver and see how much money I could make."

"Billions," I said. "And I'm pretty sure the market value just dropped 300 percent on my house since you unscrewed this door. Thanks, Dad."

With a grunt, he lifted it out of the way and set it against the wall. I glared at the four of them, especially when I saw that Nana did *not* have Ding Dongs and a burrito from Los Betos. One should not promise Los Betos if one cannot deliver, for it might make another person extraordinarily pissy.

"You done pouting?" Mom asked.

I crossed my arms and stuck out my bottom lip. "I'm *not* pouting."

"He's not done pouting," Dad told Mom.

"Okay, well, let's get this intervention started," Nana said gleefully.

They all started forward into the room, forcing me to take steps back until my legs hit the bed and I had to sit. Nana pulled out my desk chair and sat in it with a grunt, scooching closer to me until our knees bumped together. Mom sat to one side of me and put her hand on mine, and Dad sat on my other side, pressing his leg against mine. Sandy sat on the floor near my feet, and I suddenly understood what it meant to have your family smothering you.

"Who would like to begin?" Mom asked.

"We're not really doing this," I snapped. "This is ridiculous!"

"I will," Nana said as she pulled a massive pile of paper from her purse. She began to read in a flat monotone. "Paul, when you do stupid things, it makes me sad. I couldn't believe when Sandy called us and told us that you'd—"

"When in the hell did you have time to write this?" I asked, dropping my jaw. "These things *just* happened! Sandy *just* called you!"

"I already had something written," Nana said, affronted. "I modified it on the way over here. Can I finish, please?"

"Of course you can," Mom said, patting her hand.

"No, she *can't*—"

"Paul," she shouted over me, starting to read again, "when you do stupid things, it makes me sad! I couldn't believe when Sandy called us and told us that you'd gone behind your partner's back to see his mom! And then, to make it worse, you locked yourself in your room and started to cry!"

"I didn't *cry*—"

"It hurts me to see you like this! I want you to be happy, but you keep sabotaging yourself! You need to allow yourself to be happy and to stay off meth and—Wait… I don't think I got this far to change it. Hold on a second." She pulled a pen from her purse and squinted down at the paper, starting to scratch off words and muttering to herself.

"You know," I told her, "I don't know what's more unreal: the fact that you already had an intervention speech written out in case I got strung out on *meth*, or the fact that this is actually happening right now."

"I like to prepare for every eventuality," Nana said.

"I told you to open the door," Sandy said mildly. "Since you didn't, this is what had to happen."

"We're here because we love you," Mom said.

"And because Vince is pretty great," Dad said. "You'd have to be pretty stupid to let him go."

"He *made* me go," I reminded them.

"You probably just surprised him," Mom pointed out. "He wasn't expecting you to be there and it freaked him out."

"Okay," Nana murmured to herself in concentration. "I should also probably take out the part where I ask if I could have your stuff if you ever overdosed. That doesn't seem applicable here." She crossed out even more. I wanted to ask her how many pages her intervention speech ran, but didn't think I wanted to know the answer.

"You probably would have done the same thing," my dad said. "Scratch that; I *know* you would have done the same thing. But it's not *about* you. This is about him. This is about how he's going to lose his mother very shortly. This is about how he's going to need someone to lean on and that someone should be you."

I tried to stand, but they wouldn't let me. I was starting to get pissed, but at who, I didn't know. "You know," I growled at them all, "everyone keeps *saying* that to me, that he's going to need me, that he's going to depend on me, but that's bullshit. If he needed me, he wouldn't have sent me away. If he needed me, he would have told me what was going on. If he wanted me as much as he claimed, he would have fucking let me in instead of allowing me to act all stupid and do what I did. So you're right. This isn't about me. This is all on him."

"That's not fair," Mom said firmly. "It's not fair and you know it. Everything around him right now is heightened to an extreme."

"Exactly," I snapped at her, trying to ignore the hurt look on her face. "*Everything* is heightened. There's no way he would have fallen for me that quickly. There's no way I could love him this fast. Everything is just moving at light speed, and it's because of what he is going through. That's all it is. It's just that and nothing more."

Dad snorted. "You were always such a terrible liar."

"That's a good thing, though," Mom said. "Rather him be bad at it than good."

"He tried to tell me once that this singlet I found at the thrift store looked good on me," Sandy said. "But he kept twitching like he's doing now and it totally gave him away."

"Did you buy it anyway?" Dad asked.

"No. Paul made the very good point that most likely someone else's balls or vagina had been smooshed in that before I got my hands on it, and I couldn't in good faith wear it without getting grossed out."

"Oh, man," Dad groaned. "Maybe I *should* be a homosexual. Smooshed vagina? No offense, Matty, but *yuck*."

"I'll support you with whatever you decide to do," Mom told him, reaching over me to hold his hand. "I could always be your fruit fly if you do come out."

"That would be interesting," Dad said. "Do you think I could be a leather daddy?"

"You could pull it off," she said. "I know you can."

"Paul has chaps you could borrow," Sandy said, a little bit of Helena poking through. "I would have no problem seeing that. You'd be pretty hot, Larry."

"I probably shouldn't add that I'd have Johnny Depp officiate your funeral," Nana muttered, scribbling furiously. "Somehow, I don't think that would be appreciated."

"I'm pretty sure I'm the only person in the world who wishes he could be deaf," I said to no one in particular. "And blind."

"You don't wish that," Mom said. "What an awful thing to say."

"You should probably take that back," Dad said. "You don't want to piss off God and wake up tomorrow blind and deaf."

"Fine, I take it back," I mumbled. I didn't *really* want to be blind and deaf. "But if God is granting wishes, I wish you'd all go away."

"I don't think God is a genie," Sandy said. "But if he is, I wish for those two-thousand-dollar boots I saw in the boutique downtown. In red."

"I wish for world peace," Nana said. "And then six billion dollars."

"I wish for more wishes," Dad said.

"I wish for my son to stop being so pigheaded," Mom said.

We waited.

"And for Vin Diesel to come to my house and be my naked maid," she finished with a blush.

"I could take him in a fight," Dad said, flexing his arms. "I'll be your naked maid when we get home. Do you need dusting, Mrs. Auster?"

"I am feeling pretty dusty," Mom agreed, winking at him.

"I'm sitting right between you two! Gross!"

"Gee, thanks for pointing out the obvious," Dad said, rolling his eyes.

"Finished!" Nana said. "Paul, when you do stupid things, it makes me sad. I couldn't believe when Sandy called us and told us that you'd gone behind your partner's back to see his mom! And then, to make it worse, you locked yourself in your room and started to cry. I wish that things could go back to the way they were before. Like the way they were yesterday. Yesterday was a good day. Do you remember? You came over to my house with Vince and we all had dinner and I showed him Slutty Snow White and Johnny Depp loved him and Vince tried to eat your face outside after he found the bike. I wasn't supposed to see that, but it was kind of hard not to notice when you got slammed up against the side of my house. In conclusion, you should go after Vince, and never do meth because you'll lose your teeth and get weird spots on your face. No one likes weird spots." She looked up at me and smiled.

"That was lovely, Gigi," Sandy said, leaning his head against her leg. "You are such an eloquent speaker."

"Thank you, honey," she said, preening. "It goes on for an additional sixteen pages, but I felt that was enough to make my point."

"Paul, do you love him?" my mom asked suddenly.

I didn't have time to think. "Yes... oh shit. I meant *no*. Of course not. I don't know what you're talking about."

They waited.

I sighed. "Yes," I whispered. "I don't know how or when or why, but yes." I hung my head.

My dad reached up and rubbed my back. "Paul, did you know that me and your mom almost got divorced?"

I snapped my head back up. "What? What are you talking about? You guys met, everything was rosy, and a week later you were married. There was no divorce. There wasn't even an *almost*."

"No. Not completely. Oh, I knew I loved her right away, and I knew she loved me after she tried to kill me with her car, but I didn't know if that was going to be enough." He smiled over at my mom whose eyes were a bit watery. "It's one thing to love a person, but it's another to love them regardless of their faults. And I had a bunch of them."

"He really did," Mom mused happily. "So many faults."

"So many," he agreed. "So when I asked her to marry me, I was sure she was going to laugh at me, even if she did love me. It was going to be too fast, I thought she'd say. We were too young. We didn't really know a thing about each other. But I knew what I wanted, and I wanted her. For the rest of my life."

Sandy sighed and wiped his eyes. "So lovely," he sniffed.

"But she said yes. She said yes with this little laugh she has that sounds like bells. She said yes and we got married down at city hall and she moved in the next day. A week later, she moved out."

"He was a bit of a slob," Mom said. "And a jerk. He wanted things done *his* way and on *his* timeline. And, of course, that didn't work for me. At all. I was used to living my own life, and suddenly I was thrust in with this man that I really didn't know. So one day while he was in class, I packed up and moved back home.

"How long did that last?" I asked, unsure why I'd never heard this part of their lives before.

"Six months," Dad said. "I was devastated when I came home, but I understood. Or at least that's what I tried to tell myself. I went over to Nana's house and begged her to come back but she said no. I asked her if she wanted an annulment, and she said no to that too. I asked her what she wanted. She told me she wanted to date."

"We'd already gotten the falling in love part out of the way," Mom explained. "That was the hard part, and we got it done before most people would. What was left was just learning about each other to make sure the love we had was something that would last. Sometimes it's enough to love someone just the way they are. Other times, you have to work at it so that it doesn't fade away."

"Why are you telling me this?" I asked quietly. "Why now?"

"Because you love him," Dad said. "Even with all the little voices inside your head saying it's too soon, that it's not enough, that he's so much better than you are, you love him. And he loves you. And you know it as well as I do. Someone who tells you that they're going to fall in love with you, or that they're partway there, is *already* there."

"But you're not letting yourself believe it," Mom said, admonishing me slightly. "You're so used to what you had before that this is scaring you. And it'd be easier to walk away. It would be easier to pretend this never happened. But the things we want in life will never be easy, and if you want it, if you *really* do, then you need to fight for it with everything you've got. It's only yours to lose, Paul. Only you can make it go away."

"It's like all of you are after-school-specialing on me," I groaned. "I feel so cheap and used and covered in grossness, like some twink after a bareback gang bang."

"And how would you know what that feels like?" Dad asked. "Is there something we should know?"

"Not at all," I said quickly. "Just an expression gay guys use."

They looked to Sandy, who shrugged. "I understood what he meant."

I like you, I mouthed to him because I wasn't quite back to love yet. He rolled his eyes.

"So what now?" Nana asked. "I feel like this intervention was modestly successful. I don't think Paul will be doing meth again anytime soon."

"I wasn't on meth!"

"Well, if this were a romantic comedy, this would be the part where Paul would go out searching for the love of his life," Sandy said. "There'd be really cheesy music playing in the background while he went over to his boyfriend's apartment to apologize for being an idiot and to hug him and kiss him and then get down to bidness."

"Oh my," Mom said. "I think we've been watching the wrong movies."

"By 'bidness', do you mean Paul would be a pony again?" Dad asked. "I must admit, I'm fascinated by that idea now." He glanced back over to my mom. "We should get a riding crop."

"Deal," Mom said.

"I'm not a fucking pony!"

"Language," Dad scolded.

"I should just call him first," I said.

"No!" everyone said back.

"It's not spontaneous enough," Sandy said with a sigh.

"It has to be face to face," Mom said, a wistful look in her eye.

"He has to see that you mean it," Dad said, patting my arm.

"You should probably dress sexy," Nana said.

"I'm not going over to his house if I don't even know if he's there. I don't want to have to stand outside his apartment and have one of his neighbors call the police three hours later because I look creepy and bored. And lonely."

"His car was there when we drove by," Mom said without a hint of guilt. "So most likely he's already home."

I stared at them. They stared back.

"This isn't like some fucking romantic comedy," I said finally, grasping at my only and final excuse.

"Why?" Sandy asked.

"Because, this was just a fight. I think." *I hope.* "We haven't done the whole clichéd big misunderstanding, breakup thing before we get back together. That *always* happens before things get better. I don't want it to get to that. I just… I can't."

"Maybe this time will be different," Mom said.

"Or maybe it won't," Dad said. "Maybe *this* was your big breakup. Maybe it won't work out. The point is that you'll never know unless you try."

"That's reassuring," I muttered.

"And you're going whether you like it or not," Nana said. "Even if I have to drag your ass there myself. Or maybe I could just call him for you right now?" She pulled out her phone. I made a lunge for her, but Mom and Dad traitorously held me back by my arms.

"I *will* call him," Nana said.

"Why is everyone threatening me with phone calls today?" I growled.

"Because that's the only thing you understand," Sandy said.

"Oh, look," Nana said. "I just hit another button."

"You don't even have his phone number," I smirked, calling her bluff.

She read it off. She had his phone number.

"Oh sweat balls," I mumbled, knowing I'd lost. "Fine. Jesus Christ."

"I'm pretty sure I want to hug all of you right now," Sandy gushed.

Gross. "I'm leaving before there's hugging. I don't think I want to drown in the sap anymore. This has been enough family time to last me the rest of my life. Don't touch me."

But, of course, as soon as I said it, I was surrounded. It was pretty fucking lame.

Sort of.

CUE the cheesy music.

I drove faster than I probably should have. I was nervous as all hell. All I wanted to do was to have Vince look at me and tell me he loved me just so I could say it back. I wanted to protect him from all the shit that was about to happen to him. I wanted to make everything better so he wouldn't have to be upset ever again. Unlikely? Probably. Unreasonable? Sure. People do the stupidest things when they're in love, no question. And while I still doubted myself, I don't think I doubted him.

Well, not until I pulled up to his apartment at least.

And got out of my car.

And started walking toward his front door.

And looked in the big window in his living room.

And saw him up against a wall, his head rocked back, eyes closed, mouth slack.

And saw the Homo Jock King wrapped around him, his face buried in Vince's neck, his body molded into Vince's, pressing him against the wall.

And saw Vince's arms around Darren, rubbing his back, up and down.

Yeah. There was the doubt right fucking there. A whole shitload of it.

My heart broke. And I turned to walk away.

CHAPTER 18
The Clichéd Part Near The End Where We Break Up

I MADE it back to my car, numb. I knew it had been too good to be true. I knew that I wasn't the type Vince went for. I knew he'd been full of shit. I knew he'd been Freddie Prinze Junioring me this whole time. I knew he'd never wanted me to begin with. I was too fat. I was too wary. I was too sarcastic. I was awkward and clumsy and didn't have the best hair or teeth. I didn't have abs and I didn't have a fourteen-inch cock. I worked a stupid job and I lived in a stupid house with my stupid two-legged dog. I was bland. Boring. Ordinary. I was Paul Auster and I was nothing.

But that look....

That look on his face when he'd given me a star, nervous and shy.

That look on his face as he lowered himself onto me, filled with wonder.

I got angry.

Then I got possessive.

Then I said "balderdash" really loudly for some reason.

Then I almost got in the car and drove away.

Then I stopped myself.

Then I knew I wasn't going down without a fight.

I'd take Darren on if I had to.

I'd show Vince. I'd show him why he belonged with me.

I'd fight the Homo Jock King. I'd duel for the chance to win Vince's hand. Ten paces at dawn with a pistol. Or a sword. Or my fists. Whatever.

"Fuck this noise," I said, turning back around.

CHAPTER 19

The Non-Clichéd Part Where I Go After What's Mine

AND my anger/bravery/awesomeness didn't even deflate when Vince opened his door after I'd pounded on it, looking less than pleased to see me. I almost felt bad for disrupting his foreplay, but then I realized I didn't feel bad about that at all.

"Paul," he said tightly.

I pushed past him. "Sorry, didn't mean to interrupt the love fest. Darren! So nice to see you here. Get your ass outside so I can beat the shit out of you. Now."

Darren eyes went comically wide. "Excuse me?"

I got right up in his face. "You and me? We're going to duel."

He snorted. "What the hell did you smoke?"

"A can of whoop ass," I told him. Then I thought about what I'd just said. "Wait... that didn't make sense. Quick, ask me again. I can do this." I popped my neck and hopped on both feet like I was a boxer. Gettin' loose. Gettin' loose.

"What?"

"Ask me again what I smoked."

"I don't... what are you talking about?"

"Just do it!"

"Okay? What did you smoke?"

"No, you have to say it like you did before."

"How did I say it before?"

"You were slightly amused, sarcastic and angry. I think. And you have to say 'hell' again too. Makes it sound more hard core when there's cussing."

"Saying 'hell' is cussing?"

"Yeah. Well, my dad says it is."

"You are so weird."

"You and me?" I growled at him. "We're going to duel."

He stared at me.

"Say your line!" I hissed at him.

"Er. What the hell did you smoke?"

"Nothing," I said grandly. "Because I *don't* smoke because smoking kills five hundred thousand Americans every year. *Dammit*! That didn't make sense either! Why can't I think of really awesome comeback lines?"

"Oh, is that what we're doing? Do it to me now. I've got a good one. I'll start." Darren took a step back and puffed up his chest. "You and me?" he snapped. "We're going to duel."

I got a little scared at that. "What the hell did you smoke?" I squeaked.

"Your dad's pole," he snarled at me. Then he grinned. "How was that? I've got some other ones if you—"

I punched him in the mouth.

I didn't mean to. Honestly. I didn't even realize my fist was cocked back behind my head until it was too late. My arm shot forward and my knuckles collided with his lips and I remember thinking *this was probably not my best idea* while his head snapped back. And as much as I'm sure it hurt him, holy fuck, the pain that shot through my hand was *wicked*.

"Son of a bitch!" I howled, holding my hand, sure it was going to fall off.

"You just punched me!" Darren said, covering his mouth with his hand.

"Is your face made of *metal*? Are you the fucking *Terminator*? Did Skynet take over and I didn't know about it? All my bones are broken because of your face!" My hand felt like it was on fire, and I was pretty sure that bone chips were breaking off into my bloodstream and working their way up to my brain where they would become lodged, eventually leading to my death.

"What the *hell*, Paul?" Vince said angrily. "Why did you hit him?" He had his hands curled at his sides like he was getting ready to take *me* on as well. I wondered if I still had fight left in my left hand, because my right was useless.

"I *saw* you," I said, all rational reason and thought pretty much done for the day. "Through the window! He was all up on your nut sac and he wants to bone you and you've been Freddie Prinze Junioring me this whole time, haven't you!"

"You want to bone me?" Vince asked Darren, a slightly disgusted look on his face. "Dude."

"What?" Darren shouted. "No, I don't want to fucking bone you! That's gross!"

Now I was offended *for* Vince. And myself, since that reflected on my taste. "He's not gross!" I yelled back, stepping in between the two of them, protecting Vince from Darren's dangerous libido. "He's pretty fucking awesome and you can't have him! He's mine and you need to stay the fuck away."

"Paul," Darren said, "Vince is my *brother*."

"I don't fucking care if he's your *mom*, you still can't fuck him, becau—Wait. What?"

"Vince is my brother," he said again, and it made less sense the second time. He looked over my shoulder at Vince. "And I do *not* want to bone you. You're not *that* hot."

"Thank God," Vince sighed. "I thought you wanted to have sex with me and I didn't know how to tell you that incest is not something that turns me on. Well, twins, maybe."

"Twins turn you on?" I asked him, shocked. "That's... ew." But inwardly I cursed that I did not have a twin right at that moment. Not that I would have done anything with said twin. That would be wrong. Maybe.

He shrugged. "One of those things. Kind of like your box of toys hiding under your bed."

"Yeah, but dildos aren't related! And how the fuck are you brothers? I've never heard that before. Anytime you were mentioned, the news said you were the only child."

Darren smiled, but there was no humor in it. "Yeah, well, you probably wouldn't have heard that, would you? I'm the deep, dark secret."

"I am so confused," I said. Today was just another day in the weirdest week in the history of all weeks.

"Vince's dad is my dad."

"Okay?

"His mom is not my mom."

"But… not his mom?"

Darren shook his head.

I thought on it. "And how old are you?"

"Twenty-six."

"And Vince is twenty-eight. So… oh. Oh shit."

"You got it?"

I looked at Vince. "Your dad cheated on your mom?" I sounded aghast. *And she stayed with him? And she* sided *with him over her own son?* Suddenly, all the goodwill that I had built up toward Lori Taylor collapsed. I was once again angry with a dying woman. I hated the feeling, but I think I might have hated her just a little bit more. I tried to keep from showing it on my face. This wasn't supposed to be about me. At least that's what I kept telling myself.

He smiled tiredly at me before it faded. "What are you doing here, Paul?"

"I'm pretty sure I came to get you back, but now I don't even know if you went anywhere? Did you? Or, if you did, if I had any right to come after you. Did I?" I sounded idiotic, but I couldn't stop it.

He gave me a weird look. "You came after me even though I told you to stay away?"

"Er. Yes?" *Stop sounding like you're asking questions!* "Yes. That's exactly what I did. You see, my parents, Nana, Sandy, and Wheels all had an intervention after my dad unscrewed my door. Nana already had a speech written out in case I got addicted to meth which, to be honest, I never really thought about, but now that she mentioned it, I can't stop thinking about it. Uh. Wait. Not that I want to *do* meth or anything, just like… you know… what would I be like *on* meth? I don't even know what meth does to you. Is it like bath salts? Does it turn you into a zombie and you go around eating other people's faces? I don't think I'd make a very good zombie because I get really grossed out by the sight of blood and the thought of eating someone else makes me queasy. As it rightly should. So, I guess the point of this, which I hope to arrive at soon because I can't seem to shut my mouth if my life depended on it, is that I'm not a zombie. I'm not addicted to meth. I'm addicted to you and I don't want you to go anywhere without me again."

Silence. Blessed silence. Prolonged silence. Awkward silence. Excruciating silence.

Then:

Vince made a noise almost like a sob. "And you wonder why I—" He stopped himself before he finished *that* sentence, and I literally almost shat myself thinking of the possible ways it could have ended.

Here's what my mind came up with:

1) "And you wonder why I think you're insane? Did you just *hear* yourself talk? Paul, this is so over, it's not even funny. Get out of my life. I hate your face."

2) "And you wonder why I was trying to get up on my brother? Because the idea of incest is more appealing than being with you ever again. I was using my brother to wash the memory of you from my head because I'm that grossed out by you."

3) "And you wonder why I didn't tell you about my parents? I'm so embarrassed by you that I couldn't ever imagine them meeting you. Oh, and by the way, I faked all my orgasms with you."

4) "And you wonder why I decided to Freddie Prinze Junior you? You just came from an intervention at your house and are standing in the middle of my apartment after you just punched my boyfriend/brother Darren, asking me to get back together with you. What part of that makes you think I would *ever* get in your mangina again? You were a *bet*, Paul. You were nothing but a *bet*."

5) "And you wonder why I think you'll be alone forever? No one can handle your crazy, Paul. No one. Especially not me."

I almost begged him to finish the thought, but I didn't think I wanted to hear the answer. I'd pretty much embarrassed the crap out of myself (I *punched* Darren, for fuck's sake; I *punched* the Homo Jock King!), and I didn't know what else there was to say. Opening my mouth seemed to have gotten me in a shitload of trouble, and I didn't want to hurt anyone anymore.

Of course, my mouth didn't listen to my brain. I was pretty sure I needed to be medicated.

"And I wonder why you... what?" I asked Vince.

He watched me for a moment before shaking his head. "It doesn't matter. Not right now." His face went blank again, and I hated it. I hated the look on his face, and I hated not touching him when he was right in front of me. I hated feeling like I wasn't good enough to be there to help him, like he didn't think I could handle the shit he was going through.

"Why didn't you just tell me about your mom?" I asked him quietly, cringing as I yet again made it about me without meaning to. I began to look for a way to make my exit.

His mouth thinned. "Not now, Paul. Please, just go. I can't do this right now. I can't focus on you and the rest of this shit at the same time. I just can't."

I nodded, but anger flared dangerously. "I see." I wasn't able to keep it from my face.

His eyes softened slightly. "It's not... it's not like that. I just... it's not like that."

"I don't know how else it could be like," I said, my voice hardening. "Obviously you don't want me here, for whatever reason. You don't think I can handle your shit. You don't trust me enough to let me help you. But then, you've only known me a week, so I guess I can't blame you."

He took a step toward me, raising his hand. But then he stopped and dropped it back down to his side.

"Yeah," I said. "I think I get it. I'm sorry about your mom, Vince. I hope you'll be okay. I really do. You know where I am if you need me."

I turned and walked away.

I could hear Darren's angry voice as he snapped at Vince, but I didn't hear what he said. My face was burning and I needed to get out of his apartment. The entire time the awkwardness was taking place, I kept thinking how it was just the day before when he'd been above me, thrusting into me, a look on his face that suggested he'd found the only place that he ever wanted to be. It's funny, really, how quickly things can change. A week ago, I didn't even know his fucking name. A week ago, I was plain, boring, ordinary, bland Paul.

I envied that Paul. That Paul didn't have anything in his heart that would have allowed it to break. That Paul was still blissfully unaware that opening up meant getting punched in the gut.

I thought about slamming the door behind me, but hell, I'm not *that* melodramatic, even if I'd already sunk down into the cliché that I was so desperate to avoid. You know the one: toward the final act when everything should be peachy and rosy but instead comes crashing down for a stupid reason that sounds really trite but hurts like a fucking bitch anyway.

So I just shut the door quietly, hearing Darren's voice get louder before it got cut off.

It was hot outside, and I took a deep breath, taking in that heat. I rested my back against the door for a minute, trying to clear my head. Once I was sure I could walk without falling down, I moved toward my car. But I didn't make it.

"Paul!"

I turned.

Darren was jogging toward me. For a second, I thought he was going to have his revenge for the way I sucker-punched him in the mouth, and I frantically looked around for any kind of weapon I could use to defend myself. But I was standing on the only patch of grass that must have existed in the state of Arizona, and I didn't think grass stains were an effective defense, so I prepared myself to get my ass beat.

"You may take my life," I sputtered at him as he approached, "but you'll never take my freedom!"

He arched an eyebrow as he stopped a couple of feet away. "Did you just quote *Braveheart* at me?"

"Of course not," I scoffed, even though I sort of did. "I'm sorry I punched your face."

He rolled his eyes. "You didn't even split my lip, Paul. It wasn't that bad."

"I'm a lover, not a fighter."

"Now you're quoting Michael Jackson? What the hell did you smoke on the way over?"

Aha! Another chance! "Your dad's pole," I snarled at him. Then I winced. "That doesn't work anymore considering your dad is Vince's dad and the mayor of Tucson and has conservative evil running through his veins. No offense."

"None taken? I think?"

"But, *man*, that must have *really* stuck in his craw to find out he had *two* gay sons."

"Stuck in his craw? What are you, a steamboat captain?"

I grinned, forgetting for a moment that Vince was shut up in his apartment and that I was in the presence of the Homo Jock King. "No, but wouldn't that be awesome? I'd wear a bow tie and have fancy facial hair and everything."

"Andrew Taylor doesn't know about me," Darren said evenly.

My eyes widened. "He doesn't even know you exist?" I whispered, feeling awful. "That... sucks." In my head, I had this image of Darren's mother being a young secretary who used to work for Andrew Taylor's construction company and thought she was in love with a powerful man, only to get cast aside after a rough tryst in the bathroom of a Denny's after a business meeting where they talked about different types of concrete. Saddened that she could never have the love of the man she needed, she quit her job, only to find out two months later that she was with child. Instead of blackmailing Andrew Taylor with it, she kept it to herself, wanting to have a connection to the only man that ever made her feel alive. To complete her sad, sad story, she must have died during childbirth just as Darren was born, and the last words on her lips would have been professing her love for Andrew. And then she died.

"You've been hanging around Vince too much," he said with a scowl. "I don't think you were this dense yesterday. He doesn't know that I'm gay."

"And your mom died giving birth to you," I said knowingly. "It's almost romantic."

"What? My mom lives in Phoenix. She's a nurse. Seriously, I never thought Vince's brain could be contagious, but you should really go get yourself checked out."

"Why doesn't he know you're gay?"

Darren snorted. "He doesn't know a damn thing about me. I've talked to him a handful of times in the past few years. The last time he said anything to me was to remind me to keep my mouth shut around election time. Something about having a bastard child as the result of an affair not looking good to his constituents."

"You should have told him you were gay, too," I said, "just to see the reaction on his face. He should probably know that since homosexuality is hereditary, then he's the common factor here and his spunk causes gayness."

"I *really* don't want to think about his spunk," Darren groaned. "Why are you walking away right now?"

I was startled at the abrupt change in conversation. "Vince didn't want me there. My turn. Why were you pressing him against the wall and making me think you were macking on each other when in actuality you're brothers?"

He eyed me warily. "Vince was upset. I was trying to calm him down. This is harder on him than you realize."

"Yeah, obviously I don't know how hard this is on him because he hasn't told me a thing." I tried to keep the bitterness out of my voice, but it didn't work very well.

Darren sighed again. "Paul... it's not like... look. I've known who Vince was practically my whole life. We didn't actually meet until a couple of years ago, but that's still a couple of years I have on you. I know him, or at least I think I do. He hasn't been able to find the words to tell you that he compartmentalizes everything about his life. Everything is cordoned off into its own section, and while they do converge, it makes him uncomfortable. But none more so when it comes to Lori and Andrew. They've given him shit all his life, or at least their indifference, and he doesn't deal with that well. And then you came along and...."

"And what?"

He shook his head. "How can you not see it? Paul, whether you know it or not, you've changed everything about him. The way he sees things. The way he reacts to them. He wants to make you proud, but he doesn't want you to see his past."

I swallowed past the lump in my throat, only because I didn't think breaking down in front of the Homo Jock King was the best course of action. "Everyone comes with a past," I told him gruffly. "It helps make you who you are."

Darren nodded. "And I agree with you. And that's what I've told him. But Vince... he doesn't see it like that. He sees you with your perfect family and your perfect life and he doesn't know how he's going to measure up to it, given where he comes from. He thinks you're going to just focus on the bad instead of seeing all the good he has. And he has a lot of good, Paul."

"He thinks my family and I are *perfect*?" I said, incredulous. "Jesus Christ, he's spent *time* around all of us. How can he think we're *perfect*?

Every single one of us should probably be on Zoloft just to even us out! *My grandmother has a homophobic parrot named Johnny Depp.* We're so far from perfect that perfect might as well be on the other side of the fucking moon. There's a word for people like us. It's called insanity."

"Who needs normal when abnormal is the greatest thing in the world?" Darren asked with a shrug.

"That's some bullshit reverse psychology you've got going on there," I growled at him. "Has that ever really worked for you before?"

"Works on Vince all the time."

I laughed, even though it felt kind of douchey to do so.

"He's doing his damnedest, Paul, to keep you away from them, not because he's ashamed of you, but because he's ashamed of them. He thought if you knew who they were, you'd judge him based upon *their* actions and not his own. It might not have been the most levelheaded of thinking, but then Vince doesn't think like most people. He didn't want you to see them because he doesn't like to show when he's hurting. And he *is* hurting, regardless of how much they've offended him in the past. Vince can't hate. He could never hate. And losing his mother is still hard on him."

"I know," I said, even though I didn't. I never had to go through what he did. I never had to wonder if my parents cared about me or not. I never had to go through the drawn-out experience of losing one of them. I couldn't know. I couldn't have any idea. "Why are you being so nice to me? You haven't said a damn thing to me in years."

He rubbed his hands over his face. "Vince is important to me. You're important to Vince. By proxy, you're important to me now. If you do anything to hurt him, I'll kill you. But...."

"But?"

"But what he's doing to you now makes me want to knock him upside his head. Even if he thinks it's for your own good, you don't deserve to be treated this way, Paul. And I'm trying to make him see that."

I was touched, more than I thought I could be. "You're pretty weird yourself," I told him, meaning it as a compliment.

"Thanks. I think. I just want you two crazy kids to make it." He gave me a small smile.

"Uh-huh. And that's the only reason?"

He blinked. "What else is there?"

"Oh, I don't know," I teased. "A certain drag queen? One who happens to be my best friend in all the world? You could be using me to get close enough to spit some game."

"I don't spit," he assured me. Then he blushed. Jesus, what is it about men in that family and blushing? It was pretty fucking hot. Er... from an empirical perspective. "Wow... that's not what I meant to say."

I almost choked. "I'm sure Sandy will be happy to hear that."

"I don't even know what you're talking about."

"You're such a horrible liar."

"Vince was right about you, you know. I can see that now."

I was curious. "What did he say?"

Darren laughed. "Well, when he finally stopped gushing like a little girl, he said you were, and I quote, 'Pretty damn awesome.'"

"I *am* pretty damn awesome," I told him confidently, feeling a warmth that had nothing to do with the heat of the day.

"Paul?"

"Yeah."

"Don't give up on Vince, okay? You can't. You just can't. You have to promise."

I took a step back. "I...." I didn't think I was in a place to promise anything, though I wanted to. Darren could have been full of shit for all I knew, even with the earnest expression on his face that he'd had through almost the whole conversation. "That's a big thing."

He eyed me sadly and then opened his mouth and said stupid shit that I *really* didn't need to hear. "He loves you, you know. I don't know what you did, or what went through his mind when he first saw you, but he loves you. Already. He's never done anything like that in his life. He's never actually *let* anyone into his life, aside from me. And that took months before he had any sort of trust with me. You've changed him, Paul. And you can't let him change back."

"I didn't do anything," I said as honest as I could, still reeling from Darren's blunt words.

"You listened to him, which is more than he could say about most people. You didn't find him to be ridiculous—"

"Yes, I did. Because he kind of is." Awesomely so, but still ridiculous.

He glared at me. "Are you always this difficult?"

"Pretty much. It's kind of my curse. I tend to take the road less traveled just to be a pain in the ass."

"He's going to need you."

"So you and everyone else in the free world has said. *He* doesn't seem to know that."

He shook his head. "It'll happen. Trust me. About thirty minutes after you left, his mom took a turn for the worse. She's in a coma now. Her doctor doesn't think she's going to wake up. That's why Vince was a little... distraught. I was holding him up to keep him from punching the wall."

My jaw dropped. "I was just talking to her a couple of hours ago. How could she...?"

"It's been expected," Darren said. "His dad is there now, and Vince had to leave for a bit to clear his head. He's going to go back."

"Did she get to talk to him? Did she... say anything to him?"

"I don't know."

"I should go with him," I decided. "I should be there for him."

"He won't let you," Darren said kindly. "He doesn't want you to—"

"Maybe I don't give a fuck what he wants," I interrupted. "Maybe I should just do what I think is right."

"Don't push this, Paul," he warned. "He can't be worried about what you're thinking when he's starting to grieve."

I was pissed off again. "So what the fuck do you want me to do?"

"For now? Nothing. I'll have his back until he needs you."

I couldn't help the jealousy I felt at that, but I couldn't ignore the logic, either. Darren knew him better than I did. Darren had cared for him longer than I had. Darren was his family. I was not. It burned, but he was right. "Fine," I relented. "But you call me if something happens and I'm needed. You promise?"

He nodded. "Yeah. I will. I promise."

"Does he know you're out here?"

He looked down at his feet. "I kind of yelled at him for being a dick to you and he went to his room and slammed the door shut. He doesn't know. We're supposed to go back to the hospital in a few. I think he just needs time to cool off."

I thought fast. "Will you do me a favor?"

"Yes." No hesitation as he looked back up at me.

"Will you tell him something for me?"

"What?"

"Just… can you tell him that I said it's real? That if I have to, I'll tell him every day that it's real. Just… can you tell him that for me?"

"Sure, Paul."

I nodded.

And then I left.

CHAPTER 20
Lost And Found

SANDY was still at my house when I got back. He looked up from the couch as I opened the front door, and I swear to God, it was like he could see everything all at once. My face screwed up tightly as I began to shake, and he leaped up and surrounded me, whispering quietly in my ear like he was my shelter.

I didn't cry. I didn't feel like crying. I don't think I was sad. I don't think I was angry; at least, not fully. I think I was tired and worried and sick to my stomach. I was trying to fight, as I'd done the entire way home, the urge to say "screw it" and drive to the hospital almost overwhelming—promises and Vince be damned. I knew that if something had happened to *my* mom, he would be one of the few people I'd want to be there. This led to spending a few minutes considering just when I'd started thinking of Vince as part of my family. It was made worse when I realized I didn't want to think of a time when he *wouldn't* be.

Sandy petted my hair as my head was in his lap. I turned to lie on my back, staring up at him, and he smiled sweetly down at me. Wheels was asleep on the floor near my hand, where he'd been since I got home, and I stroked his fur. I felt better. Well, a little better.

"I already called in to work," Sandy said quietly. "I let them know that you both would be needing some time off, at least next week. Vince will be good to go a little longer than you. You have vacation time saved, right?"

I nodded. "Didn't really have plans to use it, so that's okay. Thank you."

He smiled softly. "Of course, baby doll. I know this is hard on you too."

"It's not about me, though, and I think I kind of made it that way."

He snorted. "You mean you asked for something for yourself for the first time in your life? You're right, Paul. That's so selfish of you. How dare you."

"Har har. Hysterical it had to happen right at this moment."

"Hey, at least it happened. I'll take that over it never happening at all."

"Yeah."

"Paul?"

"Yeah?"

"Everything's going to be okay. You know that, right?"

I did and I didn't. I couldn't figure out which was louder. I gave the easier answer. "Sure, Sandy."

He didn't believe me. "If it's not, then we'll figure out a way to make it okay."

"You're way awesome, you know that?" He was. Probably the most awesome person to ever have walked the face of the earth. It was pretty much a given that I'd have been a psychotic wreck without him.

"I do know that." He grinned. "I'm glad you can say it out loud. You should probably tell me numerous times every single day from here on out so you don't forget it."

"You're not *that* awesome."

He kissed my hand. "I pretty much am."

"Maybe you can talk to him," I said without thinking. "You know what he's going through."

His forehead creased. "Because of my parents?"

I winced. "That was an asshole thing of me to bring up. Shit. Sandy, I'm sorry." I tried to sit up but he wouldn't let me, pressing down against my chest, holding me still.

"Do you really think that would help?" he asked.

I shrugged, keeping my mouth shut so I didn't break the world in half with my stupidity.

He stroked his fingers through my hair again. "You know, I don't think that would be quite what he needs. As a matter of fact, I would think *you* would be the one more experienced in this than me."

"My parents are still alive," I pointed out, feeling like an ass saying the words out loud. "I don't know loss like you do." Though that might not have been the complete truth. Sandy's parents had been like a second set for me, and their loss was a palpable thing for a long while after they were gone. I had grieved for them like they were my own.

"They are," Sandy said lightly, letting me know he understood what I was trying to say. "And they're going to be around for many, many more years. That's not what I am talking about, Paul. You may not know what it feels like, but you've seen it firsthand. You've been through it just as close as anyone else can say."

"Sandy…."

"Hush, baby doll. Let me speak."

I nodded, reaching out to hold his hand in mine.

He took a moment before he spoke again, staring off into space. "I remember when I first heard they were gone. Do you remember where we were? It was fifth period. Mr. Cuyar's AP English class. We were talking about Flannery O'Connor's *A Good Man Is Hard To Find*, about all these different angles the story could be inspected at, and all these interpretations, every word meaning something other than what it says on the page. What did it mean when the grandmother said this or what did it mean when the Misfit said that and I remember thinking, *why can't the story just be the story*? Why can't the words just mean what they mean? Why does everything have to mean something else?

"But then the door opened and the principal was standing there, along with the guidance counselor, and I remember them looking around the room, and I knew something was wrong the moment their eyes hit mine. I *knew*. Once they found me, they didn't have to look anywhere else."

I REMEMBERED this, of course. It was a day forever ingrained in my head. I might not have remembered the specifics that he could, but when those people had walked into the room, it had gotten just a tiny bit colder, the expressions on their faces slightly grim, as if they were trying to hold back but it was leaking around the edges. They had whispered quietly to Mr. Cuyar, a small, unassuming man who lived for the written word and little else. His eyes had widened briefly and his hand had come to his mouth, but he hadn't looked at the class, hadn't looked out to Sandy. I think if he had, we both would have known right away.

The guidance counselor had beckoned to Sandy quietly, and the whispers started in the class, little snorts and giggles, people already speculating what this fierce little gay boy had done to get pulled from class. Maybe it was the makeup he wore around his eyes; maybe it was the cigarettes he smoked in between classes. Whatever it was, something had happened, and one of the bigger idiots grunted the word "faggot" as Sandy stood up. Several people laughed at the obviously bracing wit of their social leader while I prepared to launch myself at him, to smash my fists into his face until he cried out for me to stop. I knew something was wrong and it was scraping against my skin and I wanted to make someone bleed.

Sandy had seen this (he saw everything, I learned early on) and pressed his hand down on my shoulder as he walked, pausing briefly to apply pressure in a clear message of *down boy, stay down. I can handle myself. They're nothing. They're nothing to me.* His hand trailed down my arm, and I didn't care then who saw. I didn't care what names they called me. For that one moment, I didn't give a fuck. I grabbed his hand and intertwined our fingers together and squeezed. I made him feel me. I made him feel the pressure, the heat of my hand. He flashed his gaze down at me and twitched his jaw, and we knew then, I think. We both knew what was coming, though maybe not how encompassing and complete it would be. He was already struggling to hold himself together because we both knew.

I tried to get up to follow him because I was going to be *damned* if I was going to let him go through this alone, my raging little diva in skinny jeans, fat sneakers with frazzled laces trailing behind, a white belt slung low on his hips. I thought he was beautiful, and part of me, some secret part that I never let out much, wished I could fall in love with him and only him because it would make things easier. It would mean I wouldn't have crushes on the jocks who wouldn't even look at me aside from passing disdain as if I was something they'd found on the bottom of their shoes. I didn't want to want them, but I did. I wanted to want my best friend, but I didn't.

But that didn't mean I wanted to let him go it alone.

So I tried to follow him, but he shot me a look that I wouldn't recognize until years later as Helena coming forward, that hard-core bitch who didn't take shit from anyone. That look said to sit my ass down. That look said to stay where I was. That look said he loved me and he would need me soon, but he needed to take these next steps alone.

He looked so small standing at the front of the class. And then the principal put his hand on Sandy's shoulder and they disappeared through the door.

Twenty minutes later, they came back for me.

"He needs you now," the guidance counselor whispered to me as I joined them in the hall. "All he wants is you. Your parents are here with him, but he won't talk to anyone else. He says it has to be you."

"You should have brought me the first time," I snapped at her, forgetting, for a moment, that I was a fat, gay sixteen-year-old who didn't have a chance of survival in these halls. "You should have told me to come with him."

There was no response.

I heard them before I saw them, my parents and Sandy. I heard my mother's sweet, quiet whispers. I heard the low, consoling rumble from my father. But most of all, what I heard was him. Sandy.

"Paul," he said, his voice broken. "Please just get Paul. All I want is Paul."

"He'll be here in a moment," my mother whispered. "Oh, honey. Oh, sweetheart. I am so sorry. I am so sorry that this is happening."

"Paul," he said. "Please. Where is Paul?"

"Sandy?" I cried out, scared of what was happening. I didn't even think of death at that point. The worst thing my mind could come up with was that Sandy was going to be moving away and that I'd be left here behind without him, alone. A shadow of my former self. He'd been by my side for as long as I could remember, and now he was going to leave me? I was going to be trapped here without a single ally?

He snapped his head up, and his gaze was wild and lost as it found mine. For just a split second, it didn't look like he recognized me or even recognized where he was. I'd never seen that look on his face before, and I would never see it again, but for that moment, he didn't know. It passed though, and he shot up from his seat, tearing out of my parents' calming hands. It took only a second for him to crash into me, his little body shaking as he huddled in my arms, burying his face in my chest, leaking tears onto my shirt. I didn't even look up at the adults watching us. As much as they knew more about the situation, and as much as they knew more about the world, they didn't matter right then. They didn't exist. I wrapped my arms around him and led him out the office and down the empty halls, classes still full on either side of us.

He didn't ask where we were going because as much as he was shattering in on himself, he trusted me to take care of him, trusted me to take him away and make sure he could float away. He clutched at me, his hands digging into my sides, and for once, I was glad of my bulk because I was able to shelter him from everything.

I led us out the front doors, the spring heat slapping against us, hot and clean. I half walked, half carried him to my old Honda Accord near the back of the parking lot, trying not to think about the reason why my best friend was like this. I had an inkling, a faint idea, but it seemed so cosmically bigger than the two of us that I couldn't grasp it, I couldn't bring its fuzzy edges into sharper focus.

He whimpered when I opened the car door and tried to gently put him in the passenger seat. I didn't think he was going to let me go. I gentled him down a bit further, saying quietly that I was there, that I was with him, that if he let me go for just a second, I'd get us out of here and we'd go wherever he wanted. It never crossed my mind, not even once, to take him back to his house. Regardless of how much I didn't know, I knew at least that it wouldn't have been the right thing to do. There was a reason his parents weren't there. There was a reason why they weren't the ones holding onto him right now.

He finally loosened his grip as if I'd gotten through to him, and he let me close the door and walk around the front of the car. I could feel his eyes on me the entire way, watching me as if I would disappear should he look away. When I got in the car, he curled his hand in mine tightly, to the point that I had bruises for a week after. I didn't let him go.

I took him home. To my home, though he was over there enough it might as well have been his too. Enough of his stuff had accumulated in the nooks and crannies of my room and vice versa. I never needed to bring a change of clothes when I stayed over at his house because there was always something of mine there. I didn't know if that was going to happen anymore, and a little piece of my stoic armor broke off as I helped him out of the car.

I took him to my room and locked the door behind us to keep the world at bay for at least a few hours. I laid him on my bed and was going to spoon him from behind when he turned over, tears on his cheeks, eyes squeezed shut tightly. I gathered him up in my arms and pressed my forehead against his, trying to pull him into me as hard as I could so that he'd feel me there, that he'd feel the pressure, the heat, the sweat, the salt.

"Paul," he whispered. "Oh, Paul. It's bad. It's so bad."

"I know," I said, because I did, even if I didn't know specifics. "But I'm here. Okay?"

He trembled. "You're not going to go away?"

I almost hesitated with my answer, because could any of us ever make a promise like that? Could any of us actually keep that promise? But if I hesitated, he would have seen it. He would have known. "No," I said. "No I'm not going away. Not now. Not ever. It'll be you and me forever."

"I'm lost!" he cried. "Oh God, I'm so lost. You have to find me! Please, Paul, you have to find me because I'm so lost."

I could feel the shudder that roared through him then because it caused my own arms to shake. He was twitching like he was seizing, and I panicked when he started making little choking noises in the back of his throat, like he couldn't catch his breath, like his body had sunk into full-blown panic and he couldn't do anything to stop it. I did the only thing I could think of doing: I rolled over on top of him, crushing his body with mine, covering him completely like I was anchoring him to the world even as it broke.

All the air was crushed out of him, so much so that he couldn't take in another breath to allow the sobs to come again. He stared up at me with those big eyes of his, our foreheads touching, our noses brushing together. I waited until I knew it was just starting to get uncomfortable for him, when I knew he *needed* to take a breath, and then I shifted slightly and he sucked in air and let it back out, warm against my face.

His gaze never left mine when he said, "They're dead, Paul. My parents are dead."

"I know," I said, my voice rough. "I know."

"What's going to happen to me? I don't have anyone else. I don't know anyone else." Panic started to fill his eyes again. "There's no one. There's no one else."

"There's me," I said, pressing my lips against his forehead. He shook underneath me. "There's me, and there will always *be* me. I've got you.

I'll catch you. I'll worry for you. You're not lost. You're not lost because I've found you."

And he cried then, a soft sound that caused me to ache. He wrapped his arms around my neck and pulled me down and cried into me. I let him, because it was what I said I'd do. I let him break because it was what he was entitled to.

He moved in with us that very night and he stayed until we went off to college. There were good days. There were some bad days. Some nights got to be too much for him and I would hear a soft knock on my door through the haze of sleep and he'd slip in through the shadows and crawl into my bed. Sometimes I held him. Sometimes we kissed, though it never went beyond that. It was not meant to be sexual. It was meant to be comfort, and I let him take from me all he could.

He was my best friend, after all. I'd have given him anything.

"WITHOUT you, I don't think I would have made it," Sandy said, after a time. His hands were still in my hair, though they'd stilled from the memory.

I sighed. "You may be giving me a bit too much credit here."

"Only because you never give yourself enough. Seriously, Paul. How you underestimate your own worth is beyond me."

"I'm humble?"

He snorted and began to play with my hair again. "I'm not sure that's the right word for what you are."

"Meek?"

"Hardly."

"Gregarious?"

"Only when intoxicated."

"Epic?"

"Most days, sure, but not quite."

"I'm running out of ideas," I said tiredly.

Silence.

Then: "You're a lighthouse."

"Excuse me?"

"That's the best way to put how I think of you, I guess."

"That's... weird."

He rolled his eyes. "It's poetic," he said, slapping the top of my head lightly. "Lighthouses are there to help ships see through the dark. To keep them from running aground. That's what you do, Paul. You're like the beacon in the dark."

"You're a poet, and you don't even know it," I told him, feeling slightly uncomfortable with his words. I wasn't like that at all. I didn't deserve that kind of praise. I was just... Paul.

He moved his hands from my hair and cupped my face, not allowing me to turn away from those knowing eyes. "Without you," he said fiercely, "there would have been no me. I was lost, and you found me. Vince might get lost too, and he'll need you to find him. He'll need you to be the anchor. He'll need you to be the light. He'll need you."

"I don't...." But I didn't want to finish that.

"You will," Sandy said, hearing it anyway. "You know how and you will."

I THOUGHT about going to the hospital again, or calling Vince, but I wasn't sure I'd be welcome either way. I settled on sending him a text, though I didn't know if he'd get it in the hospital if his phone was turned off. It felt woefully inadequate to send him a message that said if he needed me, to call me, but I didn't know what else to say. It took me almost an hour to compose that masterpiece, and when I finally convinced myself to send it, I regretted it the moment I hit send, wishing I could take it back. I almost sent him another message, but I knew it would be followed by another and another, so instead, I tossed my phone onto the nightstand and fell back onto my bed and lay there in the dark.

Sleep was long in coming and when it came, it was thin and restless.

My phone ringing woke me later, just before midnight, pulling me from a hazy dream where I couldn't move because I was stuck to a sea cliff, shining a flashlight into the water, ships bearing down on me at high speeds, waves crashing, winds blowing. I didn't even look at the screen before answering, convinced it was part of the dream.

"Yeah?" I said.

"Paul?"

"Sure." I couldn't tell who it was in my sleep-deprived mind.

"It's Darren."

This cleared me up right quick. "What happened?"

"She's gone. Two hours ago. It was faster than they thought it would be."

"I'm… sorry. Are you okay?"

He sighed. "Yeah. I'm not calling about me."

"Vince."

"Has he called you?"

"No. Is he there with you?"

"No. He took off a while ago. He looked… wild. Confused."

"And you let him go?" I said, anger in my voice. "You let him drive away?"

"We couldn't stop him," Darren snapped. "Not without it resorting to blows. He exchanged words with our father and… it didn't go well."

"Where did he go?" I asked, getting up, planning on finding my keys.

"He said he wanted to go to his home, but I'm at his apartment, and he's not here. I don't think he came here at all."

"His home? Where else could he have gone?"

"I don't know. I was hoping you'd heard from him." He sighed. "Shit. I don't know where else he could be, unless he went back to Phoenix for some reason."

"Jesus," I muttered. "He better not have driven all the way back there with how he is. I don't—"

There was a sharp pounding at my front door. Wheels jumped up from his spot on the bed, his little barks echoing throughout the house as he rolled down his ramp and tore for the front door. "Hold on," I told Darren.

Wheels' barking turned into an excited yipping as I headed down the hall. His butt was wagging back and forth, the tires on his cart tapping on the tile. It seemed he knew who it was, and there were only two other people he responded to that way. I allowed myself to hope as I moved him out of the way, and then I flipped on the porch light as I opened the door.

Vince stood there, squinting against the light. His face was pale, his eyes clouded. "He's here," I told Darren. "I've got him."

"So that's what he meant by home," Darren said, and for a moment, the world around me got a bit brighter before I pushed it away. Darren sighed. "Keep him there, will you? I'll call you tomorrow, and we can figure out what to do then."

"Sure," I said before I hung up the phone and put it in my pocket. I opened the screen door. "Hey," I said softly, as if anything louder would spook him and cause him to flee.

"Paul?" Vince said, sounding confused. "Where...." He shook his head. "Did you find me?" he asked in a gruff voice. "I was looking for you, but... how did you get here?"

"This is my house," I said softly, my fingers aching to reach out and touch him. "You came over to my house."

He nodded slowly. "I thought I might. I think I was trying to find you, but I got lost. I drove for a while, because I couldn't remember how to get here."

"Oh?"

"I'm tired, Paul."

"It's been a long day."

He looked down at his hands and let out a shuddering breath. "Can I come inside and go to sleep? I know you're mad at me, and I'm sorry, but I just want to go to sleep. I'm real tired. I would sleep on the couch, or in the other bedroom, but I can't. I need to be right there with you, okay?" His face crumpled, his voice cracking. "I just need to get some sleep, and I sleep better when you're there. Okay? Please say it's okay, Paul. I need to sleep, and I need you to say it's okay."

"It's okay," I said, unable to hold back anymore. I reached out and took his hand in mine. He clutched at it with both of his hands, as if he'd float away if he didn't grip me as tightly as he could. I pulled him through the doorway, shutting it behind us. He kept his eyes on our hands. Wheels twisted around his feet, but even he could see something was off, and he headbutted Vince's ankle with a little growl. I shushed him quietly, and he followed us down the hall as I led Vince to my bedroom. I closed that door as well, as if to keep the outside world away.

Vince stood near my bed, like he was unsure about what to do next, like he'd forgotten the next steps. I came up behind him and wrapped my arms around his waist, laying my forehead against the back of his neck. He sagged into me with a low moan, and I gripped him tighter.

"She died, Paul," he said thickly. "I was standing right there when she...."

"I know," I said, because I didn't think he wanted to hear an apology right then.

"I thought maybe she'd wake up again. That she'd bounce back and everything would be okay because that's the way it should have been. I kept thinking that she'd open her eyes and she'd see me, she'd *really* see me, and everything would be okay and we'd laugh. We'd laugh like we did when I was a kid and she was just my mom. But you know what else I thought? You want to know what I thought the most?"

"What?"

"You," he said, leaning his head back until it rested on my shoulder, my mouth near his ear, our cheeks brushing together. "You. I thought of you. I though how I wanted to be with you. I wished that you were there with me, and I wished you weren't mad at me. I wished I'd told you everything from the beginning even though it was too much to put on a person, and I didn't want you to have to deal with it. I didn't want to bring it down on you because you were so bright. You were so clear and bright, and I didn't want it to bring you down." He shuddered again. "Darren said... he said you told him to tell me it's real. Did you say that, Paul? Did you tell him that?"

"Yes," I said, because it was the only answer that could be given. "It's real."

"Paul... I... I don't...."

His tears soaked against my cheek as I kissed them away. I told him to hush, I told him that it was okay, that I wasn't mad, not really. I couldn't be mad at him, I said, because there was nothing to be angry about. He twisted in my arms until he could look me in the eye, trying to see if I was telling the truth. I made sure he knew I was, and the wildness there receded a bit, the cloudiness parted, and a little light showed through. It was not happiness, though it was close. It was not arousal, though I didn't expect it to be. No. It was *relief,* pure and simple. *Relief* that I understood what he was saying. *Relief* that I wasn't upset with him, and I couldn't believe that I had been in the first place.

It was this relief that allowed me to pull his shirt up and over his head and fold it on top of my dresser. It was this relief that allowed me to unbutton his jeans and slide them off. I led him to the bed and followed him in, pulling the covers up to our shoulders. Our knees bumped together as we faced each other.

He watched me, for a time, without speaking, his eyes bright and wet. He reached up and traced my face with his fingertips, memorizing the skin like he'd never seen it before and would never see it again. I captured his hand in mine, bringing it to my lips, kissing his fingers just once. He sighed and turned away from me to lie on his other side. Before I could even think about what that meant, he pushed his way back until he was flush against me. He grabbed my arm and pulled it over his waist. My nose and mouth were in his hair. He trembled, but soon he stilled. He breathed heavily, but soon it quieted. He held my hand tightly, but soon the grip loosened.

And then I thought he slept. I thought he slept because I would have never whispered what I did had I thought he been awake. It was not my place. It was too soon. It was not the right time. It was not what he wanted to hear. It was not what he *needed* to hear.

But.

I had to say it. To think it was one thing; to say it aloud was another. I thought it. I thought it badly. I had to say it out loud. I had to make sure it was real.

So I did. And it was.

"I love you," I whispered in the dark.

Ten minutes later, just as the clock switched to midnight and it became the seventh day since I'd first heard his voice, he whispered back, "I love you too."

And then we slept.

CHAPTER 21
Just The Way You Are

THE days that followed that seventh day were rough. I, of course, woke up with doubts ringing through my head, sure that I wanted to take back that initial *I love you*, sure that Vince wanted to take back his response. I didn't show that fear, though, because it wasn't supposed to be about me right then. Vince opened his eyes to find me watching him nervously, berating myself for being *that* guy, the creepy one who watches his partner sleep like it's supposed to be romantic or something. I averted my eyes momentarily until I felt his fingers on my face.

"Paul," he said, his voice rough with sleep.

"Yeah?"

"Thank you."

I shrugged, trying to minimize everything. "You okay?"

He sighed as he dropped his hand. "I think so. Maybe. It's weird, you know? I hadn't spoken to her in months before this week, and I was okay with that. A little mad, maybe, but okay with it. Now she's gone for good, and I'm... what am I? Sad? Relieved? Angry?" He looked away. "I don't know what I am right now," he muttered.

"She was still your mom," I said quietly. "Regardless of what else happened, regardless of what she did later, she was still your mom."

"Yeah."

"Vince?"

"Yeah?"

I chose my next words carefully. "Everything always won't be perfect, you know?"

"I know."

"So you know you can't pick and choose what to tell me, then, right?"

"Yeah. Look, Paul, I—"

I shook my head. "Don't. I'm not mad at you for that. I'm sorry that I acted like a jerk. It wasn't my place to. I should've respected your wishes and not gone behind your back."

He was silent for a moment, then said, "I'm not ashamed of you."

I was startled. "I never said you were. I never thought that."

"Okay. I just wanted you to know that. If anything, I was ashamed of them. And jealous of you."

I snorted. "What the hell do I have for you to be jealous about?"

"Everything," he said seriously. "Your friends, your family. You. You have everything. You *are* everything."

"Vince...."

"No, Paul. How can you not see it? Why can't you see that you're perfect just the way you are?"

His earnestness was catching. I'm a sucker for earnestness. And bike shorts. Put those things together, and watch the fuck out. "I'm pretty sure your definition of perfect is skewed," I told him. "You may have a bit of a bias here."

He looked satisfied, as if I'd agreed with everything he'd said. "A very big bias," he assured me. "But it doesn't matter. Even if I didn't, I'd still see it. I just didn't want to put any of this on you. It wasn't fair. We'd just met. Hell, you would have probably run screaming, your arms flailing in the air."

"I would not have flailed my arms," I said, slightly affronted.

He smiled weakly. "A bit," he said, sure of himself. "Probably would have written in your diary all about it."

I rolled my eyes, glad to hear him joke, but also hearing the sadness in his voice. I brushed my fingers over his face. "You can tell me anything," I said. "At least, you should. It's how these things work, Vince. You have to know that."

"I just didn't want you to see pain," he said. "I didn't want you to know sadness. I didn't want you to see me like this. I just wanted you to be happy, every day, all the time."

"And what about you?" I asked him. "If you knew this was coming, why didn't you think about what *you* wanted?"

"Because I was just thinking about *you*," he said like it was the most obvious thing in the world. "You were the person who helped me through this, even when you didn't know what was happening. You were the guy who made me happy when everything else was going to shit. You were like this light in the dark, Paul. You are *my* light."

I groaned. "Sandy's *never* going to let me hear the end of this. I'm a motherfucking lighthouse."

"I don't know what that means," Vince said, confused.

"Shit," I muttered. "We're really going to do this, aren't we?"

"You talking about me and you?"

"Yeah?"

"You bet your ass we're going to do this. There's no way I'm going to let you go. We got the hard part out of the way. The rest is cake."

"The hard part?"

He leaned over and kissed me. I didn't even make mention of how much I wished he'd brushed his teeth before doing that. It seemed like it would spoil the mood. "The love part," he whispered. "I love you, so the rest will be easy."

"Oh sweat balls," I said, feeling a bit dizzy. "Are you sure?"

He nodded.

I mumbled something back.

Wheels snorted at me from his spot between us. Jerk.

"What was that?" Vince asked, a small smile on his face.

"I said I may be thinking that I might possibly entertain the idea of loving you too," I said, my face on fire.

He chuckled. "I figured as much." But then the humor slid from his face. "I think," he said, the words coming out in a choke, "that I'm about to be sad."

I curled up against him, pressing his face into my neck, wrapping my arms around him tightly. Wheels crawled on top of us, doing his impression of a dogpile. He laid his head down on Vince's thigh and watched us. "You didn't get to hear all of what she said to me, did you?" I murmured as he started to quake.

"No," he gasped. "Only the end."

"Now, you know I didn't know her, right? I only knew what I saw of her on TV and in the news."

A quick nod. A sharp breath.

"Well," I said, "she loved you, Vince. She loved you because you were her son. She loved you because you belonged to her. She may not have always told you, and she may not have told you in the right way, but she did. Even when you were apart, she did. I don't think that a day went by that she didn't think about you, and I don't expect a day will go by for you now where you won't think of her. And…." I stopped, considering.

"And what?" he whimpered, starting to break.

"And I think she knew," I told him. "I think she knew that I would take care of you. I think she knew that you would need someone after she was gone, but that she'd leave you in good hands. I think she needed to meet me to realize that. I think I needed to meet *her* to understand that.

"So you cry," I whispered, my chin on top of his head. "You cry because you're allowed to. You cry because she's your mom. You cry because she's your family. But… you have a whole other family now too, if you want it. You have another family that wants nothing more than to take you in and love you just the way you are. If you want to. If you let us."

"Okay."

"Okay?"

"Yeah. I want it. I want it bad. Paul, please. Please. I'm going to cry now, and I'm going to hurt now. Please don't let me go."

"I won't," I promised him, promised myself. "Do what you have to. I'll be here."

And he did.

And I was.

THE funeral was a big thing, a messy thing, with lots of local news coverage. I'm sure there were plenty of people hoping for some kind of delicious drama to occur between Vince and his dad, but nothing happened. As big as it was, it was still a quiet affair, with bowed heads and whispered prayers.

The only thing that could have raised any eyebrows was that Vince did not sit next to his father or the rest of his family. I'd encouraged him to do so, but ever since the morning after his mother had died, he'd taken my words to heart.

I shouldn't have been surprised when Mom called and asked what time she and Dad and Nana would be picking us up on the day of the funeral. I shouldn't have been surprised when she told me she'd hear none of what I was saying. They were going, and that was final. Family is family, she said, and she would be there to support Vince. When he'd heard these words, Vince had gotten such a look of wonder on his face that it had taken my breath away. He'd reached out and grabbed my hand, refusing to let go even when my mother insisted on talking to him herself. I could feel the heat from his hand, the bite from his grip as he said things like, "Yes, ma'am, I mean Matty," and "Thank you, Larry, I'd appreciate it," into the phone. After saying, "Say hello to Johnny Depp for me, Nana," he hung up the phone and stared at it for a moment.

"What?" I asked.

"It's like they're mine too," he said in awe.

I snorted. "Like nothing. They *are* yours too. You better hope this is what you wanted because there's no way in hell you're escaping them now. They've got their hooks in you, and even if you *tried* to get away, they'll find you wherever you go."

He eyed me. "And what about you?"

"What about me?"

"Is that what you want too?"

I shrugged, trying to play it off. "I found you first, didn't I?" I mumbled at him.

That got me a sweet kiss that turned slightly dirty. I was okay with that.

So we went, then, to support one who was becoming our own: my parents, my grandmother, my best friend Sandy, and Vince's brother Darren. Vince didn't want to sit next to his father because he didn't think he was wanted there. He'd told me the night before, as we lay in bed, that all he'd ever wanted was to *be* wanted. And since he had that, he wasn't going to waste any more time trying to pretend that everything between him and Andrew Taylor was going to be okay. I thought about pushing the issue, telling him that he couldn't just write off his dad like that, because no matter what, Andrew would always be his father. But I caught the look in his eye, almost a defiant thing, like that was what he *expected* me to say to him, like he knew what I was thinking. Vince was grieving, yes, and it hurt him greatly, but he was also showing me that he was stronger than I'd first thought. He was greater than what I'd seen.

But it was still a sight to see, especially when I realized that he was mine. He'd been right, of course, when he said we'd gotten the hard part out of the way and that the rest would be easy. I didn't tell him (though I thought it quite often) that falling in love with him had been the easiest thing I'd ever done. I think he knew that, anyway.

So the guy in the front preached about God and Heaven and about how those we love are never really gone, just as long as we can remember them in our hearts. Many people came forward and said nice things about Lori Taylor. Songs were sung and prayers were said. We stood when we were told rise, and we sat when we were told to be seated. The whole thing was very surreal, the church large and airy, the voices echoing throughout the building. Vince looked handsome in his charcoal gray suit. I looked like a sweating beaver in my black suit. I sat next to him the whole time, his hand in mine, ignoring the glares we received from his father from across the way. It wasn't about that. It wasn't about him (and, to be fair, Nana glared right back enough for all of us; there was a moment when the Tucson Boys Chorus was singing the gorgeous hymn "Abide With Me" that I was pretty sure my dad had to keep my grandmother from launching herself at the mayor after a particularly nasty look he shot Vince. You could tell Dad had a split second when he seriously considered letting his mother-in-law launch herself at one of the highest ranking people in the room. I almost motioned to let her at him, but then I realized I still didn't know if mayors had Secret Service protection and was thankful when he pulled her back. I reminded myself to ask Vince later to see if he knew).

Afterward, Vince was supposed to go stand in line with the rest of his family so that well-wishers could offer their condolences. Vince looked like he would rather get punched in the face with a fork, but I figured his mom would have wanted it. So I told him I would stand with him, if he needed me to, as the others in the line had their immediately family standing behind them. The look he gave me then was wide-eyed, but then when the rest of my family and Darren said they'd do the same, you could see his surprise like it was a palpable thing. He couldn't seem to find his words, but I thought I knew what he was trying to say.

We moved to follow him to where the family gathered before leaving for the cemetery. With his shoulders squared and his head high, he took three steps toward them. We moved to follow until he stopped suddenly. He looked back at me and held out his hand. I took it without hesitation. If he was sure about it, then I would be sure for him.

His father was not pleased.

I know what you're probably thinking: here comes the big scene, the disruption at the funeral, the father's blatant homophobic remarks cutting deeply. I'd stand next to Vince and defend him and all would hear the weight of my words and silence would fall as the mayor and I glared at each other, daring the other to speak again.

But it didn't happen. Well, kind of. I was still pretty much a badass.

Vince stood next to his father, only a few feet separating them. Both of them were stiff but aware of the other. Vince kept glancing back at me until I understood he needed to feel my presence, so every so often, I'd reach up and squeeze his shoulder, just to let him know I was still there. He relaxed further every time, focusing on shaking hands and receiving hugs from people I'd never seen before.

As if he was the opposite, the mayor grew tenser. You could see it in the lines of his shoulders, the twitch in his jaw, the little sideways looks he shot Vince, the anger in his eyes. And when the line was finished, when the last person had offered condolences, I knew the mayor was going to turn on his son. So I stepped between them while Vince was distracted by my mother.

Andrew Taylor stared at me like I was nothing better than the shit he'd scrape off the bottom of his shoe. I didn't feel bad at all about not voting for the guy. "Don't," I told him quietly, just for him to hear. "Don't do that now. It's not about you. It's not even about him. It's about your wife. So don't."

"Do you have any idea who you're talking to?" he growled like some clichéd heavyweight. I felt sad for him.

"Frankly?" I asked. "I couldn't care less. He's no longer your concern. He doesn't belong to you anymore. We've got it from here, Mayor. I'm sorry about your wife, I really am. But you don't get to make this worse for him. Not now. Not today. If I were you, I'd start focusing on what you've lost and what you can gain, rather than something that you don't agree with."

"He told us about you," he said, taking a step closer. "Me and his mother. How you'd just met. How he's certain that you're it for him. He's going to leave you, just like he did us."

I shrugged. "Maybe. Maybe not. Unlike you, I won't give him reason to."

"Paul," Darren called sharply. "We got to go."

"He'll be with me," I said, "if you ever change your mind. But if you don't, that's your choice. I don't care who you are—if you try and hurt him, I will break you in half."

Andrew laughed. "You? You're nothing."

I smiled. "Your son thinks I'm something. And that's enough for me."

And just as I pulled off that wicked awesome exit line, I spun on my heels and didn't trip and face-punch a wall or anything, even though it was what I expected. I might or might not have walked away a little bit slower and with more care than I normally did to make sure that I didn't embarrass myself before leaving the church. After all, how often does one get to tell off one's boyfriend's father in God's house and pull off some badassness before walking away practically in slow motion? One does not get to do that often.

But apparently God has a funny sense of humor because I could see them all watching me, especially Vince, and I opened my mouth to say something to him, anything to continue my streak of being amazing, but instead, I accidentally sneezed and burped at the same time and it was pretty freaking gross. And, of course, it echoed throughout the church and several conversations near me stopped as people turned to stare at me, convinced, I'm sure, that I was possessed, and a demon was trying to crawl its way out of my mouth. I expected priests to come running at me, spraying me with holy water, screaming in Latin about how the power of Christ compelled me and the demon needed to be gone from my earthly body.

"We can't take you anywhere," Sandy muttered.

"That was very manly," Dad said.

"I'm pretty sure I thought he was barking at me," Nana mused.

"He used to do that as a child," Mom reminisced. "It's even grosser as an adult."

"Is he the man in your relationship?" Darren asked Vince. "Does he tell you to go make you a sandwich in the kitchen while he sits in his recliner and scratches his balls?"

"You can't say balls in church," I scolded. "Jesus might hear you."

"I think Jesus is running away from you," Vince said.

And just because I wanted to, and just because I could, on the thirteenth day after I'd met him, I kissed him in the church.

The world, interestingly enough, did not explode.

Take that, homophobes!

WE WERE the last ones at the cemetery. Vince wanted a chance to sit with his mother after everyone else had left. I asked him quite clearly if he wanted me to go as well, but he shook his head, gripping my hand tightly as the rest of the mourners cleared out, heading to the mayoral mansion for continued services. Vince hadn't wanted to go to that, as he was almost done with the day.

It was odd, really, sitting next to the hole in the ground that contained a mahogany box holding his mother. The employees at the memorial grounds understood that we needed a bit more time and could complete their interring once Vince was ready to go. It probably didn't hurt that I reminded them who he was and who was being buried. They nodded and drifted away, starting to stack chairs and moving flowers.

I walked back over to Vince, who lay on his back in the grass next to his mother. His eyes were closed when I reached him. My shadow covered his face, and a line appeared on his forehead. "Paul," he said without opening his eyes.

"Vince."

He sighed. "Today is one of those days that I wish was already over."

"I know." And I did. Even if I didn't know what he was going through, I could imagine. No matter what I said about my family belonging to him, no matter what my family did for him today, he'd still lost someone. He still had to say good-bye to his mom. I tried to think about how I'd be if it was my mom, and I hated the thought. And I hated the idea of what he was going through.

He would need me, I'd been told.

He was going to break, I'd been told.

So far, he'd been far stronger than I think I would have been in his position. And for some reason, this filled me with great pride, knowing that he was stronger than people gave him credit for, stronger than *I* gave him credit for.

I lay beside him on the grass, not caring about my suit coat. There were more important things to worry about. Our shoulders bumped, and as soon as I was down completely, he reached over and grabbed my hand, curling it into his own.

I waited.

"I'm trying," he said finally, "to think of a good memory. Any single one that I can take with me when we leave here today."

I hesitated. "Can you find one?" I hoped he could, because he needed it. He needed to be able to say good-bye.

"I was scared I couldn't," he confessed quietly. "I thought that I'd only be able to think about the past few years and that it'd piss me off and I'd just be angry about it forever. I don't want to be angry forever, Paul."

"I won't let you," I said, ignoring how I'd essentially just acknowledged the word "forever." It didn't freak me out as much as I thought it would. "I'll be sure to kick you in the nuts if you stay angry forever."

He chuckled. "Thanks. I think."

"Did you find the memory you were looking for?"

"I think so. Can I tell you?"

I smiled as I squeezed his hand. "You can tell me whatever you want."

He turned his head to look at me. "I can, can't I?"

I nodded. "It's kind of what boyfriends are for, I guess. Though I haven't had much experience to say so."

"You've done pretty good so far."

"*Pretty* good?" I said as I rolled my eyes. "Gee, thanks for that ringing endorsement. Nothing strokes the ego like *pretty* good."

"How about amazing?"

"A little better."

"Extraordinary."

"So it's been said."

"Unexpected."

I grinned. "Likewise. What did you find to think about your mom?"

He let out a low breath and turned to look back at the sky. I followed his gaze to the azure blue. "I think I was ten or eleven," he said finally. "We lived up in the foothills in this old house on Windriver. I came home from school one day and found my mom and dad fighting. I wasn't supposed to be home that early because I had soccer practice, but it got canceled, so I just rode the bus home."

He rubbed his thumb over my fingers. "It wasn't a normal fight, like I'd heard them get into before. It was very loud. They were very angry. My mom was screaming at my dad, and he was screaming back at her. I couldn't make out what they were talking about, I just knew it was bad. My friend Jake's parents had just gotten divorced and his mom had moved away and he never got to see her and I remember thinking, *This is it. They're going to get divorced and she'll move away and I'll never see her anymore because she won't want me.* I thought that if they kept fighting, they would eventually see that they didn't belong together and they would divorce and I wouldn't know my place anymore.

"It didn't last that much longer. The voices quieted down, but they were still angry, and finally my dad left the house, slamming the door behind him. I heard the car starting in the garage before he left, and I didn't think I was going to see him again. I didn't think he was going to come back, and the only thing I wanted to do right then, right at that moment, was to find my mom and remind her that I was still there with her. That I was still alive. That I wouldn't leave her, no matter how hard it got."

His voice broke, and I thought about asking him to stop, that he didn't need to say any more, but he pushed on. I hurt for him.

"So I went to her. She was sitting on the stairs, her face in her hands, and she was crying. That scared me more than anything because for all that I could remember, I couldn't remember a time when I'd ever seen her *crying*. It seemed worse than I'd first thought, and I didn't know what I could do. I was just a kid. I was little. What did I know?"

"But you did something, didn't you?" I asked him quietly. "You helped her."

He nodded and looked over at me again. Our eyes met, and for the rest of his story, we stayed that way. "Maybe. I like to think so. I didn't know the best thing to say to her, so I sat on the steps above her, and I pulled her back into me. I wrapped my arms around her and put my chin on her head and told her the only thing I could, that it was okay. That it was all right. That somehow, I'd figure out a way to make it better for her. I asked her to stop crying because I would always be there for her and I wouldn't walk out the door. I told her I....." He stopped as his eyes grew brighter and his face trembled. "I told her that there was nothing she could do to make me leave her."

I reached over with my free hand and thumbed the tears from his face. He kissed the palm of my hand, the tips of my fingers. "What did she say to you?" I asked hoarsely, knowing she must have said something.

"She said… she stopped crying and she looked up at me and smiled. She said that she didn't know what she would have done without me. She said that she was glad that I was there for her and that she was sorry she was sad. She said that she loved me and that she always would. And then she kissed my forehead and pulled me up, and we went to the kitchen and we made peanut butter cookies and it was a good day. It was a good day, and that is what I want to walk away with. Paul, that's all I want to remember."

"Then that's what you remember," I told him. "That's what you take with you, and fuck all the rest. The rest doesn't matter. The rest isn't important."

"It's like the stars, you know?"

I frowned. "What do you mean?"

He pointed toward the sky. "You can't see them now, because it's daytime. But you know they're still there because they haven't left. Not really. It'll just be a little bit of time before you can see them again."

"Yeah, Vince. It's like the stars."

"Paul?"

"Yeah?"

"I think I'm ready to go now."

"Okay."

"Can we go back to your house? I think I just want to lay down with you for a while and not think about things."

"I think we can manage that." I stood and offered him my hand. He watched it for a moment, and then a beautiful smile bloomed on his face. He reached up and grabbed my hand, and I pulled him up with me. He put his arm around my waist and laid his head on my shoulder. I wrapped my arm around him and led him away.

We were almost back to the car when he spoke softly. "I'm glad I found you. I think someone somewhere knew I'd need you."

"Yeah," I said. "Me too."

And that was that.

CHAPTER 22
God Rides A Harley In My Very Happy Ending

TWO months later, we broke up.

I know, I know. What kind of a happy ending is that?

Sorry.

Unfortunately, it was pretty much all my fault. I hadn't meant to let it happen. There was this new guy at work who seemed to take a shine to me for some unknown reason. It was like Vince had opened the floodgates, and all the people who didn't even really know I existed before suddenly found me to be irresistible. One day, stupidly, I let new guy come over to my house and one thing led to another and Vince walked in right as new guy had his hand shoved down my pants, our lips fused together, pressed up against the wall where I'd hit my face months before getting ready for our first date—the first date I had with the guy I wanted to spend the rest of my life with.

I regret it. I regret the *shit* out of it.

The blowup was huge, and there were tears and apologies and begging and pleading. But I'd fucked up and Vince didn't forgive easily and it ended. Badly. Vince quit his job so we wouldn't see each other every day. He moved back to Phoenix, and I heard he started dating some random guy that he'd had an on-again-off-again thing with there before he'd come back to Tucson.

My parents disowned me after that, saying that they couldn't believe that I'd done that to him. I was no longer welcome in their house. Nana agreed with them and told me I that I was no better than what Johnny Depp had been calling me all along.

Sandy broke off our friendship following that whole disaster, saying that no friend of his was a cheater. He moved to Colombia, where he married a drug lord and lived a life of leisure as the madam of the house. I heard a while ago that he had a tiara made entirely of blood diamonds and a wing in his mansion dedicated to all of his wigs.

And as for me?

Disgraced, I headed south of the border and ended up in that little town in Mexico that I knew I was going to end up in. I opened my bar, Taco's Bell, just like I knew I would. I had a tiny little apartment above it that didn't have air-conditioning, and the ceiling fan did nothing to move the stifling hot air around.

On the upside, I grew a fantastic mustache and was never seen much without my poncho. The locals, initially wary of a *gringo* among them, grew to accept me as one of their own. I was eventually presented with the bride of my choice and married a tiny little woman by the name of Esmerelda Arroyo. She bore me two children—Guapo and Hortencia— and we moved out of that little apartment above the bar to a rambling old farmhouse on a spread of land right outside of town. It was hard work, but at least it was honest work. I grew wheat.

Ten years later, masked *banditos* came to town and tried to take it over, as they had decided our little haven was the perfect place for a new center of operations for their cocaine empire. Women and children were held hostage, including my beloved Esmerelda, Guapo, and Hortencia. Deciding I'd had enough, I rode into town on the trusty burro I'd named Princess Snow Cloud, given her propensity for acting like a princess and looking like a fat, white cloud.

The bloodshed was great and the violence extreme, but I emerged victorious and saved my little town from the *banditos* and rescued my family. The townspeople gathered around me and lifted me in the air, chanting, "*Gringo! Gringo! Gringo!*" A statue was erected in my honor in the middle of town, showing me riding Princess Snow Cloud. It was made from the bones of the *banditos* as a warning for any other masked hooligans who tried to take over my town.

On my sixtieth birthday, as people laughed and drank and danced around me, I was asked by a young man if I had any regrets. I told him that I had just one. He asked what that was. I told him that I regretted never finding out if I'd actually been Freddie Prinze Juniored or not.

Of course, he understood exactly what I meant because over the years, Freddie Prinze Junior had become the most famous actor who ever lived, especially after portraying such memorable roles as Hank, the gay chimpanzee who fell in love with his animal trainer, and in a stunning revelatory performance, the title role in the biopic *Material Girl: The Life and Times of Madonna.* Madonna herself said that no one in the world had ever been more Madonna than Freddie Prinze Junior.

Two minutes later, I died of a heart attack, not yet having gotten to the refried bean buffet or my piñata.

I ascended into heaven and God was waiting for me at the Pearly Gates. He looked like a Hells Angel, which I thought was slightly odd. I didn't know they had motorcycles in heaven.

"Hey," I said.

"What's up?" God asked.

I shrugged. "Nothing much. So, I guess I died, huh?"

"Pretty much," God said. "Just kind of fell over."

"Kind of a bitch way to go out, if you ask me. A heart attack? Really? Why not a blaze of glory?"

God rolled his eyes. "It could have been worse. I could have made your intestines explode. Are you going to whine the whole time you're up here?"

I scowled at him. "Are you going to give me reason to?"

"You're harshing my buzz, man," God lamented.

"I don't feel bad about that at all. I didn't know you were allowed to *have* a buzz. Aren't you supposed to be smiting people right now?"

"I'm God. I can do whatever I want." He eyed me. "You want to go for a ride on my hog?"

I contemplated this. "Are you hitting on me? Because that means two things where I come from." I wasn't sure how I felt about that.

"Maybe. But I meant on my motorcycle, not my dick. But why don't we see where it goes, and I could mean the other thing too." God leered at me and my insides felt tingly.

"Why not? You're, like, the ultimate daddy fetish."

"Damn right," he snorted. "All those 'Our Fathers' gives a guy a complex, let me tell you. You ready to rock?" A cloud descended and took the shape of a Harley. God slid a long leg over it and revved the engine. He looked back and winked at me.

"Do I get a helmet?" I shouted at him over the noise as I moved to sit behind him.

"Live a little," he shouted back. "You're already dead."

And then I rode off into the sunset on the back of God's motorcycle, clutching him as tightly as I could.

The end.

You still there?

Ha. I'm just fucking with you.

But I bet you *totally* got pissed, didn't you? Come on, admit it. For a second there, you screamed, "*Noooooooo!*" and then thought about ways you could murder me and hide the body without getting caught. I'm honestly a little hurt that you'd believe that (and a little scared about how bloodthirsty you seem to be; do me a favor and get some therapy. It sounds like you need it so you don't end up killing me or some hookers). Please. Do you *really* think I'd do something as stupid as cheating on Vince after falling in love with him over the course of a week?

Wait. Don't answer that.

Let's wrap this bitch up, shall we?

"SOMEONE obviously is going to ruin the surprise," I moaned, staring down from the balcony at the group of people amassed below at the gay bar. "I don't know why I thought I could pull this off."

"No offense to your man," Helena said, fixing her wig in her mirror, "but one does not think of the world's greatest detective when thinking of Vince. He's lucky he's pretty."

"Don't be jealous," I snapped at her. "Just because you haven't worked up the nerve to admit you want to bone Darren doesn't mean you can take it out on the rest of us."

"Girl's got claws," Daddy Charlie said with a rumble. "He's been dating Vince for six months and you'd think he was the fiercest bitch to walk the face of the earth."

Helena rolled her perfectly blushed eyes. "Tell me about it, Charlie. Hard-core, confident Paul is definitely a sight to behold. And I don't want to bone Darren. I've told you that like sixteen thousand times!"

"You are such a liar and a fat mouth," I said. "The only reason two people snipe at each other as much as you two do is when they want to be inside each other. For *days*."

"Or we could just hate each other. *That* could be a reason."

"I don't believe you in the slightest. No one in the world has that much unresolved sexual tension. Trust me, one day, you're going to come crying to me about how much you *lurve* him, and I will make fun of you forever." And I would. *Forever*. Vince and I kept devising ways for them to be alone together, and each time, it would start out okay, but then by the end, they'd be at each other's throat. Vince thought it was because they were in love already. He was such a dopey romantic sometimes. He thought that just because he loved me at first sight (which still made me feel all fuzzy inside like I was being eaten from the inside out by rabid teddy bears that pooped rainbows; it's really quite disgusting how awesome I thought that was) that everyone else in the free world should do the same. I tried to explain to him that it didn't quite work that way, but this discussion happened two months after we met, when we were moving him into my house. It was hard to argue against love at first sight when I was carrying his crap into my house.

"That's not going to happen," Helena said. "Besides, he couldn't handle Helena. And if you love me, you love both parts of me."

"How Sybil of you," Daddy said. "And I'm with Paul on this one. You go out of your way to snipe at him. That obviously means something."

She glared at both of us. "Just that I'm a sniper," she said. "Full-on, Grade A sniper. And besides, we weren't talking about me, remember? We're talking about how Vince probably already knows all about the surprise birthday party that Paul worked so hard to put together, which is now probably just ruined completely and everyone will hate him and be bored and talk about for years to come how awful of a time they had."

"You scandalous bitch!" I hissed at her. "You told him, didn't you!"

She smirked at me. "You'll never know."

"I think you will," Daddy said. "Vince isn't the world's greatest actor. If he knows, he'll probably say something like, 'Oh, gosh, now *this* is a surprise! I sure didn't know this was going to happen, no, I didn't!'"

"Better than a cheese dice," Helena muttered, straightening her falsies.

"I was a theatrical *treasure*!" I shouted at her.

"That is the gayest thing I've ever heard you say, boy," Daddy said. "And Vince told me about what you like to scream when you ride him reverse cowgirl."

"He did *what*?" I was going to murder him after wishing him a happy birthday and telling him I loved him and giving him the present that I was way fucking nervous about.

Helena's phone chimed and she looked down. "Dare said they're on their way here," she said. "They should be here in ten minutes."

I couldn't resist. "Since when do *you* have Darren's phone number? And since when did you start calling him *Dare*? Is that what you say to him? 'Oh, hey, Dare. I dare you to sit on my face and do sexy-time stuff with my butthole.' Or, you know, whatever else you would say to him."

"I will break you in half," she promised me darkly. "And I didn't say Dare. You just heard me wrong."

"No, he didn't," Daddy Charlie said.

"Even if Paul couldn't get around to it," Helena growled at him, "I *will* put you in a home, Charlie."

I reached over and wrapped my arms around the old guy. "Don't you worry, Daddy. I'll protect you from the big, bad queen."

He kissed my forehead. "Thank you, boy. It's nice to know at least *someone* appreciates me."

"I'm going to tell Vince you're kissing and cuddling with another man," Helena said.

"You do, and I'll tell Darren about the sex dream you had about him," I said back. "I would think he'd find it very interesting how you apparently liked it when he mounted you in the middle of a Sears electronics department while it was shown on a wall of TVs in front of you. Which, by the way, I don't know what that says about your psyche. I mean, Sears? *Really*? That's, like, one step up from Walmart. I feel sorry for you just thinking about it. It's like your dreams are broken and are dying slow and painful deaths."

"I knew I shouldn't have told you that," she grumbled. "What else doesn't Vince know about you that's embarrassing so I can tell him? Does he know you *really* had a diary that you wrote about him in?"

"It was a *journal*!"

"It had *Saved By The Bell* stickers on it!"

"Hey," Charlie said.

"That made it *awesome*."

"That made it a *diary*."

"Boys and girls," Charlie said.

"I'll tell Darren that you are in love with him and want to go out with him and that you borrowed my big black dildo and pretended it was him!"

"I'll tell Vince that you really got hippo shit in your mouth that time you fell into the hippo exhibit, and you had to stay overnight in the hospital because they thought you'd get some kind of weird hippo disease in your mouth!"

"Hey!" Charlie said.

"I'll tell Darren that you stare at the picture of him on your phone that you don't think anyone knows that you have!"

"I'll tell Vince what you bought him for his birthday before you give it to him, thereby ruining a magical surprise and depriving you of the look of wonder on his face!"

"Jesus Christ," Charlie muttered.

I was slightly stricken. "Do you think he'll like it?" I asked Helena quietly.

She came forward and gave me a sticky kiss on my cheek. "Oh, sugar. He's going to *adore* it. How could you think otherwise?"

"It's kinda dumb."

"And expensive."

"And crazy."

"But still the greatest present ever."

I looked up at my best friend. "You think so?"

"Baby doll, I *know* so."

"Hey!" Charlie shouted.

"What?" Helena asked, annoyed. "You don't have to shout."

"We're standing right here," I reminded him.

"Your boys are about to walk in," he said, rolling his eyes. "The bouncer just signaled they're on their way up the sidewalk."

"Oh sweat balls," I groaned. I leaned over the balcony as the DJ cut the music. "Hey, shut up!" I bellowed down.

Everyone looked up at me: friends of mine, friends of Vince's. Mom, Dad, and Nana waved up at me from where they'd cornered a Dom with his sub on a leash, obviously asking pointed questions about the bit in the sub's mouth. They still believed I was a pony. I didn't know what it would take to convince them otherwise, so I just let it go. It's easier to neigh for Vince every once in a while in their presence than to explain that I don't have a tail plug shoved up my ass when we're at home.

"They're about to walk in, so shut your faces! If any of you ruin this, I will scratch your motherfucking eyes out!"

People laughed up at me like I wasn't completely serious. Assholes.

Helena went down the stairs quickly, pushing through the crowd as everyone quieted down around her. Once she took her place on the stage, everyone went silent and the lights went out, all except for little LED lights along the floors, illuminating the walkways. The barbacks had set up a little partition that blocked the main entryway from the dance floor so that Vince would not be able to see anyone as he went upstairs.

The DJ started up the music again to cover how quiet it was as the bouncer opened the main door. I stood near the top of the stairs, listening as they climbed, Vince and Darren talking about something that I couldn't quite make out. My stomach was almost in my throat. My hands were sweating, and I felt like I was going to vomit. But vomiting was never sexy, and so I was able to choke it back down, which, now that I thought about, was even more unsexy.

"Hey," Vince said, his grin coming out in full force when he saw me. "I thought you were supposed to meet me at home. Darren said that Sandy had a queen emergency and you had to be here? Is everything okay?" He didn't even wait for me to respond; instead he crushed me into him, holding my face in his hands as he kissed me, parting my lips with his tongue. I gave a little groan and sank in his grasp, trying to remember that there were two hundred people standing in the dark only feet away and that it probably wasn't a good idea if I whipped out his cock so I could suck him off right then. He sure wasn't making things any easier. That was one of the things I loved about him the most: he kissed me every time he saw me like he hadn't seen me in years. Man, did he know how to kiss.

I managed to avoid shoving my hands down his pants and pulled back, trying to get my breathing under control. "Everything's fine," I assured him. "You know Sandy. Little things become big things."

He grinned evilly at me. "That's what I keep telling Darren, but he won't believe me."

"I heard that," Darren muttered.

"You have to do a shot with me," Vince said. "And nothing fruity." He narrowed his eyes. "But you can't spit it on another boy and try to take him home with you like you did with me."

"I don't think that's quite how it happened." I grabbed his hand. "Come here. Helena's about to go on and I want to watch."

"Why is it all dark?" he asked as I pulled him behind me. "Hey, Daddy Charlie."

"Happy birthday, boy. You ready for your birthday spanking?"

"I'm still trying to convince Paul to let *me* spank *him*," Vince confided, much to my horror. Vince thought it'd be kind of hot. I thought I liked my ass without his hand marks on it. We both knew it was only a matter of time before I caved. After all, he'd been able to convince me about the dildos. Oh *boy,* had he convinced me about the dildos. I don't know why all his little quirks had to be about things going on or going in my ass.

"Maybe I should spank *you!*" I told him quite loudly. And, of course, that was right when Charlie signaled to the DJ to cut the music, and so everyone in the bar below heard me telling my boyfriend kinky things.

"Are ponies allowed to give spankings?" I heard my grandmother almost shout in the dark above the laughter.

"I'm sure if he stays in scene, it'll be okay, as long as he's rearing up to kick his hind legs," Mom said even louder.

"I don't want to talk about my son rearing anything," Dad said. "Especially Vince."

"Mom?" Vince asked. "Dad? Nana? Why are you guys down there in the dark?"

The lights came on then, and the pictures that would be taken later would show Vince's wide, happy grin as people shouted, "Surprise!" up at him. And, of course, me, standing next to him, my red face buried in my hands, looking like I was about to die or something. Which, to be fair, I really wanted to do right then.

Helena led the crowd below in a stirring, dirty rendition of "Happy Birthday," which explicitly described the blowing of a gigantic cock. The fact that my parents and grandmother were singing right along with everyone else was enough to make me wish there were no such things as birthdays, and that it was possible for me to reach inside my own head to scrub my brain of the image. They all finished with a flourish and everyone cheered, and Vince turned to me. "You did this, didn't you?"

I shrugged. "Everyone helped."

"Paul did it!" everyone shouted.

"Jesus Christ," I muttered.

"Kiss! Kiss him!" Nana screamed. "Kiss his face off!"

Everyone else picked it up and started chanting for him to kiss my face off. It was a little weird. I felt like a goat was about to be sacrificed to a pagan god. I grinned at him as I backed away a few feet.

Vince stalked toward me. "I'm going to kiss the fuck out of you," he said as he reached for me, the crowd roaring up at us.

"Lucky me," I managed to say before I had a mouthful of Vince.

Lucky me.

WE MANAGED to escape later on, me having only taken a couple of shots so that I'd be okay to drive toward the end of the night. Vince was a little bit tipsy, but he didn't like to get full-on drunk, so I didn't have to worry about him passing out on me.

Besides, I was already worried out of my fucking mind about giving him his present.

So I stole him later, slipping quietly out the back, his hand in mine as we headed for the car. "Where we going?" he asked.

"You'll see."

And the night was perfect, warm and clear, even though it was October. We didn't talk much as I drove, him content to hold my hand, me content to be freaking the fuck out. I told myself I was being stupid, that I didn't have to be nervous, but it didn't do a damn thing to help. I'd gotten better about myself over the past six months, thanks to Vince, but since he didn't know a thing about this, it just made me all the more nervous.

He finally figured out where we were going and grinned over at me when we pulled into the parking lot of the park where he'd taken me after our first date. On the lookout for homicidal hobos with hook hands, we walked through the dark to what I thought of as our little patch of grass.

He didn't even need any coaxing and assumed his position on the ground, his stomach becoming a pillow for my head, making our T shape that we did so well. His hand immediately went into my hair and started rubbing my scalp. The stars were so bright, and for just a moment, everything was as it should be.

"Perfect end for tonight," he sighed, echoing my thoughts.

"Yeah?"

"Yeah."

"So…."

"So what?"

I almost didn't say it, but I pushed through. "So, I got you a present. You know, for your birthday."

"Yeah? Is it awesome?"

"Uh. Pretty sure. I think so. I don't know. Probably not. Maybe."

"Covering all your bases?"

I blushed. "Yeah."

"You didn't have to get me anything."

I snorted. "Bullshit. You would have given me so much crap had I not gotten you a present. Even *if* I'd thrown you a supersecret birthday party with all your friends and family, you'd have still bitched and moaned."

"Yeah, I would have made your life a living hell until you bought me something," he agreed. "But you haven't given me a bad present yet. Well, except for that neck massager you bought that I thought was supposed to be anal beads. I don't think I'll get that look on your face out of my mind as long as I live."

"You had it up your ass!"

"It vibrated," he said smugly. "Where else was something like that supposed to go? Besides, you didn't seem to mind when I pressed it against your balls."

"You know there's a homicidal hobo with hook hands jerking it to our conversation over there in the bushes."

"I don't think I'd touch my junk if I had hook hands," he said.

"How would you jerk off if you only had hook hands?" I wondered aloud.

"Easy. I'd get a plain bagel, cover it with lube, then fuck it. I'd latch it into my hook hands and just go to fucking town on it."

"We're breaking up," I told him quite seriously. "Then you can go fuck all the bagels you want, you weirdo. Keep your grossness away from me."

He laughed. "Nah. You're stuck with me, pretty much for forever."

This caught me a little in the chest. "It's real?"

He sat up, cradling my head in his lap. He bent over (for he was indeed as bendy as he had once claimed so very long ago) and kissed me deeply. "It's real," he mumbled against my lips. "Now give me my present."

I sighed and reached into the pocket of my light coat and pulled out an envelope. I almost tore it to shreds right then, but he'd already snapped it out of my hands like a greedy little child, and I tried to hide my face against his stomach. I heard him rip open the envelope and pull out the paper inside and start to read.

I knew the moment he got it once his breathing almost stopped completely. "Paul," he croaked out.

"Yeah?"

"Is this what I think it is?"

"What do you think it is?"

"An itinerary for three weeks in Asia next spring."

"Then you'd be thinking right."

He started sputtering. "I don't... how did you... fucking sexy motherfucker... I will *totally* bone you... what is...."

"Wow," I said. "That *is* kind of hot being on the other side of that."

"Paul!"

"What!"

"How the fuck can you afford this? We work the same job!"

I shrugged, embarrassed. "I've been saving." For a long time, though I didn't know for what. Then he came along, and I figured out what it was for. He wanted it, and I'd given it to him. I'd give him everything if I could.

He dropped the paper to the ground and knocked me off his lap before he crawled on top of me, covering me with his body. It happened so fast that I didn't have a chance to make a noise, much less to fight back. Our noses touched as he searched my eyes. "You did that for me?"

He was too close to be able to look away. I thought about closing my eyes, but he'd just make me open them again. "Yeah."

"We're going to Asia?"

"Parts of it, but yeah. You and me. Three whole weeks."

"Do you think we could go see the fortune-cookie factories?"

"Sure," I said, even if I didn't know if those were real things in Asia. If they weren't, I'd hunt around until I found one just so he could see it. Who cared if his dreams were weird? They were starting to become mine too.

His eyes were bright. "You're pretty much the greatest thing in the world, you know that right?" Then he smiled at me, dimples and all.

And with that, I knew all my stupid little fears had been for nothing. Every single one of them, because to Vince, none of that mattered. He was happy just the way we were, and there wasn't one more thing I could have asked for. "So you like it?"

"Paul... are you sure?"

I rolled my eyes. "I should hope so. Everything's pretty much bought and paid for already." I said this as if I hadn't been freaking out about it all for the past couple of months since I'd decided to do this. I played cool, but I knew he saw right through me. It didn't matter, though.

He smothered me in a way dirty kiss that I thought would end with me nutting in my jeans like I was sixteen years old if he kept it up, not that I minded in the slightest. I figured the homicidal hobos with hook hands didn't have any bagels to fuck, so we might as well give them a show. I couldn't even really breathe under the assault from his tongue, but breathing was overrated.

"We need to go home now," he panted, breaking the kiss, moving off me and pulling me to my feet. He pushed us quickly toward the car, his hands already down the back of my jeans, trying to get at my ass. "I'm going to Freddie Prinze Junior you so hard when we get there," he growled in my ear.

"I don't think you get the concept yet," I said breathlessly, squirming under his touch.

"I don't care," he said, a wicked curve to his mouth. "I'm going to do it anyway."

And you know what?

He did just that.

When TJ KLUNE was eight, he picked up a pen and paper and began to write his first story (which turned out to be his own sweeping epic version of the video game Super Metroid—he didn't think the game ended very well and wanted to offer his own take on it. He never heard back from the video game company, much to his chagrin). Now, two decades later, the cast of characters in his head have only gotten louder, wondering why he has to go to work as a claims examiner for an insurance company during the day when he could just stay home and write.

He lives with a neurotic cat in the middle of the Sonoran Desert. It's hot there, but he doesn't mind. He dreams about one day standing at Stonehenge, just so he can say he did.

TJ can be found on Facebook under TJ Klune.

His blog is tjklunebooks.blogspot.com.

You can e-mail him at tjklunebooks@yahoo.com.

Also from TJ KLUNE

http://www.dreamspinnerpress.com

Also from TJ KLUNE

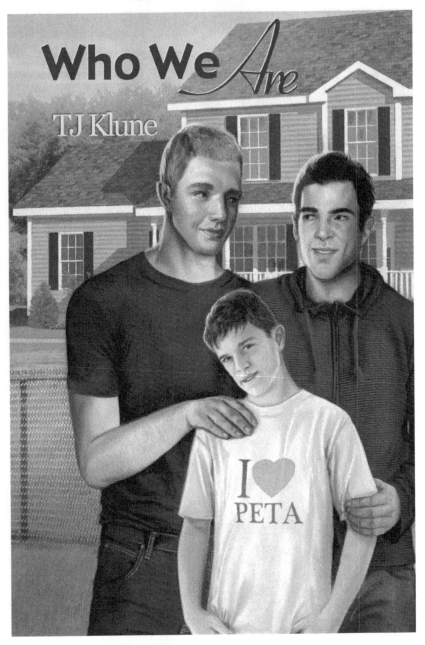

http://www.dreamspinnerpress.com

Also from TJ KLUNE

http://www.dreamspinnerpress.com

Also from DREAMSPINNER PRESS

Living Promises

Amy Lane

http://www.dreamspinnerpress.com